6/13

# SHATTERED TRIDENT

# LARRY BOND

# SHATTERED TRIDENT

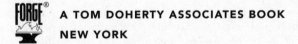 A TOM DOHERTY ASSOCIATES BOOK

NEW YORK

SHATTERED TRIDENT

Copyright © 2013 by Larry Bond and Chris Carlson

All rights reserved.

Maps by Erik Carlson

A Forge Book
Published by Tom Doherty Associates, LLC
175 Fifth Avenue
New York, NY 10010

www.tor-forge.com

Forge® is a registered trademark of Tom Doherty Associates, LLC.

ISBN 978-0-7653-3147-2 (hardcover)
ISBN 978-1-4299-4366-6 (e-book)

Forge books may be purchased for educational, business, or promotional use. For information on bulk purchases, please contact Macmillan Corporate and Premium Sales Department at 1-800-221-7945 extension 5442 or write specialmarkets@macmillan.com.

First Edition: May 2013

Printed in the United States of America

0  9  8  7  6  5  4  3  2  1

This book is dedicated to our patient and understanding wives, Jeanne and Katy, who graciously put up with the numerous long conversations, as well as the many nights and weekends we left them abandoned while we typed like madmen. Without their faithful love and support, this book, indeed the entire Jerry Mitchell series, could not possibly have been written.

# ACKNOWLEDGMENTS

We are deeply grateful to William S. Murray, associate research professor at the Warfare Analysis and Research Division of the United States Naval War College's Center for Naval Warfare Studies, for his guidance and sage counsel. Professor Murray's insight into the People's Liberation Army Navy and undersea warfare made him an excellent sounding board for us to bounce our ideas against. He also patiently helped us as we wrapped our heads around that tumultuous body of water that is the South China Sea. The generous allocation of his time and expertise is greatly appreciated.

# AUTHOR'S NOTE

Chris Carlson and I are now an established writing team, but each book is unique, requiring different approaches and techniques to help us work together smoothly to craft each story. So writing the Jerry Mitchell series has been an evolving process, but one that's been rewarding and enjoyable.

Simple communication is not enough. With numerous technical facts and interwoven plotlines, we had to be completely aware of what the other partner was doing, and intended to do next. So we talked a lot, shared story ideas, and were quick to express misgivings or problems with the draft text, regardless of who originally wrote it.

Working with another creative talent is good for me. I need someone to bounce ideas off, and to help me get moving again when I'm stuck. Chris is very good at that and many other things, and we each have complete faith in our joint commitment to making each story as believable and entertaining as possible.

# DRAMATIS PERSONAE

**USS *North Dakota* (SSN 784)**

> Commander Jerry Mitchell, Commanding Officer
> Lieutenant Commander Bernie Thigpen, Executive Officer

> Department Heads
> Lieutenant Commander Phillip Sobecki, Chief Engineer
> Lieutenant Edward Rothwell, Navigator and Operations Officer
> Lieutenant Steven Westbrook, Supply Officer ("the Chop")
> Lieutenant David Covey, Weapons Officer

> Division Officers
> Lieutenant Russell Iverson, Main Propulsion Assistant
> Lieutenant Kiyoshi Iwahashi, Damage Control Assistant
> Lieutenant Kurt Franklin, Communications Officer
> Lieutenant (j.g.) Quela Lymburn ("Q"), Assistant Weapons Officer
> Lieutenant (j.g.) Stuart Gaffney, Sonar Officer
> Ensign Olivia Andrews ("Ollie"), Chem/RADCON Assistant
> Ensign Jacqueline Kane ("Jacques"), Reactor Control Assistant

> EMCM Marco Pompei, Chief of the Boat ("COB")
> ET1 Josh Fleming, ESM/SIGINT
> STSC Halleck, Sonar Division CPO
> STS1 Andersen, Sonar Operator

STS2 Gilden, Sonar Operator
CTI3 Gus Kalinsky, COMINT Linguist


## American Characters

Gregory Alexander, Director of National Intelligence
Milt Alvarez, White House Chief of Staff
Rear Admiral Wayne Burroughs, COMSUBPAC
General Lewis Dewhurst, USAF, Chairman JCS
Commander Bruce Dobson, Commanding Officer, USS *Oklahoma City* (SSN 723)
Dr. Randall Foster, Director of the CIA
Malcolm Geisler, Secretary of Defense
Alison Gray, Deputy White House Chief of Staff
Rear Admiral Kyle Guthrie, Former Captain of USS *Michigan* (SSBN 727 Blue Crew)
Commander Warren Halsey, Commanding Officer, USS *Santa Fe* (SSN 763)
Senator Lowell Hardy (D-CT), Former Captain of USS *Memphis* (SSN 691)
Admiral Bernard Hughes, Chief of Naval Operations
Captain Glenn Jacobs, Chief Staff Officer, Submarine Squadron (SUBRON) 15
Dr. Raymond Kirkpatrick, National Security Advisor
Christine Laird, CNN Reporter
Andrew Lloyd, Secretary of State
Evangeline McDowell, President's Secretary
Joyce McHenry, Secretary of Commerce
Kenneth L. Myles, President of the United States
General Jason Nagy, USMC, Vice Chairman JCS
Commander Scott Nevens, Commanding Officer, USS *North Carolina* (SSN 777)
Commander Ian Pascovich, Commanding Officer, USS *Texas* (SSN 775)
Dr. Joanna Patterson, Deputy National Security Advisor
James Randall, Vice President of the United States
Captain Tom Rudel, USN (Ret.), Former Captain of USS *Seawolf* (SSN 21)

Captain Charles Simonis, Commander, SUBRON 15
Commander Richard Walker, SUBRON 15 Operations Officer

## Canadian Character

Hector Alexander McMurtrie, Blogger and Naval Historian

## People's Republic of China Characters

General Bao Bo, Commander Intelligence Service
Chen Dao, President, Chairman of the CMC, and General Secretary of the CCP
Senior Captain Deng Jinshan, PLAN Staff Officer
General Hu Kun, Commander of Second Artillery Corps
General Li Ju, Vice Chairman of the CMC
General Shi Peng, Political Department
General Su Yide, Chief of the General Staff
General Tian Gan, Vice Chairman of the CMC
General Wang Yaowen, Commander of the People's Liberation Army Air Force
Admiral Wei Zi'en, Commander of the People's Liberation Army Navy
General Wen Feng, Minister of National Defense
Colonel (later General) Xi Ping, Deputy Commander (later Commander) Intelligence Service
General Xiao Shen, Armament Department
Ambassador Yang Jinping, Chinese Ambassador to the United States
General Ye Jin, Logistics Department
Zhang Fei, Vice Chairman of the CMC, Secretariat of the Communist Party, and Vice President of PRC

## Vietnamese Characters

Commander Cao Van Ty, Intelligence Officer
Admiral Duan, Head of the Second Directorate (Intelligence Service)
Admiral Hieu, Chief of Staff of the Vietnamese People's Navy
Commander Nimh, Komamura's Escort

Admiral Phai, Head of the Political Directorate
Minister Vu Kim Binh, Foreign Minister

## Japanese Characters

Minister Hisagi Shuhei, Japanese Representative to Littoral Alliance Working Group

Dr. Komamura Sajin, Economics professor at Tokyo University, Author of *Navies for Asia*

Admiral Kubo Noriaki, Chief of Staff of the Japanese Maritime Self-Defense Force

Miyazaki Nodoka, Research Assistant

Commander Okubo Atsushi, Commanding officer of the *Kongo*-class guided-missile destroyer *Atago*

Vice Admiral Orihara Izaya, Military Representative to the Littoral Alliance Working Group

Minister Tadashi Hata, Japanese Foreign Minister

Ambassador Urahara Kisuke, Japanese Ambassador to the United States

Commander Zaraki Kenpachi, Commanding Officer of the *Soryu*-class submarine *Kenryu*

## Korean Characters

Minister Han Ho-Jung, Foreign Minister of the Republic of Korea

Admiral Park Uchin, Korean Representative to the Littoral Alliance Working Group

## Russian Character

Captain 1st Rank Alexsey Igorevich Petrov, Russian Navy (Ret.), Former Captain of the Russian submarine *Severodvinsk*

## Taiwanese (Republic of China) Characters

Ambassador Kenneth Leong, Taiwanese Ambassador to the United States

Admiral Wu Chen, Commander of the Taiwanese Navy

**Indian Characters**

Lieutenant Commander Maahir Jain, First Officer of the submarine
*Chakra*

Kanwal Nehru, Foreign Secretary

Lieutenant Rajat, Sonar Officer

Captain Girish Samant, Commanding Officer of the submarine
*Chakra*

N

People's Republic of China

Myanmar

Laos

Gulf
of
Tonkin

Hainan Island

Taiwan

*Philippine
Sea*

Thailand

China's
Maritime
Claims

Cambodia

Vietnam

*Andaman
Sea*

Gulf
of
Thailand

South China Sea

Spratly Islands

Philippines

Strait
of
Malacca

West Malaysia

Brunei

*Indonesia*

Singapore

East Malaysia

*Java Sea*

Lombok
Strait

0    200    400
Nautical Miles

E. Carlson © 2012

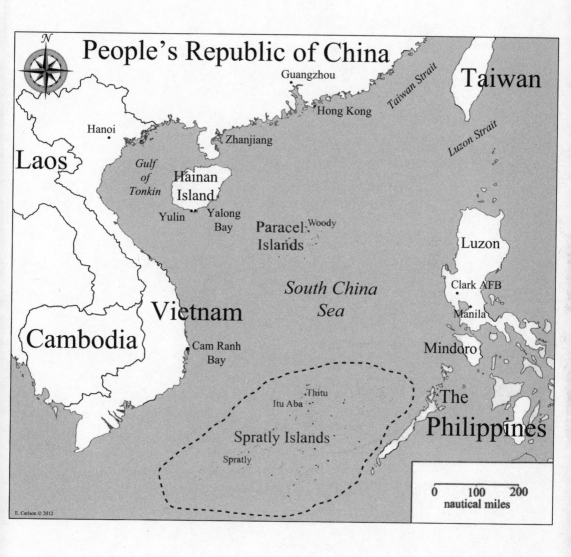

# SHATTERED TRIDENT

# PROLOGUE

18 August 2016
South China Sea

"Possible target zig by contact Sierra-three eight, based on frequency," sang out the sonar supervisor. "Contact has either turned away or slowed down."

Commander Jerry Mitchell remained silent while the officer of the deck acknowledged the report. Glancing over his left shoulder, he could see the downward shift in the tonals on the sonar supervisor's screen.

"Confirm target zig by Sierra-three eight. Contact has come right, new course three five zero. No change in speed," announced the section tracking party coordinator.

Jerry shifted his attention to a large flat-screen display; the evolving tactical situation was constantly being updated by the sub's fire control system. He shook his head slightly. It used to take several minutes and a couple of maneuvers by a trailing submarine to figure out a contact's new course after a zig. But now, they could recompute a target's course and speed in less than a minute. Somehow it didn't seem quite fair, but Jerry was fine with that.

"Something wrong, Skipper?" interrupted Lieutenant Iwahashi, the officer of the deck.

"No, there's nothing wrong. Stay with her, Kiyoshi."

"Aye, aye, sir. Pilot, right fifteen degrees rudder. Steady on course zero five zero."

"Right fifteen degrees rudder, steady on course zero five zero, Pilot, aye. Officer of the deck, my rudder is right fifteen."

"Very well, Pilot."

*Pilot,* Jerry thought ruefully. *I still prefer helmsman.* The change in some of the watch station nomenclature was but one of the many, many differences about this boat. *His boat!* Shivers still went up his spine every time the thought jumped into his mind—he was the *captain.*

USS *North Dakota* was brand-spanking-new, the first flight three *Virginia*-class nuclear-powered attack submarine in the fleet. As a class, the *Virginia*s were revolutionary in many ways. One of the more obvious changes was in the control room. There weren't any periscopes. None. No more dancing with the "gray lady." An operator simply turned the mast-mounted video cameras with a joystick and watched the output on a flat-panel display—just one among dozens that encircled the control room.

The flight three boats were the third and latest production group of the *Virginia* design, fitted with the next-generation sonar suite, built around entirely new hull and towed arrays. Without question, *North Dakota* had the best sonar suite in the world; built to find the quietest targets any potential adversary had at sea or on the drawing board. In the current situation, however, it was definitely overkill.

They had been trailing the Chinese Type 093 Shang-class nuclear-powered attack submarine for a day, hardly a challenge given how noisy these boats were. Jerry's sonar techs had first detected the Shang while she was tens of miles away, and with little effort Jerry had neatly maneuvered *North Dakota* into the Chinese boat's baffles. Once settled in the sweet spot off the port quarter, *North Dakota* diligently shadowed her target; observing everything the Shang did, recording every squeak, thump, and whirl made by her propulsion plant. It all seemed too easy, and Jerry found himself repeatedly admonishing his crew to stay focused when they started getting a little too cocky.

"Overconfidence will negate our technological advantage faster than anything the other guy could do. Stay sharp," he'd warned them. The U.S. Navy knew little about blue-water Chinese submarine operations. Every hour he stayed in contact undetected meant more data, and a better understanding of the People's Liberation Army Navy's submarine force.

"Captain, that course change puts Sierra-three eight on an intercept track with Sierra-five two," reported Lieutenant David Covey, the tracking party coordinator.

"Very well, Coordinator," Jerry responded. Then turning to Iwahashi, "OOD, show me the two tracks."

"Aye, sir." The junior officer pulled up a menu on the command workstation and zoomed out the tactical display.

Jerry studied the information on the port VLSD and did the math in his head as a quick check. The Shang was definitely closing in on the other contact, a merchant ship.

"That can't be a coincidence, Skipper. It's a perfect intercept course," remarked Iwahashi. "Maybe the Chinese captain is conducting an approach and attack drill?"

"Could be," Jerry speculated. "They certainly should have picked up the merchant by now. A Shang may be hard of hearing, but they aren't deaf. Sonar, what do you have on Sierra-five two?"

"Sir, Sierra-five two's signature matches the motor vessel *Vinaship Sea* in the database. She has a twelve-cylinder diesel with one four-bladed screw. Current shaft rate is 133 RPM, which correlates to twelve knots," the sonar supervisor answered smartly.

"Very well, Sonar," Jerry replied. And before he could even ask, the OOD spoke up.

"I have the Seawatch database entry here, sir. Putting it up on the starboard VLSD."

"Excellent, Kiyoshi."

The picture of the *Vinaship Sea* flashed up onto the starboard large-screen display. The ship looked rather unremarkable. The superstructure and funnel were aft, with a raised island at the bow and four large deck cranes spaced evenly over the ship's length.

"Looks like a buckwheat bulk carrier to me," Jerry commented.

"Yes, sir. She's 169 meters long and displaces 18,108 gross tons. Built in 1998, she is currently owned by the Vinaship Jointstock Company and is registered in the Socialist Republic of Vietnam. According to ONI, she left the Tan Thuan Terminal at Ho Chi Minh port two days ago and is en route to Osaka, Japan. Cargo is listed as coal."

Jerry studied the merchant's track. Again, his head shook slightly. The fire control system held her on course zero seven six—*That can't be right*, he thought.

"Coordinator, verify Sierra-five two's course," Jerry ordered.

"Verify Sierra-five two's course, aye, sir." A few moments later Covey reported back. "Confirm Sierra-five two's course is zero seven six, Captain."

Frowning, Jerry asked, "Is it just me, or is that course too southerly for a Japanese destination? Quartermaster, what course would we steer if we were heading for Japan from Vietnam?"

"Working on it, Skipper," replied the quartermaster of the watch. He had just selected the appropriate digital chart from the library menu and was using the trackball to lay out a rough voyage-planning route. "Sir, a better course from Ho Chi Minh would be about zero five zero, headed for the Hainan Strait. They are way too far south."

Jerry turned around and leaned over the large horizontal display screen. "Here is Sierra-five two's current track, and this is the course they should be on," said the quartermaster.

"Not very likely this is a navigation error, is it?" inquired Jerry whimsically.

"I'd say nearly impossible, sir."

Looking back up, Jerry spoke in a loud voice. "Any guesses why this ship is nowhere near where she's supposed to be?" All Jerry got were shrugs and negative replies.

"Me neither," he said. "Well, let's keep an eye on her for as long as we can. In the meantime, let's stay focused on our primary . . ."

A growing murmur from the sonar techs distracted Jerry; something was happening. The sonar supervisor didn't keep him waiting. "Sir, transients from Sierra-three eight. It sounded like torpedo tubes being flooded."

Surprised by the report, Jerry demanded confirmation. "Are you sure that's what you heard?"

"Yes, sir. Both Petty Officer Gilden and I are sure." Jerry saw the other petty officer nod his head vigorously. That was good enough for him.

"Attention in the tracking party, Sierra-three eight appears to be conducting an approach and attack drill on Sierra-five two that may include shooting water slugs. This is a prime piece of intelligence on Chinese anti-surface tactics, and we need to collect every scrap of data that we can on this evolution. The Shang may execute an evasion sequence after the shot, so stay on your toes. Carry on." Jerry was excited at the thought of recording a mock attack by a Chinese SSN. Opportunities such as this were rare, and he had a front-row seat at the fifty-yard line.

"Mechanical transients from Sierra-three eight. Contact is opening torpedo tube outer doors," announced the sonar supervisor, excitement in his voice.

Iwahashi acknowledged the report. The Shang SSN was less than seven

thousand yards away from the merchant. Ten thousand yards was the estimated outer edge of a Chinese sub's engagement envelope against a surface
ship, based on past exercises. *He'll shoot soon,* thought Jerry as he tried to
imagine himself in his counterpart's shoes.

Not even a minute later, the sonar supervisor called out, "Launch transients! One . . . no, two slugs!"

Jerry turned to look at the sonar display, but was stopped short when he
saw the color draining from the sonar supervisor's face. "TORPEDOES IN
THE WATER!" he shouted. "Two weapons bearing zero three zero!"

"I have the conn!" Jerry barked. "Pilot, right full rudder, all ahead flank!
Sound general quarters!"

The flurry of responses to Jerry's orders was only partially hidden by the
*BONG, BONG, BONG* of the general alarm. Almost immediately, additional people began piling into control as the battle stations team took their
positions. The executive officer, Lieutenant Commander Bernie Thigpen,
literally had to shove his way through the masses to reach his station.

"What the hell is going on, Skipper?" Surprise and concern were all
over his face.

"XO, our friend out there just fired two torpedoes."

"Seriously?" Thigpen asked incredulously. "At us?"

"Seriously. And I don't know," Jerry replied. "But I'm not taking any
chances. I'm cutting behind the Shang. If those weapons are aimed at us,
any anti-circular run feature should force them to shut down."

"Captain, passing zero four zero to the right. No ordered course given,"
exclaimed the pilot loudly.

"Very well, Pilot. Steer zero seven zero." Jerry had to raise his voice to
be heard over the growing buzz.

As the pilot responded to his captain's orders, the sonar supervisor
shouted out, "Captain! The torpedoes are classified as Yu-6s, bearing zero
two seven and drawing left. But I have down Doppler, repeat down Doppler, the torpedoes are heading away from us!"

"Keep it down, people!" Jerry roared. It was too noisy in the control
room and he had to hear every report properly. "Very well, Sonar."

"Concur, sir," Thigpen reported. "Weapons are not coming toward us."

Looking up at the port display, Jerry saw the Chinese torpedoes pulling
away from them—they weren't the intended target. He then saw *North Dakota's* speed climbing past sixteen knots; he needed to slow down before
they popped out of the Chinese boat's starboard baffles. At high speed even

a Shang would be able to hear them. "Pilot, all ahead two-thirds. XO, are those torpedoes heading where I think they are?"

"If you mean the merchant ship, then yes, sir," responded Thigpen flatly. "They're closing at over fifty knots; time to impact, three minutes forty-five seconds. And there isn't a blessed thing we can do about it."

In an eerie silence, Jerry and his crew watched as the dots representing the torpedoes merged with the merchant's symbol. It struck Jerry that the engagement looked just like a video game—only this time, people would die in the end. The explosion from the first torpedo was easily heard through the hull. But before the sonar supervisor could even make a report, a much louder, far more powerful explosion followed.

"Sweet Jesus! What was *that*?" exclaimed a shaken Thigpen.

"Had to be a sympathetic detonation," said Jerry dryly. "But from what? The ship was listed as carrying coal."

"Captain, I have loud breaking-up noises from Sierra-five two, bearing three one seven. She's going down fast."

"Very well, Sonar."

"Skipper, the Shang's bugging out." Thigpen pointed toward the port large display. "She's altered course to the left and has increased speed. Orders, sir?"

Still a bit stunned himself, Jerry simply stared at the display, desperately trying to understand what had just transpired. But soon he felt the weight of everyone's gaze upon him. Everyone in control was waiting for a decision from him. He was the captain. Sighing deeply, he said, "Let her go, XO. We have more pressing business."

Turning to Lieutenant Iwahashi, he continued, "OOD, make for Sierra-five two's last position. Best possible speed. We need to see if anyone survived that blast. I'm not very hopeful, but we need to at least take a look. XO, you and the commo have ten minutes to get me a draft OPREP-3 message. We've just witnessed an act of war, and we need to phone home."

# 1

# WE HAVE AN AGREEMENT

8 August 2016
Hanoi, Vietnam

Dr. Komamura Sajin took in the view of Hanoi as they drove. Much of the architecture still reflected French rule, although modern buildings were mixed in everywhere, replacing ones destroyed in "The War."

The city was filled with history. After his lecture yesterday morning, he'd visited the B-52 Victory Museum, escorted by a large party of Vietnamese officers and officials. They'd even arranged a meeting with a veteran of the war who'd flown MiGs against the Americans. Komamura was still getting used to his celebrity status, but he loved the perks that came with it.

His official escort, Commander Nimh, had chatted with the professor in English, since Komamura spoke little Vietnamese. Nimh had read the new Vietnamese translation of Komamura's book, and was obviously enthused to meet its author. Nimh made it clear that he considered the assignment a privilege, and that there had been fierce competition for the spot.

They were close to the ministry now. It occupied an entire block of Hanoi, but looked more like a college campus than office buildings or a military headquarters. Light-colored brick buildings with red roofs surrounded a grassy quadrangle with a fountain in the center. Trees dotted the grassy areas and almost surrounded the ministry buildings.

They turned out of the morning traffic and stopped at the security gate. In spite of the official car, the driver and Commander Nimh both had to present their identification. The commander showed a letter vouching for Komamura, and the guards checked him against their own access list.

There were more security checkpoints after they entered the main building and went to the top floor. As in other military headquarters he'd visited, Komamura passed relics in glass cases, paintings of battles, and several images of Ho Chi Minh and General Vo Nguyen Giap. At the last checkpoint, he surrendered his smartphone.

Komamura was nervous; he'd been treated like royalty, and had enjoyed every minute of it. But there comes a time when royalty has to earn its keep. Normally he didn't pay much attention to his appearance, but he'd dressed for the occasion in his best suit with a wave-patterned dark blue silk tie embroidered with the kanji character for "*umi*," the sea.

Nimh led him to a top-floor conference room. Instead of a large table, there were several groups of comfortable-looking chairs. Occupying three were several older naval officers. Preparing for the trip, Komamura had studied Vietnamese rank insignia. These were senior admirals.

A junior officer stepped up to translate, and the professor was quickly introduced to Admiral Hieu, the navy's chief of staff, and Admirals Phai and Duan, the heads of the Vietnamese Navy's political and intelligence directorates. He realized they'd all been at his lecture yesterday, but they hadn't been introduced to him at that time.

While Nimh served small cups of tea, Komamura took a seat next to the chief of staff. The admiral was old enough to have a puckered scar on his left arm that ran up under his shirtsleeve. Komamura had heard he'd been wounded in the south. He hadn't heard how.

Komamura was only slightly younger than the admirals, but his expensive suit contrasted sharply with their dark green uniforms. He was also nearly six feet tall, a full head higher than Admiral Hieu and the others. Komamura's large frame filled his chair, and his Buddha-like bulge would never have been tolerated in military service. Their only similarity was a lack of hair. Komamura had a fringe of white, Phai's was thin to the point of transparency, while the other two had simply shaved their scalps.

"Admiral Kubo sends his best wishes," Komamura said. "I spoke with him just before leaving Japan. He remembers your meeting in Honolulu warmly."

"At the Pacific defense chiefs' conference," Hieu remembered. "Our first discussions there were most helpful."

Once Nimh had made sure everyone was settled, he disappeared, leaving

Komamura with the three admirals and the translator. The professor knew he faced his examiners.

Admiral Phai, the head of the political directorate, began the conversation. "The new Vietnamese translation of *Navies for Asia* has been very well received here. It was even reviewed in *Quan Noi Nhan Dan,* a mainstream newspaper, although the reviewer criticized it for being 'pro-Chinese.'"

Komamura laughed, almost a chuckle. "That's what he gets for not reading carefully. Recognizing the growth of Chinese military power doesn't mean I support that growth."

"We agree with you that the Chinese threat is only going to get worse," Phai responded. "Every country bordering the South China Sea has suffered attacks on their exploration ships, unauthorized fishing in their waters, and confrontations with Chinese paramilitary vessels. The number of these incidents is growing, and China makes no apologies."

Hieu asked, "Have other navies besides Japan and Vietnam shown interest in your book?"

"I've lectured in America, and received e-mails from almost every littoral nation. Many are from naval officers. I've had to hire a secretary. I will be visiting the Republic of Korea almost as soon as my trip here is finished, and a little later, India."

"Why did you choose naval strategy for your latest work?" This came from Admiral Duan, head of the Second General Department, the armed forces' intelligence branch. "You teach economics at Tokyo University. Your earlier books have been about economics or history."

Komamura nodded. "True, but it's impossible to separate economics from politics, or politics from war. My latest book began as an analysis of China's rapid economic growth in the new century, but that massive growth demands resources, especially energy and food." He shrugged. "China has always been hungry, but now her hunger drives her to the sea. I decided to share my conclusions."

Duan continued, "You are a member of the New Renaissance Party, which promotes a strong military and reverence for the emperor. Isn't your book just a reflection of your political beliefs?"

The professor shook his head, disagreeing. "My political beliefs are rather a reflection of my research." Komamura began ticking off points on his fingers. In Japanese fashion, he raised his little finger first.

"First, Chinese economic growth requires far more resources than they have. They see those resources close at hand, in the South China Sea. The rapid growth is masking artificialities and serious flaws in the Chinese economy. If their economy slows too much, and it is slowing, it will likely collapse.

"Second, in pursuit of those resources, China is transforming her navy from a coastal defense force to a blue-water regional power. This is a clear signal of their intentions.

"Third, U.S. military power in this part of the world is waning. They are still paying the bill for two long wars, and force modernization has suffered. There are also questions about their political will. China is America's second biggest export customer, as well as her greatest importer. Furthermore, China is the largest holder of U.S. debt. I submit that we cannot depend on a distant, weary America to counterbalance nearby Chinese military power."

Komamura finished, "I joined the New Renaissance Party three years ago, and hope to advise them on economic and security issues."

Admiral Hieu had listened as Komamura made his arguments. "There are nations that would not be happy to see a stronger Japan, not only free of American support, but unrestrained by any obligations to America." Komamura knew that Vietnam had been occupied by Japan during the Second World War, although they had not suffered as badly as Korea or the Philippines.

"I do not advocate becoming stronger individually, but rather increasing our strength through alliances independent of U.S. interests, which may not be the same as our own. And what drove Japanese aggression during the Pacific War?" Komamura asked pointedly. "Demand for resources to support her rapid industrialization. Japan's military leadership in 1941 was filled with a sense of their own manifest destiny. I believe China's leaders are driven not only by national pride, but also fear. If their economy falters, they risk losing power. If it collapses, the nation could go with it. For the Chinese leadership, aggression in the South China Sea presents fewer risks."

"Dr. Komamura, how did you first contact the Japanese Maritime Defense Force?"

"They contacted me," Komamura answered. "After *Navies* was published, I gave lectures at several naval bases and the academy at Etajima. After a lecture at Yokosuka, I participated in a long discussion on naval developments with a small group of officers. Admiral Kubo himself joined the group for a short while. Afterwards, I was approached by one of his aides."

Hieu looked at the other two admirals, who both nodded firmly. He turned back to Komamura. "The original purpose of this meeting was to discuss the concept of an alliance of South and East China Sea littoral nations, an idea you have championed and your Admiral Kubo Noriaki fully supports. Unfortunately, circumstances have changed."

Komamura looked confused and uncertain. "In what way?"

Admiral Hieu spoke quickly. "Professor, the Socialist Republic of Vietnam, with the full approval of the Politburo and the Defense Council, agrees in principle with your 'littoral alliance.' We are ready to work out the details of the collaboration immediately. Every country in the region is threatened by Chinese aggression. Even working together, it will be difficult for us to stop that aggression. Individually, we don't stand a chance."

The academic was pleased and excited, but puzzled. "But this is wonderful news! I will convey your answer to Admiral Kubo as soon as I return to Japan. But what else has changed?"

"China's plans," Hieu explained, "and our infant alliance faces an immediate challenge." He turned to the translator. "Ask Commander Ty to join us."

Commander Ty was in his early thirties, and still had all his hair. While he quickly set up a laptop, the translator hurried over and sat next to Komamura, whispering to the professor as Ty began his brief.

"Good morning, Dr. Komamura, I am Cao Van Ty. I am assigned to the Second General Department, our intelligence branch." Ty bowed toward the academic, then Admiral Duan, his superior. "I will be presenting highly sensitive information about an imminent Chinese threat which affects both our countries. Professor, can we have your promise that you will not share what you learn today with anyone else, unless we give you permission to do so?"

"Of course," Komamura replied quickly. Curiosity filled him, but also foreboding. What was going on?

Ty pressed a key and a flat screen at one end of the conference room came alive with a map of the South China Sea. The Vietnamese coast lined the left edge, while Hainan Island was in the center. The Leizhou Peninsula reached out from China's southern coast toward Hainan. The mainland coast angled northeast from the peninsula until it disappeared at the upper right corner.

Ty stood next to the screen. "I'm sure you're aware of *Liaoning*'s exercises last week."

"Their new carrier?" Komamura answered. "Yes. It was even covered by the mainstream media. Inaccurately, but at least they noticed."

Ty continued. "*Liaoning* is now back at her homeport in Yalong Bay.

Her captain reports that several minor mechanical issues need to be corrected. He is also loading fuel, ordnance, and the rest of *Liaoning*'s air group. This will consist of ten J-15 fighters, six Ka-28 sub-hunting helicopters, and four Z-8 radar helicopters. He reports they will be ready to sail in five days.

"When she does sail, she will be escorted by the same six warships that took part in the exercise, three destroyers and three frigates, all armed with advanced guided missiles. The task group will rendezvous with two amphibious ships of the Type 071 class, then proceed to Guangzhou." A line appeared on the chart, starting at the southern tip of Hainan Island, heading north to the naval base at Zhanjiang, where the Leizhou Peninsula joined the Chinese mainland, then north again to the Guangzhou shipyard near Hong Kong.

"We have photos of a platform being built at Guangzhou." The screen changed to show pictures of a very large, flat structure, spotted with different colors of primer and gray paint. Open girder framework showed in many places. The images were overlaid with circles and labeled in Vietnamese. "The shipyard there builds many offshore oil platforms, but this structure is larger, and has a different configuration. But more importantly, it is armed.

"The circles mark the location of protective fiberglass domes, most likely covering point defense weapons." He pointed to one corner of the structure that did not have a dome. "The foundation here is consistent with the Chinese HHQ-10 point defense missile system. These large fiberglass structures near the front are shelters for sensor and communications antennas."

Ty pressed a control and the map returned. A bright line led south from Guangzhou deep into the South China Sea. "The *Liaoning* task group will escort the platform, under tow and accompanied by several self-loading container ships, to Thi Tu Island." Ty used the Vietnamese name for the island. The Chinese claimed it as "Zhongye Island," but the current occupiers, the Philippines, called it "Thitu Island." Thitu was the largest island in the Spratly archipelago, and even sported an airstrip. "The transit will take five or six days, depending on the weather.

"When they are close, marines from one of the amphibious assault ships will seize the island, currently held by about forty Filipino soldiers, and the platform will be anchored at one end of the island. Prefabricated containers carried by the merchants will be placed on landing craft and taken ashore, creating barracks, repair shops, hangars for fighters, and other facilities.

"Our engineers estimate it will take three days to anchor the structure. Within twenty-four hours after that, the Chinese will have a base defended

Vietnamese national masquerading as a loyal Chinese citizen,
a headquarters or on a naval base. He hoped they lived long
receive the medal they'd earned.

"...t is the chance of this information being fabricated?" Komamura
...an.

...intelligence chief shrugged. "Anything is possible, but if this infor-
...is false," he added darkly, "then our source has been compromised
...entire intelligence network in China is in jeopardy. That is another
...why we need Japan's help."

"...How?" the professor responded.

...uan answered, "The Japanese Self-Defense Forces have access to over-
...imagery, electronic intelligence, other assets that we do not. It could
...firm or disprove what we know. We will give you a flash drive contain-
...what we know. In return, we'd like your country to share what informa-
...n they have, and also begin careful surveillance of Yulin, Yalong Bay,
...hanjiang, and Guangzhou. We must be ready if the Chinese change their
...lans suddenly. And of course, Japan must be careful not to let the Chinese
...ee them watching."

Komamura replied, "I will pass your request for information to Admiral Kubo. Once he's made aware of the Chinese plan, he will very much
want to monitor their activities."

Hieu continued, "And somehow, we have to develop a joint plan with
Japan to stop the Chinese."

Komamura sighed. "That presents many complications. I can see the
Diet tying itself in knots over whether assisting the Philippines or cooperating with Vietnam is 'self-defense,' as required by our constitution." The
professor's disgust was clear in his tone.

"Let me be clear, Professor. The president and key members of the par-
liament and the party have been briefed, and we see no way to stop the
Chinese operation by ourselves. We are willing to use any means at our
disposal, including armed force, but . . ."

Komamura nodded. The idea of Vietnam's small navy facing a naval
superpower was outlandish at best. "Is there any hope for a peaceful resolution? What about revealing what you've learned to the UN or ASEAN?"

"We've considered that idea, but there's little either organization could
do, and they move too slowly. PLA units are moving now, and as Commander Ty has said, *Liaoning* sails in five days," Phai answered. "The threat
this poses to our national wellbeing is staggering. The Chinese claim the

by an integrated air-defense system, capable of op
high-performance fighters and garrisoned by a battali

Komamura was chilled to the bone. The Chinese
entire South China Sea, ignoring other nations' border
words. A strong military base would let them enforce tha
the nations surrounding the South China Sea had the fire
such a foothold. The Americans could, but he was convinc
risk open war with China, not over a collection of small, d
Even if the United States wanted to fight, they were unprep
sure the Chinese, with the strategic initiative, would be reac
just such a move.

"But one small island with forty soldiers doesn't require t
*Shan* landing ships to capture it." Ty put an image of the ship on t
It was a large, modern-looking design. "Each Type 071 landing si
carries up to eight hundred marines and eighteen armored vehicles. S
neous with the attack on Thi Tu, the Chinese will also invade Song
Island, also known as Southwest Cay, and Northeast Cay approxim
forty-four kilometers to the north. The first island is Vietnamese sover
territory, the second is Filipino," concluded Ty.

The Japanese academic fought to hide his shock and surprise.

"There's more," Ty said firmly. "Soon after China occupies key island
in the Spratly chain, they intend to invade the Senkaku Islands claimed by
your country."

Komamura was stunned. To seize so many of the disputed islands and
reefs in rapid succession was mind-boggling. The Chinese intentions, if true,
were beyond bold. One question surfaced in his mind immediately.

"This information is very detailed. I'm not an intelligence specialist, but
I've learned that naval intelligence is usually guesswork and deduction.
How sure are you of this information?"

Hieu answered, "Very sure. We don't have many of the resources available to Japan or her allies, but we have a source. Over time, it has provided
us with much valuable information on the Chinese, but this is priceless. We
are telling you of this so you will be confident when you speak to Admiral
Kubo, but you will have to convince him on your own. I won't say anything
more about this individual. Knowledge of the source's mere existence is
highly classified. Please do not speak of this source to anyone outside this
room, even Admiral Kubo."

"I understand." Komamura knew little about espionage, but he could entire South China Sea basin, right up to the 12-mile limit from our coast. It would shut down our fishing industry. Not only would a lot of people go hungry, seafood exports are important to out economy - but that doesn't matter, because with China claiming the entire South China Sea, our ports would be effectively blockaded." The urgency in Phai's voice was palpable.

"And that doesn't include the significant oil reserves," Hieu added. "I'm sure you know the numbers better than we do, Professor, but those deposits are my country's economic future."

"China has decided to abandon diplomacy for the sword. We have to be ready to meet them," Phai remarked. "But Professor, why are they moving now? Has something in the Chinese economy recently changed for the worse?"

The academic sat quietly for a moment, considering the question carefully. Finally, he said, "They resolved their own real estate 'bubble' in 2014 successfully, but only by shifting the economic pressure elsewhere. As a result, their cash reserves are dangerously low. The shortfall in oil imports from Saudi Arabia and Iran is also causing major problems, but it's not a sudden thing . . ."

He turned to Commander Ty. "How long does it take to build a platform like the one at Guangzhou?"

"Our engineers say two to three years. And more time before that to design it, of course."

"So the Chinese decided on this course of action at least three years ago," Komamura reasoned. "About the time the shortfall in Iranian oil supplies began."

Admiral Duan nodded. "It's likely. So then, this is not about some new crisis. They're moving now, because after extensive preparations, they're finally ready."

"The carrier!" Hieu blurted out. "*Liaoning*'s workups are complete. She's ready to lead the assault."

Duan nodded, his face grim, "Her pilots are likely the best in the PLA Navy. They will provide air cover for the Chinese engineers while they set up the platform. The Philippines don't have any planes that can match them. We have Su-30 and Su-27 aircraft, based on the same Flanker airframe as the Chinese J-15s, but it's over five hundred kilometers to Thi Tu from any of our bases. The Chinese would have the advantages of radar and SAM coverage, as well as the carrier to recover damaged aircraft."

"It's worse than that," Hieu emphasized. "If they establish their base, they can put a squadron of land-based fighters on the island and cooperate with the squadron aboard *Liaoning*. Those two Chinese squadrons effectively match the power of our entire air force. And they can replace any losses with more aircraft from the mainland." Nodding toward Komamura, Hieu remarked, "And it's completely out of range for planes from Japan."

"This ignores the much more important issue: open conflict with China." Duan asked, "Are any of us ready for that?"

"Not when we are so likely to lose," Hieu answered. "We're willing to fight, but there has to be some chance for success."

Komamura asked Hieu, "If the Chinese are acting now because the carrier is ready, would they undertake this operation without the carrier?"

The admiral frowned for a moment, considering the question. "I don't know. Such a grand plan is unprecedented. This is the PLAN's first large-scale offensive. If they did press ahead without *Liaoning*, they would be more exposed to air attack. Yes. Without the carrier, the odds change to favor us."

"Then stop the carrier," Komamura stated flatly. "You know where she will be for the next five days. They are not aware that you've learned their plans, so they will not be expecting an attack."

"The PLAN's anti-submarine skills are notoriously poor," Hieu conceded. "One of our submarines could easily wait at the mouth of the harbor until she sorties. We don't have to sink her. Even one torpedo hit could send her into the yards for many months."

Duan shook his head. "I'm sorry, but I disagree. The escorts would likely detect the torpedo launch, and probably the submarine itself. An overt attack would be quickly traced back to us. With the Chinese plan frustrated, but still secret, we look like the aggressor."

"Then a more covert attack," Komamura suggested. "Lay mines across the mouth of the harbor, to catch her when the carrier departs. The submarine can be long gone when they are triggered. Also, the defenses won't be as alert now as when the carrier is coming out."

Hieu ordered Ty, "Zoom the map in to show us the harbor at Yalong Bay."

Ty worked the laptop. First, Hainan Island expanded, then the southern half grew until the naval base at the southern tip filled the screen. Ty pressed another key and hydrographic information appeared.

"What is *Liaoning*'s draft?" demanded Hieu.

Ty answered instantly, "Eleven meters," and Komamura saw a small smile on Duan's face. The commander studied the legend for a moment, then pointed to Yalong Bay. "Here is the long finger pier where *Liaoning* is berthed. There are two exits from the harbor, but the northern one, near Yeshu Island, is too shallow, only seven meters. She can't get through, even at high tide. The southern exit, through the breakwater, is thirty meters deep and . . ." He worked the cursor. ". . . three hundred meters wide. The water depth changes smoothly from seventy meters to thirty in the harbor approaches from the south."

Hieu remarked, "And those approaches are completely open water. A submarine captain can pick his course. He will have to go into shallow water," he mused, "but not dangerously so."

"Bottom mines?" Duan asked.

"Of course," Hieu answered. "Russian MDM-6s. *Banh Mi* is in port at Nha Trang. I know Captain Thu well, and he's more than capable of executing this mission. We'll get her crew loading while our specialists figure out the best pattern. She can be under way tomorrow morning."

Ty had been working with the chart. "It's six hundred and seventy kilometers from Nha Trang to Yalong Bay. Transiting at fourteen knots, it will take her twenty-six hours to reach the target. I know Thu as well. He'll shave some time off that figure."

Hieu nodded. "Good. That gives her two days to scout the harbor, one to lay the mines, and a day to clear the area."

Komamura felt a little out of his element. These professionals were planning an attack on another country while he watched and listened. But he had a question. "Isn't Yalong Bay near Yulin, a commercial port? Won't other ships also set off the mines?"

Ty answered. "The MDM-6 is triggered by a combination of a ship's pressure wave, and its acoustic and magnetic signatures. We can adjust the mine to watch for a combination of all three—a combination unique to *Liaoning*. A single mine won't sink her, unless they're very unlucky, but detonating twenty meters away from her bottom?" Ty shrugged, but he was smiling.

"They'll have to move her from Yalong Bay back to the yard at Dalian, possibly under tow, then put her in dry dock. She will be out of action for months, and by then the seasons will have changed. They need over a week of good weather to tow the platform to the Spratlys and anchor it."

Phai grinned. "I like it. 'The supreme art of war is to subdue the enemy without fighting,'" he quoted.

"A Chinese proverb?" Komamura asked.

"The great master Sun Tzu himself," the political chief explained. "There is still a risk of lives being lost, but it is much reduced compared to an armed occupation, or a battle at sea."

"Absolutely," Komamura agreed firmly. Then he asked, "Has any of this intelligence been shared with the Philippine government?"

Phai sighed. "There has been some discussion at very high levels, but even forewarned, the full weight of the Philippine military could not stop the Chinese operation. And telling them greatly increases the risk to our source."

Komamura asked, "Should *Liaoning* successfully sail, would you reconsider?"

"I understand your concern, Professor," Hieu answered solemnly. "Vietnam will not allow Philippine soldiers and civilians to suffer a Chinese attack without warning. As Commander Ty said, it will take the Chinese almost a week to tow their platform to Thi Tu Island. That's more than enough time for the Filipinos to evacuate the island—or reinforce it, if they are insane enough to defend it."

"You wouldn't mind them leaving, though, so you could exercise Vietnam's claim to the island," Komamura prompted.

"Absent a Chinese task force, perhaps," Hieu answered. "We will press our claim in the proper forum. But if the Chinese occupy the islands and the adjoining seas, everybody loses."

Phai turned to Hieu. Using a slightly more formal tone, he said, "The Political Directorate approves of this plan. I will notify the Defense Council of this operation, recommending it as the only possible way of stopping the Chinese invasion without challenging their armed forces directly and risking open war. I'm sure they will approve it."

Then turning back to Komamura, he added, "And we owe you our thanks, Professor. Our intention was to ask for Japan's help in the hopes that they would find a way to assist us. It appears they have already sent us their best weapon."

"I'm sure I thought of nothing original," the professor insisted. "If you can drive me to the Japanese embassy, I will contact Admiral Kubo on a secure line."

"Of course," Hieu answered. "I know you have a flight back to Japan later today, but would you consider extending your visit? I will fly down to Nha Trang this afternoon and visit *Banh Mi* and her captain. Would you like to accompany me?"

Komamura smiled broadly. "I would like that very much."

# 2

## MISSION COMPLETED

19 August 2016
August 1st Building, Ministry of National Defense Compound
Beijing, People's Republic of China

Admiral Wei Zi'en sat dispassionately as his staff officer briefed the Central Military Commission on the vengeance strike against Vietnam. Beneath the stoic exterior, Wei was a troubled man. The Trident operation hadn't even formally begun and already they had experienced a serious setback. It wasn't fatal, but doubt in the People's Liberation Army Navy's ability to successfully execute the operation had risen immediately.

"Contact with the Vietnamese merchant *Vinaship Sea* was made yesterday at 0826 local time, here." Senior Captain Deng highlighted the area on the South China Sea chart with his laser pointer. "In compliance with his orders, the commanding officer of submarine hull 407 conducted a complete search of the area and waited until *Vinaship Sea* was isolated from any nearby traffic. He closed to a range of six kilometers, visually confirmed the target's identity, and fired two Yu-6 torpedoes at 1347. The weapons hit, causing a catastrophic secondary explosion that sank the merchant very quickly and with no survivors."

"You are certain of this?" asked General Wen Feng, the minister of national defense.

"Absolutely, sir. The South Korean container vessel *Hanjin Malta* reported seeing a large plume of smoke on the horizon over the international distress channel at 1349. They approached the source of the smoke, and issued a general distress call at 1447 when they came upon the wreckage. They found no survivors."

General Su Yide, chief of the general staff department, added, "The large secondary explosion confirms the merchant ship was carrying military arms for their outpost on Nanzai Island. This proves beyond any doubt that the Vietnamese are aware of our upcoming operation."

Wei bristled at Su's remark. "General, the Vietnamese showed their hand when they mined the entrance to Yalong Bay. And while the result of their audacious attack is inconvenient, it does not significantly affect our overall plan."

"My point, *Admiral*," sneered Su, "has nothing to do with your precious aircraft carrier, but rather that our plan was heavily predicated on the element of surprise. I think you would agree that we have lost that!"

President Chen Dao tapped the table loudly with his fingers. "Gentlemen, the question is how do we compensate for these events, not whether we carry out our plan. The operation must continue. The circumstances that have compelled us down this path have not improved. On the contrary, they have only gotten worse."

The president's reference to the growing economic crisis ended the argument abruptly. China's well-being was threatened. Scoring political points wouldn't matter if the economy came crumbling down around their ears.

Despite the economic turbulence in Europe and the United States, the Central Committee of the Chinese Communist Party had successfully managed a gradual slowdown of the economy—at least that was what the Chinese government claimed officially. In reality, the dip was far lower than desired. China had the resources, but like a juggler with an unexpected ball tossed into the mix, its rhythm was disrupted. It wouldn't take much of a jolt before balls started dropping. That jolt was oil.

Nearly two-thirds of China's annual petroleum demand came from outside the country, with half of it coming from the Persian Gulf, primarily Saudi Arabia and Iran. When scandal and the Arab Spring hit the Persian Gulf, the flow of oil began to wane.

The release of the data on Iran's failed nuclear program happened just before Iran's 2013 presidential elections. It triggered demonstrations and protests that were larger and more frequent than in 2009, plunging the country into chaos. By the end of 2015, strikes and outright sabotage began cutting deeply into Iran's exports.

On the other side of the gulf, Saudi Arabia was embroiled in demonstrations demanding democratic elections. Clerics issued fatwas calling for work stoppages. Maintenance "accidents" happened more frequently. And the second largest oil producer in the world began to waver.

By the spring of 2016, the shortfall had become severe enough that China was pulling from her strategic oil reserves to meet the economy's daily needs. At the projected rate, the shortfall would deplete China's meager strategic reserve within a year. After that, the economy would feel the reduced flow of oil directly. None of the economic estimates presented to the CCP painted a rosy picture; some were downright dire.

The leaders in Beijing quickly eliminated Africa and Latin America as alternatives. Africa was too unstable, and Latin America just didn't have the capacity. Russia wasn't even briefly considered, due to security concerns. Then China's leadership looked southward toward the huge oil and gas reserves right in their own neighborhood, in the Nansha Islands.

The Nansha Islands, or the Spratly Islands as they were known to most of the world, were scattered over hundreds of thousands of square kilometers of the South China Sea. Although made up of over a hundred small islands, atolls, and reefs, they couldn't come up with five square kilometers of dry land between them. Beneath the waters surrounding them lay potential oil and gas reserves rivaling that of Kuwait, OPEC's third-largest oil producer.

And oil and natural gas weren't the only riches; the Spratly archipelago also possessed productive fishing grounds, already an important source of food and revenue for the countries that made up its coasts, and it flanked one of the world's busiest shipping lanes.

But more than one country had claimed almost every island and reef, and decades of diplomacy hadn't resolved a single dispute. If China were going to fix her energy crisis and secure her future, she'd have to resolve the issue by force.

President Chen remarked, "I'm assuming, Admiral, that you have a backup plan for providing air cover. Or are you suggesting *Liaoning* can be repaired in time?"

Wei shook his head as he spoke. "No, Comrade President, the mine caused extensive damage to her starboard propulsion shafts, propellers, and rudder. She'll have to be towed to Dalian shipyard for permanent repairs. She will be out of commission for at least eight months, maybe longer."

"I see," said Chen. His tone and facial expression showed his disappointment. Their new aircraft carrier had been a key component in the Trident operations plan. Her availability after workups had dominated the timing of the entire operation.

"Well then, Admiral Wei, how will you provide the necessary air coverage?" Chen demanded.

"Sir, the Trident operations plan had a number of contingencies built into it. One included the possibility that *Liaoning* was incapacitated by enemy action. But it assumed that the carrier was lost *after* the first amphibious assault, not before." Wei shot a quick glance over at General Su; he was still frowning. "However, General Wang and I have a modification that would provide fighter cover and dedicated ground support for the amphibious forces."

Wei gestured toward the People's Liberation Army Air Force commander, who picked up the explanation. "Comrade President, we propose shifting the bulk of the navy and air force's tanker assets to the Guangzhou Military Region, along with the navy's Su-30MK2 Flankers from the 10th Air Regiment. These will augment the Su-30MKK and J-11 Flanker squadrons in my 6th Air Regiment and will provide an adequate force to cover the invasion objectives in the Nansha Islands."

"Won't that compromise the air defense of the motherland?" countered Chen.

"No, sir," Wang replied firmly. "In the campaign plan, the 4th and 5th Air Regiments have responsibility for air defense. The 6th Air Regiment was being held in reserve. We recommend using this reserve immediately, along with some naval fighters, to make up for the lack of carrier aviation. We need the additional combat aircraft, as well as the tankers, to sustain combat air patrols so far from our air bases."

Chen nodded and leaned back in his chair. Satisfied, he polled the other members of the CMC. "Are there any other comments on the proposal by our navy and air force commanders?"

General Wen raised his hand. "I concur with the recommendations by Admiral Wei and General Wang, however I have still not heard a response to General Su's concern that the element of surprise has been lost. We must assume that at least part of the campaign plan has been compromised. The Vietnamese are not fools. It would take a very serious provocation for them to act militarily. From their point of view, Trident would meet that criterion."

Immediately after *Liaoning* had been safely returned to her berth, the PLAN began a meticulous but quiet sweep of the channel. It took two days and many passes by mine-hunting sonars and divers before the channel into Yalong Bay was declared clear.

As the search was expanded to cover the waters just outside the marked channel, the divers discovered a Russian MDM-6 mine on the sea floor. One of Russia's most advanced naval mines, it was laid only by submarines.

The mine appeared brand-new. It had not been in the water long, and its fuzing mechanism had failed. Unfortunately, the nameplate data had been deliberately removed. After disarming the mine, Chinese ordnance engineers quickly took it apart, looking for any identifying marks or stock numbers. Several were found on some of the subcomponents, and armed with this data, the Chinese went to the Russians.

The Chinese ambassador in Moscow confronted the foreign minister directly, demanding to know who had purchased the mines. The Russians declined to answer, stating that the subcomponent numbers would not identify the specific mine. When pressed, the Russians politely refused to discuss arms sales with other nations, as they were confidential—the same terms the Chinese had insisted upon when they purchased Russian weapon systems. The Chinese ambassador walked away empty-handed, but that had been expected.

At the same time, China's 11th Technical Reconnaissance Bureau hacked into the sales database of the Rosobornexport Company, Russia's state-owned corporation in charge of all foreign arms sales. Also known as the "2020 Unit," these highly trained Chinese cyber-warriors kept tabs on Russia's military by monitoring Russian ministry of defense computer networks. They were very good at what they did.

In less than two days, they reported their findings. Both India and Vietnam had taken delivery of MDM-6 mines within the last three years. A quick review of Indian submarine operations eliminated them as the perpetrator—neither of their nuclear-powered submarines had left port for more than three days over the last several months. Their diesel submarines lacked the endurance to make such a long trip, and none were out of port for more than a week. The only other suspect, Vietnam, was exercising their newly purchased Kilo-class submarines often, and it was a very short trip from Nha Trang to Yalong Bay.

"General Wen, I agree the Vietnamese possess some knowledge of our plan," replied Wei. "But their actions also reveal their belief that the absence of *Liaoning* will force us to abandon or postpone them. If we make any observable changes to the forces or schedule we've already released on the upcoming exercise, it will alert the Vietnamese that we are on to them. It's very likely that there is a spy in our midst, who we must assume will see any changes in the units' orders and report it. Other than increasing our security measures, I don't think it is prudent to do anything."

"Of course there is a spy!" snapped Su as he stood abruptly. "My security personnel are already conducting a thorough review of everyone who has had access to the campaign plan." The general's stern gaze made it clear that included everyone present.

Su paused, his head hanging low as he took a deep breath to calm himself. His colleagues just didn't understand the source of his frustration. They didn't see the larger threat.

"I am not particularly worried about Vietnam's response to our impending military operation. They do not have the combat power to seriously challenge us. If they try, we can defeat them. Yes, we might sustain higher losses, but the final outcome is not in question. The greater issue, the more important question is, have they shared this information with any other nation? In particular, the United States."

Only silence greeted General Su's unpleasant question. If the United States knew of their plans, and chose to intervene, the outcome of the operation would not be in China's favor. Every member of the CMC knew America was still militarily exhausted and economically weakened, but no one was willing to assume America would just sit idly by while China forcibly annexed the disputed islands. Their plan was to present the United States with a fait accompli, and then dare them to act.

President Chen finally broke the awkward quiet. "General, do you have any indications the Americans are aware of our plan?"

"No, sir," he replied while stiffly shaking his head. "My intelligence department has been working closely with the Ministry of State Security's Second Bureau, and there is no evidence at this time that the Americans have a clue as to what we are doing."

"But you fear they will?" asked Wen.

"Yes, Minister, that is my greatest fear." Su stood upright and straightened his uniform jacket. "Comrades, there is an old saying: 'When two tigers fight, one is killed and one is crippled.' If the United States joins the fight, it will not end well for us, even if we are victorious."

General Wen smiled. He was an aficionado of ancient Chinese wisdom, and believed it was just as applicable in today's high-tech world as it was centuries past.

"You were always the blunt one, Yide," chuckled Wen. "However, your concerns are not without merit. What do you recommend?"

"Sir, if we no longer have stealth working in our favor, then speed is the next best thing. We must move before Vietnam has a chance to react. I recommend we advance our timetable by three weeks, and begin the invasion of phase one objectives on August 31st."

"Three weeks!" protested Wang, astounded. "There is no way we can get the air defense platform in position and operational that soon. We were cutting it close to begin with."

"I'm aware of this, General," Su sympathized. "But it is my belief that the Vietnamese will use the platform's departure as a warning indicator. They either know or at least suspect its purpose. They will be watching Guangzhou shipyard for any change in its status. The longer we delay its departure, the more relaxed our adversary will be. We have to make them believe they have been successful, that the operation has been postponed."

Wang's irritation was not soothed by Su's explanation. "That platform is crucial to establishing an integrated air defense around Nanzai and Taiping Islands. Those islands have the largest airstrips in the entire Nansha chain and controlling that airspace is absolutely essential to our success!"

"There will be far less resistance if we don't telegraph our intentions to the Vietnamese!" Su shot back. "The navy's air-defense destroyers can temporarily fill the role of the platform. We can also fly in additional surface-to-air missile systems once the islands are secured."

Wei reached over and placed his hand on the PLAAF commander's shoulder. They weren't going to win this argument, not with the minister of defense and the chief of staff in lockstep agreement. It was best to acknowledge the order and get to work on the changes needed to make the improvisations work.

Wen cleared his throat. "Comrade President, I recommend you approve Admiral Wei and General Wang's changes, as well as General Su's suggestion to advance the overall timetable."

Chen answered formally, "Thank you, General Wen. The recommended changes are approved."

Wen bowed politely, and turned toward his comrades. "I want all changes to the operational orders on my desk in two days. Do not make any large-scale unit movements. Do it in a piecemeal fashion. We must use extreme caution and deny the Vietnamese any signs that we are adapting to their strategy. Any final comments or questions?"

"Just one," replied Su. "Keep the knowledge of these changes, as well as the recovered mine, to your immediate staff and your senior political commissars. No messages, no e-mails until further notice. I know this places an additional burden on you and your people, but we must protect this vital information. If you absolutely need someone to help with the planning, contact my office and we'll get that individual cleared."

"Anything else?" Wen asked. No one spoke. "Very well, gentlemen, you have your orders. Carry them out."

19 August 2016
The White House
Washington, D.C.

Joanna Patterson leaned on the conference table in the situation room, her eyes darting back and forth from *North Dakota*'s message to an annotated chart of the South China Sea. Her right hand groped along the desktop for her morning coffee. Finding the cup with her mocha latte, she took a sip as she read the next section of Commander Mitchell's report. *Commander Mitchell.* She was still having a tough time wrapping her brain around that concept. Wasn't he just a junior lieutenant only a few years ago? Now he was the commanding officer of his own submarine. Was she really that old?

She'd made the mistake of voicing this question to her husband soon after their return from Jerry's change of command ceremony. His response was a completely deadpan and wholly unsympathetic, "Well, yeah." She threw something at him, as she recalled.

Looking at the narrative, she tried to imagine being there as the Chinese sub got into position. The shock when Jerry realized that the Chinese had actually blown the Vietnamese merchant out of the water. This had to be tied to the *Liaoning* incident; there was really no other possibility. She shook her head; the timing of these events couldn't be worse. A potential crisis with another superpower just as the president's reelection campaign was struggling to fend off his Republican adversary's attacks.

The major foreign policy success of exposing the failed Iranian nuclear program had long been forgotten. The continuing poor economic situation now held center stage. Unfortunately, many of the problems and issues affecting the stubbornly lackluster U.S. economy were offshore, in other countries, outside the president's control. Still, the aftershocks from those countries reached the United States, causing pain and hardship. And since professional politics is a "what have you done for me lately" kind of game, the president's approval rating had taken a plunge.

A knock at the door pulled her from her musings. A navy lieutenant stood there, half leaning into the doorway. "Dr. Patterson, the national security advisor wants to talk to you. Line two, ma'am."

"Thank you, Andy," Joanna replied. She walked quickly over to the phone, picked up the receiver, and hit the blinking button. "Yes, Ray."

"Joanna, grab your material on the Vietnamese merchant sinking and get up here. I managed to weasel a few minutes on the president's schedule from Milt Alvarez, but we need to be in the Oval Office in ten minutes."

"I'm leaving now," she exclaimed. Joanna tossed the receiver back onto the cradle, then rushed over and gathered her purse, notebook, Jerry's message, the chart, and background information. Running for the elevator, she wondered why she bothered to wear heels.

Dr. Ray Kirkpatrick, the national security advisor, waited for her by the security checkpoint. As she stopped to show her badge, Kirkpatrick stepped up. "Let me take some of that, Joanna."

"Thanks. I got up here as fast as I could."

"That you did. And we still have a moment or two to spare."

"Good! Let me run a brush through my hair. I must look like a mess," Joanna remarked as she dumped the rest of her material into her boss's arms.

"Actually, I would say only slightly unkempt," joked Kirkpatrick. Patterson's annoyed look caused him to chuckle. Then he said more seriously, "Remember, the navy had a piece on the sinking in this morning's read book, so the president has a good background on *North Dakota*'s report. What he hasn't heard is your theory on the linkage with the *Liaoning* mining."

"Got it. Anything else?" asked Joanna.

"Be brief. Milt is not amused that I bulled our way in this morning."

"Yes, sir."

No sooner had she spoken, the door to the Oval Office opened and a tight-lipped Milton Alvarez emerged. "Dr. Kirkpatrick, Dr. Patterson, the president will see you now."

Joanna smiled as she walked past Alvarez's stern glare. Kirkpatrick was right; he was not a happy camper.

"Ray, Joanna, please come in!" exclaimed an excited President Ken Myles. Pointing toward the couch he added, "Please, sit down."

"Thank you, sir," said Kirkpatrick as he motioned for Patterson to sit next to him. "I promised Milt we'd be expeditious, but Joanna has been working on a theory that I believe you need to hear."

A series of high-pitched electronic beeps signaled to everyone present that Alvarez had started a stopwatch.

"Oh for God's sake, Milt! Give it a rest," Myles groaned.

"Mr. President, I'm just trying . . ."

"Yes, yes, I know. The almighty schedule!" Myles's voice may have been sharp, but there was a twinkle in his eye. Looking back at Patterson, he said. "Go ahead, please."

"Mr. President, the article in today's read book provided a synopsis of the sinking of the Vietnamese merchant ship *Vinaship Sea,* by a Chinese submarine."

"Yes, it seems that our favorite submariner has found himself in the thick of it once again," replied Myles, smiling.

It was well known within the White House that Joanna and her husband, Senator Lowell Hardy, had a special fondness for a certain Jerry Mitchell that dated back to their serving together on USS *Memphis.*

Momentarily distracted, Joanna cleared her throat and continued, "This latest incident is just one of a series of events that have been part of an escalating trend over the last two years."

"To say the least," remarked the president. As an expert on Asian affairs, he'd watched the deteriorating situation in the South China Sea closely. The rhetoric and level of harassment between the disputing parties had been bad, going as far back as the 1990s. However, the number of incidents had increased dramatically following the collision of a Vietnamese warship with a Chinese fishing vessel in December 2014. The Chinese claimed it was an intentional ramming, while the Vietnamese countered that the Chinese vessel was fishing illegally within the Vietnamese Exclusive Economic Zone and was evading pursuit.

This was followed by the CCP's public declaration the following March, that the Spratly, or Nansha, Islands had become a core national interest to China, elevating the dispute to the same political level as Taiwanese independence. This red flag had generated immense concern from every nation in the region.

"It was no surprise when the PLAN announced that this year's major multi-fleet exercise would be in the South China Sea area, or that it included their new carrier *Liaoning*," Patterson continued. "We expected a very big exercise. In fact, it's been over twenty years since we've seen an exercise of this magnitude.

"Nine days ago, as *Liaoning* was departing Yalong Bay to take part in final air group training, she suffered an unknown engineering casualty and was returned to her berth. The official press release was vague, and offered no details. However, preliminary analysis of COMINT and imagery data strongly suggests she detonated a mine."

Myles's eyes popped wide open. "A mine? In Chinese waters?"

"Yes, sir. There was a reference to a 'large plume' of water, and imagery shows she has a distinct starboard list. This suggests significant flooding. Subsequent COMINT hits contained allusions to 'distorted lines' and 'bent fans' that almost certainly refer to the propulsion shafts and propellers. All of which point toward a mine; most likely a large bottom influence mine, laid by a submarine."

"But who, and why?" Myles demanded.

Joanna shot a quick glance toward Kirkpatrick, who motioned for her to go on. "I can only come up with one possible suspect—Vietnam."

"Vietnam!?" exclaimed Myles. "That's absurd, Joanna! Why would they intentionally antagonize China?"

"Vietnam has a budding submarine force with three modified Kilo-class submarines. The Russian export package included advanced bottom influence mines."

"What about India?" countered Myles. "Or South Korea, or Taiwan? All those navies have subs with a mining capability." The president looked over at Kirkpatrick, who nodded, confirming the fact. "And they all have significant disputes with China."

"I checked on submarine deployments throughout the region. We have good information on South Korea, Japan, and Taiwan, because they are U.S. allies. Nothing matches there. India's nuclear subs are accounted for, and their diesel subs don't have the endurance. We can't confirm the movements of the Vietnamese Kilos, particularly when the distance between their homeport and Yalong Bay is so short. When you add the deliberate sinking of a Vietnamese merchant ship, which was acting suspiciously, by a Chinese submarine, it all but clinches it." Joanna sat back and watched the president as he got up and started pacing.

He walked quickly, clearly agitated by the possibility. "That still doesn't answer why," Myles reminded her.

"I don't know, sir," Joanna admitted. "I suspect the Vietnamese were worried about the upcoming exercise in some way. *Liaoning* was going to be the flagship, after all. These two events, the mining and the sinking, happened too close to each other to be a coincidence."

Myles paced about in silence, worry clearly visible on his face. After about thirty seconds, he turned abruptly toward Kirkpatrick. "What do you think, Ray?"

"Sir, I recommend that you increase surveillance in the region. We don't know enough about what's behind this, and that makes me nervous. You'll need more eyes if we are going to get adequate warning, and more data so we can react properly."

Kirkpatrick handed Myles a sheet of paper. "I recommend moving some satellites, revising the deployments of our reconnaissance aircraft in the area, and increasing the number of submarines. The South China Sea is too big for just two subs. We can brief the squadron commodore and the commanding officers by video-teleconference, and then deploy the remaining Squadron Fifteen submarines. This will give you a total of four boats on station."

"Very good, Ray. We'll go with your recommendation, but with a slight twist."

"Sir?" asked Kirkpatrick, confused.

"Have the two boats already in the South China Sea head for Guam. I want the commanding officers to be briefed personally."

Surprised, Kirkpatrick was about to protest when the president cut him short. "I know there's a risk with this decision, Ray. But if Joanna is right, we have time to coordinate this properly. Besides, I've become sensitive to having a submarine exposed for long periods of time doing a VTC at sea. Only this time, it's two subs in a potentially hostile environment. I want those commanding officers to have all the time they need to ask questions. Besides, sending someone out will reinforce the seriousness of the situation. Pull them back and have Joanna go out and brief them."

"Me, sir?" Patterson was surprised by the president's order, but she quickly composed herself. "I mean . . . yes, sir."

"It's okay, Joanna, I know it's a bit of a surprise. I have to send one of you, but I can't send Ray. Sending the national security advisor out to Guam would draw far too much attention; you're less conspicuous. Give those captains everything you can and emphasize our need for more information. Get them out there and probe, but for God's sake tell them to be careful. If people are getting ready to shoot at each other, our subs should not be in the way."

"Yes, sir. I'll leave immediately."

"Give the commanding officers my personal best wishes for a safe and successful mission, and while you're out there, pass on my regards to Commander Mitchell."

# 3

# THE SUMMONS

22 August 2016
USS *North Dakota*
Apra Harbor, Guam

It was an absolutely glorious bright summer day. Jerry basked in the warm sun as *North Dakota* cleared the entrance to Apra Harbor at Guam Island. He noted with satisfaction that Lieutenant Junior Grade Quela Lymburn had "split the uprights," passing the channel marker buoys right down the middle. One of three female officers in his wardroom, "Q," as she was dubbed, was one of his best ship handlers. His XO said she was a natural and strongly recommend she conn the boat in, as the passage to Guam's inner harbor was even narrower than the channel out of Pearl Harbor. So while Q and the harbor pilot shared the confined space of the cockpit, Jerry and the lookouts enjoyed the more luxurious accommodations of the flying bridge.

Confident that his boat was in capable hands, Jerry leaned against the railing and took in the sights; this was his first visit to the U.S. territory. It was everything he expected from a South Pacific island. The water was a deep bright blue. The surface was barely rippling from the light wind, marred only by the occasional splash from one of the escorting dolphins as it leapt ahead. The cliffs of Orote Point to his right were covered with lush, thick green bushes and protruding palm trees. He strained through his binoculars to see if he could pick out any remnants of Fort Santiago, a nineteenth-century Spanish fort, or a more recent Japanese pillbox.

Down on the deck, the XO and the chief of the boat were busy with the line handlers as they prepared the fittings to moor the sub. Master Chief Electrician's Mate Marco Pompei moved with ease along the still-wet deck as he carefully checked each cleat to make sure it was secure. The diminutive figure literally sprang from one cleat to the next, his movements betraying his excitement. Pompei was coming home, and it had been a long time.

Everyone was where they should be, doing what they were supposed to in a diligent and professional manner. Jerry felt pride well up within him, as well as a sense of fulfillment. It was then that he realized this was the "feeling" that Senator Hardy had spoken about during the change of command ceremony.

It had been a typically mild Hawaiian spring day, with abundant sunshine and a light breeze. Jerry was all decked out in his dress whites, complete with several rows of medals. They clinked with his every move, and he was sure everyone would know just how nervous he really was by all the jingling. Looking toward the audience, Jerry saw his wife, Emily, his sister Clarice flown in from Minnesota, and Joanna Patterson sitting in the front row. All were brightly dressed with huge smiles on their faces—beaming the pride they all felt. He considered himself a very blessed man.

Jerry had asked his former skipper to be the keynote speaker, not because Lowell Hardy had been a particularly good commanding officer, but during a stressful combat situation he'd risen to the occasion and showed true leadership. He was also, now, a close friend and mentor.

Addressing the crowd, Hardy explained that "taking command of a submarine will be one of the most exhilarating things Jerry will ever do during his lifetime; it will also be one of the most terrifying.

"Just think about it," Hardy instructed them. "When you take command, you are responsible for over two billion dollars' worth of hardware, including a nuclear reactor, and the lives of over a hundred people. You have to make sure they have what they need to do their jobs. You have to train them, get them promoted, if you decide they deserve it, and sometimes discipline them. Their well-being is your charge; and not just the members of your crew, but their families as well.

"And you'll be surprised that even with one hundred and fifteen or so people crammed into exceptionally tight quarters, at just how lonely you will be. Every eye will be on you, superiors and subordinates alike, watching your every move, your every decision. In times of adversity, you can turn to no one else. Your chiefs and officers can provide wise counsel, but in the end, the decision rests with you, the captain. *You are where the buck stops.*"

Hardy paused to let the point sink in, and then added bluntly, "If that doesn't scare the hell out of you, then you are either not human or insane.

"Now, I have to confess that I wasn't the ideal commanding officer. I let the terrifying aspect of the job dominate my thoughts, and it had an adverse effect on my behavior. But more importantly, it had an adverse effect on my crew."

Jerry was flabbergasted. Did Hardy really just publicly admit to his shortcomings as a captain? Stunned by what he had just heard, Jerry sat in total amazement. Then the other shoe dropped.

"Stop looking so shocked, Mr. Mitchell!" Hardy commented casually. "You're not showing proper deference to your former skipper."

The audience burst into laughter, while Jerry's face flushed with embarrassment. Hardy hadn't even turned around while at the podium.

"Now, where was I?" the senator asked whimsically. "Oh yes, the fear thing. You can't get away from it. It's an integral part of the responsibility that an individual bears as a commanding officer. And though it does force you to think your decisions through, a good skipper doesn't let it dominate his thoughts and actions. A good skipper focuses on the positive aspects of command, which inevitably means focusing on the crew.

"You see, a successful command tour rests with the crew, not with a single individual, regardless of how talented he or she may be. So here is my one piece of advice, Jerry: take good care of your crew, and they will take care of you. And you'll know when you've done it right. There will be an indescribable feeling of peaceful satisfaction.

"A fortunate commanding officer will experience this feeling as his tour draws to a close. A truly noteworthy one will experience it early on. Given my knowledge of Commander Mitchell's character, I'm confident he falls into the latter category."

The crackle of the radio brought Jerry back into the here and now. Raising his binoculars, Jerry spotted the two tugs assigned to assist *North Dakota* with her landing. Tugs *Goliath* and *Qupuha* were powerful, stout little vessels. While not much to look at, they were vital in executing a good landing; particularly in tricky waterways like Guam's inner harbor. As much as Jerry loved subs, he had to admit they were pigs on the surface.

Jerry dropped to one knee and squinted at the flat-panel display.

Shading his eyes with his hands, he finally made out that they were on course zero eight three and, according to the display, were right on track. Rising, he looked through his binoculars toward the Drydock Point range. A range is a natural, or more often artificial, pair of landmarks that when lined up correctly, provided a visual reference that a ship was on a specific course. The two flashing yellow lights were squarely in line, one directly over the other—Q was dead on track. Jerry smiled.

"Captain, buoy three is just off the starboard bow," announced Lymburn.

"Very well, OOD." Shifting to his right, Jerry spotted the green channel buoy; it marked the location for their first turn. Just to the right of the buoy was the turquoise-colored water over Western Shoal. It still amazed him that in less than twenty-five yards, the water depth went from more than one hundred feet deep to two feet or less. They could literally drive right up next to the shoal and still have plenty of water beneath them. The harbor pilot, of course, would keep them at a safe distance.

As *North Dakota* slowly approached the channel marker, Jerry could see another red buoy farther behind, with the greenish waters of Jade Shoal nearby. A minute later the bridge speaker squawked to life. "Bridge, Navigator. Buoy three abeam to starboard, stand by to mark the turn."

Lymburn acknowledged the report and leaned over the starboard side of the cockpit. Constantly shifting her view from fore to aft, she watched as the buoy slid past the boat's rudder. On cue, Rothwell's voice came over the speaker, "Bridge, Navigator. Mark the turn."

The harbor pilot nodded his approval and Lymburn keyed the mike. "Pilot, Bridge. Right standard rudder, steady course one four one."

"Right standard rudder, steady course one four one, Pilot, aye. Bridge, my rudder is right standard."

*North Dakota* settled smartly onto her new course. Jerry saw the two tugs fall into line as the trio threaded their way through the shoals on both sides. With another slight turn to starboard, his boat was lined up with the inner harbor entrance. Up ahead, a small yard craft moved the boom of the barrier gate, clearing their path.

The concrete walls that lined the inner harbor entrance were even closer than the shoals, but they had good water right up to the edge, and Lymburn had no problems getting the boat through. She slowed *North Dakota* to bare steerageway as they passed Polaris Point to port. The two tugs split and moved to opposite sides of the submarine, positioning themselves to turn her completely around. Jerry saw the submarine tender, USS *Frank Cable*, jutting out stern first from Wharf A. Tied up along her starboard side were two subs, both Improved *Los Angeles*-class boats. To the left of the tender, along the channel entrance wall, was Wharf B, their designated berth. Ten minutes and one tug repositioning later, *North Dakota* gently kissed the camels along the seawall.

As the lines were tossed over to the sailors on land, Jerry handed his binoculars to one of the lookouts and said, "Well done, Q. That was an excellent approach and landing, and in a new harbor to boot."

"Thank you, sir," replied the young woman. Her face was full of pride, as well as a little relief.

Jerry thanked the harbor pilot for his assistance, and slid over the side of the cockpit onto the suspended rope ladder dangling along the sail's starboard side. Carefully, he climbed down to the deck and headed aft. The lines were just being doubled up, and a small crane was placing the brow over to the seawall onto the hull. Jerry waved to get his XO's attention. Seeing his skipper's signal, Thigpen walked over to him, gingerly avoiding the line handlers.

"Nice landing by Q," he said proudly.

"Indeed it was, and I said so," remarked Jerry.

"I figured as much." Thigpen then pointed over to a young petty officer pacing nervously by a car. "I believe your ride is here, sir."

"Yeah, I suppose so," Jerry said with disappointment. "The squadron headquarters isn't that far," he protested to no one in particular. "It would have been nice to take a little walk."

Thigpen chuckled. "I've already got a working party standing by to load the supplies the Chop ordered. Is there anything else you need me to take care of, sir?"

"Just one, Bernie. Get the COB off the boat." Thigpen opened his mouth to protest, but Jerry raised his hand and cut him off. "I know, I know, he'll complain and spew profanities like his volcanic namesake, but this is his home. We can make do without him for a few hours so he can visit family he hasn't seen in years."

"I'll try, sir. But MP can be *quite* stubborn when he wants to," replied Thigpen, smiling. Stern, uncompromising, but fair to a fault, Master Chief Marco Pompei was well respected by everyone on *North Dakota*. He would back you up without reservation if you were in the right, correct you if you were wrong, but God help you if you were just plain stupid. It was unfortunate that his initials were synonymous with "military police," an apt nickname that no one, including Jerry, used to his face.

"I hear you," Jerry said knowingly, then added with emphasis. "Make it an order. Get the whole Goat Locker to help you if necessary, just get his butt on the beach."

"Aye, aye, Skipper. Enjoy your meeting."

"Thanks, I'll try. But you know that it has to be something bigger than the incident we witnessed to haul our boat all the way back to Guam. I'll let you know what's going on as soon as I get back."

Saluting the ensign now flying at the sub's stern, Jerry walked across the brow toward the awaiting car. Behind him, Jerry heard the loudspeaker announcing, *"North Dakota,* departing." Seeing Jerry approaching, the petty officer quickly opened the door for him and saluted.

"Welcome to Guam, Captain. I'm to take you to the meeting with Commodore Simonis."

"Thank you," replied Jerry as he returned the salute. Climbing inside, Jerry watched with surprise as the young sailor goosed the car and raced down the road at a speed that easily exceeded the posted limit. The obvious urgency got Jerry wondering again. Just what the hell kind of meeting was he attending?

The Squadron Fifteen headquarters building was barely half a mile away. It wasn't even two minutes before the car pulled right up to the main entrance. Another petty officer scurried over and opened the door for Jerry. Saluting, he said, "Welcome to Squadron Fifteen, Captain. If you'll follow me I'll take you to the conference room."

Jerry was unceremoniously whisked through the security checkpoint; stopping only long enough to sign the visitor's log and collect an ID badge. Once through the turnstiles, the petty officer walked briskly down a hallway to a set of large double doors at the end. The red flashing light above the door signified a classified meeting was in session. The sailor snapped one of the doors open and stood at attention while Jerry strode through.

Inside the spacious conference room, he saw a dozen or so individuals gathered into three small groups. He immediately recognized Rear Admiral Wayne Burroughs, Commander, Submarine Force, U.S. Pacific Fleet. Whatever was happening, it had to be big for COMSUBPAC to fly all the way to Guam. To his right was a navy captain, probably Charles Simonis, the squadron commodore, and to his left was Dr. Joanna Patterson.

Surprised, Jerry came to a complete stop just inside the conference room. Joanna's face lit up when she saw him, and as he feared, she marched right on over and gave him a big hug. Awkwardly, he returned the embrace. *Well, so much for first impressions,* he thought ruefully.

"Jerry! It is so good to see you!" Joanna exclaimed. "The president sends his warmest regards."

Jerry groaned inwardly. While he didn't doubt that the greeting was sincere, or that she meant well, the circumstances couldn't have been worse. He'd worked hard to downplay his political connections. Unfortunately, his reputation as a naval officer with unusual political pull continued to dog him.

Joanna's greeting would only serve to reinforce that reputation, one that tended to complicate his relationship with his peers, as well as with senior officers. Jerry also suspected it had something to do with the nervousness of the two petty officers earlier.

"It's good to see you too, Joanna—Dr. Patterson," he replied. "But it's a bit of a surprise. Since you're here, should I assume that things are worse than I suspected?"

Instantly, Joanna's jubilant countenance transformed to one of grim concern. Patting his arm lightly, she answered, "Considerably worse, Jerry. Considerably worse."

Burroughs cleared his throat, grabbing Joanna's attention. "Dr. Patterson, I hate to interrupt, but we do need to get started."

"Yes, Admiral. My apologies," said Joanna, slightly embarrassed. As she stepped aside, Burroughs approached Jerry.

"Good to see you again, Captain." Burroughs offered his hand as he spoke.

"Thank you, sir," responded Jerry as he grasped the admiral's hand firmly. "I trust you had no difficulties getting here."

"Other than a strong temptation to find a nice spot to do some sunbathing, no, sir."

Burroughs chuckled. "I'd be willing to go along with that if I didn't burn so badly." The admiral's hair still had streaks of an intense orange-red color amongst the gray. Gesturing toward the captain, he continued on, "This is Captain Charles Simonis. He'll be your squadron commodore for the duration of this mission."

The two shook hands and exchanged greetings. Simonis then directed him to the three commanders standing by the conference table. "Commander Mitchell, these are my squadron COs. Commander Bruce Dobson, USS *Oklahoma City*."

"Pleased to meet you," Dobson said, shaking Jerry's hand.

"Likewise," he answered.

"You already know Commander Warren Halsey," Simonis remarked as he pointed to the second skipper.

"Yes, of course," replied Jerry warmly. "I wondered if *Santa Fe* was going to be pulled too, Warren."

"We're here," Halsey responded flatly. "Besides, we weren't getting a whole lot of action in our area. Not as much as your boat, apparently."

Jerry wasn't sure what Halsey meant by that comment, but he didn't have time to contemplate it as Simonis moved on to the last commanding officer.

"And this is Commander Ian Pascovich, USS *Texas*."

"Ian! Good to see you again!" Jerry eagerly grabbed Pascovich's hand.

"You too, Jerry. How's *North Dakota*? Have you had a chance to figure out all the gadgets yet?"

"She's a fine boat, Ian. And no, I'm still working on it. I learn something new every day, much to my XO's amusement," Jerry admitted. Turning toward a curious Simonis, he explained. "Ian and I were in the same PCO class together. We had a friendly rivalry going during the attack trainer phase of the course—he usually won."

"But it was close," added Pascovich.

"Ah, I see," Simonis responded, clearly unimpressed. Sweeping his hand toward the chairs he said, "Gentlemen, please be seated so we can begin the briefing."

Jerry quickly walked around the table and took a chair next to Pascovich. A yeoman immediately followed with a large binder, a dripping cold bottle of water, and a napkin. The binder was covered with colorful security markings, including TOP SECRET in large, unfriendly letters.

Nodding his thanks, Jerry opened the binder to the first page. The title caused him to stop short—"Potential for Sino-Vietnamese War." And he wasn't the only one with wide eyes. Glancing down the line, he saw that each skipper had the same look on his face.

"Gentlemen, we have a severely strained political situation in the South China Sea," began Admiral Burroughs. "For decades, the People's Republic of China has had territorial disputes with Vietnam, Taiwan, Malaysia, Brunei, and the Philippines over the Spratly Islands. There have been a number of diplomatic efforts over the years, but no results. Now it looks like the pot may be boiling over. Needless to say, the president's concern in regard to this matter is considerable."

Burroughs paused as he pointed toward Patterson. "So much so, that he decided it was necessary to send his deputy national security advisor, Dr. Joanna Patterson, out here to Guam to personally brief you on the political-military situation."

Jerry looked at the other three sub captains. They were obviously stunned by COMSUBPAC's blunt introduction. Jerry's own anxiety quotient was higher as well. If the White House was sending someone to personally brief them, it had to be bad. Like Jerry, the other three officers remained silent, still trying to take it aboard.

"Dr. Patterson, the floor is yours."

"Thank you, Admiral Burroughs. Gentlemen, it is the collective judgment of the intelligence community and the National Security Council that a war between the Socialist Republic of Vietnam and the People's Republic of China is likely. Indeed, it may have already begun. We do not understand why one, or both, nations felt compelled to adopt hostile measures, but indications of large-scale military action are growing."

*Okay, this adequately constitutes "considerably worse,"* Jerry thought to himself, as he remembered Joanna's earlier dire statement.

"But to understand the current state of affairs," Patterson clicked her remote, moving to her next slide, "you'll need a little historical background. The South China Sea has been a contentious area for nearly eighty years, but the current dispute started in 1968, when petroleum deposits were discovered in the Spratly Island archipelago. Since then, there have been claims and counterclaims by over half a dozen nations, none of which can be justified under the UN Convention on the Law of the Sea.

"Military action in the Spratlys had been rare, with only one real engagement. That battle was over the Johnson South Reef in the spring of 1988. China won handily, seizing the reef, sinking three Vietnamese ships, and killing seventy-two Vietnamese sailors and soldiers, most of whom were gunned down while up to their knees in water. Johnson South Reef, like many in the Spratly chain, is underwater at high tide.

"For the most part, the 'fighting' over the Spratlys has been done with words and the occasional raid to raise a flag on a claimed, but unmanned reef. However, the harassment of oil exploration ships, oceanographic research ships, and fishing vessels has been steadily increasing. In 2011, China and Vietnam started holding regular naval exercises in the Spratly Islands, often with live-fire drills. This has led to both nations beefing up the defenses of their outposts. Other South China Sea littoral nations followed suit.

"The situation really started to go downhill in late 2014 when a Vietnamese warship collided with, and sank, a Chinese fishing vessel. The nationalistic furor that followed this incident led to the Chinese Communist Party's announcement in the spring of 2015 that the Spratly Islands were a 'core national interest' to China. The shockwaves from that declaration sent every nation in the region to a higher state of alert."

This was huge. Between the upgrading of outpost defenses and the strong political rhetoric, the entire South China Sea was now a powder keg. All that was needed for war was for someone to light the fuze, something Jerry guessed had already happened.

"Eleven days ago, the Chinese aircraft carrier *Liaoning* triggered a bottom influence mine as she departed Yalong Bay. The damage was severe, rendering her starboard propulsion shafts and rudder useless, and causing significant shock damage to her engine rooms. The ship managed to get back to the pier, but it took the crew hours to finally contain the flooding. An official press release stated that *Liaoning* had suffered an unspecified engineering casualty.

"Exhaustive analysis by the intelligence community reveals there is only one possible mining platform—a Vietnamese Kilo-class submarine."

Jerry was as awestruck as the others by Patterson's claim. He simply could not comprehend why Vietnam would even consider attacking her much larger, and considerably more powerful neighbor. It certainly did much to explain the attack on the merchant.

"Four days ago a Type 093 SSN torpedoed the Vietnamese merchant vessel *Vinaship Sea*. Commander Mitchell's submarine witnessed the attack and his report is in your briefing binders."

All eyes seemed to focus on Jerry as Patterson continued speaking. Pascovich nudged him, his facial expression begging for details. Jerry mouthed the word, "Later."

"In his report, Commander Mitchell's noted a large secondary explosion after the *Vinaship Sea* was torpedoed. Such a strong blast was inconsistent with her listed cargo of coal. In addition, he also reported that the ship was significantly off course for her claimed destination." Patterson smiled as she advanced the slide.

"Your observations were correct, Jerry. The merchant ship was actually heading toward the Vietnamese-held island of Southwest Cay in the northern Spratlys. Her cargo, based on COMINT information, was advanced surface-to-air missile systems, radars, anti-aircraft artillery, munitions, food,

Burroughs paused as he pointed toward Patterson. "So much so, that he decided it was necessary to send his deputy national security advisor, Dr. Joanna Patterson, out here to Guam to personally brief you on the political-military situation."

Jerry looked at the other three sub captains. They were obviously stunned by COMSUBPAC's blunt introduction. Jerry's own anxiety quotient was higher as well. If the White House was sending someone to personally brief them, it had to be bad. Like Jerry, the other three officers remained silent, still trying to take it aboard.

"Dr. Patterson, the floor is yours."

"Thank you, Admiral Burroughs. Gentlemen, it is the collective judgment of the intelligence community and the National Security Council that a war between the Socialist Republic of Vietnam and the People's Republic of China is likely. Indeed, it may have already begun. We do not understand why one, or both, nations felt compelled to adopt hostile measures, but indications of large-scale military action are growing."

*Okay, this adequately constitutes "considerably worse,"* Jerry thought to himself, as he remembered Joanna's earlier dire statement.

"But to understand the current state of affairs," Patterson clicked her remote, moving to her next slide, "you'll need a little historical background. The South China Sea has been a contentious area for nearly eighty years, but the current dispute started in 1968, when petroleum deposits were discovered in the Spratly Island archipelago. Since then, there have been claims and counterclaims by over half a dozen nations, none of which can be justified under the UN Convention on the Law of the Sea.

"Military action in the Spratlys had been rare, with only one real engagement. That battle was over the Johnson South Reef in the spring of 1988. China won handily, seizing the reef, sinking three Vietnamese ships, and killing seventy-two Vietnamese sailors and soldiers, most of whom were gunned down while up to their knees in water. Johnson South Reef, like many in the Spratly chain, is underwater at high tide.

"For the most part, the 'fighting' over the Spratlys has been done with words and the occasional raid to raise a flag on a claimed, but unmanned reef. However, the harassment of oil exploration ships, oceanographic research ships, and fishing vessels has been steadily increasing. In 2011, China and Vietnam started holding regular naval exercises in the Spratly Islands, often with live-fire drills. This has led to both nations beefing up the defenses of their outposts. Other South China Sea littoral nations followed suit.

"The situation really started to go downhill in late 2014 when a Vietnamese warship collided with, and sank, a Chinese fishing vessel. The nationalistic furor that followed this incident led to the Chinese Communist Party's announcement in the spring of 2015 that the Spratly Islands were a 'core national interest' to China. The shockwaves from that declaration sent every nation in the region to a higher state of alert."

This was huge. Between the upgrading of outpost defenses and the strong political rhetoric, the entire South China Sea was now a powder keg. All that was needed for war was for someone to light the fuze, something Jerry guessed had already happened.

"Eleven days ago, the Chinese aircraft carrier *Liaoning* triggered a bottom influence mine as she departed Yalong Bay. The damage was severe, rendering her starboard propulsion shafts and rudder useless, and causing significant shock damage to her engine rooms. The ship managed to get back to the pier, but it took the crew hours to finally contain the flooding. An official press release stated that *Liaoning* had suffered an unspecified engineering casualty.

"Exhaustive analysis by the intelligence community reveals there is only one possible mining platform—a Vietnamese Kilo-class submarine."

Jerry was as awestruck as the others by Patterson's claim. He simply could not comprehend why Vietnam would even consider attacking her much larger, and considerably more powerful neighbor. It certainly did much to explain the attack on the merchant.

"Four days ago a Type 093 SSN torpedoed the Vietnamese merchant vessel *Vinaship Sea*. Commander Mitchell's submarine witnessed the attack and his report is in your briefing binders."

All eyes seemed to focus on Jerry as Patterson continued speaking. Pascovich nudged him, his facial expression begging for details. Jerry mouthed the word, "Later."

"In his report, Commander Mitchell's noted a large secondary explosion after the *Vinaship Sea* was torpedoed. Such a strong blast was inconsistent with her listed cargo of coal. In addition, he also reported that the ship was significantly off course for her claimed destination." Patterson smiled as she advanced the slide.

"Your observations were correct, Jerry. The merchant ship was actually heading toward the Vietnamese-held island of Southwest Cay in the northern Spratlys. Her cargo, based on COMINT information, was advanced surface-to-air missile systems, radars, anti-aircraft artillery, munitions, food, and fuel for the garrison—enough for the defenders to hold out for several weeks."

Jerry heard Pascovich whistle softly and say, "Hoollyy shit!"

"In conclusion," said Patterson, highlighting the bullets with her laser pointer, "both sides have taken shots at each other. However, it is significant to note that only submarines have been used to date. And while we believe the likelihood for continued hostilities is high, we simply don't understand the nature of this conflict. What triggered the Vietnamese attack? Is the upcoming PLAN exercise part of the puzzle? There are just too many unknowns right now. This is why the president is asking for your help. He needs more information if he is to respond appropriately to this crisis. The goal is to defuse it diplomatically; hopefully before a full-scale war starts. Are there any questions?"

There were plenty. Dr. Patterson went over many of the possible causes: the Chinese diversion of river water from Vietnam, significantly reducing the latter's rice crops. There were arguments over the rights to fishing grounds, and of course, China's ever-growing need for oil. The bottom line, as Jerry saw it, be it water, fish, or oil, China needed more resources to support its population and economy. In the past, they'd relied on diplomacy, and occasional bullying, to get their way. Could their need be so great that they had to up the ante?

Jerry asked, "Dr. Patterson, is there any evidence of China facing some sort of major economic problem?"

"Not that we know of, Jerry. They've had problems, but have weathered them, possibly better than we have."

"Dr. Patterson," interrupted Halsey. "In my opinion, there has to be a link between the events you discussed and the exercise. Is there a chance that the Chinese are using the exercise to hide an attack?"

"There's always a possibility, Commander Halsey. However, the Chinese have been far more open about this exercise because of its magnitude and location. Based on past exercises, with the exception of its size, there doesn't appear to be anything unusual about this one. But that's why you and Jerry were assigned to monitor the exercise, to see if their actions match their words."

"Are you suggesting that the Vietnamese are just being paranoid?" pushed Halsey.

"I'm not suggesting anything of the sort," Patterson responded tersely. "It is certainly a possibility that the Vietnamese could view the exercise as a significant threat. Whether or not that perception is real or imaginary, I can't say. But Vietnam would *only* act if it felt it had no other option, which inevitably leads back to the assumption of a Chinese first strike. We've looked into this premise hard, and we just can't find a good motivation for China to want to go to war. The repercussions would be huge, the damage to their economy significant."

"And yet, the Vietnamese have done poked the dragon in the eye," remarked Dobson sarcastically. "The Vietnamese may be paranoid, but they aren't stupid. Something is missing from this picture."

"Correct, Captain, and it's your job to find out," boomed Simonis. "Gentlemen, you each have detailed orders for your boat in your binder. But it comes down to this. You are to probe, watch, and report any movements of PLAN and Vietnamese naval vessels, and in particular submarines. Collect signals intelligence in your respective areas, with an emphasis on command and control communications. And you are to remain undetected at all times."

"Captains, I must emphasize the need for absolute stealth on this mission," echoed Burroughs as he rose. "For now, it appears that neither side is aware that we know and understand the significance of these events. That's an advantage we need to retain. Do your snooping, learn what you can, but use your good judgment when it comes to communicating your findings. I know I'm preaching to the choir, but this comes from high up the chain. You cannot be detected. Clear?"

"Yes, sir!" replied the four skippers.

Simonis walked up to the podium and brought up another slide with a chart of the Chinese coastline. "Your patrol areas are as follows. *North Dakota* will position herself off Hainan Island, monitoring the naval bases at Yulin and Yalong Bay. Commander Mitchell, you'll send one of your reconnaissance UUVs to the west to monitor the approaches from the Vietnamese submarine base at Nha Trang."

"Understood, sir," Jerry replied as he wrote down some notes. The orders would have all the details, but he needed a few cryptic reminders to make sure he covered the basics when he briefed Thigpen.

The commodore continued. *Santa Fe* would be stationed off Zhanjiang, the South Sea Fleet's main port. *Texas* was to watch Guangzhou, as well as picking up any ships coming down from the East Sea Fleet. *Oklahoma City* was to be placed off Ningbo, the East Sea Fleet's main base. She was to provide a heads-up for any ships coming from either the East or North Sea

Fleets and heading down the coast. It was a lot of real estate for four submarines to cover, but Jerry approved of the deployment.

Simonis finished up the overview of the patrol orders with the sortie schedule. "While the Chinese may or may not be aware there are four boats here at Guam right now, I don't plan on making it easy for them. As far as their imagery satellites are concerned, there is only one boat here. I intend for them to see only one on their next pass. Therefore, *North Dakota* departs first, tonight, at 2100. Three hours later *Texas* will leave. Three hours after that *Oklahoma City* will sortie, followed by *Santa Fe* tomorrow afternoon."

Dobson's head popped up; he appeared confused. Simonis saw his reaction. "I switched yours and Halsey's departure around, Bruce. *Santa Fe* has some repairs that require tender support, so she'll leave last." Halsey looked annoyed with the commodore's comment.

"Okay, people, that about wraps this pre-patrol briefing up," declared Simonis. "Are there any other questions? Last chance."

"Yes, sir, I have one," Dobson replied. "What are my rules of engagement?"

"I believe the order 'do not get detected' addresses that, Captain." Simonis's voice had an edge to it.

"Commodore, we are taking our boats into a potential war zone. I'll do my damnedest not to be seen or heard, but in the unlikely event I'm picked up, and somebody starts shooting at me, what are my options, sir?"

Jerry wanted to hear Simonis's answer to the question as well, as it was at the top of his list. There was an awkward silence; Simonis was visibly tight and glanced over toward Rear Admiral Burroughs. It was the admiral that finally answered.

"The situation is very precarious, Captain. We don't want to accidentally start a war because one of our actions was misinterpreted. There are individuals who are concerned that a loosely defined ROE would increase that risk. However, a hyperconservative one doesn't work either."

Burroughs left his chair and walked over to the conference table. Resting his weight on the table, he leaned forward, an intense look on his face.

"If after every *possible* measure has been taken to avoid detection, or to break contact if detected, if there is *absolutely* no other way to evade a hostile unit that is firing at you, you may defend yourselves. I will trust your judgment; you've been vetted and trained for independent command, and I'm not about to hold your hand. But shooting back has to be the very last course of action, and only to protect your boat. Understood?"

"Absolutely, Admiral," replied Dobson. The other three COs nodded their acknowledgment.

"Gentlemen, this concludes the briefing. Please see my operations officer, Commander Walker, in the back to get your binders wrapped for you to take back to your boats," ordered Simonis.

Jerry shook his fellow captains' hands and wished them good luck. While Dobson, Halsey, and Pascovich headed to the back of the conference room, Jerry walked up to Patterson. She was standing alone; Burroughs and Simonis were off to the side talking intensely about something.

"Joanna, one last question."

"Yes, Jerry, what is it?"

"Isn't it kind of a contradiction to say there is a high probability of war, and at the same time say there is no rational reason for said war?"

Patterson took a deep breath; she looked worn and perhaps a bit irritated. "Welcome to my world, Jerry. But yes, it's a bit of a mystery. One that we're hoping you can help answer."

Joanna looked over his shoulder, making sure no one would hear her but Jerry. "We're still working the problem, Jerry. Trust me, four submarines are not the only collection assets we are putting on this crisis. What I told you is what we know, what we don't know, and what we think. I didn't say it would make sense."

Jerry caught her slight smile at the end. Chuckling, he said, "Touché. Well, when you do figure it out, don't forget us minions in the trenches."

"You'll be kept informed. I'll make sure of that."

"Thanks, Joanna. Oh, and one thing to pass on if you think it's appropriate. My time with the SEALs beat it into me that there better be at least a Plan B, if not a Plan C. The president needs to be thinking about what he'll do if this doesn't work. Because my crew will be on the firing line, dealing with the results, regardless of whether or not there is a backup plan. It would be good to know if we can expect any help."

"I can assure you, Jerry. The president is well aware, and we are looking into contingency planning."

"That's all I need to hear," replied Jerry. "Give my best to Lowell, and you'll be hearing from me."

"Be careful, Jerry," Joanna croaked as she gave him another hug.

# 4

# COVERT ALLIANCE

22 August 2016
Tokyo University, Waseda Campus
Hongo, Bunkyo Ward, Tokyo

It had not started well. Then it got worse.

The Littoral Alliance, which appeared to be the most popular label for the new collaboration, was supposed to be a secret from the Chinese. Therefore, Komamura had suggested having the first face-to-face meeting of the principals at his university. The University of Tokyo was one of the most prestigious schools in Asia, and its Graduate School of Economics sponsored a nonstop calendar of international seminars and conferences. The Chinese would be much less likely to notice the heads of several Asian navies in one place if they met at his school instead of a military base.

It should have been trivial for one of Todai's most famous professors to reserve several seminar rooms. But the school had needed to know what conference the rooms were for. So Komamura had invented one, on "maritime economics," and then had to invent a reason why information on the "conference" should not appear on the school's Web page or in the newsletter. And he had to submit a preliminary list of attendees at least a week before the conference, and a final list within twenty-four hours of the opening session . . .

There seemed to be a hundred details, each requiring phone calls and e-mails. And with every interaction, he'd wondered if this was the one the Chinese would spot. Regardless of its innocence, each communication was a data point, a stone in the river. Given enough rocks, the Chinese might find a path across.

His classwork suffered. Even after unloading every duty he could on his hard-working graduate students, there were certain tasks he refused to delegate. Doctoral dissertations needed to be reviewed, lecture notes updated. It was work, but work he enjoyed because of his fascination with economics.

And then there were the frequent meetings with Admiral Kubo. Komamura looked forward to them, and he believed the chief of the maritime staff enjoyed the break from his demanding routine.

Kubo Noriaki was a small, square-faced man, legendary for the long hours he put in at his desk, and his love of sumo wrestling. The admiral always dressed in civilian clothes, which did nothing to change the air of authority that surrounded him. Sitting in a Tokyo *udon* restaurant, the two looked like a pair of senior executives on their lunch break. Tokyo had hundreds of such shops, and they never ate in the same one twice.

Their last meeting had not been as pleasant as most. Komamura had received word from his contacts in both India and Taiwan, on the same day, that they would not be attending his conference, even as observers. He was depressed, and it surprised him that he was so upset.

"Of course you take it personally. This alliance is your child, *sensei*." Kubo insisted on addressing him using the same honorific Komamura's students used. It could mean "teacher," or "master," and implied a level of professional respect that Komamura really didn't feel worthy of right then. Kubo also insisted, because of his civilian "cover," that Komamura simply address him as "Kubo-*san*."

The admiral was realistic. "Not everyone will think the alliance is as necessary as you do. India has reasons for keeping its distance. They are not directly threatened by Chinese expansion into the South China Sea, at least not yet. They are interested in ways of weakening their greatest enemy, but their participation is a risk with much less benefit. They will join once they believe we have a good chance of success.

"Taiwan is a different problem. They have lived next to the dragon for seventy years, and are very cautious. If China discovered the alliance, and that Taiwan was involved, it would be disastrous for us and more so for Taiwan."

Kubo asked, "If China succeeds in gaining control over the resources in the South China Sea—oil, food, minerals, not to mention control of the sea lanes—what are the long-term consequences for Taiwan?"

Komamura answered, "I covered that in the book, of course. Even a conservative—"

"I mean the *political* consequences, Professor," Kubo interrupted. "Ten and twenty years later. You said it yourself, in chapter nine. 'Political power is based on, and is directly proportional to, economic power.' You even had a chart. Can Taiwan remain independent under those circumstances?"

"Politically," Komamura mused. "With China stronger, possibly the strongest economy in the world, and all the littoral nations weaker. Taipei would have little choice but to accept unification, on Communist Chinese terms."

"Then that's the message you must give to the Taiwanese leadership. If you use only economic or military arguments, you will not convince them."

"Am I really the best man for this task?" Komamura asked. "I'm not a diplomat."

"You are the famous author of *Navies for Asia*. We believe that your independence from the Japanese government is an asset, not a disadvantage. You will speak your mind, not parrot our government's agenda. As to your lack of expertise, you've inspired three governments to work together. Considering the historical bad blood between us, you've performed nothing short of a miracle to get this far. With time, the others too will be convinced. When will you go to Taiwan again?"

"I've been invited to lead a seminar at Zuoying Naval Yard next week." He paused. "After the conference."

"It's a good time to speak to them. We will know so much more. And right before you go, there's a microbrewery here in Tokyo you should visit. Admiral Wu Chen loves their Kenji Weizen."

24 August 2016
By Water
Halifax, Nova Scotia

He'd moved to the house in Purcell's Cove ten years ago, paying far too much, but it was unthinkable to be away from the water. It hadn't been in the best shape when he bought it, and since then he'd fixed what he could by himself, and let the rest age gracefully.

Hector Alexander McMurtrie didn't care what the outside of the house looked like, and he cared even less about the yard. He'd dealt with the neighbors' complaints by planting evergreens, which had eventually blocked the view, except toward the ocean.

"Mac" left the kitchen, which also doubled as the dining room, and headed for his office at the other end of the house. He passed what could have been a formal dining room but was instead filled with filing cabinets. They lined two walls, while shelves above them were filled with ship models and nautical memorabilia. Prints and nautical charts covered every patch of wall space above chest level. The hallway was similarly decorated.

He shuffled past the first bedroom, where he actually slept, lined with bookshelves, and entered what should have been the master bedroom but was instead his office.

The house was sited on a low rise, and built so that bay windows in the kitchen and master bedroom faced the water. Mac didn't see any reason for spending his time with his eyes closed in the room with the best view of the ocean.

The shelf formed by the large bay window held his favorite relics and models: a Hog Islander his father had helped him build when he was thirteen, a small piece of the merchant ship *Mont-Blanc*, shattered in the 1917 explosion, several seashells, and other treasures, none of them tall enough to block the view.

He stood looking out for several moments, gauging the weather. Clear, with thin high stratus. A pair of binoculars sat in one corner of the window shelf, but there was nothing on the horizon to look at.

His desk, secondhand when he bought it, faced the blank wall next to the bay. All Mac had to do was turn his head to the left and he could check to see if the ocean was still there. The desk was extended on either side by folding tables. One was loaded with printers, a server box, and a wide-bed scanner, while the other was covered with papers and reference books. Behind him a bookcase had been divided into cubbyholes, each labeled and holding a project, some urgent, and some waiting years for the right moment.

Bookshelves filled the available wall space, prints and photos and maps covered the walls, and ship models and assorted maritime knickknacks occupied every horizontal surface.

Taking a large sip from his third cup of coffee, Mac was ready to get to work, although he hardly thought of it as such. Twelve years ago, when the Irving Shipbuilding Company had offered early retirement, he'd jumped at it. Now, on the high side of sixty, his second career kept him typing ten or twelve hours a day, more if he wanted. It felt like he'd always done it this way, as if being a naval architect had just helped prepare him for his real occupation.

As he'd expected, the electronic inbox was full. E-mails from friends and associates all over the world passed on bits of information on naval and merchant ships, or asked questions about naval technology. Some sent images, others brought new work: requests for two book reviews just this morning, an offer of collaboration on a photo book, and a request for an article on steampowered reciprocating propulsion plants. That was one of his specialties.

It was his own fault. Thirty years ago, he'd started a computer bulletin board on GEnie with his own mix of naval news, opinion, and outright bias. That had evolved into "Bywater's Blog," named in honor of another naval writer, Hector C. Bywater. It was also a play on words, since the mailbox in front of his home read BY WATER.

Because he was usually right, and often insightful, he'd attracted more and more readers, who had provided more and more information. Part of the fun was not just reading the latest gossip, but adding a piece, or two, to the jigsaw puzzle. One of Mac's smarter ideas had been to include the amount of new information contributed to the membership statistics. Now other naval writers, sailors from navies and the merchant service, and hundreds of enthusiasts competed to send him information.

His digital empire included an online database and daughter blogs on warship developments, shipbuilding, and maritime losses. The spinoffs had greatly improved the readability of his daily blog, but had also doubled, or even tripled, the amount of e-mail he had to answer.

From: MerchantMan
To: Maritime Losses
Subj: Vinaship Sea

I'm updating merchant ship losses. *Vinaship Sea*, sailed 17 Aug 16 from Ho Chi Minh City to Osaka Japan with cargo of coal, listed as lost by the owner 20 Aug. No cause of loss given. Do you have any info on other ships lost to coal dust explosions in the last twenty years?

"Last twenty years?" snorted Mac with amusement. "Try the last hundred."

"MerchantMan" was the handle for one of his longtime correspondents, a real-life merchant sailor who helped keep his database up to date. He'd know the answer to the coal dust question as well as Mac, but he was trying to rule out a theory.

Mac began his digital excavation. When steamships had used coal for fuel, the dust could mix with the air in dangerous concentrations. Explosions weren't common, but they weren't unheard of, either. It was suspected as the true cause for the loss of USS *Maine* in Havana in 1898, and as a contributing factor to the loss of several warships in World War I.

But the precautions against coal dust were well known, and Mac could find no ship lost to that cause since 1937. Probably not coal dust, then. But then why had she disappeared?

He called up the news reports of the loss. The media said that search planes had found nothing along her planned route, which was a well-traveled shipping lane. There had been no distress calls, which would be consistent with an explosion. The weather had been good, both for the search and for several days before. There were no navigational hazards along her route, which was well known and traveled daily by dozens of other ships.

Naval lore was littered with mysterious losses, some resolved decades later, but many still with secrets known only to the sea. Mac started typing.

From: Mac
To: Maritime Losses
Subj: Loss of Vinaship Sea

*Vinaship Sea*, bound from Ho Chi Minh City to Osaka, Japan, lost to unknown causes. No survivors. Possibilities:

1) Navigational error brought her to grief.
2) Progressive flooding from unknown cause.
3) Sudden explosion from unknown cause.
4) Hijacked and now sailing under a different name.

Please send any news of unusual sightings in the South China Sea from 17–20 August, including explosions, wrecks, unidentified vessels.

Sending the e-mail, he reflected for a moment, then wrote a short piece on *Vinaship Sea* for his daily blog. He described her disappearance, the lack of explanations for it, and pumped up the mystery as much as his conscience allowed. Then he asked for information, or suggestions that would resolve this "newest mystery of the sea."

Mac hit the "Return" key and checked his watch. Half an hour for one e-mail. He'd have to do better than that if he was going to get any time to work on the book review.

25 August 2016
Tokyo University, Waseda Campus
Hongo, Bunkyo Ward, Tokyo

In the end, they'd just placed a table at the front for Komamura and his assistants, while the delegations from Vietnam, South Korea, and Japan occupied three tables in a single row. Each admiral had brought only one aide, an intelligence specialist, and a translator. Komamura felt the absence of India and Taiwan, but it couldn't be helped, he told himself.

The Japanese support staff, heavily biased toward security personnel, outnumbered the attendees, and Komamura did his best to keep them out of sight. The Japanese were hosting the meeting, but this was not supposed to be a Japanese event, or a Japanese-led alliance.

There were no flags, no nameplates, and most strikingly, no uniforms. No one had objected to wearing civilian clothes, but all three delegations had asked about a dress code, so everyone had shown up in business suits. The South Koreans even had matching ties.

Admiral Park Uchin was visibly the youngest of the three naval leaders, and had been Chief of Naval Operations for the ROK Navy for only six months. He'd only met with Komamura once, and in very cloak-and-dagger surroundings, at a bench in Pusan's Yongdusan Park. "I'm required to report anything more than 'casual contact' with foreigners to counterintelligence," Park had explained. "I'm exercising my discretion in what is considered casual contact."

Komamura was surprised. "Are you that worried about the reliability of your own intelligence people?"

"Nobody knows about this, except people I've known personally for many years, and of course, my superiors," Park insisted. "The enemy is just a little distance to the north, and China just beyond. I am taking no chances.

"But it's worth the risks," Park continued. "We've got our hands full just dealing with the north. Someday, maybe soon, Kim's regime will fall, rotten and weak from its own corruption. We will have a moment's opportunity to unify our country, but few think it will be as peaceful as Germany.

"A dominant China will not help our cause. Better the Americans, or your alliance if the Americans are too weak. When the crisis comes, we stand a better chance of success with friends at our side."

The "conference" had begun with the formal signing of the document creating the Littoral Alliance. It was short, just two pages, and only three copies were made. Hidden like the rest of the alliance, each copy would be kept in the owner's safe until it was necessary to reveal its existence.

After a quick toast with rice wine, the admirals had listened to an intelligence brief, given by Commander Ty of the Vietnamese delegation. The three intelligence officers attending the conference, assisted by extremely small staffs, would serve as the group's intelligence arm. No one nation would command or lead the alliance. Instead temporary commanders would be appointed for specific tasks, depending on need and availability.

After reporting the Chinese Navy's status, Ty described the search for *Vinaship Sea*. Nearby merchant ships had reported an explosion and debris consistent with her projected position. There had been no sign of her crew of twenty-two. The Vietnamese shipping company had not linked those reports to *Vinaship Sea*. Instead, false positions reports, filed by the Vietnamese shipping company since her sailing from Ho Chi Minh City, had placed the freighter one hundred nautical miles northwest of Luzon when she "disappeared."

"While a formal investigation is under way, Chinese retaliation for the mining of *Liaoning* is the most likely possibility. Questions?"

Admiral Kubo smiled. "You phrased that last sentence very carefully, Commander, but is there any other possible explanation?"

Ty raised his hands helplessly. "We have no proof of any cause, only the fact of her sudden loss, and the timing. None of us believe this is a coincidence," he said, looking at the other intelligence officers, who nodded their agreement.

"If they've managed to trace the mining of *Liaoning* back to Vietnam, then the alliance is already in jeopardy." Admiral Park did not speak casually. They'd all been briefed on the basic facts of *Vinaship Sea*'s loss days ago. The Korean admiral was challenging the entire idea of covert cooperation. "How long can we act without retaliation against one or all of us? We can share intelligence, and even conduct surveillance, but an alliance in more than name demands action, and that will be the start of a war we cannot win."

Komamura, in the front of the room, broke in to the discussion. "I agree. Even acting together, we are too weak to challenge China's military strength. Even with America on our side, the issue would be in doubt. And the destruction and economic cost would be catastrophic."

Komamura paused for a minute. Admiral Park looked unhappy, even though Komamura had just agreed with him, but Admiral Hieu motioned to the other Vietnamese and tilted his head slightly toward the Japanese table. Kubo seemed unconcerned. The Vietnamese officer stated, "And you have a plan."

"Yes, Admiral, I do. I am only hesitating because I've never commanded a ship or even worn a uniform, and yet I'm standing before the heads of three navies. Please excuse my presumptuousness, but I believe the key is an asymmetric attack, matching our strength against the Chinese weakness."

"Our submarines," Hieu answered.

"Yes," Komamura confirmed. "Your attack on *Liaoning* was possible because your navy has first-line subs, and Chinese anti-submarine warfare is poor at best. In spite of the escort vessels patrolling outside the harbor, your captain was able to penetrate their screen, lay his mines, and withdraw without being detected."

Gesturing to the other two admirals, Komamura continued, "Japan and South Korea also have first-class submarine arms, at least one and often two generations ahead of their PLAN equivalents. Admiral Kubo has said that the *Soryu* class, even though it is conventionally powered, would have several advantages over even the Chinese nuclear boats, including quieting, sensors, and weapons." Kubo silently nodded his agreement.

"I agree," Park declared. He stood and bowed slightly toward the professor. "This shows great insight. Between our three countries, we can blockade almost every Chinese naval base and catch other units at sea." His expression had changed completely, his face now alight with the idea. "We can deploy covertly and coordinate our first attacks. Perhaps we can time them to catch *Liaoning* as they tow it from Yulin to Dalian, and finish her off. We can inflict tremendous damage on the PLAN in the first twenty-four hours. They won't feel safe outside their own harbors, much less the South China Sea. The shock to their navy, to their leadership, would be tremendous."

"It would be a humiliation," Komamura agreed, unhappily, embarrassed, "but I regret to say that this is not the course I envisioned. Even if such an offensive were completely successful, sending our submarines against their fleet would clearly be a classic military conflict, a clash of navies. It's impossible for our subs to repeatedly attack naval vessels, especially after the initial surprise is lost, without being detected. Even if our boats evade counterattack, detection leads to identification, which would inevitably lead to retaliation.

"China's political leadership would be compelled to respond, and to the world they would be the aggrieved party. All of our countries are within range of Chinese aircraft and missiles, and we cannot sink enough of their navy to prevent it from actions against our shipping or coastlines. It would still become a wide-scale war."

Admiral Park clearly wasn't happy. "It's a classic matchup of our strength against their weakness. Why wouldn't it work?"

The professor replied, "Because while anti-submarine warfare is a weakness in the Chinese Navy, it is not a fatal one for China. Her true weakness is her dependence on energy from abroad. If you want to make them feel pain, shut off their oil."

Nodding toward Admiral Park, Komamura explained, "I agree that a covert deployment and a timed, coordinated offensive is important, but the target should be the merchant ships bound for Chinese ports, specifically, their tankers. Their economy is balanced on a knife's edge. It would not happen overnight, but halting their oil imports will hurt them badly. They can compensate, at least at first, but the compensation itself will trigger other problems."

"Why wouldn't they respond to an attack on merchants the same as attacks on their navy?" Park countered.

"Because a merchant has no way to detect the identity of its attacker," the professor answered. "Until China can supply proof of nationality, it will be reluctant to act overtly, especially since two of our members are U.S. allies. There is historical precedent. During the Spanish Civil War, unidentified 'pirate' submarines sank Soviet merchant ships bringing supplies to the Republican forces. They were Italian subs, but while there were suspicions and accusations, the Russians could never provide proof."

"That can't last forever," Park argued.

"It won't last long," Hieu agreed. "And China won't wait to act. There will be covert responses against anyone she suspects. And we all have merchant ships, too."

"Every day of uncertainty is a day we're hurting them and they're not hurting us," Kubo answered. "We can even leak suspicions that the 'first' merchant ship lost, *Vinaship Sea*, was caused by a Chinese attack. And we can pull our merchants out of harm's way and effectively embargo trade with China at the same time. That will deny her strategic materials, sophisticated machinery and electronic imports."

"How long will it take for her economy to show the effects?" Hieu asked.

Komamura felt more comfortable with this question, and he'd researched it carefully. "They have a strategic oil reserve of ninety days at their normal consumption rate, but they've already started using it because of shortfalls in their oil imports," he explained. Seeing their faces, he quickly added, "But we will not have to wait that long. Oil prices will spike. That will cause pain by itself, and then China will see her shipping costs increase by as much as fifty percent. Together, these will cause great stress. Shortages will quickly affect many sectors of their economy."

"And your goal?" Kubo prompted, as if he knew the answer.

"At least a recession, and preferably an economic depression." Even as its author, Komamura hated the sound of it. Economists wanted to fix things, not wreck them.

"Not a collapse?" Park asked.

"No, Admiral," Komamura quickly responded, "that would be a disaster for all of us. Famine and civil unrest in the largest nation on earth? It could create the greatest humanitarian disaster in history, and nobody can predict the political consequences." He spoke with great intensity. How many would die? What would China's leaders do to stave off famine?

"It would replace greed with desperation," the professor explained. "I believe it is enough to give China's leaders a new set of long-term problems."

Park looked thoughtful. "And we do not attack PLAN vessels."

Komamura shrugged. "Except in self-defense, of course. We must do our best not to give the Chinese an opportunity to play the victim on the world stage. Their submarines are a special case. We shouldn't go looking for them, but since they can attack our merchant ships, if one of our subs meets one, we should sink it."

"When should we start this campaign?" Hieu asked.

"Now. This very minute." Komamura felt the intensity return. "Damaging their carrier threw their plan into disorder, but nobody believes they have abandoned their goal entirely. In that case, the sooner we close the valve, the better."

"This means more than just sending out our submarines," Park argued. "Our armed forces have to be prepared, our merchant ships diverted. If there's to be an embargo, we should be stockpiling critical materials."

"Any visible action may warn China," Komamura countered. "I recommend sending out your submarines immediately, but take no other detectable action until Chinese merchant ships begin sinking. After that happens, your actions can be explained as reactions to those events."

Komamura took the time to study the reaction of each delegation. He saw general agreement with the plan, but the import and scope of the consequences were just now becoming clear. Having heard Komamura's plan before, Kubo was calmest. Park looked thoughtful, but his aide was writing at a furious pace.

Hieu's face was hard, almost angry. "Our nation has been at war since *Banh Mi* mined the carrier," he declared. "All three of our submarines will be under way within the hour. The rest of our armed forces have been quietly preparing. If this conference had not ended as it has, we were prepared to begin the struggle ourselves. We have fought and won against powerful enemies before."

The Vietnamese admiral stood and bowed slightly. "The Socialist Republic of Vietnam is honored to join our cause to yours."

26 August 2016
By Water
Halifax, Nova Scotia

Mac tried to keep a regular schedule, stopping in the late evening. At his age, he felt a late night much more than he used to. But he loved communicating with friends scattered all over the globe, sharing their interests and knowledge. Sometimes it was hard to stop.

Threads of a dozen conversations passed through the keyboard, and Mac often imagined himself playing ping-pong with his correspondents, but instead of balls, batting information back and forth. It was a good game, and in the end both players won.

From: IanK457
To: Maritime Losses
Subj: Loss of Vinaship Sea

Mac,

Reports at Lloyd's of London during the period of 17–20 August include only one incident in the region. The South Korean–flagged container ship *Hanjin Malta* sighted a column of smoke over the horizon at 1349 local on 18 August. Proceeding to the scene, she sighted debris at 1447 local at 11°02′ lat, 112°35′ long. No survivors, or clues to the identity of the vessel.

Ian

Mac studied the e-mail, reading it through twice. He wished he could track down the captain of *Hanjin Malta* and ask him about the "column of smoke." That sounded like an explosion, and a big one. How high had the column gone? How far away had they been from the victim? The report didn't list *Hanjin Malta*'s starting location, but it had taken her almost an hour to reach the scene, presumably at her best speed.

That he could work with. He called up her particulars. Motor Vessel *Hanjin Malta*, call sign D977, length 289 meters, beam 32 meters, maximum speed 16.7 knots, built in . . .

He could ignore the rest. The container ship had been at least fifteen nautical miles away from the unfortunate vessel, which meant a column, what, a hundred, two hundred feet high? At least.

Mac was familiar with explosions at sea, although he'd never been in the military. If you cared about the sea, and you lived in Halifax, you knew about the December 1917 collision between the relief ship SS *Imo* and SS *Mont-Blanc*, carrying thousands of tons of TNT, picric acid, and guncotton. The force of the explosion had been calculated at three kilotons. They'd heard it on Cape Breton, over two hundred miles away.

It killed two thousand people, as well as leveling most of the town. That smoke column had ascended to twenty thousand feet, but an explosion of "only" a few hundred feet still meant tons of explosive, enough to shatter the hull of most vessels, including this one, obviously. And an explosion that big could not be caused by coal dust.

But was it *Vinaship Sea*? He pulled up a digital chart and plotted the freighter's track, based on her departure time, then started measuring. Her reported position was hundreds of miles from the site of the explosion reported by *Hanjin Malta*. But on the chart, Mac could see that the distance along *Vinaship Sea*'s track seemed the same as the distance from Ho Chi Minh City to the explosion when backtracked two days. This proved nothing, but still, two unexplained ship losses, closely related in time, and in the same region strained credibility.

Why hadn't *Vinaship Sea*'s owners made the connection? Marine losses were widely reported in the trade journals and on the Web. And one would think her owners would want to explain the loss of a vessel worth hundreds of millions of dollars.

If *Vinaship Sea* had been hijacked without making a call for help, which seemed unlikely, that would explain her position. But then what had blown her up? He wanted to solve the riddle, but part of him loved the mystery.

He made a new entry in Bywater's Blog, titled "Two Mysteries or Just One?" He laid out all the known details, and started asking questions. "The cause of *Vinaship Sea*'s loss remains unexplained. Why are there no reports of her being in distress along a heavily traveled sea lane? Instead, a second (reported) loss has appeared, with gross cause (explosion) and location explained, but no company or nation has stepped forward to claim the casualty. Rough calculations indicate the cargo included at least four tons of high explosive or its equivalent, possibly much more."

Mac stopped the entry there. He didn't need to mention "arms smuggling." It was an obvious, if fantastic possibility. It could easily be something more prosaic, but much more complicated. And even if it was arms smuggling, what made them explode?

His nautical investigation had carried him to almost two in the morning. Then it took him a while longer to fall asleep, his mind still searching for new possibilities.

The phone woke him a little after 8:00 A.M. It was a young woman's voice. "Is this Mr. Hector McMurtrie? My name is Christine Laird. I'm a journalist with CNN. Are you the administrator of a 'Bywater's Blog'?"

Her tone made it clear she was unsure of the name, but her introduction had given him a chance to force his eyes open and unstick his tongue. "Mph. Garh . . ."

"Did I wake you, sir? I'm very sorry, but we're short on time. We're preparing to run a story on the loss of a merchant ship and your blog . . ."

That woke him up completely. "You mean *Vinaship Sea*?" he interrupted as he switched the receiver to his other hand. That allowed him to reach for his glasses. He certainly didn't need them to speak on the phone, but putting them on banished the fuzzy vision and made him feel more awake.

"Yes, exactly," she said brightly, even as she seemed surprised that he'd know the name of the ship. "We'd like to quote your blog during our piece, and your claim that the *Vinaship Sea* was the victim of sabotage—"

"No," McMurtrie spoke quickly, "I never said that." It took fifteen minutes to make her understand that there were two separate locations and that the facts were complete in neither case. Trying to work in a bigger mention of the blog, he began explaining how others had worked with him to investigate the loss, but she was obviously frustrated with having to report a mystery rather than an incident. Her replies became more impatient, and he could tell she was ready to end the conversation.

Then he remembered the idea about the captain of *Hanjin Malta*.

# 5

## SORTIE

Control was buzzing with activity as they prepared to launch one of the UUVs, but Jerry's mind was elsewhere. He was back on Guam.

After the brief, Commander Richard Walker, the squadron's operations officer, quietly whispered to Jerry, "The commodore wants a few words, if you're available."

Well, of course he was available. Jerry was a commander, Simonis was a captain. Jerry was a sub skipper, Simonis was his squadron commander. He'd damn well better be available.

Simonis was waiting in his office, and stood as Jerry entered. "Commander Mitchell . . . Jerry, thanks for coming by. This won't take long. Coffee?"

Walker quickly served them both cups of what smelled like really good coffee, then left, closing the door behind him.

The commodore smiled broadly. "I couldn't say this in front of my other three skippers. I certainly don't want to show any favoritism, but I'm really pleased to have you and your boat attached to the squadron. It's a little embarrassing, but I'm not as familiar with a *Virginia* class's capabilities as I am with the *Los Angeles* boats. And I know even less about a flight three *Virginia*."

The commodore was speaking directly to him, but kept shifting his gaze downward. Jerry wondered if he'd skipped a button on his shirt, and automatically checked, thankfully not finding anything, but his hand brushed against the "fruit salad," the rows of ribbons on the left side of his shirt, under his dolphins. He was understandably proud of his decorations: the Navy Cross and Purple Heart he wore drew attention, and then mystery when people found out that he couldn't talk about what he'd done to earn them.

Simonis perched on the corner of his desk. "I've given you the hot spot, right off Yulin and Yalong Bay, because you've got the best boat and . . ." He paused for a moment, then said, "I've heard some stories, and I won't ask which ones are true, but I have high expectations."

Jerry wondered just what the commodore had heard. The submarine force might still be nicknamed the "silent service," but that only applied to outsiders. Inside the community, sea stories spread faster than the speed of truth. Jerry had heard accounts of his own exploits that he hardly recognized.

"There's no time to go over my command policies, but I encourage open discussion with my boat captains, and Jerry, I promise I will listen carefully to any recommendations you make—about your boat's capabilities, the tactical situation, anything that you think I need to know."

"Thank you, sir," Jerry acknowledged. He had wondered what type of squadron commander Simonis was. He'd heard little before coming to Guam, and obviously there'd been no time to sound out the other skippers. But this was a good start.

"There's one other matter." Simonis's tone had an uneasy note in it. Again, he didn't meet Jerry's eyes, his attention still fixed on his ribbons.

Simonis sighed, then walked back and sat down behind his desk. "I'm like most of the fleet. Politics is something you read about in the newspapers. Getting a squadron command meant learning a new skill set. I keep abreast of Asian politics. I have to, or I can't effectively implement U.S. policy out here. I get a lot of guidance from PACOM and others, but it's no different from knowing the acoustic environment around your boat."

Jerry nodded and prompted, "Of course." Was this fatherly advice? Jerry might command a squadron someday.

"This Dr. Patterson. You know her well. That's very valuable to me, Jerry. I may be up to date about Asia, but I don't understand Washington. You're an insider. Your old skipper's a senator, and his wife, the deputy national security advisor, has shown up here to give us a personal briefing on our mission. I'll be honest. I'm not comfortable with this level of attention."

Jerry wasn't surprised. Some people enjoyed being in the spotlight, but many did not. Evidently, the commodore liked to keep a low profile. Maybe he wasn't the type to take risks, or he might have doubts about his own abilities. What kind of boat captain had he been? Jerry was also a little irritated. Simonis wasn't the first officer to think he had a hotline straight to Washington, but it always rubbed him the wrong way.

When Jerry didn't respond immediately, the commodore continued, "Let me say this clearly. This is an important mission, and I'm worried that she hasn't told us everything."

He saw Jerry begin to react, and quickly added. "No, not in that sense. Of course Dr. Patterson isn't deliberately sandbagging us, but what's the background? Is there an agenda that we need to know about?"

Now Jerry looked confused, as well as a little irritated, and the commodore asked, "Do you think she could be looking for us to prove or disprove something? When you spoke with her, did she say 'We're looking for this,' or 'I need you to find out if this is true'?"

Jerry sighed. The commodore was asking an honest question, even if it implied an ugly truth. Still, Jerry resented being asked, and it was a question he never would have thought of.

"I understand, sir. No, I don't believe so. She hasn't shared anything special with me. I've known Dr. Patterson for a long time and she isn't one to grind axes." *Not anymore, anyway,* Jerry added to himself. He stated flatly, "In my opinion, sir, they're looking to us for information, to help them understand what is going on. They don't know enough yet to have an agenda—or shouldn't, anyway."

Simonis didn't answer right away. Jerry realized that the commodore was now evaluating his credibility. In his mind, anything touched by Washington was suspect until proven otherwise.

Four days out from Guam, Jerry kept going over the conversation in his mind. He thought about Simonis's worries, not about armed conflict between China and Vietnam, but about what his bosses wanted to hear. He was driven, at least in part, by fear, and Jerry resolved to remember that, both while he commanded *North Dakota*, and if he ever got a squadron. Fear replaced more useful motivations.

"Five minutes to launch, Skipper." Lieutenant Kurt Franklin, the boat's communications officer and current officer of the deck, had given him periodic updates, and Jerry acknowledged the report that began the launch sequence. Jerry wouldn't say a word unless Franklin made some mistake. "Command by negation" was all about letting your officers practice their trade and become independent thinkers. It was ironic that one of Jerry's most important duties as captain was to teach his people how to work without him being there.

Franklin ordered, "Pilot, all stop, prepare to hover."

A senior petty officer automatically repeated the command, and changed the speed setting. "Officer of the Deck, Maneuvering answers, all stop, indicated speed is four knots."

The UUVs could be launched at low speeds, less than five knots, but the smoothest launches occurred when the boat was stationary, or "dead in the water." Jerry didn't like the latter term, and discouraged its use, one of the prerogatives of command.

Franklin keyed the intercom. "Torpedo Room, Conn, we're slowing. Flood payload tube one."

"Flood payload tube one, Conn, Torpedo Room, aye." The trick was to spend as little time at a standstill as possible. Jerry had emphasized that the evolution didn't need to be done quickly, just smoothly. "Conn, Torpedo Room. Payload tube one is flood and equalized with sea pressure. Minot is ready for launch. All indications green."

"Speed two knots and falling," reported the pilot.

"Torpedo Room, Conn. Speed is two knots, unlock and open the hatch on payload tube one."

"Unlock and open the hatch on payload tube one, aye. Payload tube one hatch indicates open."

The two payload tube hatches in *North Dakota*'s bow were big, about seven feet in diameter, but tube one's now-open hatch was edge-on to the flow. It wouldn't cause much drag. The *Virginia*s were big boats, with a lot of momentum, and it took a few minutes to coast to a stop.

"Sonar?" Franklin's question wasn't shouted, but the operator heard it clearly in the quiet control room. Unlike earlier U.S. subs, the sonar operators on *Virginia*-class boats were no longer sequestered in their own little space, but located in control. A controversial design change, it was done to improve the flow of information to the captain and fire control team.

"Three contacts, the closest is Sierra-three three, bears one seven zero, range eleven nautical miles and opening, course one nine zero at twelve knots." That matched the information displayed on the big screen. They'd set up their UUV deployment box with some flexibility, so they could pick a spot with the thinnest merchant traffic.

"Speed one knot and falling," the pilot called. Jerry studied the trim indicators, although the OOD and chief of the boat were both watching them as well. Jerry knew the last knot would come off quickly. He'd actually taken time to practice coasting to a stop, timing how long it took from different speeds. Conning a sub should not involve guesswork.

"The boat is stationary." Franklin took just long enough to verify the pilot's report, then passed the word over the intercom. "Torpedo Room, Conn. We're hovering. Launch Minot."

The big ISR UUV, nicknamed "Minot," was designed for quiet launch. Using its own electric propulsion, it simply pulled itself out of the vertical tube, pitched over into a level attitude, and swam off to the west at three knots. The vehicle's entire track was programmed, along with several alternative plans that could be triggered by satellite downlink, acoustic modem, or on its own, depending on what its sensors detected.

*North Dakota*'s two UUVs, Minot and Fargo, allowed Jerry to extend his patrol area. While the vehicle's sonar wasn't as good as a *Virginia*'s, the UUV was a hair quieter and much smaller than the sub, making it harder to detect than the submarine.

By the time Minot was headed to the west, the payload tube hatch had closed and the torpedo room watchstanders began pumping down the flooded tube. Franklin had ordered the boat back to her eight-knot patrol speed and turned it toward the next patrol waypoint, all without Jerry having to say a word.

Three or four days from now, in a different spot along the western edge of their zone, they would recover Minot and replace it with Fargo, the second UUV. Until then, the submersible robot was on its own, to listen and report.

"Next waypoint bears zero seven five, twenty-two miles." Lieutenant Ed Rothwell, the navigator, had made the announcement almost as a formality. The waypoint was marked on the starboard big screen and also showed as the indicated course on the pilot's console.

The waypoints had been carefully chosen to be as random as possible, while also taking into account the current weather, the acoustic conditions at that time of day, and the likely movements of the ships they were supposed to be listening for.

*North Dakota* prowled and listened inside a bent rectangle wrapped around the southern end of Hainan Island, with the UUV's zone an angled box at the western end. *Santa Fe*'s area lay to the east, separated by a buffer zone. Although this was only a surveillance mission, it was vital that if *North Dakota* or *Santa Fe* heard another submarine, there would be no time wasted making sure it wasn't an American boat.

Slipping quietly through the water at three hundred feet, there was little for most of the watchstanders to do: no maneuvers except turning from one waypoint to the next, not even many depth changes. All the action was at the sonar watch station, as they listened and waited.

Lieutenant Stuart Gaffney, the sonar officer, watched his troops at work, making sure they and their gear were in top shape. They were, but even the best sonarman has to wait for something to hear.

"So she really hugged him? In front of everyone?" Lieutenant Lymburn's question was directed to the XO, also standing near the sonar station. She gestured toward Gaffney. "I can't believe either half of what this guy says." Gaffney, surprised at being identified as the rumor's source, did his best to fade into the bulkhead.

Thigpen nodded sagely. "I heard it from two guys on the squadron staff when they 'came by to check on our supply status.'" He gave a short laugh. "Right. What they really wanted was to pump me about how the skipper knew Dr. Patterson. I said they'd been shipmates and longtime friends, back to when he'd solved that bomb plot at the Naval Academy when he was a midshipman."

"You know, I'm right over here," Jerry remarked acidly. They'd been speaking softly, of course, but not that softly, and the well-run control room seemed even quieter than normal. "And I never did anything like that!"

"Well, sir, you did go to the academy. There could have been a bomb plot, and of course it was kept out of the papers. They thought it was fascinating."

Jerry rubbed his face and groaned. Thigpen was having far too much fun at his expense.

Turning back to Lymburn, the XO answered, "In this case, Lieutenant, Stuart is correct. The deputy national security adviser did, indeed, hug our beloved captain."

Gaffney studied the sonar consoles carefully, conspicuously ignoring the conversation.

"Wow," Lymburn exclaimed. "Did she kiss him?"

"No. He's not that beloved."

She turned to Jerry. "Sir, does Mrs. Mitchell know about this relationship?" Lymburn looked serious, and a little worried.

"Dr. Mitchell, who was Dr. Davis at the time, was the maid of honor at Dr. Patterson's wedding," the XO interjected. "Emily used to work for her. Isn't that right, Skipper?"

"*That* part of what the XO said is true," Jerry replied. He did his best not to smile, and added, "XO, didn't you have to inspect something, somewhere?"

"Yessir, I was just on my way to do that."


To her credit, Lymburn had kept one eye on the control room during the conversation, but two eyes were better. She and Gaffney remained by the sonar consoles. Since it was daytime, they weren't running with the multifunction mast up, which listened in on the local airwaves. The first sign of a contact would appear on sonar.

The southern end of Hainan Island held a large commercial port, two busy naval bases, and was home to many fishing boats and smaller craft. *North Dakota's* sonarmen constantly sorted man-made ships from the abundant sea life, and then naval from civilian vessels. They depended on a computer library of marine sounds, as well as a database holding acoustic information on warships and merchant sound signatures. Even then, the final call often came down to a petty officer's experience and judgment. Sometimes, though, the Chinese made it easy.


"Sonar contact bearing three one two, multiple sources, high blade count. Correlates with active sonars on same bearing." After a moment's pause, the petty officer added, "Sonars are SJD-5 and 7."

The sonar bearing, actually a cluster of white lines, appeared on the port VLSD.

"Pointing straight at Yalong Bay," Jerry observed. "The same time as yesterday."

A few moments later, the fire control system changed the cluster of lines to a blurry point twenty-six miles away, and added an arrow pointing almost due south. "Just leaving the eastern naval base," Jerry remarked.

The petty officer reported, "Base course is one seven zero, speed ten knots. But we're getting high-speed beats as well as slower screws that sound like merchants."

"With active sonars, they have to be escorts," Lymburn remarked. "Looks like they're still worried about submarines."

"But we've seen lots of merchant traffic in and out of Yulin that wasn't escorted," Gaffney commented.

"Could be part of the exercise they've announced," Lymburn suggested. "They're practicing wartime procedures, just as if there was a sub waiting for them to leave harbor. And maybe there's a Chinese submarine, waiting to conduct mock attacks against them."

Jerry knew the Chinese weren't practicing. He hadn't shared the details of the briefing with all of his crew. Only the XO, department heads, and the COB knew the full story. But still, she'd raised a good point.

"Let's make sure there isn't another boat lurking around here," Jerry remarked. "Sonar, keep a careful watch out for possible submarines," he instructed. "We've been innocent bystanders once. I don't want to be surprised by a diesel sub lying in wait. And make sure the Chinese aren't trying to slip one of their subs out along with those surface ships."

"Careful watch for submarines, aye, sir."

"Q, give me an intercept course at eight knots that will get us in front of them, just inside their radar horizon. We'll poke a mast up and see what there is to hear."

"Aye, sir." Lymburn glanced at the plotting board, but figured the angles in her head. "Recommend course three five zero. That will bring us within their horizon in . . . forty minutes."

"Very well." After Lieutenant Lymburn had ordered the course change, Jerry drilled her a little. "What happens next, Q?"

She considered for a moment, then said, "We should come up to periscope depth in," she glanced at her watch, "thirty-four minutes. We extend a photonics mast for ten seconds, to see if there are any close-by radars. If the coast is clear, we raise a multifunction mast and take a quick look for any comm signals. After a few minutes, we head back down to one hundred and fifty feet."

Jerry nodded his approval. "And what comes after that?"

That took a few moments for her to answer. "Close and get a periscope observation," she stated firmly.

"Correct. Get to work on the best plan that can get us within five thousand yards and then out without being detected. Remember, we're not making a torpedo approach. We just need to get close enough for a good beam-on video recording."

While the OOD worked the angles, the sonarmen continued to analyze the sounds radiated from the ships. The screws, the turbines, the electrical generators on each ship produced sounds, or "tones," that gave clues as to its identity. The thrum-thrum of the screws also let the sonarmen calculate the contact's speed, vital for tracking.

"OOD, Contact Sierra-four three is a Type 053H3 frigate, and correlates with the active SJD-5."

That got Jerry's attention. "A 53H3 frigate? That's the *Jiangwei II*. It's old, but it can carry a helicopter. OOD, allow for dipping helos in your plan. Assume they're dipping five to ten thousand yards from the ships."

The sonar petty officer reported, "Sierra-four four is a Type 54 frigate. It matches the other active sonar."

"Newer class," Jerry commented, "but it could have a towed array along with the better bow sonar, as well as a helo deck and hangar. So now they've got two anti-submarine helicopters to play with."

"Should I assume they have both up right now?" Lymburn asked.

"I would," Jerry answered. "The harbor is a high-threat area for them—for us, too, for that matter," he observed. "They'll shoot first and check hull numbers later if they detect anything this close."

Lymburn refined her solution. "Pilot, come right to zero zero zero. Sir, recommend coming to periscope depth in twenty minutes. Sonar, keep a sharp lookout for high-frequency dipping sonars."

Jerry approved her recommendation. The helos would make it harder to close on this group. Ship-based helicopters usually carried a short-ranged sonar that could be "dipped" into the water while the helicopter was hovering. The sonar "ball" was on a long cable, so it could be used to listen first above the thermocline, then below. If the sonar operator on the helicopter didn't hear anything passively, he'd then go active. If there was nothing to find, the operator would reel in the sonar and then move on to the next spot.

One helicopter could cause problems for them, but could be evaded. Two helos, using "leapfrog" tactics, could search, detect, and localize a submarine quickly. To stay quiet, a submarine has to creep at five or ten knots, but helicopters cruise at seventy. *North Dakota*'s only advantage would be that Jerry didn't want to shoot a torpedo at the ships, just get close enough to take a peek.

"OOD, we're picking up additional screws on that bearing. They were merged with the signals from the merchants, but the left bearing drift is giving us some separation now. New contacts Sierra-four five and four six."

Jerry and Lymburn both looked at the port VLSD. More of the fuzz had disappeared, replaced by two new vessels in front of the other four. The sonarman continued, "Sierra–four zero and four one are the merchants *Hai Fu 18* and *Yu He*, both Chinese-flagged container ships."

Lymburn zoomed in the VLSD to look at the formation. The two frigates were on either side of the merchants, which were steaming in column, with the two new contacts in front.

"Minesweepers," Jerry guessed, "just like yesterday. They're quieter than the others and we can't hear their mine-hunting sonars this far out."

"Seems likely, sir," agreed Gaffney, "but my guys are still working to confirm it."

"They really are treating it like the real thing," Lymburn remarked.

Watching the VLSD, Jerry saw the shift the same time as the sonarmen. "OOD, possible target zig. All frequencies have shifted, down Doppler, bearing drift is also changing. Picking up changes in blade rates."

On the big screen, symbols blurred and shifted as the fire control system struggled to predict the formation's next move. Four course arrows swung to the right, while the front two pivoted to the west, lengthening as well.

"The formation's turned east," Jerry observed. "And the minesweepers have done their job, so they're headed for the barn."

"Skipper, you're not leaving anything for my sonarmen to report," Gaffney complained.

Lymburn was bent over the horizontal display. "Sir, I'm not going to be able to get inside their horizon with an eight-knot speed. They'll pass by us to the north. If we increase to twenty knots, we can get in their forward hemisphere, but that's where their helicopters like to search. Fifteen knots will get us in trail in approximately two hours, assuming they don't maneuver again."

"I don't like either one of those options, OOD. We're too detectable at twenty knots, and you're right about the helicopters. And the trail position would be a long tail chase. We'll be too close to the eastern edge of our patrol area. What will we miss while we're running after these guys?"

It was a rhetorical question, and Jerry continued speaking before he put Lymburn on the spot. "Q, plot us a course to a spot well away from all surface traffic. We'll report to squadron. We will give Captain Halsey and *Santa Fe* enough warning so they can get in position. They can get the periscope shots."

The message upload went off without a hitch, without Jerry being anywhere near the radio room or the control. Once *North Dakota* had gotten some distance from the small convoy, he'd forced himself to go to the wardroom, get a cup of coffee, and chat for fifteen minutes before heading for his cabin.

The boat would run without him living in control. In theory, the less he was there, the more self-reliance his people developed. That was the theory.

But he didn't want to miss anything! Most sub captains had only one, maybe two command tours before being promoted or retiring. No other ship in the navy gave its commanding officer such complete one-man control over its actions, and no other ship in the fleet was so often out of touch and on its own. It was exciting, and Jerry wasn't shy about admitting that he liked being the "Guy in Charge." But captains who lived in control could die there, too. "Or smell like they had," according to Thigpen.

Immediately after taking command, Jerry and his new XO had spent a lot of time together, getting to know each other and working out Jerry's policies as *North Dakota*'s new skipper. These conferences usually involved refreshing beverages and case studies often referred to as "sea stories," but that did not diminish their value.

Prior to assuming command, Jerry attended "PCO school," a grueling three-month course that starts in the classroom, but quickly moves to a real sub operating against other surface ships, subs, and aircraft. During the "free play" exercises, Jerry practiced torpedo approaches, trailing operations, laid a dummy minefield, and simulated launching Tomahawk cruise missiles. He'd even operated against another nuclear submarine, which sounded hard and proved to be much more difficult than that.

Three months of training and thinking about command had increased his skills and expanded his consciousness. But he'd worked for three very different commanding officers for years at a time, seeing what worked for each of them. Now he had to make up his own style. He just didn't want to make it up at the last minute.


Jerry was lost in paperwork when the phone buzzed. It was Thigpen's voice.

"Skipper, would you please join us in control? We have the results from the UUV's latest data dump."

"Interesting?" Jerry asked.

"You will want to see this," the XO answered cryptically.

Lieutenant Russ Iverson, the main propulsion assistant, had the OOD watch, and gave Jerry the standard status report when he entered control, but there were no surprises. They were at depth and patrol speed, headed for the next waypoint. There were half a dozen sonar contacts, but all were civilian.

The action was in the aft starboard corner of the control room. Lieutenant Dave Covey, the weapons officer, had taken over a spare console and used it to display a plot of the UUV's activity. The XO watched over his shoulder, and made room for Jerry when he appeared.

A map was overlaid with the irregular shape of the vehicle's patrol zone. Different tracks drew colored lines through the zone, marking the progress of ships detected and tracked by Minot's sonars. One of the tracks was different, though, a tangle of lines that looked like a coil of rope.

The track of the UUV showed on the display as a different-colored line, with small deviations, for the first two-thirds of its patrol, but then it became irregular, zigging one way and sharply angling back the other in what looked like a random pattern. Only Jerry's experience with the UUV in the simulators told him this was not a malfunction.

"It's reacting to this contact," Covey reported. He highlighted the tangled track and a window with details about the vessel appeared. Time of first detection, bearings, signal strength, identity . . .

"It's a submarine," Covey explained. Jerry wasn't sure whether it was pride or excitement in the lieutenant's voice. "Just like it was supposed to, as soon as Minot figured out it wasn't a surface vessel, it started maneuvering to localize the contact, but not getting too close. What's interesting is that the contact isn't transiting."

Jerry studied the track's data carefully. It had a low blade rate, as well as low signal strength. Covey volunteered, "The acoustic data's already been sent over to our sonarmen. They're running it through the system right now."

Jerry looked up at the port VLSD. The sub was loitering to the west of Hainan Island. Minot had gotten close enough to get elevation data on the signal, which allowed them to calculate the contact's depth. The water wasn't terribly deep there, and it looked like the boat was almost hugging the bottom, creeping at bare steerageway, conserving its battery power, drawing large ovals in the water.

Lieutenant Gaffney came over from the sonar consoles. "My guys say it's a late Kilo, a Project 636. Blade rate's consistent with three knots."

Jerry had an uneasy feeling. Why would a Chinese diesel boat be hanging out to the west of Hainan Island? It was out of the exercise area the Chinese had declared, and away from the shipping lanes. "XO, did we update the intel plot during the last comms window?"

"Of course," Thigpen replied. "Squadron Fifteen's update is about three hours old."

"How many of the Chinese Kilos are we tracking?"

Thigpen sat down at the next console and called up the intelligence summary. "They have twelve Kilos, all Russian-built, purchased in '94 and '97. Two are older Project 877s, the remaining ten are the later models, Project 636." He paused for a minute, scrolling.

"And as of three hours ago, two were reported as being in the yards, and the rest in harbor. Three are assigned to the sub base at Yalong Bay, and they're still there, if the intel is right."

"Assume it was right three hours ago," Jerry said. "There's no way one could have taken station that far to the west without us seeing it."

"Not without it having a warp drive," Thigpen added. "At a top speed of nineteen knots for one hour, it would have a flat battery a third of the way to that location."

"Then we have to assume it isn't a Chinese boat. Stu, go back and tell your techs to take that signal apart. XO, punch the intelligence database and see who else might be operating a Kilo, besides the obvious answer."

Jerry studied the screen with Covey, trying to pull more information out of the display. Was the sub skipper following a pattern?

Five minutes later, Thigpen reported back to Jerry. "Aside from China, India's got ten and Vietnam currently has three. The Indian boats are early marks, Project 877. Vietnam's are Project 636s. The latest unit was just delivered this year."

Jerry nodded solemnly. "That's what I remembered, but I was hoping there was another possibility." He turned around, toward the sonarmen, with Gaffney standing behind them. Gaffney noticed the movement and hurried over.

"Nothing yet, sir," the sonar officer reported. "It's definitely a 636 Kilo. It doesn't match any of the recorded signatures, but then we don't have all the Chinese boats in the library."

"Do we have any signatures at all on the Vietnamese subs?" Jerry asked.

"No, sir. The library would have automatically . . ." He paused, processing the question. "You think this is a Vietnamese boat? Payback for *Vinaship Sea*? But why are they way over here?"

"Damfino, Stu. We need more data."

Gaffney shrugged. "Well . . . one of my techs noticed that the tonals were very 'clean.' There was very little noise around each of the lines."

Jerry understood the sonar officer's reference. New machinery ran smoothly, but as gears and bearings wore down, the sound each piece of equipment made became fuzzier, less a single tight frequency and more a band of sounds centered around the tone. Some civilian engineers used frequency analyzers to diagnose problems with turbines and generators. *North Dakota*'s sonars were sensitive enough to hear it as well, even when it wasn't bad enough to need fixing.

"So it's a new Project 636," Jerry said. "Go compare the newest Chinese 636 in our library with this signal."

Gaffney answered, "Aye, sir," and headed back to the sonar station. It only took a moment to set up the comparison, but then several minutes for the techs to examine the displays. Gaffney came back, reporting, "The latest Chinese boat we have in the library was delivered in '07. My techs, especially Andersen, can see the difference. If a cleaner signal means a new boat, then this one is newer than 2007. Maybe a lot newer."

Jerry studied the UUV's data, looking for another answer besides the ominous one, the possibility he couldn't ignore. "It would be nice to come up with some other reason for a Vietnamese diesel attack boat to take station off Hainan Island. Can any of you think of something else?"

"Something other than what?" Gaffney was still thinking about the sonar signal, and hadn't made the connection. Thigpen and Covey had figured it out.

Jerry explained, "He's waiting for a 'go' code."

26 August 2016
By Water
Halifax, Nova Scotia

Bywater's Blog
China Exercise Largest Ever?

There is information from correspondents (here) that the exercise announced by China will be the largest in its history, involving all three fleets (South Sea, East Sea, and North Sea). Information at chinadefense.com and portreporter.com shows unusual activity at naval bases as far north as Dalian.

One clue about the type of exercises has been provided by Chien585 (here), a member on Taiwan, who monitors the Chinese-flagged merchant fleet. He noted that as many as two dozen vessels have been taken off their normal runs and have congregated at Chinese naval bases.

This implies a convoy or protection of shipping exercise, but on a scale not seen before. Typical naval exercises will have one or two token merchants play the part of an entire convoy. In this case, the Chinese may be trying to see if the PLAN can successfully manage large groups of merchant ships. This is not an easy task for any navy, and the Chinese fleet is entirely new to this. They are definitely stepping off at the deep end.

Mac sat back and reread the entry before hitting the "Return" key. It would be interesting to see how successful the Chinese exercises were. They seemed to be serious about becoming a blue-water power. But now he had that article to write.

The phone rang as Mac tried to confirm the manufacturer of a ship's steam propulsion plant. This was not net research. Centuries-old copies of *Brassey's Annual* and *Scientific American* were scattered across the library floor, and he had to first disentangle himself from the pile of reference books, carefully stand, and then hurry to get the handset. He made it on the fifth ring.

He hadn't bothered to check the caller ID, but would have picked up the phone in any case. "Mr. McMurtrie, it's Christine Laird from CNN again. Is this a good time to talk?"

She barely gave Mac time to say "Of course," before she was off at high speed. "Well, you were so knowledgeable about the mystery ship and its loss that I took up your suggestion. We had one of our Asian branches locate the *Hanjin Malta* and interview its captain. They'd just arrived in Karachi, and our stringer there was able to talk to both the captain and some of the crew who saw the explosion. They were all very eager to tell him about it. One of the crew, the lookout, said he thought the explosion was 'whitish,' at least at first. Then it became bigger and dark gray or black. And several people on the bridge claim they heard two explosions, one small, and then another much larger one."

Mac remembered his earlier calculations. "Did any of them say how far their ship was from the explosion?"

"I think so." She paused for a moment, then said, "A little over sixteen nautical miles, based on their navigator's plot." After another pause, she asked, "Why would there be two explosions, and what would make an explosion white?"

Mac answered almost immediately. "The answer to the first part is straightforward, Ms. Laird. I believe the mystery ship was carrying explosive cargo, possibly even munitions. That would explain why no nation has claimed it. The first blast detonated that cargo, resulting in the larger explosion. Ms. Laird, if you can find out who owned that vessel, or where it was going, that will be a real story."

"Please, just Christine. That's what we're hoping to do. What about the 'white explosion'? Could this be some sort of gas that was released from the ship, and then ignited?"

Mac frowned and shook his head, then remembered she couldn't see his reaction. "Unlikely. To be visible at that distance, the column would have to be over a hundred feet high. I've never heard of a jet of flammable gas like that, and to be white . . ."

He paused for a moment. "What will throw a white column, not of gas but of water, a hundred feet or more in the air is an underwater explosion—a mine, or more likely a torpedo. There are dozens of photos of a torpedo exploding under a ship, creating a plume of white spray and vapor that high."

"A torpedo?" She sounded incredulous. Mac was also surprised by the thought, but it did fit the data. "But what about it being a mine, an old one left over from World War Two?"

"An old, forgotten mine, broken free from its moorings and sitting in the path of the unlucky vessel?" Mac realized he was being dramatic, but it was a dramatic idea. And highly unlikely.

"There was fighting all through that area, Christine, and I'm no expert, but I don't know of any minefields laid near that location, although it could always have drifted there from Heaven knows where." He sighed. "But more to the point, there haven't been any ships striking old mines in that part of the world for decades. Anything's possible, but I believe a torpedo is the more likely culprit."

"Adding a mystery sub to the mystery ship," she answered. "Is there any other alternative?" She sounded desperate. "My choices are the unlikely and the incredible."

"I'll work on the question, at least to rule out the mine theory," Mac offered. He decided he liked talking to Ms. Laird . . . Christine. He was willing to spend some time on it. This was more interesting than the article on steam plants. Well, a little more interesting.

"I'd be very grateful, Mr. McMurtrie. We'll mention your blog in the feature."

"Then it's my turn to be grateful, and please, just call me Mac."

"I'll call again, Mac, before we run the piece."

Mac answered, "I'll look forward to it," and hung up.

# 6

# SPOILER

30 August 2016
0200 Local Time
USS *North Dakota*
Off Hainan Island, South China Sea

"CAPTAIN TO CONTROL!" The blare from the general announcing system violently wrenched Jerry from a deep sleep. Propelled out of his rack by the sudden spasm of every muscle in his body, he was still shaking as he jumped into his loafers. Throwing open his stateroom door, Jerry dashed for the control room not more than thirty feet away. Thigpen was right behind him, equally disheveled and groggy.

Bursting into the control room, Jerry was momentarily confused. *Why isn't control rigged for red?* he wondered. As his brain dragged itself into a lucid state, he remembered, no periscopes on this boat. Electro-optics didn't need to worry about becoming night-adapted.

"Sorry for the sudden wake-up call, Skipper," apologized Lieutenant Commander Phil Sobecki, the ship's engineer and third ranking officer. "But things just got really screwy."

As the engineer spoke, he motioned for a young sailor to come forward. In his hands was a steaming cup of coffee. Still a little fuzzy, Jerry gratefully accepted the offering and nodded his thanks to the young man, who was maybe all of nineteen years old. Taking a sip, Jerry felt the world start to come into focus.

"Define screwy, Eng," he said wearily.

"Sir, we just picked up four loud explosions. Two to the west and two to the southeast."

Jerry's head snapped up from the cup. He was amazed by the report. "Four explosions? They're sure of this?" he asked while tilting his head toward the sonar techs.

"Without a doubt, Skipper."

"Show me what you've got," ordered Jerry.

"Yes, sir. Ollie, bring up the merged track data. Sonar, recall the audio on both events."

Ensign Olivia Andrews quickly manipulated a few buttons on the fire control panel, and the bottom screen on her console changed to an electronic Geoplot display. "Merged track data sent to the port VLSD, sir," she reported.

"Very well," replied Sobecki. The plot popped up onto the big screen; two bearing lines jutted out from *North Dakota*'s track. One was on a bearing of two six six, the other down one one zero. Jerry noticed immediately the lack of range information.

"You didn't get a range off the wide-aperture array?"

Sobecki shook his head. "No, sir. The explosions were pretty far away, at least thirty nautical miles. Sonar, play the audio for the western event."

The sonar supervisor acknowledged the order and soon the sound of the ocean filled the control room. At first, all Jerry heard were the noises from local biologics and the occasional fishing boat. Then came the first explosion, followed soon by the second. They were clearly explosions, and they were distant; beyond the ranging ability of the passive arrays along his submarine's flanks.

The second set of explosions was a mirror image of the first. Again, there was no doubt as to what they were. A cold chill ran down Jerry's spine. Was this just the beginning?

"The explosions in both cases were five or six seconds apart, Captain," said Sobecki.

"Sounds about right for a salvo interval from a Kilo-class boat," Thigpen interjected.

Jerry agreed. "Yes, it does. Unfortunately." Then pointing toward the western event, he asked, "Was Fargo still in contact with that new Kilo?"

"As of the last data dump, yes, sir. Our little drone was firmly in trail," Sobecki replied.

"When's the next scheduled comms window?"

The engineer pointed to an open menu on one of the command workstation's displays. "A little under three hours from now, sir."

Jerry frowned; three hours seemed like an awfully long time to wait.

"We could send it a coded pulse to command it to come up sooner," suggested the engineer.

"But that means transmitting," Thigpen warned. "Our orders are pretty explicit about remaining undetected, sir. If Fargo is still in trail of the Kilo, there's more than a good chance they would pick up the pulse as well."

"A good point, XO," Jerry conceded. "But do you think they would be able to recognize the pseudo-random noise pulse as being a valid contact? Or would they be more likely to blow it off as spurious noise?"

"Skipper, I wouldn't know a funky pulse from snapping shrimp. My point is that we don't have a good understanding of the modifications to the Vietnamese boat's sonar. We know it's an all-digital version of the older Rubikon sonar, but is it smart enough to recognize a funky pulse? I dunno, but it is something we need to consider."

Jerry nodded silently, translating Thigpen's carefully spoken "we" to mean "you." Sipping at his coffee, Jerry took a hard look at the information on the VLSD. Thigpen's concerns and Admiral Burroughs's stern admonition, "You cannot be detected. Clear?" echoed inside his head.


The Vietnamese were new to submarines, and the Russians were notorious for providing only basic system and operational training. The upgraded Rubikon sonar suite on the Vietnamese Kilos was theoretically capable of picking up the signal, but Jerry doubted very much that a newly trained operator would recognize it as something worthy of interest.

And there was the sense of urgency nagging at him. Three hours was a long time to wait for the data from his UUV. It very likely had information on the attack to the west that he needed to pass up the chain of command as soon as possible. If the balloon had just gone up, as he feared, he had to report now, not three or four hours from now. He made up his mind.

"Engineer, send the coded pulse to Fargo and come to periscope depth to receive the satellite downlink. Get the CTs ready as well; there is probably a hell of a lot of chatter going on up there right now. XO, get the commo up and prepare another OPREP-3 message. I think the war we've been told to watch for has just started, and we need to let our bosses know ASAP," ordered Jerry.

Thigpen and Sobecki acknowledged their orders, and the control room became abuzz with activity. Jerry had watched his XO's face as he gave his instructions. If Thigpen disagreed, it didn't show.

Jerry thought about hanging around in control, but that would send the wrong message. He had to show he trusted his people if they were to believe in themselves. Instead, Jerry headed back to his stateroom. He was awake now; he might as well get some work done while he waited for Fargo's data.

On his way out, Jerry overheard Thigpen telling the messenger of the watch to wake up Mr. Franklin. The young lad dutifully answered, "Aye, aye, sir," but then added, "XO, would you like a cup of coffee, too?"

"Coffee!?" uttered Thigpen cynically. "I don't need no stinkin' coffee. I have adrenaline!"

Jerry tried to review the previous week's reactor plant chemistry logs for the third time. He just couldn't concentrate long enough for them to make any sense. He knew the logs were important—reactor plant safety was a major consideration in any submarine CO's evaluation—but it was extremely difficult to focus on something so mundane when a war was starting around you. Mercifully, the Dialex phone rang, rescuing him before he tried yet again.

"Captain," Jerry answered.

"Skipper, CDO. We have the data from Fargo, and you'll want to see this."

"Very well, Engineer. I'll be there shortly." Jerry hung up and gratefully slid the chemistry logs back into his inbox. They'd keep.

Jerry deliberately walked casually toward the control room, taking deep breaths to help calm himself. He had to look composed, confident. "You should never look frazzled," he'd been counseled by Kyle Guthrie, his old skipper on *Michigan*. "The crew looks to you for stability, particularly when things start getting crazy."

Strolling past the radio room, Jerry paused and stuck his head in to see how the message was progressing. Inside he saw Thigpen, Franklin, and one of the info techs working furiously.

"How's that message coming, XO?" Jerry inquired. He really didn't need to ask, the three were clearly going at it with hammer and tongs, but every once in a while it was kind of fun to pull Thigpen's chain. You never knew what kind of response you'd get. Jerry remembered, with the type of fondness that only comes with the passage of time, how often Guthrie had tugged on his line.

Thigpen was hovering over the console, twitching as he pointed toward the screen. "No! Move that part here. No, not there, here! Yes, right there. Good!" blurted the XO. Looking up and seeing Jerry in the doorway, Thigpen held up one finger as he bounced from one foot to the other. "Give us another minute, Skipper, then we'll have something for you."

Jerry smiled, nodded, and continued on. Upon entering control, he saw LT David Covey hard at work on the spare console. The port VLSD had the output from one of the photonics masts on it, while the electronic support system's audible signal kept beeping in the background. Sobecki sounded a little stressed as he gave rudder orders. The track display on the starboard big screen showed a large number of contacts. It sure was busy up here.

"Command Duty Officer, report," Jerry ordered.

"Sir, we've downloaded Fargo's data and you were right, she saw the whole thing. Dave has been busy sending the highlights to the XO for the OPREP-3 message," responded Sobecki.

Before Jerry could ask for any details, a warning alarm suddenly sounded in control.

"Conn, ESM. Have an APS-504 radar, signal strength three, bearing zero one three, closing fast."

Sobecki didn't acknowledge the report right away; he had to move quickly, as a Chinese Y-8 maritime patrol aircraft was getting dangerously close. The aircraft's surface search radar was a significant detection threat to the two exposed masts.

"Lower all masts!" he cried.

The optics mast operator and copilot echoed the command as they manipulated their controls, dipping the masts below the ocean's surface. Jerry could feel the tension rising in the air. The watchstanders had acted properly, but they were all on edge.

"Sorry, Skipper, it's been hectic," apologized Sobecki. "A lot of search-and-rescue traffic popped up in the last fifteen minutes. That was our second Y-8 MPA, probably one of their alert aircraft."

"You're doing fine, Phil," Jerry reassured his third in command. "Now, tell me what's going on."

Sobecki wasn't able to utter a word before Thigpen interrupted him, "Here you go, Skipper. This is the *Reader's Digest* version of the story; if you're happy with this we can send it out as soon as the airspace clears."

Jerry took the hard-copy message from his XO and quickly scanned it.
He skipped through the preamble after making sure the "Z" prosign for
"Flash" precedence was present. Jerry was less interested in proper format
right now than he was in the content.

Jumping to the body of the message, he noted the location of the first
set of explosions—latitude 17° 54' N, longitude 108° 46' E—almost forty-
nine nautical miles to the west; the time, 0159 local; and the tactical assessment. His eyes quickly homed in on the sentence: "ISR UUV acoustic data
showed two TE-2 torpedoes fired by probable Vietnamese Kilo-class submarine at a Chinese merchant, subsequently identified as the China Ocean
Shipping Company tanker *Yan Shui Hu*, 25,428 gross registered tons."

Jerry shook his head as he continued reading. The information content
of the message was good; its implications were anything but. He moved on
to the second set of explosions, which had far less data. However, the conclusion that it was possibly due to another submarine attack made it just as
stark. Grunting his approval, he handed the draft back to Thigpen.

"Send it, XO."

"Yes, sir," replied Thigpen, visibly relieved. As he headed back to the
radio room, Jerry called back to him.

"XO. Nice work, Bernie."


Ten minutes later, with *North Dakota* back down to 150 feet, the atmosphere
in control began to ease. Jerry hovered over the spare common console as LT
Covey walked him through the engagement. The Kilo had positioned itself
off the starboard beam of the tanker and fired a two-weapon salvo at a range
of 4,500 yards. It was a textbook Russian attack, deliberate and premeditated;
there was no other way to describe it.

While Jerry, Thigpen, and Sobecki dissected the Kilo's tactics, one of
the electronics technicians poked his head out of the ESM bay. "Skipper,
XO. We picked up something you'll be interested in."

Jerry and Thigpen crammed themselves into the tight ESM shack,
while Sobecki leaned in from the doorway. "What goodies did you vacuum
from the ether, Petty Officer Fleming?" asked Thigpen with a lighthearted
tone.

Fleming smiled as he pointed toward a young third class. "Petty Officer
Kalinsky here has been going over the material we collected while we were

uploading the message, and he found some pretty interesting stuff. Go ahead and tell the skipper, Gus."

Kalinsky was one of the CT riders, a cryptologic technician attached to *North Dakota* in support of the special operations mission. Linguistic experts are often added to a submarine's crew to provide on-the-spot information by monitoring the local radio frequencies. Many an intelligence gem had been harvested in the past by the careless transmission of someone who thought they wouldn't be heard.

"Yes, sir, Captain," stammered the young sailor. "While the boat transmitted the message, I picked up a lot of voice traffic from the port authority at Yulin. Most of the chatter was from rescue ships asking where they needed to go to assist. Well, one of those rescue ships was heading in the direction of the second set of explosions, and that dude was really confused. The guy at the port authority started shouting at the captain and repeated the location and identification data for another ship. I wrote it down as quickly as I could. Here it is, along with a rough translation."

Jerry took the sheet of torn paper and looked at the hastily written notes. The top lines contained Chinese characters. Sloppily written, they looked like a child's chicken scratches. Below them, however, were neatly printed English words—their meaning electrifying. Jerry read them out loud.

"Distress beacon transmission, merchant vessel *Chang Chi*, lat 17° 25'N, long 111° 10' E. No response to radio hails." Jerry handed the notes to Thigpen. "Eng, look up the *Chang Chi*."

"Already did that, sir," Fleming exclaimed. "It's another tanker, Skipper. Motor vessel *Chang Chi*, crude oil tanker, 27,155 gross registered tons, owned and operated by the Nanjing Tanker Company." Fleming handed the report chit to his CO.

"Well done, Petty Officer Fleming. You too, Petty Officer Kalinsky. That was mighty fine detective work." Jerry was pleased with his people's performance. He briefly looked again at the *Chang Chi*'s information, and a frown formed on his face.

"Two tankers. Just a coincidence, or an indication?" Jerry asked openly.

Thigpen chuckled. "Just a coincidence, Skipper? An ice cube has a better chance in a blast furnace. These were deliberate attacks. In my opinion, it's an indication." Then, deftly snatching the report chit from Jerry's hand, Thigpen added, "Well, it looks like I have another message to write."

"I believe you do, too," agreed Jerry.

30 August 2016
2100 Local Time
USS *North Dakota*
Off Hainan Island, South China Sea

Jerry paced back and forth in his stateroom. There hadn't been any response from squadron on his two messages, nothing. There were snippets of information in the routine broadcasts that hinted at possible attacks elsewhere along the Chinese coast, but nothing with any substance, no details. Adding to his frustration, Fargo had lost contact with the Kilo. Whoever the captain was, he knew his business. He craftily merged with a small fishing fleet before he started snorkeling. The UUV's autonomous detection algorithms couldn't differentiate one marine diesel from another, and dutifully locked on to the loudest source around the Kilo's last known bearing—a large fishing boat. The sonar techs had plowed through the last data dump and were confident the UUV had been tracking the fishing vessel for at least an hour.

"I don't want to let this guy go," he had said earlier to his XO and department heads. "He's a known bad actor, and I've got a nagging feeling we've only seen the beginning."

"But Skipper, why couldn't these two attacks just be a tit-for-tat retaliation for the 093's sinking of the *Vinaship Sea*?" asked Rothwell.

"That's a possibility, Nav, but the dots don't stack up very well for that hypothesis," Thigpen argued, referring to the fire control's visual display of a neat vertical line of bearing dots when the solution was a good one. "This would be the second rotation on the retaliation merry-go-round. Remember, the Vietnamese mined the carrier first. I doubt the Chinese will let these attacks go unanswered."

"The XO's correct," observed Jerry. "But it doesn't matter what the Kilo skipper's motivation is right now. We need to find him, and pronto."

"And do what, sir?" objected Thigpen testily. Jerry noted the fatigue in his XO's voice. Both men had been up since the initial attacks some twenty hours earlier. Thigpen rubbed his forehead, then continued with a more restrained tone, "It's not like we can shoot him to get him to stop."

"That's a reasonable question, XO. I don't know what we can do, if anything. But we can still learn something by observing his actions, even if all we do is watch him kill more ships. However, the first order of business is finding the guy." Jerry then looked down at the electronic navigation chart on the horizontal large-screen display, and motioned toward the left-hand side of a large square drawn on the chart. "So, we'll head toward the western edge of our patrol box and look for him. Once we reacquire the Kilo, we'll direct Fargo back into contact and then turn about and head back east."

"But that means we'd be leaving the Chinese navy bases uncovered, won't it?" Covey asked hesitantly.

Jerry shook his head. "No, we'll leave Minot behind to keep the bases under surveillance while we head off to find the Kilo."

Covey looked confused. "Sir, I thought you didn't want to deploy both UUVs at the same time?"

For a brief instant, Jerry felt a little irritated by his weapons officer's response. Then Jerry remembered that he too was very tired. Taking a deep breath he said, "That was the original plan, Dave. Circumstances have changed, and the plan needs to adapt accordingly. Now, launch Minot, get her on station, and then get us heading westward at best tactical speed."


The electronic ring of the phone dragged Jerry back to consciousness; he'd fallen asleep while reviewing the chemistry logs. Groping for the handset, he yanked it from the cradle. "Captain," he mumbled.

"Skipper, CDO. My apologies if I woke you, but we've reacquired the Kilo."

"Ahh, excellent. I'll be right there," Jerry croaked.

Stumbling into the head he shared with Thigpen, Jerry nearly collided with his XO as he tried to splash some cold water on his face. Amused by Jerry's semi-comatose expression, Thigpen hunched over and shrieked softly, "It's alive!"

Jerry looked over the towel as he dried his face; he attempted to give Thigpen an evil stare, but failed, his eyes only opened halfway. "That, Mr. Thigpen, is a matter of debate," he finally replied.

Thigpen laughed as he finished combing his hair. "Was that Phil?"

"Yeah, we've picked up the Kilo again."

"Oh goodie! Just in time for my CDO watch," exclaimed the executive officer.

"What time is it?" Jerry asked, confused. He still wasn't entirely awake yet.

"It's 2330. Give or take a couple of minutes."

"Really? Is it that early? The Kilo must have been heading east the whole time," said Jerry, more to himself than anyone else. His brain was beginning to process data again.

"Sounds about right. He was heading easterly when Fargo lost contact," answered Thigpen. Looking down at his watch, he added, "I need to go do the prewatch tour with Q. I'll see you in control in about twenty minutes."

Jerry acknowledged the XO's departure with a curt wave. His mind was on the Kilo. After a quick rinse with mouthwash to get rid of the old-sock taste in his mouth, Jerry headed up to control. He'd just closed the door when he heard the sonar supervisor announce, "New sonar contact. Designated Sierra-seven nine, bearing zero five one. Sounds like diesel engines starting up."

"Very well, Sonar Supervisor," Covey responded, then, turning to the section tracking party, ordered, "Begin tracking Sierra-seven nine."

Walking up to the command workstation, Jerry saw Sobecki and Covey hunched over, focusing on one of the displays. The engineer was furiously moving the trackball, while Covey punched some buttons. Both looked a little worn.

"CDO, report."

"Yes, sir. Our friend is contact Sierra-seven eight. He bears three two zero, range about eight thousand yards, drawing right." Sobecki pointed to the port VLSD, where all the pertinent data was enlarged just above the tracking symbol. Jerry noted they were on the Kilo's starboard beam and drawing behind him, very nice. They would soon be in his baffles and they could close from that advantageous position.

"We've just picked up a new contact, Sierra-seven nine, off to the northeast. We're working on a solution now. Say, Skipper, do you want me to get you a cup of coffee?"

"No thanks, Eng, I probably drink too much anyway," Jerry replied as he studied the tactical situation on the display. "Have you attempted to contact Fargo?"

"Not yet, sir. The last fix we had indicated the UUV was still well outside of acoustic modem range; it won't be close enough for about another hour."

"Hmmm, I guess we'll have to dog this fellow ourselves for a little while then," lamented Jerry with feigned inconvenience.

"What a shame," Sobecki replied cynically. Both men sported large grins. This was exactly the kind of action that any submariner worth his or her salt longed for.

"OOD," sang out the sonar supervisor, "Sierra-seven nine is classified as a Type 039 Song-class submarine, snorkeling."

Jerry, Sobecki, and Covey all looked surprised. There was nothing in the intel reports that suggested a Song-class boat had deployed. "Very well, Sonar Supervisor," said Covey over his shoulder. "This complicates things a bit."

"Indeed it does," Jerry admitted, "but we're still in a good position to control the tactical situation."

Sobecki nodded his agreement. Then, leaning past Covey to get a clear line of sight to the tracking party, he grumbled, "Hey, Ollie, don't you have a solution on Sierra-seven nine yet?"

"Coming up now, Eng," Andrews shot back. "It should be up on the port VLSD."

The data popped up on the display along with a tracking symbol in the approximate position and an error circle. The Song bore zero four eight, range ten thousand yards, heading due south at three knots.

"He's chugging along, fat, dumb, and happy, recharging his battery," Covey observed.

Jerry frowned. The picture just didn't look right. "CDO, what's the range between the Kilo and the Song?"

Sobecki spun the trackball, moving the cursor over the Kilo, and then dragged it to the Song. "Range is about 12,800 yards, Skipper."

Jerry's frown morphed into a disappointed grimace. "Are you serious? They shouldn't have any problems at that range hearing the Song when it's making such a racket!"

"Maybe their sonar isn't as good as we've given them credit for, sir," commented Covey.

"My aunt Agatha with a hearing trumpet couldn't miss that!" Jerry's voice was laden with sarcasm. The Vietnamese were new at this game, but surely they weren't incompetent.

Standing there staring at the large-screen display, Jerry wrestled with the inconsistency. Maybe Covey was right and the updated Rubikon sonar wasn't all that the advertisements claimed it to be. But still, even the older version would have been able to detect a relatively loud target this close. It just didn't make sense. Perplexed, Jerry started going over possible alternatives in his head. He didn't get far before the sonar chief blurted out, "Possible target zig, Sierra-seven eight, based on frequency. Target has either turned towards or sped up."

"Confirm target zig, based on bearing rate," cried Andrews. "Sierra-seven eight has altered course to starboard."

The expression on Jerry's face must have changed, as Sobecki started chuckling. "There, are you happy now, Skipper?" he teased.

His head hanging low, Jerry let out a long sigh. "Well, at least it now makes sense. But . . ."

"But," interrupted Sobecki, "the Kilo is now heading straight for the Song."

"Yup, that about sums it up."

"Do you want me to summon the XO to control?"

"Yes, please, Engineer."

As Sobecki called for Thigpen over the 1MC, Jerry moved closer to the large display on the port side—his thoughts focusing on the tactical picture. The situation was degrading slowly. It would be at least half an hour before the Kilo would reach a firing position, assuming the Song didn't change course. But what could he do with that time? Would it even be possible to break up the attack? His orders were pretty straightforward, and everything that came to mind violated those orders.

It didn't take Thigpen even a minute to reach control, and by then the fire control system had determined, conclusively, that the Kilo was on a perfect intercept course. There was no mistaking what was happening. The Vietnamese Kilo captain was getting into position to ambush the Chinese submarine. Jerry's mind was racing. Shooting tankers was bad enough, but attacks against another country's naval vessels kicked things up a notch. And then there were the safety concerns for his own boat. They weren't far enough away to be immune from a stray torpedo. Should he just bug out and put more distance between the warring parties? He really didn't like that option, but there seemed to be nothing else he could do. If only they could come up with a way to spook the other subs without giving themselves away.

"Skipper, I understand your desire to prevent bloodshed, but what can we do without revealing our presence?" pleaded Thigpen.

"That's what I'm trying to figure out, Bernie!" snapped Jerry. He stopped and took several deep breaths. His XO wasn't the enemy and Thigpen was only doing his job—perhaps, annoyingly, a little too well at the moment. His mind refocused, Jerry reapproached the problem.

"Okay. Active sonar is out. It's a big neon sign that says 'shoot here.' The UUV is too far away, so we can't use it as a diversion. And the mobile de-

coys are tuned for acoustic homing torpedoes." Jerry ticked off the options on his fingers one at a time.

"And we can't use any of our ADCs, as their electronic noise would be easily ID'd as American," added Thigpen.

It was Thigpen's last words that suddenly gave Jerry an idea. One that just might work. "Weps, we still have a few of those old NAE Mark 3 beacons on board, don't we?"

"Yes, sir. We use them during exercises. They're a lot cheaper than an ADC Mark 4."

"Captain . . . what are you thinking?" Thigpen asked suspiciously.

"It's quite simple, XO." Jerry looked around for a piece of paper to draw on. Then remembered that there weren't any paper plots—there wasn't any room for them with all the electronic displays in a *Virginia*-class sub's control room. Grabbing a pen from his pocket, he pointed to the geoplot display on the command workstation.

"We pull in behind the Kilo, overtake him, and drop an NAE with a time delay *between* the two boats. We then pull off to the north before either party has a chance to figure out what the hell happened."

"But, sir, we'll give ourselves away if we drop a countermeasure. They'll detect it and know we're here. There is no way to avoid that!" insisted Thigpen.

"You're right, they'll detect the NAE—but they won't know it's us. They won't suspect it's from an American sub!" Jerry exclaimed.

Thigpen was confused, frustrated, and it showed. "Huh? Come again? I'm not following you, Skipper."

"Okay, look. The NAE is a very old countermeasure; the first models were designed in World War Two, over seventy years ago. It generates noise mechanically, not electronically. Neither the Vietnamese nor the Chinese would suspect the U.S. still has, or would even use, such a low-tech device.

"Also, when I was reviewing the log entries from *Michigan*'s engagement with the Iranian Kilo, my skipper, Kyle Guthrie, noted that the countermeasures deployed by the Iranian boat sounded almost exactly like an NAE. Don't you get it? Both sides have Russian gear, including acoustic countermeasures! Each captain will think the other guy detected him and shot out a decoy! They'll both be spooked and start evasive maneuvers, while we slink off to the north."

Thigpen still wasn't convinced. "But they'll both be able to hear us when we pull in front. We'd be, what? Maybe two or three thousand yards away for either sub. We're really quiet, but that's way too close."

"Correct again, we'd be *too* close. Both the Kilo and Song captains are boresighted toward the surface. The Song, so he doesn't get run over by a passing merchant, and the Kilo as he's setting up his attack. Neither sonar system can look at more than one depression/elevation angle at the same time. So we come in right off the bottom, below their sonar's field of view. The water is shallow here, which will help hide our signature, and we have a negative sound velocity profile down to the bottom—everything is in our favor. Trust me, this will work!"

Jerry watched as Thigpen worked the problem through. He was still unsure, but his CO's confidence overwhelmed him. Swallowing hard, Thigpen finally said, "It's your call, sir."

With a beaming smile, Jerry slapped his XO on the arm. Turning to Covey, Jerry ordered, "Weps, load an NAE in one of the signal ejectors. Set a two-minute time delay."

"Aye, aye, sir," replied Covey.

Looking back at Thigpen, Jerry nodded and said, "XO, man battle stations."

Once the crew was at general quarters, Jerry explained his plan to the control room watchstanders. He took extra care to make sure everyone understood what they were about to do, and why. The junior officers were awestruck and excited; the more senior ones were apprehensive. Even though the odds were very much in their favor, this was not a risk-free evolution.

As soon as the Kilo was on their starboard beam, Jerry made a sharp turn to the northeast and moved *North Dakota* into the Vietnamese boat's baffles. Blocked by the submarine's hull, the large cylindrical array in the Kilo's bow couldn't hear them and Jerry accelerated to fifteen knots.

It was a long, slow overtaking geometry, but twenty minutes later, the Kilo was five hundred yards to port and a hundred feet above them. With only fifty feet between the hull and the sea floor, Jerry slowed to ten knots as *North Dakota* slowly pulled in front. For the next six minutes, hardly a sound was made in control; even the watchstanders' breathing was hushed. When they reached the designated point, Jerry ordered the NAE launched, turned north, and slowly increased speed to twelve knots. Thigpen started a stopwatch on the command workstation and called out the time in fifteen-second intervals.

"Fifteen seconds . . . ten, nine, eight . . ." Thigpen's voice was just above a whisper.

"Pilot, ahead standard," Jerry commanded.

"Ahead standard, Pilot, aye, Captain. Maneuvering answers ahead standard."

"Very well, Pilot."

Seconds later the NAE fired up and began rotating the rings of ball bearings inside at high speed. The noise it made was deafening.

Both the Kilo and Song were taken by complete surprise. The Kilo popped a countermeasure of its own, and accelerated to the southwest. The Song stopped snorkeling and headed north at flank speed. Not a single torpedo had been launched.

In *North Dakota*'s control room, a low cheer broke out as soon as it was clear the two hostile submarines had bolted in opposite directions without firing a shot. The plan had worked perfectly.

"Well done, all! Your execution was flawless," gushed Jerry, clearly pleased with his crew.

"I think there are some drawers that need a changin'," remarked Iwahashi cheerfully.

Thigpen shook his head. "Mine would if I was blasted out of the blue with Metallica at 150 dB!"

Jerry was still smiling. "Attention in control, we'll stay in contact with the Kilo as it finishes its evasive maneuvers. After it settles down, we'll get Fargo back in contact and then we'll head back east. Carry on."

A visibly relieved Thigpen moved closer to Jerry. "Congratulations, Skipper, your plan worked."

"Thanks, XO. I was confident it would."

Thigpen shook his head again. "You know, Captain, I think you're a little too smart for your own good."

Jerry laughed, but he heard his XO's message nonetheless. "After Fargo is back in trail, we'll break off and report in. This should make the commodore's day after all the bad news we've sent in."

"I don't know, sir," Thigpen replied. His face was skeptical. "Somehow I don't think our new commodore is going to be all that pleased."

Jerry was puzzled. "What makes you think that, Bernie? Neither side had a clue we were here, and we prevented more deaths. Surely that has to be a win in anybody's book. I think once I explain it to Captain Simonis, he'll agree it was the right thing to do."

# 7

# CONSEQUENCES

31 August 2016
0800 Local Time
USS *North Dakota*
Off Hainan Island, South China Sea

Jerry couldn't have been more wrong. Simonis was absolutely furious with his new commanding officer, and he wasted no time in saying so.

"What were you thinking, Captain? Your orders were to remain unde-tected, observe and report! Not to reveal yourself by interfering!"

Jerry swallowed hard; the severe dressing-down had caught him by surprise. Simonis's reaction was immediate, almost visceral. Jerry had badly misjudged his new boss's risk tolerance.

"Commodore, I am confident neither side knew a U.S. submarine was in the vicinity. My approach made the best use of the tactical situation and the environment; the other two submarines have inferior sensors and were too engrossed in what they were doing to notice our presence." Jerry's at-tempts at explaining his actions only succeeded in making Simonis angrier.

"Notice your presence!? Even if they didn't pick up your boat, they couldn't help but notice the countermeasure!" screamed Simonis. "How can you possibly defend this flagrant violation of your orders?"

Jerry took a deep breath, calming himself. He would have only one chance to get his point across. Responding with an angry tone would simply make matters worse. "Sir, as I stated in my report, an NAE is virtually identical to the Russian MG-24 countermeasure that both Vietnam and China have on their submarines. I took special care to make sure the NAE was placed between the two subs; their first impression would be that the other guy popped the decoy. The mutual evasion conducted by both boats, with no attempt to follow up and acquire me, proves that assumption was correct."

"And if they recorded the acoustic signature, they'll be able to discover the countermeasure's identity after conducting post-processing," Simonis countered.

"Commodore, if they recorded the signal, with a calibrated system, and a competent ACINT analyst processed the data, they *might* be able to make a distinction. But Vietnam doesn't have that capability, and China's ACINT program is still in the early stages of development, their people only have a few years of experience. Their first inclination, if they find a difference, is that the Russians provided a modified version of the MG-24 to the Vietnamese with their more recent Kilo purchase."

Thigpen bumped lightly into his captain as he finished up his argument, and subtly pointed to a scrap of paper on the control panel. Written on the paper was a single sentence. *You may win the battle, but you'll lose the war.* Jerry gave his XO a slight nod, acknowledging the message.

Simonis's nostrils visibly flared on the radio room display. His patience was all but gone. In a voice that was carefully metered and forceful, he said, "I am not interested in theoretical discussions, Commander Mitchell. And I am very well aware of your academic credentials. But this isn't a laboratory; it's the real world, and it's not as forgiving or controllable. You're in a war zone, Captain, and you need to begin acting accordingly. Now, are you going to start following your orders, or do I have to pull you off station and replace you with someone who will?"

It was an empty threat, or at least Jerry thought it was. There was no way Simonis would get permission to yank *North Dakota* off station, not now, not with a war starting. But, the message behind the words was quite clear. Jerry had lost the collar check and needed to toe the line. Simonis's absolute hostility to Jerry's actions had badly shaken his confidence. Jerry thought they had walked right up to the edge, but still turned away in time. Now, he wasn't so sure. Simonis and his own XO believed differently, that he had exceeded the limits of his orders. Regardless, Simonis was the squadron commodore, his superior; there really was only one correct answer to his question.

"No, sir. That won't be necessary. I will conform to my orders as instructed."

"Good," replied Simonis, satisfied. Then in a lighter tone he added, "I've found your reports to be most valuable, Captain. I'd hate to lose the insight you're providing."

"We'll keep you apprised of the situation as it evolves, sir."

"Very well. Squadron Fifteen out."

As the screen went dark, Thigpen whistled softly. "Your reports are most valuable. Man, talk about faint praise!"

"So much for 'I will listen carefully to any recommendations you make,'" whispered Jerry to himself.

"Come again, Skipper?"

"Oh, it's nothing, XO." Jerry looked up at Thigpen and smiled. "Looks like you were right. I got a little too cocky."

"If I remember correctly, sir, I said I thought you were a little too smart for your own good. I never said anything about being cocky."

"I believe the distinction was lost on our commodore. He certainly was . . . annoyed with me," lamented Jerry.

"Annoyed!? Is that what you call it?" cried Thigpen, amazed. "Did you see the muscles in his neck? They were throbbing like that guy in the first *Star Wars* movie . . ."

Jerry raised his hand and cut his XO off. "Bernie, please."

"Yes, sir. Sorry," Thigpen said apologetically.

"Well, now that we've had our orders clarified for us, we'll continue to observe and report—nothing more, nothing less. If you need me, I'll be in my stateroom working on all that paperwork you keep giving me." Jerry gave his XO a quick smile as he spoke, but it was forced, and it showed.

As Jerry headed out of the control room, Lieutenant Iwahashi and Ensign Jacqueline Kane walked over to Thigpen.

"We couldn't help but overhear, XO. The commodore was sure pissed at the skipper," commented Iwahashi quietly.

Thigpen frowned as he tried to find the right words. There was no way to whitewash the ass-chewing his boss had received, but at the same time he had to be supportive. "Yeah, well, that happens from time to time with COs that get creative. And one thing's for certain, our captain is a very creative guy."

The vague allusion to Jerry's past prompted Kane to ask, "Sir, I've heard the rumors about the skipper, just like everyone else. Did he really fight his way out of Iran?"

Thigpen suppressed the desire to groan. How many times had he been asked that question? And why did everybody think he knew the answer? Sighing, he replied, "Jacques, I honestly don't know for sure. The skipper has never said a word to me. But you can take this to the bank; you don't get a Navy Cross and a Purple Heart from the president of the United States for just being a damn good executive officer—however wonderfully you performed your duties. No, our skipper did something very unusual and very important to merit those awards."

He neglected to mention the circular scar he'd seen on Jerry's left shoulder after he had showered. In such close quarters, where even the two seniormost officers shared a common head, it was nearly impossible to hide something so obvious, and yet so personal.

"He looked really depressed," empathized Kane. "Will he be all right?"

"He'll be fine," insisted Thigpen confidently. "A little flame-spraying every now and then is good for the soul, builds character. He's a big boy. He'll get over it." Left unspoken were the words, "I hope."


## Squadron Fifteen Headquarters
## Guam

Commander Walker stood by the information systems technician as he logged out of the VTC system and turned off the video camera and large flat-panel display. The young man then quickly departed, leaving Walker alone with the commodore. The chief staff officer and the rest of the staff had also vacated the conference room within moments of the VTC ending. Walker completely understood why the others wanted to clear datum; Simonis was still fuming. Wonderful. His commodore was going to be very cranky for the rest of the day.

"You don't approve," Simonis spurted without warning.

Walker wasn't sure if it was a statement or a question, but either way it was a loaded comment. One that he had to tread carefully around. "Excuse me, sir," he said.

"My handling of Mitchell. I can read body language fairly well, Commander. I take it most of my staff thought I was being too harsh on our new captain."

"Commodore, it isn't my place to say one way or the other. This is your command . . ."

"Damn it, Rich! Stop dancing and tell me what you think!" roared Simonis.

Trapped, Walker gestured toward a chair. Simonis nodded, and the operations officer tossed his notebook onto the table as he sat down.

"Well?" Simonis demanded impatiently.

"In a nutshell, yes, sir. I think you were a bit hard."

"Why?"

Walker took a deep breath; he had to carefully phrase his words. Simonis wasn't a bad commodore; on the contrary, he was quite successful. He ran a tight squadron at the end of a long logistics train and kept things moving on track, on schedule. No, a better description of Simonis would be that he was tough and demanding. He wanted everything done at the right time, the right way, for the right reason. Deviating from the approved plan was not advisable or tolerated. His rigid, almost legalistic interpretation of rules and regulations always brought him into conflict with those individuals who regarded official edicts as being somewhat elastic, having a little give, depending on the situation.

"Commodore, while he may have not followed the exact letter of the law in regard to his orders, he did follow its spirit. What Mitchell did was well thought out and perfectly executed. And I agree it's likely neither the Vietnamese nor the Chinese will conclude that a U.S. submarine broke up the attack."

"But he revealed himself when he dropped that NAE!" Simonis insisted angrily.

"Sir, you're implicitly assuming that revelation automatically becomes useful, incriminating knowledge. In this case, I think that's a bit of a stretch."

Simonis stood up abruptly and started pacing. Everything about Jerry Mitchell seemed to annoy him, grated his sensibilities. "I still believe he overstepped his bounds," he grumbled.

"Yes, sir, he did. But he had his orders in mind when he dropped an antiquated NAE instead of a more modern countermeasure. If I may, Commodore, it appears to me that you're more upset that Mitchell decided to interfere with the attack in the first place, not necessarily with how he went about doing it," observed Walker.

The commodore paused, considering Walker's last statement. His operations officer was right. He was irritated that Mitchell had become actively involved when their orders had directed them to be passive observers. And while the orders hadn't explicitly restricted them to that role solely, there was a strong inference to that effect. Simonis inwardly cursed the sloppiness with which the whole operation had been thrown together. Rushed, ill-conceived, a typical Washington solution to a dangerous situation. It was a response that allowed the powers that be to say during an election year campaign that something had been done, while at the same time limiting the United States' involvement. A response that made little sense from a military perspective, and put his entire squadron potentially in harm's way.

"Point taken, Rich," Simonis granted. "Well, I hope the additional instructions I provided Commander Mitchell will preclude any further shenanigans."

Walker noted the reduced volume in his boss's voice, but there was still something in the background. "Hope, sir? You sound uncertain. Mitchell didn't strike me as a man who is openly insubordinate or reckless. In fact, everything I've heard says he's an outstanding officer."

Simonis shook his head as he plopped back into his seat. "Same here. I've even spoken to Rear Admiral Guthrie, and he was effusive with his praise. He said Mitchell was intelligent, innovative, calculating, thorough, and responsible. Everything I would have wanted to hear about a new skipper assigned to my command."

Walker was now puzzled. He'd thought the problem had been identified and dealt with, but now he wasn't so sure. Something else was gnawing at his commodore, something other than Mitchell's novel tactics. *North Dakota*'s CO was certainly at the heart of the matter, but he wasn't the only factor. There was something else, thus far unspoken.

"I'm sorry, sir. I guess I'm not following you. What is it that has you concerned?" asked Walker with a hint of frustration.

Simonis grinned warily, surprising Walker. "Washington," said the commodore bluntly.

"Washington? I don't get it."

"This operation is a Washington-inspired idea, and Mitchell is their local man on the scene. I'm not sure they'll take my disciplining of their fairhaired boy very well."

Walker struggled to hide his skepticism. He was well aware of Simonis's aversion to Washington politics, but this was a bit much. How would they even know, unless . . .

"Sir, you're not suggesting Mitchell would contact them directly? Bypassing the entire chain of command?" exclaimed Walker, aghast.

"Of course not!" Simonis snapped back. "But I have to report this up my chain of command, and Admiral Burroughs will pass it on to PACOM, who will pass it on to the CNO, et cetera, et cetera, until it eventually gets to Patterson."

"The deputy national security advisor?"

"Correct!"

"Begging your pardon, sir. But why would Dr. Patterson even bother to get involved over such a minor issue? I know she and Mitchell are friends, but she has a lot more important things on her plate right now," countered Walker.

"Because, Commander, she has a proven track record of getting her mitts into other people's business. She and Mitchell are very close, and she has inserted herself into the picture every time he's gotten into trouble." Simonis sprang back to his feet and started pacing again.

"And of course, this will ensure that I'll receive additional guidance from on high. Politically motivated guidance that will complicate my life to no end. God! I wish Mitchell hadn't been so impulsive!" Simonis moaned.

There it was, at last. The real reason behind Simonis's objection to Mitchell's successful interference ploy was based on the commodore's fear of having to deal with instructions from armchair generals, or admirals in this case, during a significant political crisis. Walker couldn't help but appreciate the irony of the situation; the micromanager par excellence was worried about being micromanaged. Added to this was Simonis's own personality type and sense of responsibility that made him duty-bound to report the altercation with Mitchell, even though the commodore was convinced that doing so would result in the undesired guidance he so feared. No circle could have been more vicious.

A loud sigh told Walker that Simonis was finally calming down. The operations officer waited in silence. Nothing he could say would make the bitter pill easier to swallow. After about half a minute, Simonis turned abruptly to Walker and said, "Oh well, there's no point in delaying the inevitable. Have the CSO contact Admiral Burroughs's chief of staff, I need to speak with the admiral ASAP!"

"Aye, aye, sir," replied Walker as he jumped for the door.

31 August 2016
1300 Local Time
USS *North Dakota*
Off Hainan Island, South China Sea

Jerry plowed through the stack of logs and reports that had been sitting in his inbox for days. In a way, Simonis's stern rebuttal had refocused Jerry's mind on the proper execution of all his duties as a commanding officer, including the less than glamorous day-to-day admin. And while it was a bit tedious at times, in the end it was good to get this stuff off his plate. Jerry took a perverse sense of pleasure when he had to start dumping reports on Thigpen's rack after filling up the XO's inbox.

Pulling the last folder from his stack, Jerry saw the bare wood beneath and mentally cheered. It would be a short-lived victory, of course. Since Mother Nature abhorred an empty inbox as much as a vacuum, more paperwork would naturally be flowing his way, but for now he was done. Well, almost. The last folder contained the mid-term counseling forms for both his junior lieutenants, Lymburn and Gaffney, and while the comments were of interest to Jerry, he was actually more interested to see how well their department head did in putting them together. It was a career management exercise for all three individuals.

Jerry quickly reviewed the forms, made a few minor changes, and initialed them. Finished, he had just closed the folder when there was a knock at his door. Looking up, Jerry saw his supply officer, Lieutenant Steven Westbrook, in the doorway.

"Excuse me, Captain," said Westbrook, "but I have next week's menu ready for your review."

"Come on in, Steven," Jerry responded, waving for his "Chop" to enter the stateroom. "You must have sensed that my inbox was empty."

The supply officer was the only staff corps member on Jerry's crew. Sometimes called the "Suppo" or "Pork Chop," a reference to the Supply Corps oak leaf insignia that looked like a pork chop, on submarines they were usually just called the "Chop." Responsible for everything from spare parts to food stores, the supply officer made sure the boat had everything it needed to go to sea and perform its mission. He or she was also responsible for managing the ship's checkbook and ensuring the ship's store was well stocked with ball caps, uniform patches, candy, and other creature comforts.

When under way, the daily meals were an important morale booster for the crew, and the CO reviewed and approved the weekly menu.

"Let's see what you've got," Jerry said as he reached for the sheet of paper.

Westbrook handed his captain the menu and noted, "We missed you at lunch today, Skipper."

"Yeah, well, I wasn't very hungry," replied Jerry solemnly as he started reading.

"We had your favorite, fried chicken with mashed potatoes and gravy."

Jerry looked up. A tinge of disappointment briefly flashed across his face, then acceptance. "It's probably for the better that I didn't have lunch anyway. The scale in sickbay is a blunt, cold-hearted messenger. It said I'd gained four pounds already."

The supply officer nodded. "I hear you, sir. I added another fifteen minutes on the bike to help keep my expanding borders in check."

"I hate that accursed device," Jerry growled with disgust. "I already have enough trouble sitting there for forty-five minutes, going nowhere." As a runner and hiker, Jerry found the stationary bike to be a thoroughly unpleasant way to burn calories. Staring endlessly at the same pipes and valves was downright demoralizing.

Jerry continued reading, nodding his head on occasion, then stopped when he came to the last entry, the Wednesday dinner for the following week. His right elbow fell to the desk, his hand supporting his head as he groaned, "Aggh! Steven, you are an *evil* little man!"

"Sir?" questioned Westbrook innocently.

With a scornful voice, Jerry read the entry back to the supply officer. "Wednesday night is Italian night with creamy bacon chicken on penne pasta. Caesar salad, and tiramisu for dessert. What are you trying to do, give me a heart attack!?"

"Absolutely not, sir! But the kickbacks I get from the cardiologists is a sweet gig," snickered Westbrook.

Jerry hurriedly scribbled his signature and threw the piece of paper at the Chop. As Westbrook snatched it from the deck, Jerry pointed forcefully toward the door and cried, "Get behind me, Satan!"

"Yes, sir. I'm glad you approve, sir," Westbrook mocked.

"OUT!" thundered Jerry, rolling his eyes.

As Westbrook left the CO's stateroom, he turned forward, toward the door leading to the control room, and gave Thigpen a thumbs-up. Smiling, the XO retreated back inside and quietly closed the door.

In spite of the wicked menu Westbrook had brought him, Jerry found his spirit buoyed by the exchange. He then recalled a piece of wisdom his XO on *Seawolf*, Marcus Shimko, had given him. "When you find yourself alone and depressed, tour the ship, talk to the men; it is a curative balm for a troubled soul."

Jerry realized that he had voluntarily isolated himself from his crew following the dressing-down by Simonis. Sitting in his stateroom alone, stewing silently over his mistakes. True, useful work was accomplished, but in fact he was hiding in his room, pouting like a scolded child. *Wrong answer, mister,* he thought to himself. Heeding the advice from his old XO, Jerry left his stateroom and headed aft.

He started in the engine room, stopping to talk to the watchstanders, seeing how their day was going. The entire crew knew about the commodore's rebuke within moments of it ending. In a ship so confined, there were few secrets. Jerry made sure he visited every watch station, and spent a little time with each individual. He had just finished chatting with the torpedo room watch when the 1MC blared.

"CAPTAIN TO CONTROL."

Jerry quickly scrambled up the ladder to the middle level and ran toward control. A sailor plastered himself against the bulkhead to make way for the captain. As he approached the door, the messenger of the watch opened it for him. Striding up to the command workstation he barked, "CDO, report!"

Sobecki was back on watch and he immediately pointed to the port VLSD. "Skipper, we have three new contacts. All are submarines sortieing from Yalong Bay, two Kilos and one Song. There could be more in the harbor that we just can't see yet. It looks like the Chinese are starting to flush their boats from their bases."

It certainly looked that way to Jerry as he evaluated the track data on the large screen. Two of the tracks were angled in their direction, the third to the southeast.

"CDO," sang out the sonar supervisor. "There is at least one more boat, probably a Kilo by the sound of it, behind Sierra-nine two."

"Very well, Sonar."

"There goes the neighborhood," remarked Covey. "It's going to get a bit crowded around here."

"Mm-hmm," agreed Jerry. He was considering his options when Thigpen walked up behind him.

"Now what's going on?" asked the XO. His voice sounded groggy. He looked like he had been taking a nap.

"We've got company, Bernie, lots of it," Jerry replied, pointing to the port VLSD.

Thigpen focused on the large-screen display. It didn't take him long to assess the situation. "Uh-oh."

"That about sums it up." Jerry turned and spun the trackball on the horizontal display. Thigpen and Sobecki joined him around the console. "Okay, let's head to the south to give these guys some room. Eng, come to course . . . one nine zero, and goose us up to ten knots."

"Change course to one nine zero, increase speed to ten knots, aye, sir."

While Sobecki turned *North Dakota* around, Jerry and Thigpen started discussing how they should deal with the rapid influx of PLAN submarines. Suddenly the WLY-1 acoustic intercept receiver started whooping an alarm.

"CDO! Two new active sonars, bearing zero one five and three five zero. High-frequency systems, probably helicopter dipping sonars."

Jerry turned and saw the two datums on the port large screen. They were still over sixteen thousand yards away, but things were definitely getting out of hand. The situation wasn't immediately dangerous, but it could get that way if he didn't do something soon. Simonis's voice echoed in Jerry's mind, "You're in a war zone, Captain, and you need to begin acting accordingly."

"Mr. Sobecki, sound general quarters."

# 8

# ESCALATION

31 August 2016
1400 Local Time
August 1st Building, Ministry of National Defense Compound
Beijing, People's Republic of China

The Central Military Commission usually received a carefully polished and rehearsed intelligence brief before each meeting in their posh conference room. This time, though, they'd assembled in the operations center, below ground level.

Admiral Wei Zi'en watched the near-chaos of the intelligence staff as they updated the screens and plotted what little data they had on the attackers. He appreciated what they were going through, and knew what they had to work with. The data was pathetically thin and conflicting; he shared their frustration. This was his problem, his fight, his responsibility, and he felt as helpless as the workers updating the master plot. Maybe more so. At least they had useful work to do.

Colonel Xi Ping, one of the deputy commanders of the intelligence service for the General Staff, was the senior officer currently in charge of the operations room. Xi explained, "General Bao regrets not being here to brief you personally. Unfortunately, he is still heavily involved in counter-intelligence issues. I have just spoken with him, he sends his apologies and asks your indulgence in allowing me to brief you."

Wei could hardly complain. Normally, the brief was presented by a major or an ambitious captain. But the general's absence had been noted by several members of the commission.

The operations room walls were crowded with maps and flat-screen displays, as well as the obligatory portraits. The staff paid little attention to the visitors crowded in the back, although they must have noticed that some of them matched the pictures on the wall.

"The status boards there, and there," Ping said, pointing to the opposite wall, "display merchant traffic and the movements of all known foreign naval vessels, including submarines. The white symbols on each board show where our merchant ships, all tankers, have been attacked."

Admiral Wei barely listened to the brief. He'd already received the bad news over the course of the day, and in more detail than it was being presented here. He knew the real reason the intelligence staff had brought them to the operations center. It was to show the Central Military Commission that the intelligence section, so surprised by the earlier Vietnamese mining of *Liaoning*, was now making every effort to avoid further embarrassments. And if there was so much bad news, it wasn't their fault.

After an unsatisfying report, the council's twelve members, including the president and the entire General Staff, elected to stay below ground level, and trooped across the hall. There was no point in going back up five floors just to have a meeting.

The utilitarian conference room was less opulent than their normal meeting place. It was large enough, and obviously well used. Posters on the walls showed comparisons of Chinese and foreign military hardware. The classroom-like setting seemed to encourage the colonel to use a more casual manner than he might have otherwise.

"Please, ask your questions," Xi prompted.

General Shi was head of the political department. He said, "During the brief, you continually referred to the 'unknown attackers.' Why can't you tell us who is sinking our tankers?" Shi's frustration was clear.

The colonel answered, "As long as they only attack unescorted merchant ships, we have no way of detecting them, making identification impossible. Passive sonar could pick up a submarine's acoustic signal, enabling us to identify the class, and thus the nationality of the attacker. But they have avoided our warships so far. It's a clever strategy."

"So you approve." Shi's tone was almost threatening.

"Only of their tactics," Xi quickly responded. "They attack anony-mously with no risk to themselves. We don't know where to strike back."

"There is one obvious choice," Shi replied.

"If we attack Vietnam now, without proof, we become the villain," Vice Chairman Li Ju countered.

"They're behind it," Shi affirmed.

"If it is the Vietnamese," Xi was careful to say, "they cannot be acting alone. They only have three Project 636 subs in service. It's physically im-possible for only three submarines to cause this much destruction over such a wide area."

"More than one nation? Has Vietnam shared its information with oth-ers? Is it the Americans?" Wei could hear genuine fear in Shi's voice. He wasn't as concerned as Shi, but American naval superiority was still a fact of life for China. If they threw their full weight against his PLAN, the out-come might be grim. Just their submarine forces alone . . .

"How can they know which ships to attack?" Vice Chairman Li asked.

Xi answered patiently. As a PLA general, Li Ju was unfamiliar with the maritime environment. "There are automated communication systems in place that allow the real-time tracking of virtually all merchant vessels. The information is widely available. Unlike during World War Two, when sub-marines had to search for their targets, now they can steer straight to them."

Xi sighed. "In a way, we're lucky our enemies are concentrating on tankers. It takes them some time to move from one to the next. If they were to simply attack all Chinese merchant ships, the losses in the last thirty-six hours would have been far greater."

"This is quite bad enough," replied Admiral Wei. "And of course we can't easily suspend our participation in the system while our ships are at sea." His voice was full of irony. "With only Chinese tankers being targeted, the rest of the world's merchant fleets will make doubly sure they are clearly identified."

"What about introducing false data, altering their identification?" Shi asked.

Xi shook his head. "Hostile naval intelligence would be quick to pounce on a ship that suddenly appeared in the same place a tanker disappeared. General Bao's people in the cyber warfare section are investigating ways to switch two ships' identities, but it's not trivial."

"Then should we be escorting our tankers?" Wen Feng, the minister of defense, asked Admiral Wei. He was careful to include General Su, the chief of the General Staff and Wei's superior, in his question, but Su deferred to the admiral. Wei was the expert.

The admiral sighed. "It's the obvious counter to a submarine campaign, but it would mean deploying escorts to many commercial ports, then waiting for enough merchants, or in this case tankers, to arrive before sailing. Once they have been convoyed across the danger area, the escort group must either return to the first port or exchange roles with another group that takes its place."

Looking around the room, Wei saw everyone nodding understanding, including General Su. Wei continued, "It's resource-intensive, requiring large numbers of escort vessels—numbers we currently lack. It would also reduce oil imports by as much as twenty-five percent because of the delays inherent in the convoy system. And that's assuming no more ships are lost."

Wei paused for a moment, then added, "Of course, if we were to begin convoying, those escorts would have to be taken away from our upcoming 'exercise.'" Even in this supposedly secure area, Wei was circumspect. "We would probably have to cancel it altogether."

The council's expressions at that suggestion ranged from simple frowns, to shock, to near anger.

General Shi, listening to Wei's explanation, turned back to Xi. "Colonel, I apologize. Our opponents are more than clever. They know our plans and present us with an unpleasant choice."

"We have taken some steps," Wei continued. "Patrol aircraft are flying along the routes of the heaviest shipping. It's impossible to be everywhere at once, but they can react more quickly to news of a sinking than surface ships, and hopefully catch a submarine after an attack. Even if they can't sink it, they can lay sonobuoys and possibly record its acoustic signature."

"So we can't prevent them from robbing another bank, but we may, with luck, be able to get the criminals' license number as they speed away." General Ye of the logistics department didn't sound pleased.

"Confirming their identity is exactly what we need, General." President Chen Dao had been silent since the start of Xi's briefing in the operations room. Everyone turned to listen. "Economists on my staff say that on average, it takes a large tanker a day to meet China's oil import needs. Thus, we've lost over twelve days' supply in the past thirty-six hours," he swept everyone in the room with his gaze, "without a hint of how to stop it. This will mean drawing even more heavily on our strategic reserves."

Chen stood and moved toward the front of the room. Xi quickly stepped aside and sat down in an out-of-the-way corner. "Our enemies have correctly identified and struck at our greatest weakness. This does not change our needs. It highlights them. The 'exercise' will proceed with all possible speed. Its success will remove our vulnerability. It will also give our enemies something else to think about.

"China is strong enough to endure this attack, even if it grows worse. I will tell our economic planners to prepare for additional losses, so we can follow our chosen path without distraction.

"Colonel Xi, thank you for your hard work. Redouble your efforts to identify our antagonists. Also, inform General Bao that I wish to see him immediately. I have several questions for him.

"General Su, at this time we may not be able to demonstrate that Vietnam is behind this, but we must have a plan in place when their culpability can be proved. Develop one that inflicts punishing damage on their economy and armed forces, particularly their submarine base. However, do not use any of the units needed for the 'exercise.'" Su nodded, but looked worried.

"Admiral Wei, determine if there is any way to speed up the timetable for the exercise. The sooner we consolidate our position, the better. Have a report ready by the end of the day."

After Chen left, the commission members headed back aboveground. Wei at least felt hopeful. They had a plan, and he had something useful to do.

31 August 2016
USS *North Dakota*
Off Hainan Island, South China Sea

Jerry sat in the wardroom, fidgeting, fighting the urge to go to the control room. The troops had seen his disagreement with Thigpen, and had heard about his dressing-down by Commodore Simonis. Although he'd done his best to stay positive, he was still frustrated. The crew picked up that vibe and their tension rose.

Bernie Thigpen poked his head in. Seeing that the wardroom was empty except for the captain, he came through the door, and after pouring a cup of coffee, sat down near Jerry. He wasn't near enough to crowd his skipper, but close enough to show something was on his mind.

"What's the latest scuttlebutt, XO?"

"A lot of the crew is wondering what we're up to out here. One of the snipes described it as, 'All the risks of combat but none of the laughs.' A lot of them also think the Vietnamese are nuts starting a war with the Chinese."

"What do you think, XO?"

Thigpen sighed. "I'm worried about what happens when you decide to stretch our orders again."

He paused, waiting for a reaction, but Jerry didn't respond immediately. Thigpen continued, "Nobody on this boat has ever done this before. That makes everyone nervous, me included, and the last thing the crew needs on top of the external situation is a disconnect between the CO and the XO."

"Do you think I was wrong?" Jerry kept his tone even and nonconfrontational. He wanted a discussion, not an argument.

"It isn't about being right or wrong. You're the skipper, and it's your call, but I think you violated the spirit, if not the letter of our orders. I understand why you did it, and I'm glad it worked. I like it when nobody dies, especially us. But the commodore was seriously pissed, which confirms my suspicion that the brass wants us to keep well clear."

After a few moments, Jerry nodded. "You're right, of course. I thought we could walk right up to the line without crossing it. In hindsight, though, I did cross the line, and you were right to point it out. But I can't promise that something else like it won't happen in the future."

Thigpen made a face. "Where does that leave me, Skipper? It's my job to warn you at times like that, but we can't be seen disagreeing by the crew, especially now."

"Also right," Jerry answered. "Do you believe me when I say I'm listening when you raise those objections? That I'll always act in the best interests of the mission and the boat?"

"Of course," Thigpen answered almost automatically. Then he added firmly, "No doubts, Skipper."

Jerry smiled. "Good. Doubts are my job. Since my orders have been 'clarified' by the commodore, I'll do my best to follow them precisely. But you're also right that this is a unique situation. If I have to leave our guidance behind, I'll listen hard to your counsel, but it's always going to be my decision."

"And I'll do my best to implement it," Thigpen confirmed.

"If you want to take notes, or keep a separate log, I understand. If the fertilizer starts flying because of something I did, I'll do my best to keep it away from you."

"Thanks, Skipper, but that's negative thinking, and the last thing I need is more paperwork. We'll get it done somehow."

The XO got up and left, his coffee untouched. Jerry thought about what Thigpen had said. Nothing had changed, really, but it was good that each had spoken his mind. And Bernie had started the conversation. Jerry felt he'd been assigned a very good XO.


Jerry made it a point now to always be in control during the UUV data downloads. The vehicles were on a four-hour collect-and-report cycle, sending their accumulated data to a satellite. He wanted to look at the data immediately, and was willing to risk coming shallow at predictable four-hour intervals to get that information the instant it was available. Of course, *North Dakota* did it at a different spot each time, and always made sure nothing was nearby.

Putting a communications mast up also allowed them to get the latest intelligence update from the squadron and to take a sniff of the local airwaves. That gave Jerry three good reasons to be in control.

Thigpen was working with Lieutenant Covey in the same back corner of the control room as before when he reported, "Skipper, you will want to see this." The XO sounded worried.

As Jerry walked over, he tried to sound positive. "At least Fargo's earning its keep."

Thigpen didn't smile. He just pointed to the display. "It's another submarine."

The screen showed a familiar mix of lines—the straight lines of merchants' tracks, clustered to the north, as they sailed from Point A to Point B; the irregular shape drawn by Fargo's path; and a highlighted line that entered from the southwest corner of the screen. It zigged once to the west, and some time later turned north again.

"This track data was collected ninety minutes ago. I'm starting the replay from that point. This is at ten to one." The XO pressed a key and then stood aside.

Jerry watched the highlighted line advance. It seemed fast, even with the replay in fast-forward. He paused the display and checked the readouts. "He's transiting at ten knots. This is not a diesel boat."

"We both concur," Thigpen replied. "It's not a Chinese nuke, either. The quick ACINT analysis says it's an Improved Akula I, so it has to be *Chakra,* the attack sub India leased from the Russians."

"The Indians?" Jerry was so shocked all he could do was stare at the display, disbelieving.

"It's the only thing that fits. I have sonar confirming the signature, but it can't be the Russians. I checked the latest ONI data and all the Russian PACFLT Akulas are either in port or in the local operating areas. Which leaves only the Indian Akula. And watch what happens." He pressed the key to resume the playback.

The submarine made another small course change and closed on one merchant's track. Jerry didn't need the computer's help to see it was an intercept course, and a perfect setup for a torpedo attack. As the range closed, Jerry slowed the display rate down to three to one. The boat continued to close on the unsuspecting vessel, and at four thousand yards, almost point-blank range for a modern torpedo, the sub fired four weapons. They hit a few minutes later, with the explosions appearing on the display as a series of bright bearing strobes. The merchant's track stopped moving and ended at the point of intercept.

The attacking sub turned away from its target and headed west. It was still in the UUV's patrol zone when the playback ended ten minutes later.

Jerry had just watched what could have been a simulation in the attack trainer, or a video game. He was chilled by the destruction the attack had caused, but also felt detached. He had to make a conscious effort to remind himself that this was real.

"Four weapons, four hits. It must be—" He corrected himself. "—must have been a big one. Do we know who it was?" he asked.

"Thanks to the intelligence update, yes. It was MV *Hai Tun Zuo,* 43,718 gross registered tons. She's a tanker last known headed for Tianjin, China, with over 75,000 tons of refined petroleum products. Chinese-flagged, too. You were right, Skipper, for a target that big they would have used four torpedoes. She sent out an incomplete distress call less than an hour ago, and her emergency-position-indicating radio beacon has been activated. There was no information on survivors, or even her crew size."

Jerry tried to estimate their chances of survival. A big ship like that could take a lot of damage. Depending on where the weapon hit, the crew could be hundreds of feet away from the impact point. But the crew quarters were right above the screw, if the weapons were Russian wake-homing torpedoes . . .

That wasn't his problem. "Did the update from squadron include anything about this?"

The XO answered, "No, which is why we're doing the analysis. They got Fargo's sensor log the same time we did—" Thigpen glanced at the time. "Fifteen minutes ago."

Jerry almost laughed. "So do you think they're taking this any better than we are?"

"This isn't the only thing they've got on their plate, Skipper. If this is the local situation, here's the big picture." He gestured toward the starboard VLSD. Jerry saw the image zoom out from the local area to include the entire South China Sea. The shipping lanes were marked by dozens, perhaps over a hundred symbols for merchant ships moving along the coast, and through the different straits. A heavy band of traffic moved straight across the middle, cutting from southwest near the Vietnamese coast and heading northeast, passing south of Taiwan.

Dotting the shipping lanes were red circles, each with a time. Jerry could see four, including one that corresponded with the loss of *Hai Tun Zuo*. He checked the times.

"All in the past eight hours?" Jerry asked incredulously. The circles were scattered all over the South China Sea and just south of Taiwan. He shook his head sadly; the attacks had already claimed twelve ships. Resigned, he said, "It's become a war. Twelve ships lost while we sat here and watched." Thigpen heard his CO's frustration.

Jerry started looking at the information on the ships that had been sunk. Maybe there was a pattern he could squeeze some data out of.

He didn't have to work too hard. "Look at this. They're all tankers, and all bound for Chinese ports."

"Which means they're loaded," Thigpen continued.

"At least we know their intentions," Jerry remarked. "Shutting off Chinese oil imports. This is going to get very bad."

31 August 2016
0415 Local Time
Georgetown, Washington, D.C.

Ray Kirkpatrick had called Joanna at her home. There was no need to explain, nor could he give her details over a cell phone. And it didn't really matter that it had been 3:30 A.M., after a very long day.

By the time Joanna had dressed and given her happily sleeping husband a good-bye kiss, the car had arrived. The streets were empty, of course. She used the ten-minute ride to check her smartphone and clear away the last of the cobwebs.

She was in the situation room ten minutes after that. Kirkpatrick didn't even bother greeting her. "We went to DEFCON III in the Pacific an hour ago. All exercises have been canceled. Detached personnel recalled to their units, the whole banana. The president gave the order and went back to bed. I doubt he'll get much sleep, though. There have been three more sinkings since you left."

"Have there been any attacks on U.S.-flagged ships?" she asked.

"No, only Chinese-flagged and -owned tankers bound for Chinese ports. It's probably the only thing that will keep oil prices from tripling tomorrow morning. They'll still go up somewhat, of course, but that's somebody else's problem.

"And frankly, I'm glad we're at DEFCON III," Kirkpatrick remarked almost casually. "It means we're better able to react, and the rest of the world knows it, too. But there's more bad news: the Indians have joined the party."

Joanna was pouring coffee and almost dropped the pot. She did spill some, and had to force herself to carefully set it down before answering. "I don't suppose the Indian government's issued any statement about the South China Sea lately."

"Not a one," Kirkpatrick said calmly. "We should be so lucky. The latest sensor dump from *North Dakota*'s UUV shows *Chakra* sinking a Chinese tanker. You can pull it up and watch it later, if you have the time. You probably won't. Squadron Fifteen says they are ninety-five percent certain of their analysis. Commander Mitchell's crew came up with the same conclusion. That isn't why I woke you up, though."

Patterson had just started processing the implications of Indian involvement in the crisis. "What could be worse than that?"

Kirkpatrick pointed at the screen displaying the South and East China

Seas. It was overlaid with the four subs' patrol zones. "Commander Dobson's boat, *Oklahoma City*, is up in the East China Sea, and he sent in a disturbing contact report that Squadron Fifteen just forwarded. He picked up a very faint submerged contact and spent almost an hour trying to close and get a better look. It moved off before he could identify it, but he is convinced that it was quieter than any Chinese boat or a Vietnamese Kilo."

"He lost contact?" Patterson was surprised. *Los Angeles* subs had very capable sonar suites, and could maneuver quietly at speeds that would exhaust a diesel's batteries in a few hours.

"Oh, he's still looking," Kirkpatrick explained. "In fact, according to Commodore Simonis, he's pissed. He's not used to losing. More to the point, this was the first indication . . ."

A naval officer, almost breathless, came up to the pair, stopping short, but then offering Kirkpatrick a sheet of paper. "Another sinking," the officer explained, "the tanker *Da Ming Hu*, 84,855 GRT, Chinese flagged, near Wenzhou, north of Taiwan."

"That's in Dobson's patrol area," Patterson remarked.

"The first one that far north, as well. Look," he said, pointing to the Chinese fleet boundaries, "and the first one in the East Sea Fleet area."

"So the Vietnamese . . . and the Indians have the southwest, and somebody else the northeast?" Patterson asked.

"Does Mongolia have submarines?"

"Don't joke about it, Ray," scolded Joanna.

"India seems about as likely," Kirkpatrick countered. "And now somebody else? We don't even know why Vietnam is fighting. The only thing India and Vietnam have in common is that they both see China as a threat. So who else doesn't like China?"

"That's a long list," Joanna replied.

"Good point." Already frowning, Kirkpatrick asked, "How do we know it's only one more player?"

She didn't bother giving the obvious answer. Patterson felt frustrated by being so clueless, and fearful for the future. If you don't know where you are, it's hard to know where you'll end up.

She thought about the latest tanker to be sunk. The printout said 84,855 gross registered tons, deadweight tonnage 160,000 tons. Deadweight tonnage was a measure of a merchant ship's carrying capacity.

Years of working on environmental issues kicked in. At a little more than seven barrels per ton, that meant something over a million barrels of crude oil was spreading though the East China Sea. The prevailing winds would carry the slick into the Pacific Ocean . . .

"Now you know why I called you in," Kirkpatrick observed. "I'm forming a crisis team. You're in charge, of course. I've already notified State, DoD, and CIA to send reps, and not low-level ones either. Also, you're getting someone from the council of economic advisers. We have to know just how much pain China's feeling. If you think of anybody else, don't even bother asking me first, just grab them and fill me in when you can."

She'd done this before, Joanna reminded herself. But she still felt chills. War was breaking out, and they didn't even know who was fighting, or why. And she had to find answers.

"My charter is to give the president options to guide U.S. policy. I believe the best U.S. policy right now is to find out what the hell is going on." Kirkpatrick sighed and took a long drag on his own coffee cup.

"You haven't slept yet, have you?" she asked.

"No, and I have to brief the president at 0700 hours this morning. That gives you," he glanced at his watch, "less than three hours to come up with intelligent suggestions for me to offer the president. Don't be subtle. The rest of the world is going to start reacting to the sinkings very soon. Wake people up, reach out to anyone in the government you think can help. I'll be back here at 0630."

"Are you going to get some sleep, I hope?"

"No, I've got a few bodies of my own to exhume. If they have anything useful, you'll be the second one to know."

# 9

## TIDINGS

31 August 2016
0700 Eastern Daylight Time
CNN Headline News

The two anchors on the CNN morning broadcast did their best to look grim. Happy faces were not appropriate to the news. "War has broken out off the coast of China, although so far a one-sided war, and a secret one."

The image on the screen was frightening, but fascinating. "This was the Chinese-owned and -flagged tanker *Hai Tun Zuo*, en route from the Persian Gulf to Shanghai, loaded with over half a million barrels of crude oil." The massive vessel, broken in two, listed drunkenly on the ocean's surface. The two parts of the ship were enveloped by flames, fed by a dark black slick that spread out hundreds of meters. The bow and stern were elevated as the torn midsections took on water, exposing the red lower hull. The white upperworks on both parts were scorched and stained. Rescue ships stood off upwind from the oily black smoke that half-hid the shattered vessel.

"At a little before dawn local time, *Hai Tun Zuo* suffered a disastrous explosion, leaving her on fire and sinking. Normally, a disaster like this would have to be investigated and its cause determined, but this was not an isolated incident."

A map replaced the burning tanker, with a flickering point of fire marking the ship's location to the west of Hainan Island. The map then began to fill with other points of flame.

"In the past forty hours, over a dozen merchant ships, all Chinese tankers loaded with oil, have suffered deadly explosions, dotting the ocean with desperate calls for help. Naval experts all agree that someone has begun torpedoing Chinese tankers."

The image shifted to show a white-painted rescue vessel with a red band angled across the bow and Chinese characters along the side. "China's Maritime Safety Agency, responsible for search and rescue at sea, has mobilized its entire force to respond to the distressed vessels, any one of which is a major disaster. The Border Guard, a separate Chinese paramilitary force, is also assisting, as well as hurrying to the defense of other Chinese vessels.

"Other merchants have approached the distressed vessels and offered what aid they could, but the wrecked ships are often on fire, and many of the survivors require more medical care than the civilian ships can provide. In all the attacks so far, at least seventy merchant sailors are known to be dead or missing, with twice that many injured."

Images of stretchers being carried away from a helicopter were replaced by a seated Chinese official, flanked by military officers. Chinese characters scrolled across the bottom of the screen. "Officials in Beijing have condemned the sinkings as 'terrorism,' but have refused to identify their attackers, or explain this refusal. The Chinese ambassador at the UN also declined to comment, and would not speculate on possible Chinese actions. The only conceivable reason for not naming the perpetrators of the sinkings is because the Chinese do not know who they are.

"Insurance rates are already rising, although so far only for ships headed for the new war zone. And within the last hour, Lloyd's has announced it will no longer issue insurance for Chinese-owned or -flagged ships.

"The belligerents' goal is obvious: to starve the world's largest nation and fastest-growing economy of oil. Rumors of other measures, including cyber attacks against Chinese interests and sabotage of Chinese refineries, are circulating, but have not been confirmed."

The Lloyd's of London logo was replaced by shots of Chinese warships steaming in formation. "Although called 'terrorism' by the Chinese, no known terrorist group has the resources to operate even a single submarine, and naval experts agree that an attack on this scale would require several vessels. The U.S. Navy refused to speculate on the identity of the mystery subs, and categorically denied making any attacks. They would neither confirm nor deny the presence of U.S. submarines in the South China Sea. The White House is preparing a statement for release later in the day."

The picture shifted back to the stricken tanker. "In the case of *Hai Tun*

*Zuo,* the crew was able to send a distress call, and because her emergency beacon was activated, rescuers were able to arrive relatively quickly." The camera panned over to a helicopter hovering while a sling was lowered to a bright orange lifeboat.

"Most of the twenty-three-man crew were rescued, but three are known dead and another five are still missing. Pushed by the prevailing winds and ocean currents, the slick is expected to arrive at the Leizhou Peninsula in a day or two.

"As of this morning, the Chinese are losing a war with a phantom submarine fleet. It remains to be seen if they can stop or even identify their enemy. Please stay tuned for further developments in this fast-moving crisis. A list of all the vessels attacked is available at our Web site."

31 August 2016
0900 Local Time
By Water
Halifax, Nova Scotia

Mac had split off everything about the sinkings onto a new daughter blog. He'd also shelved all his projects in a desperate effort to keep up with the insane amount of traffic. It wasn't the news of the sinkings themselves. There'd been eleven in the past twenty-four hours, and after the first three, he'd set up an online database to display what was reliably known: location, identity, casualties, and so forth.

He'd been very careful to post only official information, and that only after he'd thoroughly reviewed it. The Chinese government wasn't obligated to tell the truth, after all.

War had not been declared, but truth had already become a casualty. His notoriety in the naval community was now working against him, as would-be contributors inundated him with rumors. Most were disappointed when they found out that their data was old, inaccurate, or just plain wrong, but they accepted it. Others were convinced of their information's accuracy, gleaned from some "inside source" or "inspired deduction." Those individuals would not take no for an answer, and accused him of being narrow-minded or biased, except for one person who accused him of being in the pay of the Chinese! Mac loved a good exchange of information via e-mails. These were nothing like a good exchange.

But he wouldn't stop reading and answering his mail. There'd been a few gems. Reports of a fire at a Chinese shipyard had been confirmed indirectly by the local media. His correspondent at Lloyd's had allowed him to break the news about suspending insurance on Chinese tankers. Christine had appreciated his phone call on that one, although she'd acquired the same information only moments after he did.

Now he was calling her again. She'd given him her cell number, because she was so rarely in her office. "Mac!" She sounded rushed, but also pleased. "What news by the water?" she joked.

"It's about *Vinaship Sea*."

"That's last week, Mac." She sounded a little disappointed. "Have you seen the news today?"

"I won't dignify that with an answer," he huffed, but both knew he was joking. "There is a connection, Christine."

"What? I may not be an expert, but *Vinaship Sea* was Vietnamese, and it wasn't a tanker."

"Bear with me for a moment." Mac spoke quickly. "I've had several correspondents in Asia tell me about information that's being leaked on Chinese blogs and Web sites, probably by a government office or the intelligence service. It claims to be a list of *Vinaship Sea's* actual cargo—a surface-to-air missile battery, anti-aircraft guns, and ammunition, all destined for the Spratly Island chain."

"That would explain the large explosion!" she remarked, almost happily.

"That part fits, but more important than that is her destination," Mac explained. "I've plotted her course based on the new information, and it matches the location where she was sunk perfectly. The Vietnamese lied about her destination, and even filed false position reports. So if she was torpedoed, it had to be by someone who knew her true position."

"And the Chinese knew," she concluded. "Doesn't this mean the Chinese are saying they sank the ship?"

"Indirectly, yes. The Spratly Islands are contested by Vietnam and China, among others. If Vietnam was secretly moving arms to the area, China may have decided to stop them just as secretly. And now they want other people to know."

"So the tanker sinkings are payback by Vietnam?" She sounded skeptical. "That's a lot of revenge for losing one ship."

"And it's also a lot more ships than the Vietnamese Navy could possibly sink. They only have three diesel-electric submarines. We did the math. You need a lot more than three."

"So probably the Vietnamese and almost certainly some other navy are trying to damage China's economy by sinking tankers." She paused, then said, "That's not a real strong headline."

"It's more than you knew five minutes ago," he countered. "How about, 'A Secret International Conspiracy, Aligned Against China'?"

"That sounds much better. I'll have to rush, but we can probably get this into the next hourly feed. Please send me what you've got. And I'll make sure your name gets mentioned."

He pressed a key. "You have it."

31 August 2016
1155 Local Time
Pentagon City Metro Station
Arlington, Virginia

Senator Lowell Hardy stepped off the Yellow Line Metro train at the Pentagon City station and reluctantly took the escalator up to the street level. The thick heat of Washington in August poured down the angled steps, and Hardy took strength in the restaurant being close—just across the street and four blocks down.

He hadn't picked Siné Irish Pub, although it was a good place to meet. Good faux-Irish food and decent Irish beer. Not too noisy to have a conversation, or too quiet to stand out.

He suppressed the last thought, but it was a mysterious message, after all. A fellow submariner and a friend of Jerry Mitchell's wanted to meet. The matter was extremely urgent, and he had suggested noon at Siné. He hadn't left a name, or number where he could be reached. Hardy wondered if he'd pick up the tab.

The message hadn't mentioned red carnations, so Hardy had simply walked in, expecting to be met. Nobody came up to greet him, but there was a short line waiting to be seated, and he joined it. When it was his turn, he asked, "Reservation for Hardy, twelve o'clock?"

"Yes, sir," the hostess answered brightly. "Your other party has already been seated."

Hardy followed her to a booth, where a single man waited. In his late forties, maybe early fifties, Hardy judged, the stranger was fit, blond, with a broad round face that screamed "Russian!" He was wearing jeans and a polo shirt, but on him the clothes looked like a disguise. Hardy started to feel uneasy, but it was too late to back out now.

The hostess left, and the stranger offered his hand. Hardy took it automatically while the other man introduced himself, "Senator Lowell Hardy, I am Aleksey Igorevich Petrov," in slightly accented English. "Thank you for coming."

They both sat down, Hardy's mind whirling. He'd been in Washington long enough to know that not all spy stories were fiction, but a meeting, out of the blue, with a Russian? The message said, "a former submariner." And the name "Petrov" jarred old memories. And he was a friend of Jerry Mitchell.

Petrov had sat silently for the moment it took for Hardy to recognize the name. The senator finally said, "The captain of *Severodvinsk?*"

The Russian nodded solemnly. "Former captain, yes. On her first and only voyage. You and I have never met, but Jerry has spoken of you many times. He and I keep in touch by e-mail, and he was very proud when you were elected a senator. And now Jerry has his own command."

"Yes, I was at the change of command ceremony when he took over."

"He will make a good captain." Petrov smiled. "Not that I am qualified to make such a judgment."

"Jerry said the Russian Navy let you retire without punishment," Hardy offered.

"Losing my command and eighteen of my crew was punishment enough," Petrov replied softly. "I and the rest of the survivors will always be grateful to Captain Rudel, Jerry, and the rest of *Seawolf*'s crew." Although he smiled, the lines around his eyes showed his melancholy.

Petrov shook off the mood and straightened a little. "I have stayed close to the navy and submarines since I retired. I am now a naval constructor at the Admiralteiskie Verfi shipyard in St. Petersburg. My government knows about my friends in the U.S. Navy, and when they offered me this task, I accepted gladly. I have a message. It is not an official communication, but this meeting has been approved by the highest levels of my government."

Hardy had already decided to take Petrov at his word. Jerry had said good things about the guy. He'd trust Jerry's judgment, but Hardy chose his

words carefully. "Is there something that your Foreign Ministry doesn't want to say to the State Department?"

Petrov didn't have a chance to answer. The hostess appeared, and Hardy distractedly ordered a burger and iced tea.

As soon as she left, Petrov explained, "This is not a matter for either the Foreign Ministry or the State Department. It is best if they do not learn of it. In fact, it involves information we obtained from within the Japanese Maritime Self-Defense Force."

Hardy couldn't hide his expression, and Petrov paused for a moment, almost apologetically. "You can understand that we would not normally share this type of information with you, but in this urgent matter our interests coincide."

What could be so important, Hardy wondered. Then he remembered the morning's headlines. "Does this concern . . ." he paused, "the waters around China?"

Petrov leaned forward slightly and spoke softly but clearly. "Japan, South Korea, India, and Vietnam have entered into a secret military alliance to cripple China's economy. They are using their submarines to sink Chinese merchant ships, and the Chinese Navy if they get in the way."

Hardy had been about to sip his iced tea. Thankfully, Petrov's bombshell had reached him before that happened. He quickly set the glass down as the possibilities swirled around him. "Nice. As long as they conceal themselves, the Chinese won't know who to strike back at."

"Correct," Petrov answered. "And if they do, Japan and South Korea are U.S. allies, and your country must come to their defense. They can't stay hidden forever, but if they can do it for long enough, they can cause tremendous damage."

"Did this source mention why Vietnam and the others are doing this?"

The Russian shook his head. "I asked the same question. The information only refers to an 'imminent Chinese threat.' They may believe that if they don't fight China now, they will have to later, when China is even stronger and they have no other option." He smiled. "They also don't have a very high opinion of America's willingness to confront China."

Hardy didn't react to the last part. "When they do find out, China's going to get really mad," Hardy remarked, then caught himself. He wasn't discussing the day's headlines with a friend at lunch. This man was the unofficial and secret envoy of a foreign power. "I'm assuming you are confident of the information's reliability."

Petrov nodded silently.

"You know that immediately following this meeting, I'm going to give this information to my government's intelligence service."

"We'd rather it was passed directly to your decision-makers. That's what your CIA would, or should do with it anyway. I believe your wife, Dr. Patterson, works closely with the national security adviser. We met, once, after the inquest was over. Please give her my regards."

"I'll consider your suggestion, but I make no promises," Hardy answered. "I also can't promise where the information will go once I've passed it on."

"To your president, I hope," Petrov replied, "and I ask for no conditions. But we believe the information is true. It is also in our best interest to convey this to your leadership. We have a long border with China. 'If your neighbor's house is on fire, you must look to your own property.'"

"Is that a Russian proverb?" Hardy asked.

"Chinese, actually."

Hardy laughed, but agreed with the sentiment. Russia couldn't be seen openly helping the United States, hence the covert nature of the communication.

"Is there anything you can offer that corroborates this information?"

Petrov looked puzzled for a moment, but then said, "If you mean some visible proof, watch the reactions of the Japanese, Vietnamese, and South Koreans in the next few days. They will react quickly and effectively, because they knew about this ahead of time, and similarly because they are sharing information.

"Also, I must apologize. I was chosen because of my personal contacts within the American Navy. My first choice was Captain Rudel, but he's retired now. Evidently, he's a history teacher in Ohio."

Hardy nodded and laughed. "Tom wanted something a little less stressful. Somehow, I don't know if a room full of high school kids qualifies. He also runs their NJROTC program at the school."

"I am disappointed that I did not have the opportunity see him. If you are in contact with him, please give him my greatest respects and good wishes, likewise to Commander Mitchell. I know *North Dakota* is based in Hawaii. Since he was not available, Dr. Patterson or you were our next choice. I gather your wife has been very busy lately. I could not reach her."

Hardy didn't explain what Joanna was involved with. "I'm not offended, Captain. I'm glad to be on the same list with them."

"Good. One other thing." He held up a hardcover book. "With the Pacific so much in the news lately, I found this at Heathrow Airport while I was making the connection to come here." He slid the volume across to Hardy. The cover appeared dark blue from a distance, but close up he could see it was actually a map of Asia and the Pacific. The title, in gold letters, was *Navies for Asia,* by Sajin Komamura.

Petrov said, "I read it on the flight, and it's very informative."


31 August 2016
1415 Local Time
The White House
Washington, D.C.

They waited in Kirkpatrick's office.

"You had lunch at Siné and didn't invite me?" Joanna looked angry and hurt. Hardy wasn't sure whether she was serious or not. Better to play it straight.

"I couldn't invite you. Besides, weren't you busy here?" Hardy protested.

"Yes, and I had my usual turkey sandwich. I'm getting too many of my meals from the White House food service." She sounded unhappy. "You could have called and asked, and I could have turned you down."

"I had no idea what the meeting was about—none at all. I certainly didn't imagine Alex Petrov was going to be there."

"It would have been wonderful to see him again."

"The idea was to keep a low profile. You would have made a fuss and hugged him, just like with Jerry."

"You heard about that?" She sounded surprised. "At the squadron briefing? On Guam?"

"It's a small community. Word gets around," he said casually.

She shrugged. "I admit it. I'm a hugger."

"And it's one of your many virtues."

Ray Kirkpatrick ducked his head in the door. "The president's ready for you."

It was only a short distance, but they still hurried. Hardy tried to keep his focus. This wasn't his first trip to the Oval Office, but it wasn't what he'd planned for the afternoon. The air seemed a little thin—at least that was one explanation for his light-headedness.

The president's office was crowded. In addition to Myles and Milt Alvarez, the secretary of state, Andy Lloyd, and the director of national intelligence, Greg Alexander, were also waiting. Neither looked happy.

Myles met them almost as they came in the door. "Joanna, Senator Hardy . . . Lowell," he corrected himself, while shaking their hands. "You've performed yet another valuable service."

"The Russians contacted me, Mr. President. I can't take credit for this."

"But you carried the ball perfectly when they passed it to you. Please, have a seat." Myles gestured to the two couches in the center of the room. Myles and Hardy shared one couch, while Alexander and Patterson sat across from them. There was plenty of room for Lloyd, but he remained standing. He looked like he wanted to pace, but was fighting it.

Alexander said, "The folks at CIA are still going through the CD that was tucked into the book he gave you, as well as examining the book itself. The disc has a series of reports from the source Petrov mentioned. It matches the story he told you, and we now have a name: the 'Littoral Alliance.' Plus we get a little bit of their timeline, but not much about the 'imminent threat' they're so concerned about."

"Imminent implies near-term, does it not? What, if anything, are the Chinese doing that could have all these nations so spooked?" Myles asked.

"If that's even the correct word," Lloyd grumbled. "The reports are in Russian, but apparently were translated originally from Japanese, and now into English."

Alexander ignored the SecState's comment and answered Myles's question. "The only thing the Chinese are doing in the near term that we're aware of is the large exercise in the South China Sea, and we already knew the Vietnamese were concerned enough about it to mine the Chinese carrier."

Kirkpatrick volunteered a different definition. "A better word might be 'alarmed,' Mr. President. And whatever Vietnam knew has now convinced three other countries to join them in a covert war."

"We'll do our best to find out if there's something going on besides the exercise," Alexander assured them. "There's always the possibility that it was being used as a distraction or cover."

"Andy, do you have any questions for the senator?" inquired Myles.

Lloyd shook his head quickly. "No, sir, I don't, and thank you for your service this afternoon, Senator."

As Hardy nodded his acknowledgement, Lloyd continued. "To me, this is a logical move for the Russians. Like us, the last thing they need is China at war. If things got bad in China, the refugee problem alone could be disastrous for Russia.

"We have more influence in the region, with Japan and South Korea as formal allies, and our security arrangements with Taiwan. With this warning, we can work to limit the crisis and position ourselves to keep our people safe, and limit our own involvement."

"Is that your recommendation, Andy?" asked the president.

"Boiled down to the basics, yes, sir. My staff is still drawing up our formal recommendations, but that's what my experience says. Wars always last longer than the people who start them think they will, and the longer a war lasts, the more it spreads. What if North Korea tries to take advantage of the situation? Can Taiwan stay out of it even if it wants to? And what about the strains of a war on the Chinese economy? We know it's fragile, and this 'Littoral Alliance' is chipping away at the supports."

Myles held up his hands. "Too many questions, too little information. This meeting is about the Russians' message, as delivered by the honorable senator from Connecticut."

He turned to Hardy. "Given the nature of this message, I think we all would have liked to speak to the messenger ourselves. Still, I'm satisfied the Russians have provided information that they believe is true." He stood, and the others did as well. Myles shook Hardy's hand again. "Lowell, know you've got a friend here if you need one."

"Thank you, sir. One quick question." He turned slightly to face Greg Alexander. "Do you think the CIA's lab is done with the book yet?"

Alexander was surprised for a moment, then answered, "Of course. It was a gift from Alex Petrov. I'll make sure the lab doesn't mangle it, but it will take a few more days before they're done. Is that all right?"

"Yes, sir. But I wanted to read it as well."

"You should probably get another copy, then," replied Alexander, smiling.

Myles said, "Joanna, can you come back right away, please? We have more to discuss."

Taking the hint, she left with her husband while the others sat down again.

Myles waited for the door to close before asking Alexander, "What's Petrov doing now?"

The DNI glanced at his watch. "It's been a little over two hours since we received Hardy's report. Petrov arrived in the U.S. this morning at Dulles airport with a diplomatic visa. We've made a quiet search of the

Crystal City area without spotting him. He has not visited the embassy, and is scheduled to fly out this evening from Dulles at 9:45. Did you want to question him further? We can detain him there, if you wish."

"Detain him? Are you nuts?" Myles exclaimed. "No, just the opposite. Get someone to Dulles and make sure Petrov has no issues getting to his flight. No TSA screw-ups, no random searches. I owe that guy a steak dinner. The least we can do is make sure he makes his flight home."

Patterson returned within minutes, carrying an armful of documents. She handed them to Kirkpatrick while she slipped into her chair. As he started to skim them, he said, "Go ahead, Joanna."

"All the armed forces in the region have gone to heightened states of readiness. No surprise there. It's the logical move. There's no general pattern that we can point to, but specific incidents do support the Russians' claim. They've held air-raid drills in Vietnam, South Korea, and Taiwan.

"All available Aegis ships in the Japanese and South Korean navies are at sea, with heavy escort. They are taking positions to protect those countries from ballistic missile and air attacks originating from Mainland China.

"Vietnam has reinforced its border with China, and ELINT shows that some of their best air-defense units have been deployed there as well.

"As far as we can tell, there's been no unusual military activity by India."

Lloyd remarked, "Keeping a low profile, no doubt. And submarines?"

She sighed. "A lot of their subs are missing from their home ports, more than enough for a campaign against China. But countries do their best to hide sub movements, even in peacetime. Nobody can be ruled out, or in, based on that criterion alone."

"No smoking torpedo tube, then." Myles's frustration was clear. "Andy, has there been word from any of these four governments, or China for that matter?"

"The Chinese are still keeping mum. All of the countries in the region have issued the usual statements about 'preparing a response to this grave situation.' Usually that means they don't have a clue what's going on, except now we know that four of them know damn well what's happening!"

"If we act on our knowledge of this 'Littoral Alliance,' won't we risk tipping our hand to China? We know what's going to happen when they find out who's behind the attacks," cautioned Patterson.

Ray Kirkpatrick replied guardedly, "We won't be giving that much away. China must have suspicions, including Vietnam, of course. And reports are circulating in the media now about an 'international conspiracy' behind the attacks, and naming Vietnam as one of the actors."

"All right, then." Myles sounded almost relieved. "Let's try the front door. Andy, draft a note to the four countries involved, asking what they know about the sinkings. Make sure it says that we're only asking those four countries."

"A formal first-person note?" Lloyd confirmed.

"For my signature," Myles replied. "Nothing public, of course. We'll just ask them flat out."

"And when they lie and say they don't know?" Lloyd asked.

"They won't. They can't stay hidden from China forever. Asking only those four makes it clear we've got some idea of what's going on. What we need from them is why this is happening. Andy, your job is to come up with ways to keep this from turning into an open war."

"Oh, I thought it was going to be something hard."

Myles laughed along with the rest, but warned, "If China directly attacks Japan or South Korea, the U.S. is compelled to respond. If that happens, it's out of our control and nobody can predict how far this will go, or who lives and who dies."

# 10

## DECISION

"We need to know, Doctor, what will the Americans do?" Hisagi Shuhei was an assistant to Foreign Minister Tadashi, and if he was being accurate, spoke not only for the Japanese Foreign Ministry, but in this case for the other Littoral Alliance members.

"The last meeting accomplished nothing," Hisagi complained. "Everyone was shocked that the alliance had been 'discovered' by America, even though it had to happen sooner or later. Perhaps this crisis has come on us too quickly. The alliance has no process for collaborative decision-making."

*Or planning*, Komamura thought to himself. He had locked the door to his office and was listening to Hisagi on headphones while he watched the diplomat on the monitor. The man was visibly worried, stress adding years to his forty-something appearance.

"When you're dying of thirst, it's too late to dig a well."

"Another Chinese proverb?" Hisagi asked.

"Japanese," Komamura answered. "Instead of discussing the question beforehand and having a plan in place, the alliance leadership prefers to wander aimlessly. No wonder they are easily surprised. They cannot reach a consensus even after the event." Komamura knew he was scolding Hisagi, but he needed scolding.

Along with Admiral Kubo, Hisagi was Japan's political representative on the "working group," the ambiguous-sounding name for the Littoral Alliance's advisory body. Each of the four nations sent two representatives that coordinated the alliance's actions. The civilians were supposed to set broad policy, while the military ran the war. It had worked so far, but the only policy decision they had made was to begin the war.

"I've mentioned before that you needed to be ready for this," Komamura mused. "I don't have any special insight into the Americans' intentions."

"With respect, *sensei*, I disagree. Everyone on the council, civilian and military, respects your wisdom."

That was not as comforting as Hisagi intended. To be truthful, Komamura was dismayed when he thought about the chaos his book had caused. His "wisdom" had taken life and wrought violence. But if one accepted his arguments, it was inevitable. That Komamura could see the problem clearly was a tribute to his academic experience. Still, it made him a reluctant advisor.

He'd tried to keep clear of the alliance's decision-making processes, but it appeared that plan was doomed. All right, then, if they needed him to assume the role of grand vizier that badly, then he'd assume it fully.

Komamura asked, "Is there any sign that the Chinese have confirmed the identities of the four countries?"

Hisagi shook his head. "None of the alliance intelligence arms has any indication, Professor. And besides, if the Chinese did, they wouldn't keep quiet about it."

"They might if they were preparing a surprise counterstroke," Komamura countered, "but the Chinese would not wait long. That blow would fall quickly. And it is only a matter of time until they have their proof."

"But how do we answer the Americans?" Hisagi persisted. "They know."

Komamura fought back impatience and frustration. Coalition warfare was difficult at best, and Hisagi was inexperienced at this type of thing. The members of the working group had been picked by their governments because they were not top-ranking officials whose movements would attract unwelcome attention. They were competent, of course, but unused to speaking for their governments.

"And what power does their knowledge have?" Komamura asked. Then he reasoned, "If we say, 'Yes, there is an alliance, join us,' the Americans will refuse. That gives us nothing. If we say no they will know we are lying, but they will not tell the Chinese either."

He saw Hisagi sit back in his chair, working through the logic. "So we gain nothing by admitting our involvement, and lose nothing by denying it."

"Certainly this was discussed by the working group," Komamura stated.

"It was, indeed, but one person was worried that if we denied it, the Americans would be offended . . ."

Komamura laughed, but quickly stopped. "That is why silence is better than a lie. I hope it wasn't one of the foreign service officials."

"No, Professor, it was one of the naval officers. Another expressed hope that while the Americans might not participate, they would publicly support our cause, or perhaps act as an intermediary between the alliance and China to negotiate a cease-fire."

"Really?" Komamura's tone made Hisagi smile.

"Are the Chinese close to breaking, Professor?" Hisagi sounded like a man looking for a reason to hope.

Komamura immediately answered, "No, not yet. It's only been a short while. We have dealt the Chinese a heavy blow, but they are powerful and no less determined than we are."

The professor gestured to the documents on his desk. "I've done nothing since the campaign started except work on the answer to that question. After this crisis has passed, I must instruct the alliance's intelligence people on how to gather economic data. Much of this 'secret information' is neither secret or informative."

Komamura paused. "Please excuse me, I'm complaining to a man with much larger problems. Given time, our plan will work." He tried to sound confident.


2 September 2016
1300 Local Time
White House Situation Room
Washington, D.C.

Patterson was giving the briefing. Kirkpatrick had given her as much warning as he could, a little less than thirty minutes.

Myles had called for a meeting of the National Security Council as soon as the Littoral Alliance's "nonanswer" arrived. Everyone had shown up. No deputies this time. The secretaries of state, defense, the chairman and vice chairman of the Joint Chiefs, the director of national intelligence, even the director of Homeland Security sat close to the head of the table, but much of the cabinet had also decided to attend: energy, treasury, commerce, even the attorney general.

The president was late, and he'd sent word to start without him, but the empty chair distracted her. It also meant he wouldn't hear her opening, but they couldn't wait any longer. Ray nodded to her, and she stepped up to the podium.

"Ladies and gentlemen, China has mobilized for war, as have most of the nations in the Western Pacific." She pressed her remote and a map appeared on the screen showing military unit movements from India eastward, all the way to South Korea.

"I am going to summarize the situation in the region. A detailed accounting would take more time than we have. Dr. Kirkpatrick can provide any of you with—"

A rectangle of light appeared to one side, and President Myles came in, hurrying. "Apologies, everyone. My conversation with Prime Minister Keyes went longer than I expected." He paused, then added, "but the British can add nothing to what we already know." Settled in his chair, he looked over and said, "Dr. Patterson, please continue."

She pressed the remote again, and the map zoomed in to frame China. Unit symbols littered Chinese territory, but clustered near the borders. "Of the eighteen group armies that make up their main ground forces, all but two have mobilized, and of those, all but three have left their garrisons. The regional troops in all seven military districts have been put on alert, and this morning President Chen Dao signed an order requiring all reservists to muster with their units."

Patterson used a light pointer. "Ground and air forces are concentrating in the south, along the Vietnamese border, in the Chengdu and Guangzhou Military Regions. The 13th, 14th, and 41st Group Armies will be in position to attack Vietnam within twenty-four hours. There has been no appreciable concentration across from Taiwan; in fact, elements of the 31st Group Army are heading westward. Some mobile units have been sent to reinforce the northern border, but this seems to be more of a precautionary measure, as they are second-line formations without the latest equipment.

"There are also indications that China has seized several islands and reefs in the Spratly Island archipelago, SIGINT reporting indicates fighting on Namyit and Spratly Islands and Southwest Cay. All three are Vietnamese-claimed islands.

"Every nation in the area, including those in the Littoral Alliance, has gone to a full war footing. In the three Pacific Littoral Alliance countries, U.S. attachés and other U.S. nationals have been barred from military bases 'for their own safety.' This has not applied to our joint-use bases in Japan and South Korea. Instead, Japanese and South Korean units are being moved from the joint bases to ones exclusively under national control."

The map shifted west suddenly, framing India. "Delhi has ordered an alert in the north, 'because of China's history of past aggression.' Indian Army and Air Force units in the area are deploying to defensive positions. Their ballistic missile forces have also begun moving to dispersal sites."

Patterson brought the map back east, expanding it to include the entire western Pacific. "Merchant ship traffic in the South and East China Seas has dropped by fifty percent in the past four days, with many ships reaching their destination and not leaving, or in some cases, simply heading for the nearest safe harbor. This includes, as of eight o'clock this morning, seventeen U.S.-owned vessels."

She checked the time. Good, five minutes flat. "Questions?"

General Jason Nagy, the Joint Chiefs vice chairman, raised his hand. "Dr. Patterson, the Vietnamese islands you mentioned, they span the entire length of the Spratlys?"

"Yes, General," Joanna replied. "Southwest Cay is in the north, Namyit Island is in the center, and Spratly Island proper is in the south."

"Thank you, ma'am, for makin' my point," answered the Marine Corps general with a heavy southern drawl. "That's a maritime front over two hundred nautical miles long. It would take at least three amphibious assault groups to conduct that many landin's simultaneously."

"You're correct, sir." She nodded. "Three of China's Type 071 Yuzhao-class LPDs are in the South China Sea AOR, and the Marine Corps Intelligence Activity has assessed they are the primary units behind the attacks."

General Nagy smiled broadly. "Yes, ma'am, I've talked at length with the boys in MCIA, but doesn't it strike you as a very fortuitous coincidence that the Chinese have the necessary assets all together and ready to go on a moment's notice?"

Joanna felt uncertain. What was the general getting at? "Well, General Nagy, they were scheduled to participate in the major exercise, but that is obviously OBE. Since the units were available, the Chinese put them to immediate use attacking islands belonging to at least one of their adversaries."

Nagy chuckled. "Well, I wouldn't know about that. But it seems to this dumb grunt that an amphibious campaign of this magnitude would require a helluva lot more time to plan and prepare for than just three or four days."

The lightbulbs suddenly came on, as everyone present comprehended what the marine general was saying.

President Myles leaned forward, his gaze intense. "General, are you suggesting these invasions were preplanned? How much time would you need to organize such a campaign?"

"Mr. President, all I'm sayin' is that it would take months to get everythin' planned and in place, the people trained and properly supplied. Particularly for a navy and a marine corps that hasn't done anythin' like this before. Now some pretty smart folks are suggestin' the Chinese are more flexible and could turn their forces around much quicker than we can. And with all due respect to their considerable credentials, Mr. President, that's a pile of manure."

"The 'imminent Chinese threat,'" Patterson blurted out, referring to the Russian CD. "If the Vietnamese had knowledge of a planned invasion of their holdings in the Spratlys, that would explain the mining of the Chinese carrier—the flagship of the invasion force."

"My God!" a weary Lloyd exclaimed. "This is the reason why the Littoral Alliance went to war!"

"Hold on, Andy. It only provides an explanation of why Vietnam went to war. It doesn't do us any good for the other three nations," retorted Malcolm Geisler, the secretary of defense. He was the newest member of the cabinet, having replaced the ailing James Springfield.

"But it does, Malcolm. Japan and South Korea have similar issues with China in the East China Sea. Remember that tiff over Japanese oil and gas exploration by China near the Senkaku Islands last year? And what about the growing number of incidents between Chinese fishing boats and Japanese and South Korean coast guard ships? Same story, different location," Lloyd argued.

"And there is still no resolution on the overlapping EEZ disputes between those countries," added Commerce Secretary Joyce McHenry.

"All right, what about India?" Geisler asked.

"There's disputed territory there as well, just not quite as picturesque," Lloyd responded, stifling a yawn. "India and China actually went to war in the early 1960s over the Aksai Chin area. China kicked the Indians' butt, but ultimately declared a cease-fire and withdrew. The Indians haven't forgotten that unpleasant episode. They've also taken great umbrage over China's occupation of Tibet."

"The Indians have also actively opposed China's development of civilian ports in Pakistan, Sri Lanka, Burma, and Bangladesh. The 'string of pearls,' as they are called, is part of China's strategic plan to reduce the vulnerability of their sea lanes," McHenry concluded.

"So, there is a rationale that supports a preemptive strike by an alliance of weaker nations with similar grievances against China," Dewhurst summarized.

"It's a reasonable theory, General," observed Kirkpatrick.

"But can we prove it?" Myles demanded.

"We'll get right on it, Mr. President," said Alexander. Then turning to Nagy, "General, let's discuss your theory after the meeting. I'd like to work out the details to help MCIA run this to ground."

"It would be my pleasure, sir," Nagy replied.

Myles said, "Well, I'm encouraged. Maybe we can finally get our hands around the root cause of the war. I'm not surprised that it involves an aggressive move by China, but I'm perplexed as to why the Chinese think it's necessary.

"I'll sit down with Andy and chew on this one." He looked over at his secretary of state. Lloyd's eyes were at half-mast.

"Andy, I'm sorry," sympathized Myles. "You've been at this all night. Please brief the others on the response from Littoral Alliance."

Lloyd stood slowly, as if with great effort. He looked very tired. "All four nations responded to President Myles's note with exactly the same words, at the same time, saying that they 'could not respond to our inquiry.'" He smiled as he said it, but he was clearly not amused. "They didn't deny it, but they didn't answer it, either."

"Did you expect them to admit it, Andy?" asked Myles.

Lloyd sat down, sighing. "They did admit it, of course. They sent us a clear message by acting in unison, but without giving us a staring point for a discussion. I'm a diplomat. We love to talk. I could ask them why they started this war, or what their goals are. Of course, I'd also encourage them to stop shooting, but I don't think they want to stop."

"Hard to make them stop when you didn't know why they started." Myles sounded frustrated. He'd taught Asian studies before getting into politics. That knowledge wasn't giving him the answers he needed. "Gregory, has the intelligence community come up with anything to shed light on Andy's idea?"

Greg Alexander, the director of national intelligence, answered hesitantly, "We have few resources in South Korea or Japan, of course. We rely on attachés in those countries, as well as our bilateral relationships. Our sources in Vietnam and India haven't given us any information beyond details of their respective mobilizations. It's clear they are serious, even scared.

"As for the Chinese," he continued, "they're scared, too, but not in the same way. Our sources within China gave us no hint of the approaching crisis, and now there's word that the General Staff's intelligence arm has launched an all-out hunt for 'enemy agents.' We suspect they're looking for the Vietnamese spy that stirred up so much trouble with the information he or she stole."

Alexander paused for a moment, as if considering the possibilities. "As a result, most of our people have gone to ground. It's hard just sending them a request for information, much less expecting anything back."

"Too bad we can't find the spy first. He could answer so many questions." General Dewhurst sounded half serious.

"I'm afraid that isn't very likely, General, as much as I agree with your sentiments," snapped Alexander, with a hint of annoyance in his voice.

The conversation was wandering, but the president pulled back on task. "Let me lay this out clearly," Myles stated. "Right now this war does not involve the U.S. directly, but it's begun to hurt us economically, and the longer it goes on, the more damage we will suffer. And the longer it lasts, the greater the chance we will be involved, directly. That means open war with China and an impossible cost in blood and treasure. What pressure can we bring on the two sides to stop fighting?"

Lloyd sighed. "With only one side doing the shooting, pressure on China is pointless. And if we publicly act against the Littoral Alliance countries, we give China its targets. So whatever we recommend has to be as covert as the conflict itself."

The silence that followed Lloyd's reasoning was suffocating.

General Dewhurst finally remarked, "In 1971, we sent *Enterprise* into the Indian Ocean to help end the Indo-Pakistani war. That worked."

"And the Indians and Pakistanis are still mad about it," Lloyd answered. "And don't forget that China was just as irate when we sent carrier battle groups off Taiwan in the mid-1990s. A mere display of military force isn't going to help us this time. You need superior power to enforce a cease-fire."

"That's not entirely true," Alexander countered. "Commander Mitchell managed to stop an attack by a Vietnamese Kilo on a Chinese sub. One could call that 'local superiority.'"

General Dewhurst visibly winced at the mention of what was already called "the Mitchell incident." Lloyd scowled, and Ray Kirkpatrick almost scolded the director. "Mitchell was lucky. Poking your nose into the middle of a sub-on-sub engagement is begging for trouble."

Confused, Myles asked, "But when you briefed me on that, Ray, you said that Mitchell's sub was far superior to the other two, that as long as he handled himself well, there was little chance of him revealing his presence."

"Yes, sir, the odds were definitely in his favor, but there was still a risk of being discovered, and a smaller risk of getting shot at. It would have been better if he hadn't intervened at all."

"But when he did, he kept the casualty list from growing," Myles insisted. "One of the reasons wars go on is because of the price both sides have paid in blood. After a while, even if the original reason no longer matters, you keep on fighting because you don't want all those deaths to be in vain."

Patterson could see the president was warming up to something. "What if we don't care whether they know we're there? What if we use our submarines to spoil attacks, whether it's sub on tanker or sub on sub? And it doesn't matter who's doing the shooting. We show ourselves to be completely neutral by disrupting any attack by either side."

She listened to the exchange, mentally rolling the facts around in her mind. Like the others, Patterson wanted to find a way to stop the conflict before it spiraled out of control. She agreed with Myles's goal, but this . . . It just didn't feel right. She wanted to say something, but what? She wasn't afraid to speak, but she had no idea what to say. She wasn't alone.

Lloyd, the president's closest adviser, broke the silence that had followed Myles's suggestion. "Mr. President, I don't believe U.S. forces have ever been used in that way."

When Lloyd paused, searching for a second sentence, General Dewhurst added, "The Squadron Fifteen boats are already risking their lives just to 'observe and report' in the middle of a war zone. I understand our critical need for information, that's why I haven't recommended getting them out of there. This strategy puts them directly in the line of fire, at far greater risk for no gain."

Lloyd nodded. "I agree with the general, Mr. President. We could lose a sub by getting involved in someone else's fight. And it will just make both sides mad at us."

"I don't mind that if you don't, Andy." Myles was smiling, but his tone

had a grim edge. "Actually, that's one of my goals. Two U.S. military allies have begun a secret war, without a word of explanation to us. When we ask them, they stonewall. This will get their attention, and maybe convince them to start talking to us."

Myles continued, "It also buys us time for Gregory and his people to confirm the rationale for a preemptive strike that Andy put forth. Once we know that, our people can be pulled out of the area."

"Sir, what if we agree with them?" asked Geisler hesitantly. He saw everyone's reaction, and immediately added, "I'm not suggesting that the U.S. start sinking tankers, but the countries in the Littoral Alliance did not go to war lightly. This invasion theory is certainly reasonable justification; at least for Vietnam."

Lloyd answered, "I agree, but it all comes back to the Littoral Alliance not informing us, even after the shooting started. The Russians have given us more information than our 'Pacific allies.'"

Alexander added, "The Russian may have given us more than we thought. When Senator Hardy said he was interested in reading the book that Petrov had given him, I wondered what it was about. I haven't read *Navies for Asia*, but there are summaries and reviews all over the Web, especially on Pacific and Asian Web sites. Komamura's an economist and historian, but the book is about Asian seapower. He compares the growing strength of countries like Japan and South Korea with fading U.S. influence in the region. He posits an alliance of Asian countries, able to 'act without U.S. constraints,' against regional threats. And he has a whole chapter on the Chinese threat."

"It's a blueprint for their alliance," Geisler remarked.

"Except they didn't withdraw from their treaties with us first," Lloyd countered.

"Because that might have telegraphed their intentions," Myles completed. "It all makes sense, right up to the time the shooting started, and after that, it's all about pride. They're showing us they can handle China without our help."

Alexander nodded. "That's what Komamura said in his book. One of the chapters was titled 'Sailing Alone.'"

Dewhurst said, "'Alone' is a tall order. The Littoral Alliance is trying to cripple the Chinese economy quickly, but Alexander's economists estimate they will need to keep this up for weeks, maybe months. The Chinese won't sit still for that long, even if their opponents manage to stay hidden."

"I concur," Geisler added. "If China approaches the crisis point without

a clear target, they'll start lashing out randomly. But it's more likely they'll get the proof they need, and then their anger will have a focus."

President Myles stood and turned to face down the length of the table. "Every scenario we've discussed ends up with a bad situation getting considerably worse. If the only way to change the dynamic is by using our submarines as spoilers, then that's what we'll do. Does anyone else have a better idea?"

General Dewhurst said, "Four submarines aren't enough to stop a war, if that's even possible. In a few days we'll have two carrier strike groups assembled off Japan's east coast . . ."

"Who will we use them against, General? My official policy is to find out what's going on. The spoiler strategy will pressure the Littoral Alliance into communicating with us, while hopefully keeping the casualty count from climbing."

"Somebody will accuse us of being the 'world's policeman' again," Alexander observed.

Myles shook his head sharply. "Absolutely not. The world's too small for conflicts like this anymore. If two neighbors next door are feuding, and it's likely to endanger my family, then it's in my interest to stop it. Let me worry about justifying this to Congress and the American people."

"Excuse me, Mr. President, I'm loath to bring this up, but I believe it's necessary," Kirkpatrick interrupted hesitantly. "This course of action you are considering has considerable risk, politically. It would be quite damaging to your campaign to insert U.S. forces into this conflict. Your opponent would be able to capitalize on this move, and your poll numbers are not as . . . as robust as we would like."

To everyone's surprise, Myles laughed. "Ray, I appreciate your concern. But my Republican opponent will criticize me just as vigorously if I choose some other course. Since I'm damned if I do, and damned if I don't, I might as well get skewered for doing something."

He turned to Dewhurst. "General, in consultation with Dr. Kirkpatrick, the CNO, and Secretary Geisler, write orders that turn Commander Mitchell's tactic into a plan for spoiling attacks by either side. The goal is to limit the violence to both sides while minimizing the risk to our people."

Dewhurst was writing furiously as the president spoke, and when the general paused to look up, Myles added, "And get some more submarines into the area immediately."

2 September 2016
1430 Local Time
Old Ebbitt Grill
Washington, D.C.

---

Joanna had called and asked him to take her to lunch at the Old Ebbitt Grill. It was one of her favorite places, and Hardy knew immediately she was upset.

They both liked the place—dark, warm décor, great food, and bustling without being too noisy. She'd met him inside, out of the late-summer heat. She smiled, but it was thin, almost forced. He'd started to worry with the phone call, and that now blossomed into full-blown concern.

They'd been seated immediately, with Hardy watching her every movement. They both knew the menu well enough to immediately order their meals. The waiter had barely disappeared with their choices when she asked, "Did you ever have to carry out an order you didn't agree with?"

Surprised but relieved, Hardy asked, "In what way? Illegal, immoral, or just stupid?"

Patterson shook her head and gestured as if brushing the question aside. "It's not illegal or immoral, and I'm almost sorry it isn't. That would be easy."

Hardy almost laughed out loud, but suppressed all but an amused snort. "Not for some people in this town. What's this about?"

"I can't go into details. It concerns my current assignment."

"So it's stupid, but important."

"Yes. Very important," she answered. "But let's change 'stupid' to 'bad idea.' And can I pass it on if I don't think it's the right thing to do?"

Hardy sighed. "It's an old story. I was in command of a nuclear submarine, master of all I surveyed, except for the 'in' box in the radio room. Whoever you are, whatever rank you are, there's usually somebody with a higher rank, telling you what to do."

"Not in this case," she replied. "Nobody outranks this person. He gave the order, and it's passed down to me, and now I have to tell someone else to do it."

"I understand why this is hard, Joanna. I've had the 'chain of command' philosophy drummed into me since the academy. It doesn't take a full day there before you find out that not all orders make sense, and that some of them aren't just bad ideas, they're downright stupid. With anyone in the military, following a legal order should be automatic."

"I can't be just a robot," she protested.

"You're not a robot," Hardy insisted. "I said 'automatic.' That doesn't mean you stop thinking. You're allowed to have your own opinion, but it's the big guy's call to make. Wait a minute. Did he come up with this on his own, or was there discussion?"

"Lots of discussion." Their drinks arrived, and she took a good-sized pull on her glass of wine.

"Do you have information that he doesn't?"

"No."

"Then you've got nothing to worry about," he explained. "It really is his decision to make, and your duty is now to carry it out to the best of your ability, especially if you think it's a bad idea. The orders you agree with are the easy ones. Now is when you earn your lunch money."

"I can't help but feel that by cooperating, it's my fault when it goes bad."

"Now you're just whining." Hardy's voice was still warm, but it had a hard edge. "That's why people look at the top of the chain when things go bad. He gets all the credit, and all the blame."

Hardy leaned closer, and spoke softly, but with great feeling. "What your boss needs right now is everybody working in the same direction. If it's a near thing, your efforts may make all the difference. You make it happen, *his* way, and no second-guessing."

As Hardy sat back, he suddenly smiled. "Besides, you can never tell how things will work out. Some years ago, when I was in command of *Memphis*, I got a presidential order that I was certain was insane. Can you believe he wanted me to take two civilian women with me on a northern run?"

She made a face at him. "And it's been nothing but trouble ever since."

He shrugged and grinned. "There have been some positive aspects."

"All right," she sighed. "It's my job, and I'll do my best, but can you please give me some guidance on what to say? Captain Simonis is going to like this even less than I do."

"The commodore of Squadron Fifteen?" Hardy had started out in a normal speaking voice, but lowered it to almost a whisper as he realized they were veering toward classified realms.

She nodded silently.

"Does this thing have to do with his submarines?"

"Yes," she answered simply.

Standing quickly, Hardy reached for her hand. "Come on. You don't have a leisurely lunch with operational orders waiting to be sent." As Hardy pulled out his wallet and threw a couple of bills on the table, their server spotted them. Hardy explained, "I'm sorry, something's come up. That should cover our order."

Hurrying out of the restaurant, he said, "I'll coach you on a few things you can say, and a few more you shouldn't."

The thick, hot air was a shock after the air-conditioned interior, but it was only three blocks to the White House's staff gate. "Don't worry," he continued as they walked. "Simonis knows the drill. He'll protest, and probably ask questions, maybe even pout, but if he's any kind of an officer, he'll eventually say, 'Aye, aye' and make it happen."

2 September 2016
1615 Local Time
The White House
Washington, D.C.

Captain Simonis's image appeared almost immediately. It was a little after four in the morning in Guam, but he'd been close by, evidently. "Dr. Patterson, good . . ." He glanced at something off camera. ". . . afternoon in Washington." He didn't smile. Captain Glenn Jacobs, the squadron chief staff officer, and Commander Walker were both visible in the background. In the lower corners of the screen were insets showing Admiral Bernard Hughes, the chief of naval operations at the Pentagon, and Rear Admiral Burroughs, COMSUBPAC in Hawaii. Patterson saw Simonis's eyes narrow as they darted back and forth, looking at the screen; he saw the two flag officers.

"I apologize for the early hour, Captain, and I won't waste your time. Has anything significant or unusual happened since your 2000 report?"

"No, ma'am. All boats are on station and operating as ordered."

"Good. The National Security Council has decided to make a change in our tactics. We've decided to become more proactive."

Simonis frowned, mixing confusion and concern. "I'd hoped my boats had gathered enough data that we could think about withdrawing from the middle of a war zone."

"Unfortunately, Captain, we are still missing several critical pieces of information. Although we know who is participating in the Littoral Alliance, they refuse to acknowledge the fact to us. The president is also very concerned about the damage the alliance is inflicting on China."

Simonis paused before answering. "If that's the case, then things are going to get a lot worse. The Chinese Navy is having absolutely no luck in tracking the alliance subs, much less sinking them."

"That is why your new orders are to actively interfere with the alliance and any Chinese submarine attacks they observe. Distract them, disrupt and confuse them, whatever it takes to make the approach fail and allows the potential target to get away."

Simonis paused again, but his expression was unusual—wide-eyed and blank-faced. He seemed to be considering different responses, evaluating the pros and cons of each alternative. He finally settled on verifying the content of her last statement.

"Are you directing us to deliberately involve ourselves with a hostile submarine as it approaches a vessel it intends to attack?"

"Yes, with the purpose of preventing that attack, either by alerting the target or distracting the attacker." She was pleased with her answer.

"I've never heard of such a thing," Simonis replied, almost to himself, but it was clear that he did intend for her to hear it. "What do we hope to gain by this tactic?"

"First, to reduce the casualty count. If the Chinese lose too many ships, they will be compelled to take more aggressive military action as a face-saving measure. Second, to compel the Littoral Alliance to open a dialogue."

"I guarantee it will get their attention. But what if our subs are detected, or mistaken for an enemy boat? What if they are fired on?"

"It's no longer necessary to remain undetected, but your rules of engagement regarding counterfire remain unchanged," Patterson replied calmly.

"I like being undetected. If they can't see me, they can't shoot at me. Deliberately revealing ourselves in the presence of not just one, but possibly two potential enemies, while tying our hands behind our back, goes against all my training. It's not what submarines are supposed to do!"

The captain paused, and took on a calmer tone. "This is taking what Mitchell did and asking everybody in the squadron to do it—repeatedly. Are you sure the president has been properly informed on the capabilities and vulnerabilities of our submarines?"

"He was well briefed, Captain." Patterson chose a firmer tone. "The detailed orders are being sent right now by secure communications."

Simonis was visibly shaken. "Mitchell was lucky, and *North Dakota* is a flight three *Virginia* class—a step up from *Texas* and at least a generation more advanced than my two Improved *Los Angeles* boats. They won't have the same acoustic edge over the alliance boats. The Chinese, perhaps, but not a Project 636 Kilo or India's *Chakra*."

"But they still have superior sensors and fire control systems, and we are also sending reinforcements; at least three more submarines are being sent to you. USS *North Carolina* left Pearl Harbor earlier today." Patterson took a deep breath. "I appreciate your concern, Captain, we all do, but all your boats have to do is interfere with an attack, not sink them."

"Sinking is easier!" he shot back. "Leaving a hostile sub that's detected you alive invites disaster. I can't even begin to assess the increased risk to my boats. Is the return on this change in tactics worth the lives of my crews?"

His question went straight to her heart, and although Patterson tried to hide her reaction, the effort may have given her feelings away. She'd been ready for this, though. Lowell had taught her.

"Captain, you have your orders. I expect you to do your best to carry them out."

# 11

## DIVISION

Simonis sat motionless; he simply stared at the now-blank screen. The staff members present, amazed by the orders Patterson had just given them, were likewise stunned. They looked hesitantly back and forth between each other and their commodore in awkward silence. The only discernable noise was the whirling blades of the cooling fan on the VTC computer.

Everyone in the room waited anxiously for the other shoe to drop. The commodore's temper was a fact of life in Squadron Fifteen, and collectively the group couldn't decide whether to beat a hasty retreat, or stay and watch the fireworks.

After an uncomfortable length of time, Simonis's head slowly began to fall. He took a deep breath, the expected prelude to a monumental rant. But when he finally spoke, his voice was calm, emotionless, the volume restrained.

"Captain Jacobs, I want a draft message ordering the four boats to break away and establish a SATCOM link with squadron headquarters at . . ." Simonis paused as he looked at his watch. ". . . 0600 their local time. Flash precedence. You have seven minutes."

"Aye, aye, sir," responded the chief staff officer. Rising, the CSO pointed to an information technician to follow him. Both quickly left the conference room.

Simonis took another deep breath, then looked around the room. Struggling, he said, "With the exception of Commander Walker, everyone else is dismissed."

As the staff filed out of the room, Walker moved up to the main table and gestured for the last man out to close the door. Pulling a chair away from the table, he quietly sat down, pen and notebook at the ready. By the time Walker had situated himself, Simonis's face was crimson, his body shaking visibly.

"Rich, I have never, throughout my entire career, ever considered disobeying a lawful order from a superior, until now," Simonis rasped through clenched teeth. Suddenly he lashed out with his right arm, striking a wooden chair next to him. A sharp snap and flying splinters testified to the force of the blow. Rising abruptly, he kicked the damaged chair out of his way. Stomping angrily around the table, he slammed the top with his fist and bellowed, "What is the president thinking!? Does he even have a clue as to what he's telling me to do!?"

Walker shook his head ruefully. "The CNO and COMSUBPAC didn't look thrilled at all. Neither did Dr. Patterson, for that matter."

"Any sentient human being could see there is no way that four attack submarines, by themselves, can stop a war between five nations even if they expended every Mark 48 in their torpedo rooms!"

Simonis spun and paced, raising his arms in frustration. "And yet, we've been ordered to insert ourselves into a shooting war, under a 'weapons hold' provision, with the stated goal of interfering and frustrating the attacks by both sides! Is it just me? Or is this manifest insanity!?"

"Sir, Dr. Patterson didn't say we had to 'stop the war,' just slow it down a bit to give the president a chance to force this Littoral Alliance to engage and resolve the crisis diplomatically," Walker responded carefully.

The enraged commodore turned and thumped both of his hands on the table. "ELECTION YEAR BULLSHIT, COMMANDER!" howled Simonis. "To execute these orders, we not only have to give up our stealth advantage, but our boats will also have to get far closer to the hostile submarines if they are going to pull this off. Which means they will be far more vulnerable to hostile fire, and I'm not talking about shitty TEST-71 torpedoes either. The Indians have the UGST, Japan the Type 89, China has the Yu-6, and South Korea the White Shark—all top-of-the-line weapons."

Simonis had placed both hands firmly on his head, holding it tightly between them, as if trying to contain an explosion from inside his skull.

Suddenly, he stopped and threw his hands in the air. A resigned sigh escaped from his lips, followed by his head and shoulders drooping over. Looking toward Walker, he uttered tersely, "I tell you, Rich. If we don't lose a boat over this fool's errand, it will be a miracle."

The operations officer remained silent; there was really no way to argue with his boss. From a military perspective, Simonis was absolutely correct. But a decision by a president was almost always based on political considerations; internal, external, or both. Sometimes, those political considerations required military forces to be deliberately placed in harm's way, doing things they would normally not do. As a staff officer Walker could look at the situation dispassionately. He was thankful he wasn't in the commodore's shoes.

A knock on the door broke the uncomfortable silence. Captain Jacobs opened it and marched over to Simonis with a single sheet of paper. Taking it, the commodore leaned against the large table and read the draft message. A facial twitch showed he'd read something he didn't like; he made some quick annotations to the draft. Thrusting it to Jacobs, Simonis ordered, "Send it, CSO. You have two minutes."

Jacobs grabbed the message and literally ran from the room. Walker struggled to contain a smile as he watched his CSO sprint down the hallway. Even in this situation, conflicted as he was, Simonis would get a "Flash" precedence message out within the recommended ten minutes. The man was totally obsessed with following procedures to the letter.

"Well, that's that," exclaimed a depressed Simonis. "In a couple of hours we'll discuss this change in orders with our four COs and then send them off to play referee."

Walker chuckled lightly. "I don't think that's a very good analogy, sir. At least referees are protected by the rules of the game. Last time I checked, rules are a little hard to come by in war."

"True. But that is exactly what the president has told us to become, referees in a fight where there are no rules," countered Simonis sternly. "And for the near future, those four crews are going to feel very lonely."

"But Commodore, Dr. Patterson mentioned that additional boats had been ordered to reinforce us," said Walker, reading from his notes. "She said *North Carolina* was already en route."

Simonis smiled cynically. "Yes, she did. But do the math, Rich. There are thirty attack submarines in the Pacific Fleet. Assuming eighty percent availability, that means twenty-four can go to sea. Of those, about eight boats are currently at sea, based on one deployed submarine for every three available boats. Thus, this squadron already has about half of the deployed submarines in the entire fleet!

"*North Carolina* left Pearl yesterday. Even at flank speed she'll need about six days to get to the South China Sea. It would take a deployed submarine in the CENTCOM AOR another day or two to get there. The boats in port will take even longer. And you did notice that no one said a word about a carrier strike group? No, for most of the coming week, we are on our own. This mission is ours to execute, whether we like it or not."

3 September 2016
0600 Local Time
USS *North Dakota*
South China Sea

Jerry, Bernie Thigpen, and the IT senior chief were the only ones allowed in the radio room during the video conference with Squadron Fifteen. Simonis wanted to keep the audience to an absolute minimum, thus only the top leadership and one tech from each boat were permitted to participate. Jerry certainly could understand why. The new orders they had received an hour earlier initially had the caveat, "Commanding Officer's Eyes Only." It was only after Jerry had read them that he was allowed to clue Thigpen in.

"Hoollyy Shit!" the XO had said as he started reading the new orders in Jerry's stateroom. "Are they frickin' serious?"

"It would seem so," Jerry answered nonchalantly.

Thigpen's eyes peeked over the orders. "You know, this is your fault," he stated frankly, an accusatory expression on his face.

"Yesss, it would seem so," replied Jerry with a sheepish look.

The XO kept reading. As he worked his way down the message, his facial features underwent dramatic change. First, his left eyebrow cocked up, then his mouth fell open, finally his face transformed into a visage of utter disbelief. Thigpen's eyes darted back and forth from the message to his CO. His face screamed, "This just can't be right!" Shocked, he began reading the text aloud.

"'You are authorized to use any means at your disposal, with the exception of launching weapons, to interfere, frustrate, or spoil attacks by Littoral Alliance or Chinese submarines. The previous requirement to maintain absolute stealth is rescinded. It is expected that overt actions will be required during the execution of these orders that will reveal your presence to the belligerent parties.'"

Thigpen slowly placed the message on the desk, his awestruck face staring into space. "This is just plain crazy!" exclaimed Thigpen. Then, focusing on Jerry, he added, "You've created a monster!"

Jerry raised his hands and shrugged, admitting his guilt. "It would seem so."

"Can you *please* say something other than that?" wailed a frustrated Thigpen.

"Like what, Bernie!?" Jerry replied, discouraged. "I had no idea the president would take that one event, with circumstances hugely in our favor, and turn it into the linchpin of a campaign!"

"Yeah, one that's going to get our ass shot off."

"That's a distinct possibility," agreed Jerry quietly.

"I . . . I don't get it," mumbled a resigned Thigpen, sitting down. "How does a lowly commander, no disrespect intended, sir, have such a significant influence on the president of the United States?" He paused and leaned forward, confused and uncertain. "Why does what *you* think matter so much to him? It makes me wonder, Skipper, what kind of man am I working for?"

Jerry initially remained silent. His brain raced while he ran his fingers through his hair. The questions, though uncomfortable, were nonetheless valid. And his XO deserved answers. Hesitantly, he began, "I'm sure you've heard the rumors."

"Of course, sir. Who on this boat hasn't?" responded Thigpen. "But I've also seen the nickel-sized scar on your shoulder."

"It's not that large!" Jerry protested.

"Fine, dime-size then, but that was still a damn big bullet that hit you!"

Jerry sighed and rubbed his face; disobeying a direct order from the CNO not to discuss the Iran mission with anyone who wasn't properly cleared wasn't something Jerry wanted to do. And his XO most certainly wasn't cleared. But if he was going to violate that order to restore his XO's confidence, then it was a worthy cause.

"All right, then, but nothing I say leaves this stateroom, understood?" he warned sternly. "Or I'll make you walk home!"

"Cross my heart," said Thigpen eagerly, adding the gesture for good measure.

"Okay. Yes, I was stranded in Iran with four SEALs when the ASDS self-immolated. And yes, we got into several firefights. Two were absolutely, unbelievably intense, something I'd never want to repeat. The only reason I'm here is because those SEALs are incredible warriors. I hope we have some SEALs embark with us sometime down the road. Then you'll see what I mean.

"Anyway, towards the end of our 'visit' we were hunkered down in a grove of trees, surrounded by IRGC units. And I mean completely surrounded, both landward and seaward. I, uh, had a disagreement with the SEAL platoon leader about our next course of action, and I basically pulled rank and ordered an escape by sea. We stole a fast boat and hightailed it across the Persian Gulf."

"No shit," whispered Thigpen with rapt attention.

"Oh, it gets better. While we were making our getaway, the Iranians sent three boats after us. There was no way we could outrun them, and *Michigan* couldn't help us because she was busy playing tag with an Iranian Kilo. One of the SEALs, the leading petty officer, took out one of the boats with the luckiest shot I'm ever likely to see in my lifetime, but another one worked us over pretty badly with machine-gun fire. In short order, the platoon leader, the LPO, and myself were all hit. It felt like someone had swung a bat hard against my shoulder, and then my left arm just stopped working."

Thigpen's face scrunched up into a grimace as Jerry described the sensation. "I bet that hurt like a son-of-a-bitch," he commented.

Jerry paused as he mentally replayed the events after being struck. "Actually, XO, I don't remember it hurting all that much. Oh sure, I was in shock. A 30-caliber bullet had just blown through my shoulder blade, for God's sake. But I don't recall feeling a lot of pain. That came later when I went through physical therapy. Now *that* was painful."

The laughter in Thigpen's voice was a welcome sound to Jerry's ears. His XO was finding his feet again, his attitude getting back into battery.

"So there we were, down two shooters and I'm trying to steer the boat with one hand. The two remaining Iranian boats are closing in to finish us off, when out of nowhere there was this loud *whoosh*. The next thing I know, one of the boats just evaporates. *Woof*! Gone! There, off to our right, is a MH-60R, coming in low and fast. A split second later he shoots another Hellfire and that was it. I think I passed out right after that, because I don't remember a blessed thing until I woke up in USS *Decatur*'s sickbay."

Thigpen shook his head, marveling at his CO's tale. "Now that is one hell of a sea story!"

"Yeah, one that I'm not supposed to tell anyone." Jerry chuckled lightly. "But to answer your *real* question, I need to tell you what happened at the award ceremony. During the reception, the president made it clear that he believed I made several critical decisions that enabled him to keep our country out of a war with Iran. I tried to politely dissuade him from that notion. It was very much a team effort, and I thought he seriously overplayed my part in the whole operation. So here we are with a similar situation: a war has started, one that involves longtime allies and threatens to drag the U.S. in, and he thinks, 'That Mitchell guy is out there. He's pulled rabbits out of the hat before . . .'"

Thigpen's face lit up with revelation. "And your unusual tactics only reinforced his belief!"

"That's how I see it," Jerry answered flatly.

"It makes sense," replied Thigpen, nodding. Suddenly, a cynical grin popped up on his face. "Did I ever mention that I think you may be too smart for your own good?"

Jerry sighed. "Yes, XO, I believe you've said that before."

"So what do *we* do now?" asked Thigpen.

Jerry was encouraged by his XO's emphasis on "we"—Bernie Thigpen was back on an even keel again. "*We*, XO, are going to start contingency planning. If there is one thing I learned from the SEALs, it is that one can hope for the best, but should still plan for the worst. We'll start looking at possible scenarios, come up with a set of tactics to deal with each one, and then try to break it, find the holes in our thinking and plug them. That's what we're going to do."

The radio room display showed the Squadron Fifteen headquarters conference room in the center, with the four submarine COs and XOs along the bottom. None of the participants looked very happy.

"Gentlemen," Simonis began. "By now I'm sure you've read your new orders. I will not read them verbatim, but I will emphasize the key points. First, consider any submarine contact as potentially hostile. A sufficient buffer separates your patrol areas, so there should be no issues with mutual interference. If you pick up a submerged contact, it will almost certainly belong to one of the warring nations, and you are to treat it accordingly.

"Second, use any means at your disposal, with the exception of launching weapons, to interfere, frustrate, or spoil attacks by Littoral Alliance or Chinese submarines. Stealth is no longer a critical consideration. Do what you can to cause the attacking submarine, or submarines, to break off and evade.

"Third, while it is not anticipated that either side will deliberately target a U.S. submarine, it is possible that weapons could be fired in reaction to the unexpected appearance of one. Use your acoustic advantage to position yourselves so as to minimize the possibility of an effective shot. If weapons are launched at you, use evasive maneuvers and countermeasures to their fullest extent before giving any consideration to counterfiring.

"You are only authorized to fire after every possible option has been taken to evade a vessel that is deliberately attacking you. This is a weapons hold provision, gentlemen. Your first line of defense is your speed, countermeasures, and anti-torpedo hard kill systems, not Mark 48 torpedoes. Is that clear?"

Every commanding officer answered in the affirmative, but Dobson and Halsey looked the least pleased with this aspect of their orders. Jerry was sympathetic to their less than desirable position; they had the two older, less advanced boats.

"Finally, gentlemen," Simonis concluded, "exercise extreme diligence and caution in executing these orders. You'll need to plan each encounter carefully. Make the maximum use of the environment and your superior stealth; only reveal yourselves when you are in the best possible position to spoil an attack, *and* you have a clear avenue of escape. Questions?"

Of course there were questions, and every one was a "what if" situation. Simonis dealt with each in stride, but became noticeably impatient after the sixth one. As Dobson started off on this third hypothetical question, Simonis cut him off.

"Gentlemen, you are *commanding* officers, and I expect you to command. I can't clarify every possible scenario. This is a new situation with too many unknowns. There will always be situations that fall outside your guidance. The navy spent a lot of time and money training you to develop good decision-making skills—use them!

"I won't try and blow sunshine up your skirts. These orders are . . . difficult. Interfering with another boat's attack is far more complicated than your standard approach and attack evolution. I appreciate that it's not something that we've specifically trained for; however, you have all the skills necessary to fulfill this mission. I suggest you get with your wardrooms and chiefs and figure out how to get the job done."

Admonished, Dobson and the others acknowledged the commodore's instruction. Simonis then personally bid each skipper good luck. He initially started to say "good hunting," but caught himself. As soon as he finished each farewell, Simonis had that CO dropped from the VTC. Jerry wasn't surprised that he was the last one that the commodore got to.

"Captain," Simonis opened sternly, "I trust you've realized that your actions have had significant, if unintended consequences."

Although embarrassed by the commodore's statement, Jerry was still grateful that Simonis hadn't aired this in front of his peers. "Yes, sir. And I regret overstepping my orders earlier. It won't happen again, Commodore."

"Good. Your reputation is exceptional, Captain, and even though I was quite upset over your unusual tactics, you handled yourself well."

"Uh, thank you, sir," Jerry replied, confused. This wasn't what he expected at all.

A brief smile flashed across Simonis's face. "We didn't have a lot of time to get to know each other, to learn how each other thinks, so I have to assume some of the responsibility for what happened earlier. And if I was less than clear when you were here in my office, I hope that you now have a better appreciation for my expectations."

"Yes, sir. I do."

"Very good." Simonis nodded. "And now, Captain, I have one last item for you."

"And what would that be, Commodore?" asked Jerry.

"All our intel says the Indian Improved Akula is still in your neck of the woods. I want you to find him, and dog him. That boat is far and away the best one in this Littoral Alliance, and its superior capabilities in stealth, mobility, and firepower make it a greater threat than three of their conventional submarines. If you can contain his actions, that will go a long way to meeting the president's goals."

"Understood, sir. We'll stick to her hull like a barnacle," Jerry stated confidently.

Simonis smiled again. "Good luck, Captain. Squadron Fifteen out."

3 September 2016
1400 Local Time
PLAN Frigate *Sanming*, hull 524
East China Sea

Commander Ma Hongwei was a frustrated man. For the last two days his frigate had been running from one reported periscope sighting to another. So far they'd found a floating log, a chair, even a dead seabird, but nothing that looked remotely like a submarine's periscope. Part of him wanted to throttle those merchant mariners who constantly radioed in false alarms. The other part of him realized that they were all running scared, and with good reason. So far, unknown assailants had sunk eighteen tankers. Eight of them had been torpedoed in the East Sea Fleet's area of responsibility, and the fleet commander was incensed that not one prosecution had taken place.

Ma raised his binoculars and looked at the merchant ship on the horizon. It was the tanker *Lian Xing Hu* en route to the port of Shanghai. The navigation radar operator on the bridge said she was making just a hair under fifteen knots, which would be flank speed for this vessel. Her master was obviously in a hurry to reach the safety of the harbor. Smart move.

"Captain, the helicopter has been stowed in the hangar. The flight crew has begun repairs and refueling," reported the officer of the deck.

"Very well, Lieutenant. Let's head over toward that tanker before we go to the next supposed periscope sighting," said Ma, pointing to *Lian Xing Hu*.

"Aye, sir."

As *Sanming*'s bow started swinging to starboard, Ma took another look at the tanker. The two ships had been closing, and the merchant's hull was now fully above the horizon. She wasn't a VLCC, but she wasn't small either. She was riding low in the water; full of crude oil that China's economy lusted for. Ma frowned as he looked the ship over, there was a lot of rust on the tanker's hull. *She could use a little attention,* he thought critically.

Suddenly, a sharp glint caught his attention, a bright flash from the sea surface. It was from something between him and the tanker. Searching the area carefully, he soon found a small wake trailing behind a tiny fuzzy object—a periscope! It had to be from a foreign submarine; no Chinese subs were authorized to be in this area. And judging by the flash of sunlight off the periscope head, this submarine had an inexperienced commander.

"Submarine off the starboard bow! Sound Combat Alert!"

The loud ringing of the alarm galvanized the crew into action. Men ran to their positions on the bridge while Ma kept his eyes firmly on the submarine's periscope, one arm pointing toward the spot. The intruder was clearly moving into position to attack the tanker. He had to stop it!

"Activate the sonar, sector search centered on bearing one one five! Signalmen, tell that tanker to alter course to starboard! Inform fleet headquarters we are attacking! Provide our location!" barked Ma.

"Captain! Sonar contact bearing one one six degrees, range four point three kilometers," shouted the OOD.

"Very well. Stay on this course. Helmsman, ring up ahead full. Prepare anti-submarine rocket launchers for firing."

Ma watched as the wake faded and then disappeared. "She's going deep!" he cried.

Fear for the tanker gripped the frigate captain. They were still too far away to attack with the rockets; they'd need at least another three minutes before they were close enough. The submarine would certainly shoot long before then. He needed to do something now, or that tanker was doomed, but what? *Sanming* wasn't equipped with ASW torpedoes, and her helicopter would never be able to take off in time.

"Fire ASW rockets!" Ma shouted in desperation.

The OOD looked up, surprised. "But sir, we aren't in range yet."

"I know that, damn it! Fire anyway!" roared Ma. He could only hope that the submarine's inexperienced captain was a little gun-shy and would choose to evade rather than press home the attack.

From the ship's bow, the two six-tubed launchers started spewing rockets at regular intervals. Arcing gracefully in the air, they pitched over and struck the water in a preset oval pattern a little over a kilometer ahead. Acrid smoke billowed around the bridge until the wind of the ship's passage swept it away. Seconds later, the water boiled as the twelve depth bombs exploded. As the smoke cleared, Ma could see his crew busily reloading the launchers.

"Captain," sang out the bridge phone talker, "sonar reports they are being jammed. Last good bearing to the submarine was one one nine, range two point five kilometers."

Ma swore but nodded. The submarine had dropped a noisemaker. He'd expected this, but it still made his job considerably harder. Running back into the bridge, he stopped at the plotting table and looked at the sub's reported positions. She had been drawing right, it was reasonable for a submarine to change course after deploying countermeasures, but her commander would also want to disengage. After a moment of assessing, he acted. "Helmsman, come right to course one two five."

"Captain!" shouted the phone talker. "Sonar reports multiple passive contacts clearing the jamming zone! Moving at high speed, drawing left, bearing zero nine eight!"

Ma hung his head in despair—torpedoes! He bolted for the port bridge wing, and raised his binoculars. He didn't have to wait long. Less than a minute later, a huge column of water formed under the tanker's bow. A second weapon detonated just a little aft of the first. The bow, torn free from the rest of the ship, was pushed under by the force of the tanker's momentum. Giant geysers of black oil erupted from ruptured tanks. A third blast jumped out of the water farther aft, under the bridge. The damaged hull buckled from the explosive shock and the heavier aft section was literally wrenched free. Flames ignited around the stern of the tanker, sending a huge column of pitch-black smoke skyward. *Lian Xing Hu* was dead, murdered by the underwater assassin.

Seething, Ma screamed into the bridge, "Where is the submarine!? Find that bastard!"

"Sir, sonar reports an active contact bearing one two eight, range one point one kilometers," announced the phone talker.

Ma smiled. The enemy was right where he thought she'd be. And this time she was within range. "Fire ASW rockets!" he bellowed.

The bow of *Sanming* was once again covered with fire and smoke as the two launchers disgorged their contents. Ma watched with satisfaction as the bombs exploded, heaving the water up in a neat chain of white circles. He had just turned to head back into the bridge when he felt his body being lifted from the deck. Confused, he struggled to find his feet, but before they touched back down, the ship lunged again and Ma was slammed into one of the bridge wing frames. Dazed, his head wracked in pain, Ma attempted to stand, but his left hand slipped off the railing. He stopped to look at his hands, and after straining to get his eyes to focus, he saw they were covered in blood.

In the distance, he could hear someone shouting, "Mayday, Mayday . . ." Ma thought it sounded like the officer of the deck, but he wasn't sure. Finally fighting to his feet, the captain found it difficult to stand. The ship had a pronounced port list. Still confused, Ma looked aft. What he saw left him quivering. The ship had been torn in two, just forward of the stack. The aft portion was taking on water fast, as he could see huge bubbles of air around its shattered hull. With an almost perverse fixation, Ma stared as the aft section first went vertical, then plunged beneath the waves. He was still watching the swirls when the rest of the ship jerked to port. Between the dizziness and his slippery hands, Ma lost his grip and was thrown over the railing. He hit the water flat on his back, knocking the air out of him. The pain in his head was excruciating.

Ma fought his way back to the surface; his body in agony with each stroke. It seemed like an eternity before he finally cleared the water. Coughing and gasping, he grabbed a life preserver that was floating nearby. Safe for the moment, he struggled to turn in the water and see what was going on. As Ma turned around, he was just in time to see his beloved frigate roll over and come crashing down upon him.

3 September 2016
0225 Local Time
By Water
Halifax, Nova Scotia

Mac had fallen asleep at his desk for the third day in a row. He was barely semiconscious when he heard the electronic *ding* signifying the arrival of a new e-mail. Groaning, he began searching for his glasses with his right hand. They had to be somewhere on this desk. After failing to find them, he patted his head and discovered his glasses hanging precariously from his ears. Pulling them down over his eyes, Mac sat up straight to look at his screen. The sharp pains accompanying the crunches and pops were an unpleasant reminder that he was too old for this kind of thing.

As his eyes came into focus, he saw that he had received over two dozen e-mails since he had dozed off. But it was the subject line from a colleague at the Keelung Port Authority in Taiwan that grabbed his attention.

From: ShipKeeper
To: Mac
Subj: URGENT—More East China Sea Attacks

Things are heating up in the East China Sea, Mac. Another tanker was attacked, *Lian Xing Hu*'s EPIRB went active at 1412 Hotel time.

The ship was en route to the port of Shanghai with a cargo of crude oil. No voice communications could be established. Ship data as follows:

GRT: 43,153 tons
DWT: 75,500 tons
Length: 229 meters
Beam: 33 meters
Max Speed: 14.8 knots
Call Sign: BOGK

But it gets worse. At 1414 Hotel time the PLAN Jiangwei II class frigate *Sanming* (FF 524) issued a Mayday over Channel 16. The individual on the Chinese frigate was near panic and said the ship had been torpedoed while prosecuting a submarine that had just attacked a tanker. The posits for the two vessels put them very close to each other. Whoever is behind these attacks, they've just upped the ante. Nothing good will come of this. ☹

Mac had to read the e-mail twice, just to make sure it said what he thought it said. He then looked at his watch. The attacks were not even fifteen minutes old! The fact that the Chinese frigate used the international distress channel meant everyone and their brother would know about this attack soon. An attack on a warship was big, big news. He typed out a quick acknowledgement of the e-mail and promised to get back to him later. Fumbling for his cell phone, Mac chuckled with sadistic delight; *he* was going to wake Ms. Laird up this time. As he pulled up his speed-dial list, his eyes caught an earlier e-mail from a friend in the Philippines. He was a fisherman by trade, but he also had great sources of information that kept him clued in on anything going on in the Spratlys. Mac put the phone down and clicked on the e-mail.

From: Tag Fishrmn
To: Mac
Subj: Rumors are True

Regarding rumors of China invading islands in the Spratlys, it's true. Attached is a photo of Chinese landing craft from a friend at

Loaita Island—19 nm southeast of Thitu Island. Both of these islands are claimed by the Philippines, and are not part of this tanker
war—we don't have any subs. So why is China doing this? Please
post on your blog. Thanks man.

Opening the file, Mac saw a line of three air-cushion landing craft and
a Chinese Type 071 amphibious assault ship in the background. The image
was of poor quality, but it was clear enough for Mac to identify the vessels.
His heart began to pound. Tag was right, the Philippines couldn't possibly
be involved in the submarine campaign, and yet here was a photo of Chinese marines coming ashore on a Filipino-claimed island. *This war is getting
way out of hand*, he thought.

He grabbed his phone and hit Christine Laird's number. While her
phone rang, Mac pulled up his now all-consuming blog covering the tanker
attacks and changed the name from "Chinese Tanker Attacks" to "The
Great Pacific War of 2016." He had just finished when a very sleepy woman's voice answered.

"Hello?"

"Christine, it's Mac, and I have some very disturbing news."

# 12

# DECLARATION

4 September 2016
1210 Local Time
Shinjuku Gyoen
Tokyo, Japan

They'd bought *bento* lunch boxes and gone to the park to eat. Admiral Kubo still had business at the Maritime Staff Office, located nearby in the Shibuyun district, although these days he was spending most of his time in Yokosuka, at the fleet headquarters.

In earlier days, the Shinjuku Gyoen had been the private estate of a noble family, later taken over by the Imperial house. It was now administered as a national park. Similar to Central Park in New York, it was the largest green space in the Tokyo metroplex, a natural world set among the steel and concrete sprawl.

They'd picked the English formal garden, along with what seemed like most of Tokyo, salarymen and office ladies enjoying a break from the muggy summer heat. Kubo and Komamura had both dressed casually, in slacks and open-collared shirts, as if they'd spent the morning at the links.

Kubo had arranged the meeting, with information to share and questions to ask. Komamura was more than willing to meet with someone he now thought of as a close friend. The admiral had started by asking Komamura for details on China's oil status, and the professor was pleased with the questions he asked. It was clear those "udon economics lessons" had not been wasted. His answer was no different than the one he'd given Hisagi a few days ago—the Chinese were not going to buckle this week.

Then it had been Komamura's turn to be the pupil. Kubo actually looked left and right, as if checking for eavesdroppers. "Last night, *Kenryu* reported being attacked as she approached a tanker."

Komamura's alarm was clear in his expression. "She must have survived, or she would not have been able to report. But how did the Chinese find her?"

"We don't think it was a Chinese submarine. Captain Zaraki had a good solution on his target and was just outside firing range. He'd just opened his outer tube doors when a powerful active sonar pulse struck his submarine. It was so strong that it was audible inside the pressure hull."

"That meant he was close by," Komamura offered. "But you said that submarines rarely use their active sonars."

"That's right," Kubo agreed, "but one of the few times it might be used is if the attacker is not sure of his fire control solution. Then he would send a 'ranging pulse' to confirm a target's position just before firing. If you're about to shoot, revealing yourself with active sonar is not as important."

"And was he fired on?" Komamura asked.

"Zaraki didn't wait to find out. He deployed a noisemaker and maneuvered violently to evade any possible torpedo. He heard nothing on passive sonar, either from a torpedo or another submarine. Since our standing orders are to avoid any warship capable of detecting a submarine, and he'd depleted his battery avoiding the unknown submarine, he abandoned his attack on the tanker and reported to us."

"And there was no further sign of the other sub."

"The attack came from almost the same bearing as the tanker. It may be that the submarine was masking its own noise with the tanker's."

"Isn't that hazardous for the sub, staying that close to another ship?"

Kubo nodded. Finishing his meal, the admiral tucked his chopsticks into the box and replaced the lid. "Zaraki transmitted his recordings of the sonar pulse to us, along with his request to be immediately relieved from command."

"Because he allowed himself to be detected by another submarine, who may have recorded his acoustic signal and thus revealed our identity to the Chinese." Komamura was sympathetic. "I can understand his distress."

"Zaraki is very dedicated. He certainly was detected, although we are not going to relieve him. In this case, we don't have to worry about our identity being compromised, because our analysts have identified the signal as coming from an American BQQ-5 sonar."

"An American?" Komamura was surprised, which grew to shock as he considered the implications. "So not an attack. But then what?" It was distressing enough to discover an American submarine in the area, and near one of China's vessels, but interfering in *Kenryu*'s attack?

"We were hoping your wisdom could give us some insights, *sensei*."

"Please don't use that word," Komamura protested. "My wisdom hasn't gained us much, and has set us all on a dangerous path."

"Please," Kubo persisted. "You are not so close to the problem. I have a theory, which my staff disagrees with, and I need another viewpoint."

Komamura closed his own lunch box, long since finished, took the admiral's, and threw them into the trashcan next to the bench. He stood, and the two men began strolling along the paths that twisted through the park. Ahead and behind, the security men who had watched them eat stood and walked as well.

Komamura sighed, working through the news as it followed its own path in his mind. Having heard about this just a moment ago, he needed to grasp all the implications. Finally, he replied, "An American submarine prevents a Japanese submarine from attacking a Chinese tanker. Has the world gone mad?"

"One fool on my staff suggested that Americans defending Chinese ships meant they had formed an alliance."

Komamura stated flatly, "No. That gains the Americans nothing. I believe this is their response to us not properly answering their diplomatic note. The timing of the incident is consistent with this hypothesis."

"Defending Chinese ships?" Kubo asked. "What does that accomplish?"

"Not defending them so much as frustrating us. It shows that they can't be ignored, that they are involved whether we want them to be or not. Which was always true," added Komamura.

"But it was your recommendation to not give an answer," Kubo protested.

"And it still is. We don't want the Americans joining the fight."

Kubo said, "Eventually, the Chinese will have proof they can take to the world, and they will bring the war to our countries. When that happens, we might welcome the Americans' help."

"Both the Americans and Chinese have nuclear weapons. If the

Americans were to become directly involved, and the course of the war favors us, as China faces defeat, she will become desperate. She could demonstrate her resolve to use nuclear weapons without actually striking the American homeland by using one of us as a target."

The admiral paused for half a beat, before continuing to walk. "I had not considered that."

"It is my nightmare," admitted Komamura. "Our goal is to inflict crippling economic damage on China before they have a chance to strike back effectively. We must focus on that task, and continue moving forward."

"So will the Americans continue interfering?" Kubo asked.

"It's likely. Only experience can tell what effect they will have on Chinese losses. Have you decided what our subs will do if they detect an American submarine?"

"That's easy. Definitely *not* fire at it," the admiral replied. "That will be my recommendation to the working group. That, and send out more submarines to compensate for American interference."

Komamura asked, "Have you made a recommendation about what we should do when China calls out the alliance openly?"

"Those plans are ongoing, but yes, a plan is in place."

"Then please tell the working group my recommendation is that we continue as before."

4 September 2016
1600 Local Time
PLAN Frigate *Yancheng*, Hull 546
Yellow Sea, South of Qingdao, China

*Yancheng* was only four years old, and Jiang Wu was only her second captain. She was sleek and clean in her light gray paint, with an angled superstructure designed to reduce her chance of being detected by hostile radars. She was armed with first-line missile systems to engage surface and air targets. But more to the point, she carried a helicopter and a towed array. The Type 054A frigates were the most capable anti-submarine platform in the PLAN.

Looming dangerously close, the tanker's aft deckhouse blocked Jiang's view forward and to starboard. Following the guidance of the experts at North Sea Fleet headquarters, Commander Jiang had tucked *Yancheng* in tight against the tanker's stern.

Motor vessel *Da Qing 435* was laid out like most tankers, with a long, low hull, a slightly higher bow, and a deckhouse at the stern, housing the propulsion plant, the crew's quarters, and the bridge, all clustered in a single high superstructure. Hopefully, a submarine on a periscope approach wouldn't notice the smaller frigate behind the deckhouse's bulk. More important, the noise of the frigate's engines should be hidden by the tanker. The Type 054As, designed with sub-hunting as one of their missions, had a quieter acoustic signature to begin with, while the tanker's diesels sounded like a New Year's celebration.

Thanks to the tanker's noise, the frigate's bow sonar was nearly useless, but the passive towed sonar array, streamed two kilometers astern, was working well. It was more sensitive than the bow sonar, and while the forward-looking beams would be filled with the tanker's noise, the other beams that looked past the tanker were unaffected. That would give them their first warning.

Ever since rendezvousing with *Da Qing 435* two days ago, Jiang had lived either on the starboard bridge wing or in the sonar cabin. The two ships had followed the shipping lanes along the China coast, first east, then curving north. Plodding at twelve knots, the tanker's best speed, it would take another day to reach Dalian harbor and the oil piers.

He was sure Captain Xin was counting the minutes. He'd had no choice, indeed no notice, about being used as bait for the mystery submarines. Jiang's frigate had simply shown up and taken station near the tanker's stern.

It had been a tense, but boring two days. Three hundred meters between the two vessels sounded like a lot until you thought in terms of ship lengths. Jiang wasn't worried about his *Yancheng*. She was a gazelle compared to that hippopotamus of a tanker, but if the tanker maneuvered without warning, his smaller ship would suffer the most. Although only a third longer than his frigate, the tanker was exactly twice his beam and eight times his displacement. Apart from the damage a collision might cause, and the failure of his mission, he'd have to shoot himself from the sheer embarrassment of it.

The winds were offshore, from the east, and the seas were relatively mild, just sea state three. Environmental noise, caused by wave slap and even breakers on the shoreline, mixed with the sounds made by fish and other sea life and the noise of engines from other ships nearby. This was called "ambient noise," and the whisper of a submarine's approach had to be picked out of this cluttered background.

Theoretically, the submarine had a similar problem, but the tanker's engines were much noisier, plus the sub knew where to look. Jiang had worked it out several times. There was an even chance that their first warning of an attack on the tanker would be the sound of torpedoes in the water. That was why his two pilots had slept in the helicopter for the past two days, allowed out of the cockpit only for the demands of nature. *Yancheng*'s helicopter stood ready, fueled and armed.

Jiang had reviewed all the possibilities, drilled his crew, studied what little intelligence the navy had, and now could only wait.

It came while he was visiting the sonar cabin. The operator reported, "Contact, bearing zero four zero." The "waterfall" display screen showed the towed array's entire frequency range, left to right. Sounds at different frequencies showed up as bright lines along the top edge of the screen. Technically, there were two possible bearings, 040 and 340 degrees, but the second bearing pointed toward the nearby shore, so the valid bearing was obvious.

A moment later, the sonar took another sample of the incoming sound, and then another. Each sample extended the line, pushing the earlier sample down the screen. This created a "waterfall" effect. Random noise that appeared and faded quickly showed up as faint dots or misshapen blobs, but a constant sound showed up as a line, marching down the display.

It could still be a "biologic," a school of mackerel warning of a predator, for instance. But man-made mechanical sounds tended to be narrow, sharp lines, while natural sounds were broad, even fuzzy. That's why sonar operators went to school. Jiang had gone to the same school as his sonar operators, and then done another six months of theoretical work on top of that.

The operator listened carefully to the sound, as well as watching the distribution of acoustic energy on the computer display. He needed both senses to solve this problem. Classifying a contact was a slow, exacting process. They'd had dozens of false contacts that afternoon, each one analyzed and examined until it could be confirmed as "not a submarine." This time, the operator was taking longer, and Jiang fought the urge to grab a second set of headphones. He could see the screen, and the line was narrow and very bright.

The rating looked up at his captain and nodded confidently. "It's not natural."

That was all Jiang needed to hear. He picked up the handset for the intership phone system and ordered, "Launch the helicopter and send it northeast. We'll give them a precise steer once they're in the air." With that urgent task done, he ordered, "Put the crew at combat alert against submarines. Add that it is not a drill." He'd run the crew ragged practicing, and he didn't want anyone making foolish assumptions.

The sonar techs ignored the alarm klaxon and the bustle behind them as more people came into the space. As soon as Jiang hung up the phone, the tracking operator reported, "He's tracking right, with a fast bearing drift. He's close."

Which meant he was close to firing. Jiang had no illusions. Any modern submarine's sonar was going to be better than his equipment. If he could hear the sub, it was nearby. His only advantage was surprise.

Jiang ordered sharply, "Check the datalink."

The tracking operator reported, "The link is up. We are sending."

Jiang smiled approvingly. He picked up the phone again. "Warn the tanker, 'Sub off your starboard bow, prepare—'"

"Torpedoes in the water, Captain!" Jiang could see the weapons appear on the display, three bright strong lines.

" —belay that, tell him to turn *now* to . . . one zero zero, and warn our helmsman to watch for his stern!" Jiang had taken the time earlier to brief Captain Xin on torpedo evasion.

*Yancheng* had to steer a straight course, unfortunately. If she turned, the towed array streaming behind her would kink at the point where she turned, and be useless until it stabilized. He couldn't afford to lose his primary search sensor for even a few moments, much less several minutes. Luckily, his ship wasn't the target.

A rating stood at the door. "Helicopter is airborne."

Good, things were happening fast, as they had drilled. Jiang acknowledged the report, then instructed the sonar team, "Watch for the sub's signal to separate from the torpedoes. He's not expecting an escort, so he won't try to clear his firing point as quickly." The operators nodded their understanding, already deep into the search.

Jiang stepped from the sonar cabin into the command center, now fully manned at combat alert. He found the helicopter controller, one of his junior officers, hunched over his display screen. "We don't have a range yet. Run him straight down the towed array's bearing and have him search at five kilometers." Certainly the sub had been at least that far away when he fired. The controller acknowledged the order and began guiding the aircraft.

Jiang noted the time. Forty-five seconds since the torpedoes had been launched. It was unfortunate, but one useful piece of information would be the time it took for the weapons to strike their target. Most torpedoes cruised at roughly forty knots, or just over one kilometer a minute. The time of their detonation would give him a rough idea of how far away the sub was when it fired.

With the rest of his men, Jiang watched the time fall away, seconds passing as distinct moments. He glanced at the navigational radar. "Is the tanker turning yet?"

The phone talker passed the question forward to the bridge. "They've just started," he replied.

Jiang shook his head. "Too late, far too late." The trick was to be somewhere else when the torpedoes' own sonars activated. If there was nothing in front of them, the weapons would have to circle and search, which dramatically reduced the chance of a hit. And while they circled, the target moved in the general direction of away. But the tanker, like all tankers, turned like a cement truck.

Running back up to the bridge, Jiang arrived to see the distance between the two ships growing slowly. Another reason for the turn was to get some separation from the torpedoes' intended target. He didn't want to be nearby, and in nautical terms, that was measured in miles.

He didn't get miles. Luckily, *Da Qing 435*'s new course took her almost directly away from the frigate, but she was still a little less than a mile away when the vessel seemed to shake, as if she'd struck a submerged object. The water around her hull churned to a milky froth, then erupted in a white tower. It all happened silently, until the sound reached him a few seconds later, first as a deep rumble, then an explosive roar that staggered him and rattled the frigate's hull.

The perfect geometry of the column was destroyed a moment later, when the second torpedo detonated. The force of the first explosion, just a little aft of amidships, had actually pushed the massive tanker up out of the water by a meter. Jiang could clearly see a band of red showing below the ship's normal waterline. Now the second explosion, just a little forward of the first, pushed the tanker's bow up even farther, so that the bow stem actually cleared the water for a moment.

Amidships, the ruin created by the two weapons extended well up from the waterline, and the ship began to sag in the middle, like a swayback horse. Thick coils of black smoke were starting to appear, and through binoculars he could see the crew struggling across the tilting deck to reach the lifeboats.

His first impulse, from years of training, was to get his own boats in the water and go to their aid, but he checked the thought almost immediately. He would have to stop to lower any boats, which would not only disrupt his towed sonar, but would also make him a sitting duck if the submarine chose to attack. First things first.

Jiang stepped back into the command center, checking his watch. Just over four minutes. Call it four and a half kilometers. Pleased with his close guess, he started to talk to the helicopter controller, when sonar announced, "The third weapon has missed the tanker. It passed underneath without detonating."

So the turn had made a difference, just not enough. "Fine," Jiang acknowledged, "keep tracking it, but don't stop looking for the submarine."

"Understood, sir." The sonar rating turned to go back in the sonar compartment when a shout came out of the open door. "The third torpedo! The bearing drift is changing! It's turning!"

Jiang felt ice form in his chest, but he quickly told the controller, "Keep working with the helicopter," then turned and hurried toward the sonar space. The door was open, and he called, "Which way?" before he'd even stepped inside.

The answer, in a relieved tone, was, "Starboard, away from us!" and Jiang could breathe again.

Many torpedoes had "wire guidance," thin wires that actually spooled out as the torpedo left the submarine. Miles long, the wire allowed the sub to see what the torpedo's own seeker saw, and the launching sub could also steer the torpedo if the target maneuvered radically. In this case, the submarine captain knew the third weapon had missed, and was turning it back toward the tanker. Miles away and underwater, he didn't know that the merchant ship was finished.

"Where's the sub now?" Jiang demanded.

"Heading south, Captain, and speed has increased to eight knots."

Jiang smiled. "Good, keep feeding those bearings to the helicopter—"

The other sonar operator, tracking the weapon, reported, "Sir, it's still turning. It's gone past an intercept course for the tanker, and is turning toward us!"

The guidance wire can break. If that happens, the torpedo automatically circles and searches on its own. But Jiang quickly discarded the idea. He couldn't take the chance.

He picked up the handset again. "Bridge, increase speed to flank, turn us to starboard, and pass as close as we can to the sinking tanker!"

"Sir, the towed array . . ."

"Forget that! Do it now!"

Jiang didn't wait for an acknowledgement, but hung up the phone, and hurried out of the sonar cabin, through the combat center, and onto the bridge. The sinking tanker, with black smoke pouring out of the hull, was swinging across his field of view as the deck officer turned the frigate hard to starboard. The deck, tilting with the sharp turn, vibrated as the screws tried to push the hull faster and faster.

"Steady us on . . . one one five," Jiang ordered after taking a bearing, and the deck officer acknowledged with a worried look. Jiang knew his bridge watchstanders would be too cautious and pass too far away from the hulk. They'd hidden behind the tanker before, now perhaps the dying ship could absorb the torpedo meant for his frigate. The tanker would appear as a much larger target to the weapon.

"Sonar, what's the torpedo doing?" he demanded.

"We've lost it on the towed array, but our bow sonar still sees it, sir. It's headed straight for us. Very strong signal."

He'd guessed right, then. Jiang stepped out onto the port bridge wing. The burning hulk loomed fine on the port bow, and Jiang tried to judge if he could steer closer. *Yancheng* was responding wonderfully, speed building from twelve knots, and was already past twenty-two. It was much more responsive than any tanker, but it still took some time for 3,800 tons of steel to accelerate. They had to close the distance between . . .

The deck officer put down the intership phone. "Captain, sonar reports the torpedo's seeker has activated, and the weapon's speed has increased!"

"Hard left rudder! New course back toward the weapon!" Jiang sighed. He'd lost the race. At attack speed, the torpedo would swim at forty-five knots or more. Their only hope now was a sharp turn inside the weapon's arc.

*Yancheng* was continuing to accelerate, and the bow swung sharply to port, putting the tanker on the other side now. A cold wind cut at his face and tugged his clothes. He stepped back into the bridge and studied the plot, watching the angles. He ordered the deck officer, "Tell all hands to brace for impact!"

4 September 2016
1830 Local Time
Shinkansen Control Center, Kansai Region
Japan

The Japanese "bullet train" system is one of the most efficient and fastest in the world. With speeds close to two hundred miles per hour, trains operate on dedicated rail lines, separated from slower-moving freight and local trains. First operating in the early 1960s, the ever-expanding network has dramatically shortened travel times across the mountainous country, revolutionizing transportation and commerce in Japan.

Obata Takeshi had the duty at the Kansai control center when the trouble began. The three large flat-screen displays didn't give any indication, and none of the communications staff had reported any problems.

The central display showed the Kansai region, his responsibility, in the south central part of Japan's main island of Honshu. Heavily urbanized and populated, it holds Kyoto, Osaka, and many other major Japanese cities. The electronic map showed not only the cities and the rail lines, but could display local traffic, emergencies like fires, and even precipitation levels.

The position of each bullet train was updated constantly, using transmitters on the trains and sensors placed along the track. The Osaka–Tokyo line, one of the major runs in the system, could have as many as a dozen trains an hour in each direction, neatly separated by five-minute intervals.

The phone at the control desk connected to the first responders rang, and Obata grabbed it quickly. Nothing showed on the board, but it could be a drill, or a warning. "Obata, Kansai Control."

"This is Battalion Chief Kawaguchi at the Fushima station. We're rolling everything we've got. Who is the on-scene commander?" The firefighter's tone was urgent, but professional.

"What?" Obata's astonished question was loud enough to attract the attention of others in the center, and he punched a button that put the conversation on the loudspeaker. In the background, they could hear sirens and the roar of diesel engines.

"Who is in charge at the scene, dammit? We're losing time. Can't you people follow your own procedures? It's bad enough we had to hear about this from civilians who saw the accident. I need to know if I should sound another alarm. Two—no, three trains, what is that? It's over a thousand passengers per train."

"Battalion Chief, I'm not showing any problems on any of the lines." Obata's confusion was obvious.

Kawaguchi replied quickly, "Your board is wrong. We've gotten dozens of mobile phone calls about trains colliding about five kilometers west of Shin-Osaka Station. At first, it was just two trains, but we're getting word of a third train that's plowed into the mess. And you don't show any of this?" The firefighter's question, shouted a little to be heard over the sirens, ran through Obata like an electric charge. The rest of the staff had the same reaction, and began furiously checking their systems.

Obata, thinking in terms of time and distance, shouted, "Emergency stop all trains to Shin-Osaka now! Call them on the secondary circuits!" Dozens of questions leapt into his mind, and he fought to control them. Did the trains' conductors see what he saw here? If what Kawaguchi said was true, then the third train might be followed by a fourth, and others unless they could be warned off. "Don't depend on the readouts! Get voice confirmation."

"Can you tell me anything?" the firefighter demanded.

"Chief, you will have to be the on-scene commander, because I have no information here." Hand shaking, Obata hung up the phone. His mind filled with images of cars full of people already dead if they didn't get them stopped in time.

He turned to his deputy, Moritaka. The man's face was as pale as the moon. "Take over. Call the regional director. Assume a major disaster, and a major communications failure. Get people busy finding out what's wrong. I'm going to the scene to find out what's happening. It should be only a few kilometers from here. I'll report when I know something."

4 September 2016
0600 Eastern Daylight Time
CNN Headline News

The anchor looked hurried, and although he spoke quickly, he kept his tone even and professional. "Good morning. Welcome to CNN's continuing coverage of the crisis in the Pacific. We begin with the stunning announcement by the Chinese government that they have proof of Japanese involvement in the covert submarine campaign against their merchant tankers."

As he spoke, images appeared on the screen and were replaced by new ones: maps, a burning tanker, a warship, and a submarine. "The Chinese have released an audio recording of a submarine attack on a merchant ship and escorting warship. Although both vessels were sunk, the acoustic signature was transmitted by computer datalink back to shore, which allowed it to be analyzed and classified as a Japanese *Soryu*-class submarine.

"The Chinese have posted the audio file on the Net, and several navies are examining the file, not only to confirm the Chinese accusation, but for evidence of tampering or falsification.

"The Chinese have also accused Vietnamese submarines of taking part, and have demanded both nations immediately cease attacks and agree to reparations, or face 'the gravest consequences.' The Chinese have also frozen all Vietnamese and Japanese funds in Chinese banks, and forbidden the trading of the yen."

New scenes appeared, of a Chinese embassy guarded by Japanese police, almost surrounding the building, then a crowded airport full of worried travelers. "Chinese embassies in both countries are closed, diplomatic personnel are preparing to leave, and Chinese nationals have been instructed to leave immediately. The same situation applies to Vietnamese and Japanese nationals in China, which includes tens of thousands of tourists.

"Beyond these public announcements, reports and rumors of attacks are popping up over the entire region.

"Early yesterday, Philippine sources reported Chinese ships and aircraft operating near their possessions in the Spratly Islands, followed shortly by a total loss of mobile phone and radio contact. Ownership of the Spratlys is disputed by China, Vietnam, Taiwan, the Philippines, and other nations. Sources online have confirmed the presence of Chinese naval vessels, and probably Chinese troops there.

"The Vietnamese government has reported scores of aircraft attacks along its border with China, and ballistic missiles falling in both Hanoi and Haiphong, with deadly results. The government has ordered the entire country 'mobilized to repel the Chinese invader.' The Vietnamese claim to have shot down almost a dozen aircraft in the initial wave of attacks.

"And this footage was just received." A tangled complex of pipes and storage tanks appeared, billowing with black smoke and surrounded by emergency vehicles. "This is Sinopec's Guangzhou Branch refinery in Guangdong province. Witnesses reported seeing cruise missiles striking the facility, triggering massive explosions and fires, with heavy loss of life."

The anchor paused, as if to draw a breath before continuing. "On any other day, this disaster would be the lead story. Hundreds of people have died in the first-ever fatal accident of the Shinkansen, the Japanese 'bullet train.' One train, at full speed, collided with another train inexplicably stopped in front of it. Before word of the accident reached the controllers, a third train slammed into the other two."

The footage showed rescue workers in helmets and brightly colored vests moving amid tangled wreckage. It wasn't recognizable as a train wreck until the view changed to a longer shot, showing the tracks and parts of the train still on track. Then the image shifted to show a Shinto priest praying in front of dozens of white-draped bodies. "Hospitals in the area have been flooded with casualties, and the total count of the dead and wounded rises by the hour."

## White House Situation Room
## Washington, D.C.

Kirkpatrick switched off the set. "That's a good summary of what the rest of the world has to work with."

Patterson, General Nagy, and Admiral Hughes all nodded. Nagy, the vice chairman of the JCS, asked, "Have we confirmed that the Japanese disaster was a cyber attack?" He was asking Kirkpatrick, but also looked at Dr. Foster, head of the CIA.

Foster answered, "Yes. The Japanese and our people came to the same conclusion. The control system was hacked. First it sent an 'obstacle' message to just one train, causing it to stop, but only that train. It then took over the communications network, suppressed all the real-time data, and replaced it with synthetic information. The controllers never saw any problems because they were looking at an animation."

Patterson asked, "And the Chinese were behind it?"

"It's likely," Foster said. "Electrons usually don't leave fingerprints, but we traced the hack back to a location associated with past operations run by the Chinese. Whoever did it had to be real good, because the Japanese network protections were top-rate."

Kirkpatrick added, "We'll see more of that in Japan now. They're a U.S. ally, so the Chinese are pushing first covertly, to see if they can make Tokyo say uncle. We don't have the details yet, but we think the Chinese are going to make some sort of move that will devalue the Japanese yen."

General Nagy observed, "They don't have that problem with Vietnam. That news report is the tip of the iceberg. The Chinese haven't committed any ground troops yet; it looks like they're taking a page from Desert Storm and pummeling the Vietnamese from the air for a while before they invade."

Patterson asked, "How long before the Chinese cross the border?"

The general shrugged. "Soon, but they'll want to make sure they have an overwhelming force before they attack. The Vietnamese are unlikely to cave in easily; they fought the Chinese before, back in 1979 and gave them a whuppin'. But in the meantime, the Chinese are inflicting a lot of damage with only moderate losses. That release from Hanoi didn't mention that the Vietnamese have lost a lot of their own fighters trying to stop the Chinese raids."

"And you were right, General." Kirkpatrick smiled. "Dumb grunts can be pretty smart. EP-3 intercepts and satellite images show Chinese troops and ships all over the South China Sea, seizing islands and reefs that have been disputed territory. They're concentrating on ones with airfields, so this is only wave one. Intel has been backtracking the movements of Chinese units, now that we know where to look, and they've been prepping for months."

"And the Vietnamese mined the carrier to disrupt the operation," Patterson concluded.

"Except it didn't," Kirkpatrick explained. "Beijing pressed on. But now that we know who started the ball rolling, the president can get to work. He will see the Chinese ambassador later today. And in the meantime, the State Department is advising U.S. citizens to get out of China and all the countries bordering it—basically, most of Asia. Who knows where trouble is going to pop up next?"

# 13

# REVELATION

5 September 2016
0830 Local Time
Tokyo University, Waseda Campus
Hongo, Bunkyo Ward, Tokyo

Komamura stared at his computer screen with a mixture of apprehension and dismay; his right hand shook as he reached for his cup of tea. The professor had once again locked his office door before calling up the CNN news feed, a precaution that was becoming all too common these days. He didn't want someone barging in on him while he watched the press conference. He had little confidence he would be able to hide his emotions. The Littoral Alliance was going public.

The debate the night before had been long, intense, and at times, heated. Komamura had argued vociferously that anonymity was still a useful weapon in the alliance's arsenal. As long as the Chinese were uncertain as to whom they faced, their actions were constrained. Once the veil of doubt was removed, the Chinese leadership would be free to escalate the conflict—undoubtedly resulting in more casualties among the civilian populations. Many of the military participants argued that revealing the alliance's members, as well as the current war, would allow them to invoke civil defense measures that would preclude another disaster such as the Sanyo Shinkansen train wreck.

The elderly academic had shivered when General Ijuin, the chief of staff of Japan's Self-Defense Forces, mentioned the multiple train crash just outside of Shin-Osaka Station. At the height of the evening commute, the two sixteen-car trains and the one eight-car train carried over 3,200 people. The death toll was now just over 2,700, and expected to rise, as the vast majority of the survivors were in critical condition. Only a fortunate few had limped away from the scene.

Having ridden Japan's bullet train system often, Komamura had trouble banishing images of the carnage that would be created when one train traveling at three hundred kilometers per hour slammed into another. The preliminary accident report showed no indication of a mechanical failure. The black boxes had been recovered quickly and the data showed all three trains were functioning normally, with the exception of the automatic train control system input. The Nozomi train recorded a track-obstruction warning signal that caused it to come to a stop; the other two trains not only didn't show the same warning signal, they weren't alerted that they were getting perilously close to another train.

The only possible conclusion for this highly improbable failure was deliberate sabotage. This meant someone had to hack their way into the Shinkansen's control network and alter the signals sent to the three trains. That the incident occurred almost simultaneously with the PRC's press release alleging Japan's involvement with the tanker war all but proved Chinese culpability for the cyber attack. Indian cyber warfare specialists agreed.

As costly as the Shinkansen cyber attack was, Komamura had stressed that once the alliance membership was announced to the world, the cork in the nuclear genie's bottle would be removed. Identifying India as an alliance member could potentially have the same negative effect that inviting the Americans would have. India was a nuclear power, and a desperate China could send a "message" to the alliance by using a single nuclear weapon on one of the nonnuclear members. Given the lingering psychological scar from World War II, that made Japan the most likely target. Komamura understood this scarring all too well. His mother had died of radiation-induced cancer two decades after the Nagasaki bombing.

"Dr. Komamura," replied Vu Kim Binh, Vietnam's minister of foreign affairs, politely, "while I appreciate your concerns, I believe you are being overly cautious. All three superpowers have lost wars without resorting to nuclear weapons to ensure victory: the U.S. and China with my country, and the Soviet Union with Afghanistan."

"Yes, Minister, you are correct, sir. But this conflict is fundamentally different from the ones you just mentioned," countered Komamura. "In those conflicts, the superpowers were never threatened at a national level. Their pride was damaged, but not their homeland. We have intentionally targeted China's economy. We *want* to cause national harm, to rein in their aggressive behavior. The current conflict is on a far greater scale, which comes with far greater risk."

"Which is why we must conclude this campaign as soon as possible, Professor. And to do that, we must increase our pressure on the Chinese. This alone requires that the war, and the reason behind it, be made known to our countrymen," interjected Japan's foreign minister, Tadashi Hata.

"I agree with you, Minister Tadashi," echoed India's foreign secretary, Kanwal Nehru, over the VTC speakers. "And in that regard, the Republic of India is prepared to enforce a total blockade of the Strait of Malacca and Lombok Strait. This will shut the PRC off from its primary oil suppliers in the Middle East and Africa. It will also extend the blockade to their bulk cargo carriers, denying them the raw materials for their factories."

"Gentlemen, I am encouraged by your devotion to our common cause," Vu said with noticeable emotion. "My country has borne the brunt of the PRC's aggression and we have suffered considerable losses. Our sympathy goes out to our Japanese ally, but such losses will only continue to rise if we do not take bold steps to increase China's pain."

"Minister Vu," interrupted General Ijuin, "have you been able to confirm the rumors that the Chinese have implemented their original invasion plan in the Spratly Islands?"

"Yes, General. Even though we ordered our spy to make good his escape, he bravely sent us another report before doing so. He provided a copy of the revised timeline as well as the order for the PLA Navy to begin the amphibious invasions of numerous islands across the entire breadth of the Spratly archipelago. Not surprisingly, their initial targets were those islands with airfields.

"Based on sparse reports, both Thitu and Itu Aba Islands fell almost immediately. The Vietnamese garrison at Dao Truong Sa, excuse me, Spratly Island, is giving the Chinese a good fight, but I regret to report they too will soon fall."

"Can anything be done to lend them assistance?" asked the Japanese general. Concern filled his voice.

Vu's expression was resigned as he shrugged. "We've sent a naval squadron to engage the Chinese invaders, but even if they are successful in stopping their amphibious operations, I fear our navy will be horribly mauled in the process."

An ominous silence fell upon the group. The arguments had been made; there was nothing further to say. Several sharp wooden raps shattered the silence. Tadashi lowered the gavel onto the sound block. "If there is nothing more to discuss, I recommend that we put the motion of declaring the Littoral Alliance's existence to a vote."

Komamura watched in silence as the vote was three to one in favor of revealing the alliance to the world. Only South Korea voted against, concerned that the PRC would turn the North's army, effectively a mercenary force, south. Foreign Minister Tadashi assigned one of his adjutants to arrange the press conference for the next morning.

It was early in the morning when Komamura finally returned to his Tokyo apartment. He collapsed into the recliner, loosened his tie, and took a long drink of sake, emptying the cup. He refilled it, and without thinking picked up the TV remote. The flat screen flashed to life and immediately showed news coverage of the train wreck. Komamura gasped as the screen was filled with dozens of first responders carrying body bags toward a line of waiting military trucks. The camera zoomed in on one of the trucks, showing the thick black bags stacked up inside the bed like cordwood. Shaking, the elderly professor quickly turned the TV off, and drank in the dark.


"Good morning. The purpose of this press conference is to inform the world about the secret war our four nations have been fighting with the People's Republic of China, and alert them to the threat our enemy poses to all of us." Foreign Minister Tadashi's introduction wrenched Komamura from his drowsiness. Sitting up straight in his chair, he leaned forward as Japan's leading diplomat continued with his formal announcement.

"I know many are asking, 'Why would they do such a thing?' The short answer is that we had exhausted all other options, other than surrender. China has grown more assertive over the preceding two decades, as their economy and technology base expanded at a fantastic rate, but within the last few years that assertiveness has taken a militaristic path.

"The People's Republic of China has *demanded* we cede to them some of our territory, they've interfered with the exploitation of the natural resources in those territories, arrested our fishermen for fishing in our waters, and threatened our nations with dire consequences if we did not comply. They've used extortion on one of our members; pay or we'll no longer be able to hold our allies to the north in check. They've provided weapons to terrorist groups around the world, furthering the pain and anguish of the indigenous population for political and/or economic gain. Our countries have made diplomatic attempts to try and resolve the issues peacefully. But the answer was always the same, accept their demands and then there would be peace. The world has heard this story before."

Tadashi paused as he let his carefully tuned emotional appeal sink in. He had to reach the people of the Littoral Alliance countries, and, hopefully, the world.

"Recently, we discovered the Chinese planned to resolve the issue of sovereignty of disputed territories in the South China Sea through military conquest. What were we to do? Acquiesce and reward the Communist bully? Encourage him to become even bolder? This aggressive move is but the beginning of a carefully crafted campaign designed to also seize even more territory in the East China Sea and the Yellow Sea.

"Should we cower in fear and let China take what is not theirs to secure a short-lived peace? Or do we stand up for our democratic principles, our heritage, and our people? Given the choice, we *collectively* chose to stand against the bully, to defend our countries, to defend our people."

Komamura was impressed with Tadashi's oratory. He was pushing all the right ethnic, cultural, and political buttons designed to raise the righteous indignation of the Japanese people. His words would probably have a similar effect on the other alliance populations, and perhaps Western Europe. And while Tadashi's message would resonate with some in the United States and Russia, it wouldn't be sufficient for their governments to be convinced they needed to become directly involved.

Japan's foreign minister then expounded on the alliance's knowledge of the Chinese threat, explaining the chain of events in vague terms and linking them to the current amphibious operations in the South China Sea. This was in deference to Vietnam's request to not provide too much information that could jeopardize their spy's safety. Still, it was enough to show that the People's Republic of China had been planning a major military operation in September to seize control of most of the Spratly Islands. Tadashi wrapped up his portion of the press conference by reiterating that their only choices were a preemptive attack or surrender—and the alliance had chosen the former.

The Vietnamese and South Korean foreign ministers both spoke briefly, essentially adding their country's stamp of approval to Tadashi's statement. But it was the Indian ambassador, standing in for the foreign secretary, who dropped the final bombshell.

"Since the Littoral Alliance is at war with the People's Republic of China, we must, regretfully, declare that all shipping lanes in the South China Sea, the East China Sea, and the Yellow Sea are war zones. Any merchant ship sailing through those waters will be at risk. Any ship heading to a Chinese port will be attacked and sunk without warning. We will no longer confine our attacks only to tankers.

"Lastly, the Indian Navy will begin a total blockade of the Strait of Malacca and Lombok Strait effective immediately. Any ship attempting to pass through either strait will be boarded, their registry and cargo manifest examined. *Any* cargo bound for the People's Republic of China will be confiscated; vessels bound for other Far East destinations will have to take the long way around. If a ship refuses to heave to and be boarded, they will receive but one warning before shells are fired at the bridge."

4 September 2016
1950 Eastern Daylight Time
CNN Headline News

The transition from the press conference in Japan back to the New York studio took the anchorwoman by surprise. She hesitated for a moment, as she struggled to comprehend what the entire world had just heard, but recovered quickly as her producer waved feverishly behind the camera.

"That . . . that was astounding! We are witnessing history in the making! That was the representatives from the new Littoral Alliance formally declaring that a state of war exists between them and the People's Republic of China. This brings out into the open the hidden conflict that has been raging under the sea for nearly a week. And yet, our own Christine Laird has been able to keep on top of developments through the use of an unusual blog site. She joins us now to talk about this interesting Web site. Good evening, Christine."

"Good evening, Jackie."

"Christine, tell our viewers about this phenomenal Web site you've been using."

"Certainly, Jackie. The blog has undergone a number of name changes over the last two weeks and it is currently listed as 'The Great Pacific War of 2016.' I first came upon it when the blog's administrator, Mr. Hector Mc-Murtrie, a noted expert in maritime affairs, wrote an interesting entry on the loss of the Vietnamese merchant ship *Vinaship Sea*. In hindsight, this ship was probably the first casualty of the war. I contacted Mr. McMurtrie shortly thereafter, and he has provided a steady stream of incredibly accurate information and insight, long before our usual sources. I've asked Mr. McMurtrie to join us on Skype to talk about the situation in the South China Sea. Good evening, Hector, thank you for joining us."

"Good evening, Christine," Mac replied. He looked up at the TV behind his desk and he saw his face. This was all very strange. His initial thought was the tie he was wearing was the wrong color; it made his face look pink. But he didn't have a whole lot of choices. Mac hadn't worn a tie in years, and the popular colors back then tended toward the louder hues.

"Hector, the Indian ambassador to Japan just announced the blockade of the Strait of Malacca and Lombok Strait. What is the significance of these two waterways?"

"They are two of China's main lifelines. The Strait of Malacca is one of the busiest ocean highways in the world, with twenty-five to thirty percent of all oceangoing traffic passing through it each year. A lot of China's inbound and outbound trade uses this strait. But as important as Malacca is, it's rather shallow, only about twenty-five meters deep, which prevents the passage of oil tankers. They use the much deeper Lombok Strait."

"So if India can block both straits, China is largely cut off from Middle East oil?"

"It's much worse, Christine. This cuts China's access to oil and other natural resources from both the Middle East and Africa. Ships carrying these vital raw materials will have to sail around the Philippines and approach Mainland China via the East China Sea—an approach that is effectively under Japanese military surveillance."

"Hector, if the Littoral Alliance is successful in bottling up China's merchant fleet, what are the implications for the rest of the world's economies?"

"At the very least, raw materials and imported goods will cost considerably more, which will be an unpleasant shock to everyone. Rising insurance rates and fuel costs are already having a significant impact, and it will only get worse the longer this war goes on. People need to realize, Christine, that nearly ninety percent of the world's trade is moved by ship.

"And it only gets worse. China is the world's largest exporter of finished goods and the second largest importer of crude oil. Her merchant fleet carries the lifeblood of her industrial engine. If the Littoral Alliance successfully strangles China's trade, her economy could implode. The shock waves from such an event would ripple across the globe with frightening speed and effects. A worldwide depression is not out of the question."

"That's not an encouraging picture you're painting, Hector. What do you think that China could—"

"Excuse me, Christine," interrupted the anchorwoman. "We've just been told that President Myles will be addressing the nation at 9:00 P.M. eastern daylight time, undoubtedly to inform the American people on the actions his administration is taking. If you don't mind, Christine, I'd like to ask Mr. McMurtrie a question."

"Not at all, Jackie."

"Mr. McMurtrie, given the negative economic implications you've described, what impact do you think this will have on President Myles's re-election bid?"

Hector chuckled; the question was a minefield that he had no intention of entering.

"Jackie, I'm Canadian, and my personal opinions on the elections of my neighboring country are irrelevant, as I don't have a say in the matter. What I think is about as useful as a used lottery ticket."

Laird grinned at Mac's response; it was a good answer to a difficult question. Behind the camera she could see her producer making a slashing motion with his hand across his throat. She needed to wrap the interview up.

"Well, that's all the time we have for tonight. Thank you, again, Mr. Hector McMurtrie, for sharing your insights with us."

"You're welcome."

"And now back to you, Jackie."

Mac saw his face vanish from the TV screen and immediately he yanked off the wretched tie. He took a deep breath, relieved that the interview was over. He hadn't felt such pressure in a long time, and he wasn't certain he wanted to again. Suddenly, Christine Laird's face popped onto his computer screen. "That was awesome, Mac! My producer is thrilled!"

Mac jumped in his seat. The abrupt appearance of the CNN reporter startled him. Wiping the sweat from his brow, he wagged a finger at her and scolded, "Christine, I'm not a particularly young man and jolts like that have been known to cause heart attacks. So, if you want me to be alive for the next interview, please, don't do that again." He smiled at the end, to let her know he wasn't angry.

Laird looked appalled. The thought of her killing off her star "talking head" was horrifying. "I'm sorry, Mac! I was just so excited by how well the interview went, that's all."

"So I see," he replied wryly. He was about to suggest that she might want to consider drinking decaffeinated coffee when she hit him with another shock.

"My producer wants to do more focused interviews. How soon can you get to New York?"

"What?" asked Mac, dumbfounded.

"He wants us to put together a number of features on the Chinese merchant fleet, the tankers that have been sunk, and the strategy of the Littoral Alliance. And we want you close by in case there are other fast-moving stories. The best way to do that is for you to come to New York."

"Absolutely not!" answered Mac sternly.

Now it was Laird's turn to be surprised. "Why not, Mac? We'll put you up in one of the finest hotels in Manhattan, close to our studios in the Time Warner Center."

"Christine, I don't like going into downtown Halifax, let alone a city with a population over ten times that of my entire province! I'm not a fan of concrete!"

"I promise, you won't have to worry about a thing. I'll make sure you're taken care of," Laird protested.

"And who will keep my blogs updated?"

"You can do that here just as well as from your home. We'll give you an office with all the IT support you could possibly need," argued Laird.

Mac took off his glasses and rubbed his eyes. He was very tired, and could feel himself getting curmudgeonly. "Young lady, not all of my references are electronic. In fact, I often use hard-copy articles, and these quaint oddities that are called 'books.'" He emphasized his point by lifting a large volume of *Jane's Merchant Ships*.

"We'll move whatever you need." Laird was now pleading.

"Hardly," Mac snickered.

"Mac, please—"

McMurtrie quickly raised his hand, stopping her in mid-sentence.

"Ms. Laird, I'm going to stay here and keep my group's blogs up to date. It's what I like to do, and it's my responsibility. I'm afraid you and your producer will just have to learn to deal with that."

4 September 2016
2015 Local Time
Oval Office, the White House
Washington, D.C.

Milt Alvarez knocked on the door before opening it. Inside the Oval Office, President Myles and Secretary of State Lloyd were sitting in the easy chairs going over their strategy to confront the Chinese.

"Mr. President, the Chinese ambassador is here."

"Ah, excellent, Milt. Please show him in," responded Myles as he stood up.

"Took him long enough," grumbled Lloyd.

"Be polite, Andy," whispered Myles, smiling.

The chief of staff returned, opening the door wide, and ushered in the People's Republic of China's representative to the United States. Yang Jinping was a short, slightly portly man with a full face that always seemed to have an infectious smile. He was a seasoned diplomat, having served as China's representative to the United Kingdom and the UN.

"Welcome, Mr. Ambassador. Welcome to the Oval Office," greeted Myles in Mandarin Chinese.

Yang's smile grew larger. He stopped, bowed, and said, "It is an honor to be received in my native tongue, Mr. President. I must say your pronunciation is quite good."

Myles laughed, while shaking his head woefully. "You are being very diplomatic, Mr. Ambassador. But I fear my Mandarin instructor would not share your views. He always complained that my nasal tones sounded like I was about to throw up."

Yang erupted into a full-blown belly laugh. The ambassador's laugh sounded genuine; that was what Myles wanted to hear. The conversation he was about to have with Yang was going to get tense enough as it was; the president didn't want it starting out that way. Coming forward, Yang shook

Myles's and Lloyd's hands. Gesturing to the chairs, and switching over to English, Myles said, "Please, have a seat. Would you care for some coffee? Or perhaps tea?"

"No, thank you, Mr. President," Yang said solemnly. "We both know we have a difficult discussion ahead of us, and I'd prefer that we just get to it."

Myles saw the smile fade from the elderly statesman's face. He *really* didn't want to have this meeting. Perhaps he was uncomfortable with what he had been instructed to say. "I appreciate your candor, Mr. Ambassador. But I prefer to discuss our mutual problem, even if strong words are used."

Yang's smile returned briefly. Straightening his coat, he sat upright as he spoke. "I must first apologize for being unavailable, until now. But it was felt necessary by my government that we both have the same information. I trust you watched the announcement by the Littoral Alliance representatives?"

"Yes. Secretary Lloyd and I watched the news conference together."

"Your impressions?"

"We have a very bad situation on our hands, one that is likely to get much worse if measures aren't taken to stop the bloodshed."

Yang's eyes narrowed, carefully scanning the American president. "If I may, Mr. President, just who are you referring to when you say 'we'?"

"The world, Mr. Ambassador," Myles answered bluntly.

"That is very noble of you, Mr. President. But need I remind you we were attacked first," countered Yang.

"If you mean that the Littoral Alliance fired the first shot, then you are technically correct. However, the Vietnamese would never have mined the *Liaoning* if you hadn't already put into motion your plan to seize most of the islands and reefs in the Spratly Islands by force. The plan you are currently executing."

Yang's face showed no response. The man was indeed a professional, but he hesitated slightly and Myles pressed on with his prepared plan of attack.

"Yes, Mr. Ambassador, we know quite a bit about Operation Trident. Catchy name, I must admit, three prongs on a trident, and three attack vectors into the Spratlys, one to the north, one in the middle, and one to the south. We didn't figure it all out at first, but after one of your Type 093 submarines torpedoed *Vinaship Sea*—"

"Really, Mr. President! I must protest!" interjected Yang indignantly.

"My dear Ambassador," Myles responded lightheartedly. "One of my nuclear-powered submarines witnessed the whole attack. They'd been trailing your submarine since it left port the day before. We know the Type 093

fired two Yu-6 torpedoes, and we know about the large secondary explosion that followed. I'm willing to provide a copy of the recorded sonar files and fire control plots if you'd like.

"No, Mr. Ambassador, the People's Republic of China is not an 'innocent victim' in this case. The Littoral Alliance may have fired first, but that's only because they found out about your plan and beat you to the punch."

"We have suffered terrible losses, Mr. President, far more than the Littoral Alliance. This is unacceptable."

"That is not true, Mr. Ambassador, and you know it." Myles heard the ambassador inhale deeply through his nose. He was insulted by Myles's accusation that he was lying—good. Whether or not the ambassador knew what his countrymen had done was immaterial; the president now had the opportunity he'd been looking for.

"Oh yes, we also know the Fourth Technical Reconnaissance Bureau is responsible for causing the Sanyo Shinkansen tragedy. They hacked into the bullet train's control circuit and caused the deaths of nearly 2,750 civilians. Your cyber intrusion specialists in the 61419 Unit are very good, so I'm told, but they left behind some electronic fingerprints."

Yang remained silent at first, and swallowed hard. The American president seemed very well informed, far better than expected. There was no point in trying to fence with Myles given his disadvantaged position.

"What would you like us to do? Surrender?" he sneered.

"No, Mr. Ambassador. But your country is the key to ending this conflict. Withdraw your troops from the islands you invaded, and request a cease-fire. I will fully support it and will put considerable pressure on our allies to accept it. Once the fighting has been stopped, I will propose a mediation plan to resolve the dispute."

"So you expect us to just absorb the losses inflicted by your *allies*, and then throw ourselves at *your* mercy. I seriously doubt my government will see any advantage in that."

"I concede that it's not the most palatable solution, but the alternative is far, far worse," pushed Myles. "We have not supplied any of this information to any of our allies. Not even the British know what we know. I'm offering the People's Republic of China the 'right of first refusal.'

"I also don't appreciate the position you've put me in by invading territories belonging to nonbelligerent nations that have security agreements with the United States; in particular, the Republic of the Philippines, which has absolutely no ability to threaten your country. If China continues down

the current path, I sincerely doubt I'll be able to keep my country neutral. And if that happens, then the information I've shared with you will be used against China. This will undoubtedly tip Western Europe over into the Littoral Alliance's camp. You've seen the news reports as well as I; there are many who are already advocating such an action."

"Are you now threatening us, President Myles?" Yang shouted angrily.

"No, Ambassador, I'm just trying to minimize the possibility of a misunderstanding. Your job is to faithfully inform your leaders where the United States stands on this matter. I need to be clear if you are to perform your duty properly.

"But consider this. With the rest of Asia's trade already lost to you, if Western Europe and the United States join them, China's economy *will* implode. This will plunge your country into chaos, along with the rest of the world. We don't want to see that happen any more than you do. The economic and political repercussions would be severe, affecting virtually every nation on the globe, including my own country. And I doubt Russia would come to your aid. They would welcome seeing both our nations knocked down a notch."

Myles noted that Yang was visibly shaking. The ambassador was incensed with the president's message. But after an awkward moment, the elderly diplomat nodded his understanding, rose, and said, "I will convey your message to the Central Committee."

"Thank you, Mr. Ambassador," replied Myles as he stood. "I abhor being so blunt. It's not my normal modus operandi to deal with a foreign government's representative in such an unpleasant manner, but the current situation demands that I do nothing less."

Yang nodded, looking depressed and suddenly much older. He extended his hand. Myles grasped it firmly and said, "Good evening, Mr. Ambassador."

As Yang was escorted out of the Oval Office, Lloyd leaned over and whispered, "You were awfully generous with our information, Mr. President. Was it really necessary?"

Myles sighed. "I know, Andy. And that decision may come back to bite us in the future, but I had to convince Yang that we had detailed knowledge on everything China was up to. That information is one of the few weapons I *can* use. I can only hope he's running a little scared right now."

"Well, if it's any consolation, he looked pretty miserable to me," observed Lloyd.

Myles smiled and patted his friend on the shoulder. "Yes, I'm afraid our

friend Yang looked none too happy. And his night will undoubtedly get worse."

5 September 2016
1100 Local Time
INS *Chakra*
South China Sea

Captain Girish Samant surveyed his central post: the control room on a Russian-designed submarine. Everything was as it should be. The men were alert and attending to their duties as expected, despite the fact they'd been at action stations for several hours now. The war with China was only six days old and *Chakra* had already bagged four tankers, including one VLCC. Samant judged their performance thus far as adequate, but tankers are easy prey. Now they were hunting bigger game, a more elusive adversary, one that could fight back. Looking to his left at the Omnibus fire control consoles, he could see his first officer huddled with the two operators. The three men were having an animated discussion, their voices raised and excited. One of the operators pointed toward his circular display and commented on the target's lack of proficiency. Samant frowned at such undisciplined behavior.

"Status, Number One," he demanded sternly.

"Yes, sir. Contact four seven is heading westerly at four knots. Range estimate is ten thousand four hundred meters and opening. Recommend changing course to three one zero to intercept."

"Very well, Number One. Helmsman, starboard fifteen, steer three one zero."

The Indian captain was certain the fire control solution was inaccurate; he seriously doubted they could detect a new Type 041 Yuan-class submarine on the battery at ten kilometers. Still, the recommended turn was in the correct direction, and while *Chakra* swung to her new heading, he mentally ran through the math.

Girish Samant's reputation as the finest submariner in the Indian Navy was not without justification. Not only did he finish at the top of his class in every course of instruction, he consistently had the highest ratings on the submarines he served on. But far and away his greatest accomplishment was that he was the first Indian naval officer to successfully complete the Royal

Navy's Submarine Command Course, or "Perisher." Initially one of five officers in his class, and the lone foreign officer, he was one of only three who successfully made it through the demanding six-month course. The other two failed, or "perished." Upon graduation, Samant was cited for possessing an exceptionally ordered mind and coolness under duress.

When he had been selected as *Chakra*'s second commanding officer a little over a year earlier, Samant considered it to be the pinnacle of his career. But then India joined the Littoral Alliance and he suddenly found his submarine thrust into war. With this change in perspective, his peacetime accomplishments abruptly seemed unimportant, trivial. Being the best submariner in the Indian Navy was no longer good enough. Now he was determined to become India's most successful captain ever. So driven, he set out to sink as many ships as fast as he possibly could. And while tankers ran up the tonnage, sinking combatants, particularly submarines, brought more glory. This Chinese boat would not escape him.

As he studied the fire control solution at his command desk, a nagging feeling began poking at him. The bearing rate seemed a little too high, and this reinforced his earlier thoughts; the contact was closer to him. "Number One, reduce the contact's range to seven thousand meters and recompute target course and speed," he ordered.

"Aye, aye, sir," replied Lieutenant Commander Maahir Jain. Within moments he reported back to Samant. "Captain, sir, revised target course is two eight zero, speed three knots. The starboard flank array has also picked up the contact, revised range estimate is seven thousand eight hundred meters."

Samant's expression remained an impassionate mask. Even though his range estimate was vindicated as accurate, the flank array's information merely confirmed a fact. There would be no premature congratulations; it would have to wait until the target was sunk. "Very well, Number One, stand by for target setup. Helmsman, right fifteen, steer three four zero. Deck officer, set combat quiet condition."

## USS *North Dakota*

"Confirm target zig, Sierra two-nine has changed course to the right," reported Thigpen.

Jerry looked up at the port large-screen display. It didn't take a lot of imagination to guess where the Indian was going. "Well, that cinches it. He's heading straight for the Yuan."

"Yes, sir. But it also means he's turned toward *us*," Thigpen replied with emphasis.

"Yeah, that too," Jerry conceded. The geometry of the encounter was terrible. Turning to parallel the Akula made the most sense, except that it drove them toward the Yuan. Trailing six thousand yards off the Indian's starboard quarter meant they risked getting closer, sooner to the Chinese boat. Worse yet, being loosely between the two hostile submarines increased their risk of getting caught in a cross fire.

"OOD, bring us parallel with the Akula, but slow us down to five knots. I need to consult with the XO."

"Aye, Captain, come right and parallel the Akula, slow to five knots," acknowledged Iwahashi. Jerry nodded his approval and stepped out of the way. As the junior officer started the course change, Jerry saw Thigpen turn and approach the command workstation.

"Our position stinketh, Skipper," he lamented.

"It most certainly does, XO, and I don't think we can get to a better spot before the Akula reaches his firing position. Do you concur?"

"Absolutely. Either we pound his ass now, or we break off and go with Plan B."

"I'm leaning toward the latter, Bernie. We need to separate ourselves from these two before they start shooting at each other."

"We could just slow down more and let the Akula pull farther ahead," Thigpen observed. He placed his finger by the icon representing their boat on the geographic plot display and pulled it back to demonstrate a growing distance.

Jerry considered his XO's suggestion; it solved the problem with the Akula, but not the other boat. It would take too long to get the desired angular separation. The Chinese captain would likely launch at least one weapon when the Indian reacted to Jerry's interference. *North Dakota* could still get caught within the acquisition cone of one of the torpedoes.

"That doesn't get us far enough away from the Akula, XO," Jerry said. "Let's come more to the right. If we steer forty-five degrees off the Indian's course, we'll pull away from his position faster, but still keep both targets out of the end fire beams of the towed arrays."

"Works for me, Skipper," nodded Thigpen. "Then we can bring Minot

in and hit the Akula with her bow mine-hunting sonar. That should scare
him off."

Turning back to the geographic plot display, Jerry noted that Minot was
five thousand yards off the Akula's port quarter and a tad shallower. He'd
have to get the UUV to move up along the Akula's flank if both of the submarines were going to detect the high-frequency pulses.

"All right, XO. Let's increase Minot's speed to nine knots and position
her off the Akula's beam. Then turn her to . . ." Jerry adjusted the position
of Minot's icon with the trackball until it was aligned with the Indian
Akula and the Yuan. ". . . zero two one and have her go active on the bow
mine-hunting array. And use the lowest power setting on the acoustic modem. We don't want to draw attention to ourselves."

"Increase Minot's speed to nine knots. When abeam of the Akula,
come right to zero two one and have her say, 'Tag, you're it,' aye, sir."


## INS *Chakra*

"Captain, contact four seven is steady on course two eight zero, speed three
knots. Range estimate is six thousand eight hundred meters and closing.
We have a good solution," reported Jain.

"Very well, Number One." Samant looked at the clock on the bulkhead.
It had taken his fire control watch about eight minutes to obtain a firing
solution. That was acceptable.

"Bring tubes one, two, seven, and eight to action state," he ordered. The
first two tubes held UGST torpedoes, the second two, MG-84 mobile decoys. Samant was taking no chances. He completely expected the Chinese
commander to counterfire once he detected *Chakra*'s torpedoes.

"New contact, bearing two three zero, off our port side," announced the
sonar operator over the intercom.

Samant reached for his microphone, while simultaneously spitting out
an order to his fire control team. "Begin tracking contact four eight. Be smart
about it, Number One."

Keying the mike, he said, "Sonar, identify new contact."

"Captain, contact four eight is weak. No discernable bearing drift or
tones. Possible submerged contact," responded the sonar operator.

*Another submerged contact*, thought Samant. The possibility of an ambush
crossed his mind, but that would require a detection and coordination

capability well beyond what the Chinese were known to possess. But even if it were just a coincidence, the second contact had shown up at a most inconvenient moment and he had to deal with it.

"Bring tubes three and four to action state. Stand by for deliberate fire, contact four seven. Firing sequence tubes seven, one, and two."

## USS North Dakota

"Captain, Sierra two-nine is flooding tubes and opening outer doors," said the sonar supervisor.

"Very well, Sonar," responded Jerry. "XO, command Minot to go active."

"Aye, sir. Command sent."

## INS Chakra

The acoustic intercept receiver suddenly began wailing its torpedo warning, followed immediately by a panicky voice over the speaker. "Active torpedo, bearing two three zero! Torpedo is close!"

Samant didn't have time to evaluate the situation; he had to react. Wasting no time, he responded with a fusillade of commands. "Fire tubes seven, one, and two. Rapid fire, contact four eight, tube three. Helmsman, ahead flank, right twenty-five, steer one six zero."

## USS North Dakota

"Torpedoes in the water!" cried the sonar supervisor. "Four weapons were launched!"

"Pilot, ahead standard," Jerry ordered. "Sonar, where are the torpedoes heading?"

"None are closing, Captain. Two were fired at Sierra three-zero, the Yuan. Another was fired toward Minot. The fourth is heading directly away along Sierra two-nine's course, possibly a decoy."

"Very well. Keep a sharp eye on those weapons," Jerry demanded.

"My God, that boat just barfed out a ton of torpedoes!" exclaimed an impressed Thigpen.

"It helps when you have eight tubes and a rapid-firing system," Jerry replied dryly.

"Captain, Sierra three-zero has launched an acoustic countermeasure. Sierra two-nine is rapidly changing course to the right. He's starting to cavitate!"

"Pilot, ahead full!" shouted Jerry.

The fire control party watched the large-screen displays as the tangled weave of sonar contacts quickly began to sort themselves out. The Indian Akula had spun about and headed southward at high speed. The Yuan turned toward the north and retreated as fast as she could, popping more countermeasures in her wake. The Indian torpedoes, jammed by the countermeasures, passed by where the Yuan was and were now spinning about in reattack circles, searching in vain for their target. The one fired at Minot never found its diminutive prey.

Out of the cacophony of noise emerged a lone Chinese Yu-6 torpedo that ran after the Indian's decoy. Frustrated by the lack of a hull to hit, the Chinese weapon kept making pass after pass as the decoy ran to the northwest.

With all the torpedoes running about to the north, Jerry altered course to follow the Akula, which was still fleeing the scene at thirty-plus knots. Four torpedoes fired, with no hits. Jerry was understandably pleased with his crew's performance.

"Well done, everyone!" Jerry announced, beaming with pride. "You too, XO," he added with a wink.

"Gee, thanks, Skipper," Thigpen responded indignantly. Both men broke out laughing.

"No, Bernie, seriously, your team did really well. That stunt worked better than I had hoped."

Thigpen slowly shook his head. "You pulled another rabbit out of the hat, Skipper. I was pretty well convinced that Yuan was toast."

"I had my doubts too, XO. But everything worked out well in the end—at least from our perspective."

"That Akula skipper is probably one honked-off son-of-a-bitch right now," Thigpen remarked ruefully.

"Yes, I suspect he's quite peeved," agreed Jerry with a smile on his face. "He'll just have to get over it."

# 14

# CONFRONTATION

5 September 2016
0600 Eastern Daylight Time
CNN Headline News

---

"The Indian naval base at Visakhapatnam was attacked last night in a major assault by Maoist terrorists. First appearing in the late 1960s, the movement is especially strong in the southeastern state of Andhar Pradesh, where Visakaphatnam is located."

Images of Indian uniformed security forces, heavily armed, appeared, followed by corpses arranged in a row, their faces covered. All were dressed in ragged civilian clothes and spattered with blood. Automatic rifles were neatly arranged at the feet of each one.

"The attacks began shortly after dark, when small groups of gunmen charged police stations and an army barracks near Visakhapatnam with rifle fire and grenades. The attacks were not pressed home, but lasted for several hours."

The scene briefly shifted to a map, showing the location of the two bases halfway up India's east coast, then back to a dark scene with armed men running. Lit by searchlights, a high wall in the background was stained and marked by explosions, and the camera occasionally shook as the operator ran, with gunshots echoing nearby.

"The real targets were revealed twenty minutes later, when the naval bases at Visakhapatnam and nearby Rambilli were each swarmed by as many as a hundred men. Visakhapatnam is the Indian Navy's largest base on the east coast.

"At both locations, terrorists outside launched distracting attacks while infiltrators, already inside the perimeter, used heavy weapons, including rocket-propelled grenades and satchel charges. At Visakhapatnam, they attacked the ammunition magazines, and managed to get through the perimeter defenses, but were stopped short of the ammunition bunkers.

"Rambilli is a separate naval base located some twenty-five miles south of the main base, and is the home port for INS *Arihant*, the Indian Navy's first indigenously produced submarine. At that base, Maoists overpowered the guards on the pier and planted explosive charges near the submarine's stern and propeller. Video of the rebels at work was transmitted during the attack, and showed divers with snorkels near the back part of the submarine, then soon after pulled from the water."

Good-quality video matched the description, with men in diving gear working while others on the pier pointed spotlights down onto the water. Occasional shots could be heard in the distant background as the rebels shouted to each other. After the divers were clear, the camera view shifted to a more distant view of the submarine and the pier, followed by explosions and a spray of water.

"Launched in 2009, *Arihant* underwent an extensive period of sea trials before being commissioned in the Indian Navy in 2013.

"The Indian Navy has not released any photos of *Arihant* since the attack, although it claimed the damage was 'limited to the after-part of the vessel.' They also claim that over fifty Maoists were killed and an undisclosed number wounded or captured. Thirteen Indian security personnel were killed, and another twenty-three wounded.

"In a related story, several nations, including Brazil, Germany, and Iran, have all submitted resolutions to the UN general assembly calling for an immediate cease-fire in the conflict to avoid further loss of life and disruption of trade."

5 September 2016
1700 Local Time
Maritime Staff Office
Shibuyun District
Tokyo, Japan

There was no need for secrecy anymore, but it still felt strange to simply walk into the headquarters building. The guard at the main gate to the compound phoned ahead after seeing the professor's identification.

There were more guards now, armed with assault rifles, patrolling the grounds and clustered around the entrance to the main building. One checked his identity again, but after he nodded, two more by the main entrance opened the doors and snapped to attention.

The building's lobby was spacious, and decorated not only with the Japanese flag and the naval ensign with its familiar red-on-white sunburst, but with a new crest—for the Littoral Alliance. It showed a circular blue field with four stylized warships sailing in line abreast, trailing long white wakes. Each was in a different color, to symbolize the four nations, and the group was turning in formation to face north.

He had only a few seconds to study it before he noticed a square-faced commander standing near the entrance. He came up and bowed deeply. "Welcome, Professor Komamura. I am Commander Sato. The admiral is waiting for you upstairs."

Admiral Kubo was waiting alone in his office. He motioned Komamura to a chair, but did not offer tea, and barely let the professor sit before saying, "I wanted to tell you before we went to the brief. It's official. The Taiwanese will declare neutrality at noon." He said it as flatly as possible, but his expression made it clear he considered it bad news. When Komamura didn't reply immediately, he added, "It may be for the best."

Finally, the professor said, "It leaves a large gap in our campaign to encircle China."

"You sound like a military man," Kubo remarked. "But as a military man, even I can appreciate the political risks if Taiwan joined the alliance. It could push China over the edge, and force them to act immediately."

Komamura nodded. "It was the smart move for Taiwan. If we prevail, she can join later. And if we don't, America still guarantees her security, at least in the near term. For the long term . . ." The professor shrugged.

"Has the working group drafted a response to the UN?" Komamura sounded worried. "If we stop the campaign before enough damage has been done, this will have all been a waste."

The admiral shook his head. "There will be no 'official' response. We have friends who will delay the motion for as long as possible, and even if it passes, the alliance will simply ignore it. But it makes your trip all the more important," Kubo observed. "We need to end this conflict quickly. If we can get Indonesia, Malaysia, or Singapore to join us, our grip on Chinese seaborne trade will be nearly total." Kubo smiled broadly at the thought.

"It will help politically, of course. What matters is the oil," Komamura insisted.

"With the Indian blockade in place, we've already turned off that spigot, Professor. We have to look for other ways to inflict pain on our enemy."

"By widening the war." Komamura sighed tiredly.

"Let's go to your brief," urged the admiral. He led the elderly academic into a briefing theater, half full.

Commander Sato was among those waiting. Kubo said, "With your approval, Commander Sato will accompany you, as your 'secretary.'"

Komamura turned and gave the officer a closer examination. In his forties, and almost as tall as the professor, he seemed eager. "If he has your endorsement, Admiral, then I am sure he will do very well."

The commander bowed deeply. "It is an honor to work with you, Professor. I will work hard to earn your trust."

Komamura bowed in return, but replied, "We will have to see how much honor this war leaves us. I put myself in your hands."

A small woman in her twenties stood next to Sato, dressed in green-patterned fatigues and gleaming black boots. "This is Captain Yoruichi of the Special Forces Group. She will be in charge of your security detail," Kubo explained.

Komamura tried to hide his surprise. "I hadn't expected a security detail at all." To himself, he thought, *I have a niece older than you.*

"We will do our best to stay out of sight," she said softly. She bowed, and a ponytail tied high on her head bobbed.

The professor also bowed slightly. "Please take good care of me."

Kubo explained, "They will sit in on your briefing." He glanced at the wall clock. "We'd best get started. Your plane leaves in four hours." He nodded to a staff officer while he motioned Komamura to a seat.

5 September 2016
1700 Local Time
Vietnamese Frigate *Ly Thai To*, HQ-012
West of Spratly Island, South China Sea

The battle was still going on. The Chinese just didn't know it yet, and if Trung was lucky, they wouldn't find out until it was too late.

The bright afternoon sunshine did not lend itself to concealment, but the beachhead was over a hundred kilometers away, on Spratly Island. Resistance had ended about an hour ago, with the last voice transmissions describing deadly airstrikes by helicopter gunships and naval gunfire.

Captain Trung Hu had listened to the radio transmission with tears in his eyes. They were too late. The Chinese had secured Spratly Island, and captured the all-important airstrip. Intelligence said that a container ship accompanied the task force, loaded with air-defense weapons, supplies, and equipment. The Chinese would turn it into an all-weather air base capable of supporting a squadron of Flanker fighters.

His squadron had raced to the scene, but the landings had started two days earlier and the garrison just couldn't hold on. He'd been forced to listen helplessly to the increasingly desperate calls for assistance. They were almost two hundred kilometers out when the last transmission came through.

He hadn't known the officer speaking—an army captain, but he'd been brave and defiant, and now Trung had to honor his sacrifice. The race for the island was lost, but Trung had adopted a new strategy.

Trung's ship was a new Russian-built Gepard frigate. *Ly Thai To* had only been commissioned in 2011, and it was well armed, with a 76mm gun, anti-ship cruise missiles, torpedoes, even a Ka-28 helicopter on a pad aft. She and her sister were the two biggest and most capable ships in the Vietnamese People's Navy, and Trung was proud to be her captain.

For this operation, he'd actually been made a commodore, in fact, if not the actual rank. A squadron of Molniya missile patrol boats had been placed under his command. They were smaller than his frigate, but they were also well armed.

He could see them now, not in a neat formation, but in a very ragged line abreast, with his ship in the center. Any spit-and-polish naval officer would throw a fit at such poor station keeping. Each ship was on a different course, although all tended eastward. Each ship was at a different speed, although none was slower than eight knots, or faster than sixteen.

Aside from his own ships, he could see half a dozen other vessels, a mix of scruffy little fishing boats and larger coastal freighters, all going about their business. This part of the South China Sea was thick with coastal freighters and fishing craft. The war, if they were even aware of it, was over the horizon, and they hoped it stayed there and left them alone. Some of the fishermen waved to the warships as they passed.

Trung could see some boats with Vietnamese flags; others were Filipino. He didn't see any Chinese vessels, and while nobody would ever mistake his gray-painted squadron for coastal freighters, on radar they would look the same as the civilian craft, and he made sure they acted the same.

To see them at all, an observer would have to get within twenty kilometers or so, and about half that to "classify" them, or identify them as warships. Trung was working hard to make sure that the Chinese never came that close.

He stepped off the bridge wing, through the bridge, back to the command center. The cramped space was filled with equipment and men, wherever there was a place to stand. Three were clustered around the plotting table; all that would fit. One was the radio talker, another the recorder, and the third was Lieutenant Commander Mai, his executive officer. Trung didn't even try to ask Mai a question. He just watched as the recorder called out rapid-fire bearings from the other ships in the squadron. The recorder quickly copied them down, and Mai busily plotted them on the display.

Although his ships were all fitted with radar, every set was off and red-tagged to stay that way. Radar could help a ship see hundreds of kilometers away, but it also sent out a signal that told anyone who wanted to listen exactly what direction you were in, and what type of radar you were using. In the empty expanse of the ocean, that information was very useful to an enemy.

Trung didn't need radar to know where the Chinese were, and they didn't care who knew. Given they'd invaded Spratly Island, concealment had been overtaken by events. The ships in the Chinese task group had lit off everything they had—air search, surface search radars, scanning the sea and sky for threats. Mai was using those signals to track the Chinese ships' positions.

Each one of Trung's ships had a Garpun-Bal or Monolit targeting system with a high-resolution passive radar receiver capability, and as they scanned the frequency spectrum, they passed the bearings of the different Chinese radars to Trung's frigate, the flagship. Cross-bearings from two or more ships revealed the Chinese ships' exact positions.

The Vietnamese surface group wouldn't be close enough to be detected by Chinese shipborne radars for some time, but the Chinese had also launched a search helicopter. Its primary mission was to patrol for submarines, but it had its own search radar, and its close approach half an hour ago had made Mai the busiest man in the South China Sea.

It was a Kamov Ka-28 "Helix," and Trung was very familiar with its capabilities. A nearly identical machine sat on *Ly Thai To*'s fantail. The VPN operated the same model, with the same sensors. Like the Chinese surface ships, the signal from its "Octopus" radar allowed Mai to plot its much more rapid movement.

Doing his best to avoid distracting Mai, Trung leaned over to study the electronic plot. They were at the edge of the helicopter's detection range, which was good news. It had been closer for the past ten minutes, and Trung could only watch and hope the radar operator was too busy looking for periscopes.

Helicopters were too fast for a ship to outrun, and because they were higher than a ship's mast, they could see farther. The sea surface didn't offer any place to hide, so the only course was to pretend to be something other than a warship, and hope that they would not attract the radar operator's interest.

"It's headed southeast, Captain," Mai reported triumphantly. "Look here." He pointed to a cluster of dots some seventy kilometers away from the island in their direction. "My plot shows him dipping five times in that sector, just like the one before."

There were several clusters of dots, and as the helicopter darted from one sector to another, the dots marking its positions began to describe a circle centered on the island a hundred and fifty kilometers across. A much smaller circle, only forty kilometers in diameter, showed the positions of the Chinese destroyers and frigates as they patrolled their sectors. Near the center, right next to the island, two stationary symbols marked the big amphibious ship and the container ship anchored alongside, while the rest of the task force encircled them protectively.

"How soon can we increase speed?"

Mai answered immediately. "Now, sir. He's opened the range to a hundred kilometers from us, and he's moving away at one hundred forty-five knots—his maximum speed." He smiled. "We won't catch up."

"And you're sure it's a southerly course," Trung asked.

"Absolutely," Mai confirmed, nodding.

"Good, then tell all units to increase speed to twenty-five knots with less radical course changes. And tell 'Miss Tham' to continue straight south."

"Right away, sir."

Trung was back out on the bridge as the helmsman advanced the throttle. It felt good to speed up, now that it was safe to do so, but there was no point in racing toward the Chinese at flank speed. In addition to his five ships, and "Miss Tham," their own support aircraft was inbound. All their movements had to be coordinated with an uncooperative Chinese helicopter. Everything had to be timed very carefully.

And the Chinese task force, tied to the island, wouldn't stay there forever. The amphibious assault ship had used helicopters and air-cushion landing craft to carry troops and armored vehicles to the island, while the destroyers provided artillery support. With their conquest secure, the ship was now ferrying back the wounded and any troops that would not be part of the permanent garrison.

Trung knew the defenders had left booby traps all over the island, and especially on the pier. Those would all have to be cleared away, but once that was done, and the container ship docked, the task group would leave and his chance would be gone with them.

Mai stepped out onto the bridge wing, facing the wind and stretching. He saw Trung's worried look and reported, "The chief has taken over watching the plot. The helicopter is heading to a southeastern patrol zone. No other changes. And our 'air support' has arrived. I wish it was something more potent than a patrol plane."

Trung smiled. "Right now, over half the People's Air Force is pummeling the Chinese base on Woody Island. It's true we don't get any fighters, but the Chinese won't get any, either. Would you like to have an air battle right over our heads? Hard to make a stealthy approach."

Mai laughed. "It's broad daylight, our ships are roaring east at twenty-five knots, and we're being stealthy?"

Trung laughed with him, then said, "That's enough fresh air. Get back in there and make sure we stay hidden in plain sight." Mai saluted and left.

5 September 2016
1730 Local Time
PLAN Destroyer *Lanzhou*, Hull 170
Near Spratly Island, South China Sea

Admiral Sun Lin had decided to make *Lanzhou* his flagship, even though the amphibious ship *Jinggang Shan* was fitted with a flag plot. He'd visited the landing ship and inspected the facilities before they sailed, but he knew that once the operation started, his attention would be pulled to the island and the thousand problems even a successful landing would present. He'd let General Tian and his staff, in charge of the marines, take over the spaces.

For Sun, the threat lay in the other direction, toward the open sea. The bare horizon was not reassuring. It was only forty-five kilometers away, but the enemy had missiles that reached three times as far. *Lanzhou*'s own weapons had even greater range, but he had to find the enemy before he could kill them.

And what did the bright blue surface hide beneath it? The greatest danger was from submarines, which had already wrought so much damage to his country. But his task group was not made up of defenseless merchant ships. They had sonar and anti-submarine weapons, as good as any in the PLAN. But he'd been in the navy too long, and watched too many Chinese submarines infiltrate formations, to ignore the threat.

By rights, he should have had two helicopters working the screen, but he'd lost two machines during the landing, one to gunfire and the other to a shoulder-fired SAM. A third had blown a compressor stage in one of its engines, and could not be fixed at sea. He could only afford to keep one aloft, busily darting from sector to sector, hurriedly searching in each with its dipping sonar.

And even without an enemy in sight, there were still problems.

The radio talker called, "Admiral, I have Colonel Xu on the radio." Xu was the air force commander of the base on Woody Island.

Sun virtually snatched the handset from the junior officer's hand. "This is Sun. What's your situation?"

"We've got the fires out, Admiral, and we're working to clear the wreckage," the colonel reported happily.

"I don't care about the fires, Colonel. When will your runway be operational?" Sun demanded.

"Sir, some of the fires were *on* the runway, and another threatened my ammunition storage. Now that they're out, my ordnance people are making the area safe. Then we can start repairs to the runway surface," he explained. "It will take another six, perhaps eight hours."

"That's unacceptable. The standard for repairing damage in a battle is two hours. You know that."

"Sir, this is a forward base. A regular air base has far more heavy equipment and personnel. The Vietnamese scattered air-dropped mines all over the place, and the wrecked planes can't be removed until the mines are cleared. I'm using unqualified personnel to assist my ordnance specialists already. After that, I'll use every able-bodied man to make the runway serviceable, but it will take at least six hours, and that assumes nothing else happens."

Sun forced himself to listen, then simply said, "Very well. Keep me informed," and slammed the handset into its cradle. No air cover, while his ships were still committed to defending the beachhead. This was when they needed *Liaoning,* and when he missed her the most. Damn the Vietnamese for crippling the carrier. And the enemy had to know they were here, had known since they'd launched the assault two days ago.

The radio operator stood quietly, trying to look attentive while avoiding the admiral's direct gaze. Unhappy admirals could be more hazardous than the enemy.

"Contact General Tian and find out how much longer it will take to clear those demolitions." Sun's tone made it clear he wanted to get some good news.

## Ly Thai To

Trung checked his watch and keyed the intercom. "Check the helicopter's position again."

Mai replied instantly. "Sir, he's been dipping in the northeast sector of the outer screen for five minutes. He's eighty kilometers away from Miss Tham, and slightly farther away from us."

It was what Trung wanted to hear, but he couldn't bring himself to smile. Not yet. "Tell Miss Tham to get ready."

"Right away, sir."

"And tell our boatswain to put up our battle ensign."

"Yes, sir!"

Trung stepped out on the port bridge wing and looked aft. A sailor was already standing next to the main mast. The wind tore at his clothes, but he stood, bracing himself against the ship's motion, and waited.

The signalmen appeared just a moment later with a red bundle. While one rating held it, another clipped it to the signal halyards, and then hauled away. The small package flew up to the top of the forward mast, about twenty meters above the main deck. The second signalman now pulled on a cord wrapped around the package and trailing down from it, and a red flag with a bright yellow star burst open, fluttering tightly in the twenty-five-knot wind.

It was the same naval ensign that *Ly Thai To* normally flew, but that flag was less than a meter long. Their battle ensign was three times that size, and the color stood out vividly above the gray-painted warship.

Trung heard a few cheers from the bridge, as well as some improbable suggestions involving the Chinese and seagulls. The other sailor had hauled down the smaller ensign, and was carefully folding it.

He checked his watch again. That had taken two minutes, and it was still far too soon to hear back from Miss Tham. He looked out to the northeast. She was as close as they'd been all day, perhaps fifty-five kilometers away. That was still well out of visual range, of course. He wouldn't see her, even when she launched. Of course, neither would the Chinese.

Trung had given her that name, although she actually had two others. The first was *Dong Du,* a medium-sized Vietnamese-owned container ship. The second was *Ora Bhum,* which was the name she would answer to if challenged by the Chinese. It hadn't felt quite right to use the alias, but Trung was reluctant to use the container ship's real name, even on his own ship.

*Ora Bhum* matched the size and configuration to *Dong Du,* and the freighter had even been repainted in the other ship's colors, with the false name in white on the bow and a Singaporean flag at the stern.

Her cargo was a battery of Bastion coastal missile launchers, four vehicles each carrying two Yakhont supersonic anti-ship missiles. Lashed securely to the deck, they'd been hidden by the shells of cargo containers cannibalized to serve as camouflage. The deception was good enough to withstand even a close visual inspection.

It would take the freighter's crew more than a few minutes to remove and discard the covers. This was the period of greatest risk, but the helicopter was the only Chinese unit that could expose them, and it was too far away.

The Russian Yakhont was faster and newer than the 3M24E Uran missiles his own ships carried, but it was also far larger. None of the VPN's ships could be fitted with them, especially once the crisis had begun. But Vietnam had already purchased the land-based launchers from the Russians for coast defense. Now they were at sea, in a lashed-together arrangement that wasn't pretty, but would work.

Even though the Yakhonts would be launched after his Uran missiles, the subsonic Urans would arrive after them. In the low trajectory mode, the Yakhont cruised at Mach 2.0, giving the target only moments to react as it came over the horizon. The Yakhont's seeker package was also much smarter than the Uran's. It could be set to home in on the signal from one specific type of radar, like the Dragon Eye radar on a Chinese guided missile destroyer. And to top it all off, as the Yakhont attacked, it maneuvered, making it a harder target than the straight and steady Uran.

Trung had time to review the tactics, and all his choices, several times as he waited for Miss Tham's signal. They should be done soon, but the camouflage had been improvised. Was there a problem with the wind? Had the camouflage damaged the launchers or the missiles in transit, or as it was being removed?

The intercom came alive and Trung ducked back into the bridge. He'd been expecting Mai's voice, but not his report. "Sir, our patrol aircraft reports the container ship has probably weighed anchor. She is no longer stationary. Speed is three knots and increasing."

"Tell Miss Tham they've got five minutes, and recalculate the time on target."

Mai answered quickly, "Understood."

Trung tried to put himself on the merchant ship's bridge. They did not have the acceleration of a warship, but all they needed was to get to ten knots or so. The wind had them facing west at anchor, and he would have to turn to sail around to the south side of the island, where the pier was located. Once the island was in the way, one of Trung's two primary targets would disappear. But merchant ships turned slowly, especially at low speeds. Was there time to reprogram the Uran missiles on his ship? If he added waypoints . . .

"Sir, Miss Tham is ready, all launchers at the vertical. If we launch in sixty seconds, she launches sixty seconds after that."

That matched his own rough calculations. Trung ordered, "Launch in sixty seconds, then." He released the intercom key, then stepped over and closed the door to the port bridge wing. A watchstander on the other side did the same thing with the starboard door. As Trung dogged it down, a siren howled, loud even over the wind.

Trung stepped over to a small console next to the captain's chair. As he waited, a large red button, engraved in white letters with PERMISSION TO FIRE, lit up. He immediately pressed it, holding it down for the required count of three, then walked over to the intercom. "Permission to fire confirmed."

The Uran tubes were located midships, in the gap between the stack and the after mast. Even muffled by the wind, and through the closed doors, the roar of the rocket motors was loud, and seemed to go on forever.

Missiles burst out from the launch tubes at three-second intervals, climbing and immediately turning sharply east. A rocket booster, with a flame as long as the twelve-foot missile, burned for a moment before the missile's turbojet engine took over. At that distance, Trung could only make it out as a small black shape, skimming the water.

The frigate's eight missiles were all gone within ten or fifteen seconds, by his watch, and as Trung undogged the starboard door, the missile officer's voice came over the intercom. "Launch successful, all eight weapons functioning normally."

Trung used his glasses to check the Molniya missile craft closest to him, *HQ-375*. She was still launching. The Molniyas carried sixteen missiles instead of eight, in four quad launchers on either side of the ship, and each missile appeared on a column of flame as it erupted from the launcher, followed seconds later by the next one. The wind of the ships' passage swept the exhaust off the ships' decks, but it formed a billowing gray smoke trail behind each vessel. The beginning marked when each ship had started firing, and its abrupt end showed when it was complete.

A radio speaker on the bridge let him hear the reports as the four missile craft reported successful launches. Keying the intercom, Trung ordered, "Mai, execute turn to two two five, all ships flank speed." They'd done their duty for the Socialist Republic, and now it was time to look to their own welfare.

## Lanzhou

Admiral Sun was still speaking to General Tian. With the pier cleared, the container ship would dock, and Tien had sufficient troops to unload it, so . . .

"Low-altitude contact to the northwest! Missile alert!"

"Engage!" That order had come from *Lanzhou*'s weapons officer, and almost before he finished saying it, Sun heard the roaring forward as the destroyer's vertical launchers rapidly salvoed air-defense missiles. Seconds mattered.

The radar operator passed information without wasting time on extra words. "Forty-five kilometers, eight contacts, supersonic! Speed . . . 1,320 knots—Mach 2." The operator was speaking quickly, but the attackers had already covered half the distance to the ship during his report.

Sun watched the display, symbols moving almost too quickly to follow. Their outbound interceptors were even faster than the attackers, and the two groups came together as if pulled by strings. A string of characters appeared next to the hostile missiles—"Yakhont." Sun grimaced. He knew what that meant, and could only hope they were lucky.

Three, then four of the oncoming missiles disappeared. It was a good result, out of five engaged, but there was no time for another salvo.

A harsh rattling sound carried through the bulkheads. The ship's 30mm point-defense gun had opened fire, and a *BANG!* from the bow showed even the 100mm gun was firing, for all the help it would be. Again, no order had been given after the first one. There was no time . . .

Someone called "Brace!" and Sun tried to comply, then discovered he'd already done so. He barely had time to think about finding a better position when the first shock came, a crash that turned into a rumble under his feet. The deck jerked suddenly, but that was all, and Sun was starting to think about damage control when the second and third missiles slammed into the ship within seconds of each other.

This time the shock was brutal enough to knock Sun and everybody else to the deck. A pressure wave passed over him, and the stench of burning metal and plastic made him cough, then gag. One deafening crash followed another and another, and his mind gave up trying to understand what was happening.

The crashing stopped, but was replaced by a roaring sound—it was a fire, a big one, and close by. Sun could also hear screams and moans, and then metal bending and tearing, as if under great stress.

Sun pulled himself up, first kneeling, then standing, although a sharp pain ran up his left leg into his back. Battery-powered lights were the only illumination, making white beams in the haze. He could still see through the smoke, although his eyes burned.

The admiral drew a breath, coughed, then drew another and managed to croak, "Everybody topside." Most looked at him dumbly, and he said, a little louder, "We're finished here."

## Ly Thai To

The report from the targeting systems matched the patrol plane's exactly. At the same moment the aircraft's radar showed the incoming Yakhont missiles reaching one of the Chinese destroyers, the signal from the Dragon Eye radar had abruptly ceased. "The contact also appears to be slowing," the radar operator reported.

Trung let them cheer for a moment. The linchpin of the Chinese defense, a Type 052C guided-missile destroyer, had been disabled. Perhaps it would sink, if they didn't beach it on the island. It might limp home and eventually be fixed. But it was out of the fight.

Their own Uran missiles were only moments away.

Trung moved to the Monolit console. The combat center was much less crowded now, since they didn't have to track the Chinese formation so closely. Instead, they watched the radar picture data-linked from the aircraft, and compared what they saw with the Monolit operator's report.

At this point, Trung was as much a spectator as the rest of his crew. He'd made all the decisions before launching his missiles. All that was left was reporting the results and defending his ship.

"I'm getting new radars," the operator reported. "Type 354, Type 344G, Russian MR-123 radars—those last ones are point defense."

Mai pointed to a pair of blips. One was the stricken destroyer, the other a missile frigate. "That's the only ship directly in their path. For everyone else, our missiles will be crossing targets." A missile passing across a ship's line of sight, instead of holding steady, was harder to shoot at—much harder.

With the most powerful missile ship out of action, the patrol plane had been able to get closer to the formation. Its radar was sharp enough to actually provide rough images of the different ships, and could see the Uran missiles as they closed. It was also smart enough to identify ships by class, and labels appeared next to different blips as the radar's computer identified the vessels: two Type 054A missile frigates, a Type 052B missile destroyer, the Type 071 landing ship, a Russian-built *Sovremennyy* guided missile destroyer, the container ship, and two older frigates, not counting the crippled destroyer.

His eyes were on the two targets: the landing ship and the container ship. Altogether, his force had launched seventy-two missiles, an unholy amount of firepower. He'd been tempted to use part of them to attack the frigate, but it was a moving target in its patrol zone. The two primaries were stationary, or had been, and that made for easier targeting. The moving container ship was a worry, but with luck, it would not have time to get too far from the aim point.

Trung knew they wouldn't be able to see the defender's fire, but he could watch their Uran missiles disappearing, as defending missiles and guns had their effect. The Type 054A had a good SAM system, and it was well placed. The Urans wouldn't attack the frigate because Trung had ordered the missiles' radar seekers to stay off until they were past the ring of defending ships.

He tried to count, and quickly lost track. He knew that analysts would play these recordings later and count the losses, refining their estimates of the Chinese weapons systems. All he cared about now was seeing enough missiles reach their destination.

He saw an older frigate in between the missiles and the container ship. It was close enough to absorb some of the missiles. Had the captain done it deliberately?

By rights, he needed only four or five missile hits on each target to cripple it, but he didn't want to just cripple them. Crippled ships could be repaired, their cargo salvaged. He wanted to destroy the invaders. Killing the entire formation would not be enough to satisfy him, but killing the two largest ships would be a good start.

"Captain," Mai pointed to the radar screen, "the helicopter has disappeared." His voice was full of concern. "How long has it been gone?"

"It didn't land," Trung remarked. It hadn't approached a ship. That meant it must have climbed to a higher altitude. The Vietnamese patrol aircraft's radar was designed to detect ships and aircraft close to the sea surface. The Chinese Helix was above the radar beam now.

"Find the helicopter's radar! Plot its position!" Trung ordered. People scrambled around the plotting table, setting up the tracking team again.

The missiles reached the center of the formation, and Trung cheered inside every time a small radar blip reached one of the ships. "That old frigate is absorbing some of the missiles meant for the container ship," Mai observed.

"Just find the helicopter!" Trung ordered, although the climax of the battle was hard to ignore. Clusters of blips raced toward the ship symbols and disappeared. The amphibious ship had its own point defenses. Had those missiles been shot down? Or had they reached their target? The container ship was defenseless, but the old frigate guarding her was serving much the same purpose by absorbing some of the missiles.

The radar receiver operator reported, "I can't find the helicopter's radar signal. It's gone." There was no emotion in the report. He didn't understand what it meant. The Chinese knew that their opponents could detect the radar signal. Now Trung had no way of finding its position. Their enemy's move was obvious: fly down the launch bearing, then snap on the radar to search for their now-fleeing attackers.

But how far would it fly? In which direction? The Chinese knew the maximum range of the Uran, but could they know that Trung's ships had fired from much shorter range? Trung turned on the intercom. "Bridge! Double the lookouts. Keep your eyes peeled for a helicopter."

Trung's ships were running west at flank speed. His top speed was twenty-seven knots, but the Molniya boats could make almost forty-three, and were already several kilometers ahead. That was fine. There was no security for them in a formation.

Run, or slow and mimic fishing boats again? If they could get far enough away from the Chinese warships, then they'd be out of missile range and they could thumb their noses at the helicopter.

But it had only been a few minutes since they'd launched, then turned. The Chinese YJ-83 missiles had almost double the range of his Urans. It would take hours at flank speed to be completely clear.

"Captain, we've picked up the Octopus radar again."

"What bearing?"

"Northeast, on our starboard quarter," the rating reported.

Trung waited while Mai quickly plotted the bearings from several of the ships in the squadron. It was a neat fix. "The helicopter is about fifty kilometers aft." Mai's voice made it clear he understood what it meant. It had them.

Trung cursed his indecision. His heart was made of lead, and it was suddenly hard to breathe. He should have ordered his ships to slow, then searched for the helicopter. Now it was too late.

He noted the time. It would take a minute for the helicopter to report, then another minute, maybe two, for the Chinese missiles to be programmed and launched. "Tell the formation, 'Man air-defense stations,'" he ordered.

He tried to do the math while he watched the time. Even with a destroyer and that old frigate knocked out, there were at least five ships fitted with eight cruise missiles each. Their warheads were about the same size as the Uran's, but while it had taken more than a few missiles to knock out each of his targets, one missile hit would be enough to cripple his small frigate. And a single hit would severely damage, if not sink, the even smaller Molniya craft.

He counted the seconds, then it was time. "All ships, turn left ninety degrees now. Energize all radars." If he'd timed it right, the Chinese missiles were in the air, and it was time for a vigorous zig away from their flight path. They were subsonic, so he expected to see them in about a minute and a half at the radar horizon.

"All radars active, Captain, all air-defense stations manned and ready." One minute.

Trung said, "Prepare to engage air targets to port."

The gunnery officer repeated his order. *Ly Thai To* didn't have any SAM systems, and the guns could not open fire until the last moment.

Thirty seconds. Trung left combat central and went onto the bridge. All eyes were on the portside horizon. Normally he'd reprimand the deck officer, but there was open water ahead of them for miles.

He started to step out onto the port bridge wing, but remembered the Palma weapons mount just forward of the bridge. It had two rotary 30mm cannons, and when it fired, the noise would be brutal.

Any moment now.

"Radar reports high-speed contacts bearing zero seven three!" A moment later the intercom added, "Eight missiles." The radar operator's report was immediately followed by Mai's command. "Chaff."

Dull thuds amidships would have been alarming if Trung was not familiar with the sound. Explosive charges were firing cartridges filled with reflective material into the air. Hopefully, the missiles' seekers would find the cloud a more attractive target than his frigate.

The missiles were across the horizon now, but how far away could you see a missile, head-on, with a diameter of what? Less than half a meter? He couldn't remember exactly. With a turbojet engine, there would be no smoke trail . . .

"There, on the port beam!" The lookout's warning triggered a fusillade of fire. The Palma system roared, like a giant's chain saw cutting metal. Bright flames a meter long leaped from the muzzles. The 76mm gun on the bow thudded once, twice. Trung knew there was another rotary 30mm aft adding its own fire to the others.

Streams of tracers reached out, and that gave him a cue to his own search. They were also much closer now, and easier to spot. A puff of smoke several kilometers out marked the destruction of at least one missile. Was the chaff having any effect?

The first missile reached *Ly Thai To* a few seconds later. The warhead waited a few milliseconds after hitting, so that it penetrated inside the ship, rather than exploding on the outer hull plating. The explosion tore a hole ten meters in diameter amidships a few meters above the waterline. The damage was severe, but if that had been the only attacker, *Ly Thai To* might have survived.

Then the other three missiles arrived, at three-second intervals.

# 15

## DELIBERATION

Their well-appointed meeting room had become a command center. Considering that China had not fought any kind of conflict in almost forty years, Chen thought he and his staff were adapting well. Of course, knowing that they were rusty, they could have thought ahead, at least a little, Chen admitted to himself.

The room's flat-screen display, usually used by briefers for carefully polished presentations, had been augmented by two other large displays and a standing bulletin board. Extra tables had been brought in to line the sides of the room. There was plenty of room, and they gave the new support staff places to work. Tea and coffee urns at one end of the room were always kept full. At least it was good tea.

The buzz of conversation washed over Chen, sitting at his customary place at the big table. It rose and fell as messengers arrived, or different working groups debated and discussed.

It was the pace and scope of the war. He understood that now. Chen and the other members of the Central Military Commission were used to making major decisions, of course, ones that would affect China for decades to come. But the decisions didn't usually arrive piled one on top of another, or require split-second verdicts that could invite catastrophe. And they were all too well aware that the time they took to consider an issue was measured in lives.

Important decisions had to be made at any hour of the day or night, usually after subject matter experts and advisors were consulted. And what advisor wanted to be asleep when opinions were sought?

They resorted to catnaps and hurried meals. A doctor had been assigned to the staff to monitor everyone's health and administer prescription medications as needed. After all, Chen was nearly seventy, and he was not the oldest man in the Central Military Commission.

With the exposure of the Littoral Alliance, problems could no longer wait for thorough analysis and the 0800 briefing. Finally identifying their enemy should have solved their greatest problem —who and where to strike. The announcement had answered that question, but the hundreds that replaced it now shouted for attention.

Chen sat at the head of the meeting table. He'd been there since five in the morning, and that was after only three hours' sleep. His mind would not stop racing, like a rat on a wheel.

Vice Chairman Li Ju came into the room and approached Chen. The president greeted Li by pushing the tea set on the table toward an empty chair. "Join me, please," Chen invited.

The general sat down tiredly and said, "Good morning, Comrade President," as he helped himself to a cup of tea.

"Is it a good morning?" asked Chen expectantly. He'd set Li to work yesterday evening, and doubted that the general had slept at all.

"Yes, I believe so," Li answered, with a satisfied tone. "We finally received the programmers' report twenty minutes ago. The problem with the numerically controlled machines was not a virus. It mimicked a virus, though, so we would waste hours taking the wrong countermeasures. When we weren't stopping its 'spread'—"

"General Li," Chen asked patiently, "what was the cause?"

"A back door in the control software. Camouflaged and appearing to function normally until it received the activation signal. Then it came to life and tried to wreck whatever device it controlled. Every controller that malfunctioned was imported from Japan, and not all from the same manufacturer."

"And the countermeasure?" Chen asked.

Li shrugged. "Shut down every piece of manufacturing equipment in China that uses a Japanese controller, especially the ones that haven't malfunctioned yet. Forgive me, but I gave the order in your stead some ten minutes ago. We've already lost too many machines, millions of yuans' worth. Then there are the factory workers that have been killed, and many others injured."

Chen shook his head, as if to clear it. "So, after losing millions in damaged machines and goods, we lose billions more in manufacturing capacity. And since the Japanese made the best control units, we used them in our most important factories. But it cannot be helped. We will all endorse your order." Others around the table nodded.

"Our technicians will replace the firmware," Li explained. "They have to remove the back door, of course, and make sure there aren't any others. They expect it to take about a week, perhaps two. And to be sure it doesn't happen again, they're removing all networking capability. The machines will be less efficient, unfortunately."

Chen laughed a little. "And we may have problems obtaining spare parts in the future." His smile disappeared. "I wonder how many bombs it would have taken to do this much damage to our industry."

"General Xi's cyber warfare people are expanding their security screens. It's the best we can do." Xi, looking a little uncomfortable with his new rank and new job as head of intelligence, simply nodded quickly, but remained silent.

The other two vice chairmen, Vice President Zhang and General Tian, had joined the group, listening silently to Li's report. Others came to listen as well. The "factory sabotage" had become the biggest story in China, after the war itself. By the time Li had finished his explanation, the Central Military Commission was assembled. In the edges and corners of the meeting room, others continued their work.

After Chen signaled that he was satisfied, Li turned to General Tian. "My condolences on the loss of your younger brother, General."

Tian nodded his thanks. "Tian Ma was only one of hundreds that died on *Jinggang Shan*, not to mention more on *Lanzhou, Xiangfan,* and the container ship. I will miss my brother greatly, but I mourn them all."

Chen added, "Admiral Wei is at Zhanjiang, but he sent me the total casualty list: six hundred and thirty killed, almost a thousand injured, three ships sunk and *Lanzhou* crippled. Sinking four Vietnamese missile craft is hardly adequate compensation."

"It's the only defeat we've suffered," General Shi Peng offered. He was head of the political department.

"If you don't count the massive tanker losses, the damage to our industry from sabotage and missile strikes, and the economic sanctions the West is beginning to impose." Vice Chairman Zhang Fei replied sharply. Along with a handpicked team of experts, he'd taken on the task of limiting the damage to China's economy. They now understood that was the Littoral Alliance's true target. "We could use the political department's help with the workers. Wild rumors about 'killer viruses' are spreading. We've had walkouts, disturbances, and even sabotage at some factories."

Zhang paused for a moment, then asked, "General Shi, will the political department support immediate fuel rationing? No personal travel. Nonessential industries shut down. Blackouts during the evening hours."

Everyone at the table reacted with alarm, and Shi, horrified, protested, "We don't need to do that—we aren't starved for oil, not yet, anyway."

"And the sooner we start rationing, the longer that will be," Zhang responded quickly. "With the loss of all oil imports, we will be drawing heavily from our strategic reserve, which if you remember was *not* at full capacity when this war began. Vehicle fuel consumption is tripled because of the movement of army units. Jet fuel, marine diesel fuel demand has quadrupled at the very least, it could be even higher. It turns out our strategic reserves were based on unrealistically low wartime expenditure rates, and did not assume such a complete cutoff of imports."

President Chen stated flatly, "It is necessary, Shi. Do you want to use our strategic reserve to supply civilian cars?"

"No, Comrade President, the political department will not object."

"The political department will do its best to prepare the country for the hardships it will have to face," Chen said firmly. "Zhang, how long do we have with the rationing implemented?"

Zhang didn't answer right away. Finally, he said, "By law, it is supposed to sustain us for ninety days. Even with rationing, we have at most five weeks. After that, we'll have to start making more dramatic cuts—it appears the war effort will consume most of our indigenous production."

Chen's mind whirled with the implications. China needed fuel to run its farms, to move the food, for cooking and heating. It was late summer now, thank goodness. They had fuel for the harvest, but after that . . .

"We must do more!" Shi insisted.

Zhang, unhappy at having had to deliver such bad news, was visibly irritated with Shi's remark, and started to speak, but then closed his mouth abruptly and sat back, glaring.

"Admiral Wei is in Zhanjiang organizing a submarine campaign," Chen explained. "We will sink anything afloat with a Vietnamese or Indian flag, naval or civilian. Pakistan is willing to provide intelligence on Indian ship movements. There will be more cyber attacks, as well."

General Su, chief of the General Staff, nodded approvingly, but added, "Unfortunately and obviously, we can't attack Japanese or South Korean vessels. We can't give the United States a reason to involve itself. My junior commanders, and even a few of the senior ones, want us to 'take off the gloves.' They want to punish them all, but my officers don't want to consider the price we would pay."

"What about North Korea?" General Wen Feng asked. "Can they act for us? Could they increase their sabotage campaign against the South? They have an extensive network of agents in Japan and South Korea."

"No!" Chen and General Shi both answered at the same time, and so forcefully that Wen sat back in his chair, open-eyed with surprise.

Shi sighed, explaining, "Pyongyang has become a nuisance, agitating for more food and increased fuel supplies so they can increase their readiness to attack the South. Nobody in my department actually believes they intend to do so. And they are full of wild schemes to injure or embarrass Japan and South Korea, whatever the consequences. We have not shared these with all of you, because there are more important matters to consider.

"Besides," Shi complained, "That 'extensive network' of agents is useless. It didn't give us a hint of warning about Japanese or South Korean participation in the submarine campaign. If Pyongyang had discovered any useful information, they would have passed it on to us—for a price, of course, but they would not sit on something as valuable as that."

General Su added, "And an increased threat from North Korea would require the United States to send more military units to South Korea. We must avoid anything that draws more American forces into this region.

"We will begin our ground campaign against Vietnam soon," Su continued. "Our aircraft losses are higher than we'd like, but we are clearly taking control of the air. Once that is secured, we will seize control of Vietnam's oil fields. That will be the beginning of their repayment . . ."

7 September 2016
0800 Local Time
USS *North Dakota*
South China Sea

"Watch her." Dave Covey was the OOD, and Jerry watched silently as he conned *North Dakota*, following *Chakra* through another turn. It was obvious the sonarmen were watching the Indian sub closely, but Covey's imperative referred specifically to the size of her turn. He needed to know when she was going to stop turning, or if she wasn't going to stop at all.

"Doppler has not changed, OOD, she's still in a slow starboard turn." The sonar operator's report involved a lot of subjective judgment, but after several days in close company with *Chakra*, they had gotten used to the way she moved.

"Pilot, make turns for three knots," Covey ordered. The more the other boat turned, the slower *North Dakota* had to go if she was going to stay in her trailing position. The U.S. sub was well astern and offset to starboard, on *Chakra*'s "quarter." The Indian's hull-mounted sonars were blind at this angle, and at ten thousand yards back, her towed array would not detect the *Virginia*-class boat, mirroring her movements.

"Doppler shift is zero—she's steadied up," the sonar operator reported. A moment later, the fire control computer finished its analysis. "New course is zero two zero," announced Ensign Andrews.

Covey checked the time, doing the math in his head for the fourth time on this watch . . . twenty seconds . . . and *now*. "Pilot, right fifteen degrees rudder, steady course zero two zero. Make turns for five knots."

"Right fifteen degrees rudder, steady on course zero two zero, make turns for five knots, Pilot, aye."

"Sonar, is there anything out there in front of *Chakra*?"

"No, OOD, the nearest contacts are in the first convergence zone, thirty-plus miles out, and thirty degrees to port. And this is not even close to an intercept course."

Sitting in one of the empty fire control console chairs, Jerry speculated aloud. "Heading north to close on the shipping lanes?"

"Except there's not a lot of shipping traffic left, Skipper," Covey replied.

"Valid point, OOD. But whatever the reason, where he goes, we go."

"Aye, sir. UUV operator, how's Minot doing?"

"Minot is on station, five thousand yards abaft the port beam, matching *Chakra*'s new course." Keeping the vehicle on station was trivial compared to *North Dakota*. Much smaller than any submarine, and quieter, she could turn on a dime. Software on the UUV actually calculated any course and speed changes, so the operator's job was usually just making sure Minot was behaving itself.

"Watch the range, OOD. Make sure we don't drift too far aft."

"Aye, aye, Skipper. Sonar, keep an eye out for another maneuver. Pilot, make turns for six knots."

Jerry watched his OOD and was more than satisfied with his performance. Covey had been busy like this since he'd taken over the conn, and had handled it well, but they were trailing a tiger on the hunt. This was a very different situation than when he'd trailed that Chinese Shang-class boat not so long ago.

Back then, Jerry had fought to keep his watchstanders alert, trailing a boat with the acoustic signature of a heavy metal band. The Russian-built sub was a different animal entirely. She was still noisier than *North Dakota*, but not by that much. And to make matters worse, he had to stay tucked in close. He could have trailed from twice this distance, or just let Minot track and report the Indian's movements, but Jerry had to be ready to move in and spoil any attack *Chakra* attempted to make.

Jerry's only hope was to use his smaller signature and better sonars to stay one step ahead of the Indian sub skipper—figure out what he was doing, and if it involved a potential target, get in his face. But it all depended on knowing what the other boat might do next.

## INS *Chakra*

"There, sir. Do you see it?" The sonar operator pointed to a faint trace on the waterfall display, more a loose series of dots than a true line.

"I see something, but it's not distinct enough to be a man-made source." Captain Samant pointed to a different part of the screen. "This trace looks exactly the same. Probably a biologic."

"But that one will drift aft. This one keeps a constant bearing. I've been watching it for some time now. When we made that starboard turn just now, it dropped aft, with a left drift, then drifted right again until it was at the same relative bearing."

Samant didn't appear convinced. At this point, Lieutenant Rajat, the sonar officer, added his opinion. "Sir, I compared this signal with the recording of the submerged contact two days ago. This type of trace was on that same bearing right before the torpedo appeared."

"What's your recommendation, then?" Samant was willing to let the sonar officer have his say. He certainly didn't want to discourage this type of independent thinking, even if the boy was likely full of nonsense.

"There are no contacts nearby. Let's attempt to close on it. Go and say hello. If we force it to maneuver or reduce the distance to the contact, we may get a decent acoustic signature."

Samant considered the idea. The area was clear, and if there was indeed some extremely quiet platform out there, he wanted to know about it before it fired another torpedo.

"All right, Lieutenant, get your best people on the equipment." Then, sticking his head out of the sonar room, Samant called to the deck officer. "Lieutenant Parul, sound action stations."

## USS *North Dakota*

"OOD, rapid left bearing drift, down Doppler . . . and now a speed increase! *Chakra* has turned sharply to port."

"Pilot, make turns for seven, correction, eight knots. Make your depth two hundred fifty feet." Covey's response was immediate and correct. Jerry nodded his approval. If they were on the outside of the turn this time, they'd have to speed up to keep station.

Like everyone else in control, Jerry felt a jolt of adrenaline at the sonar supervisor's report. Dave Covey was coping, but he looked worried.

"Skipper, he doesn't normally increase speed when he clears his baffles."

"Concur, OOD. Sonar, what's the blade rate?"

"The rate jumped up quickly, sir, passing ten knots. Slight cavitation."

This time both Jerry and the OOD frowned. "He's not interested in staying quiet," Jerry remarked. "What's he up to?"

Covey looked at the port VLSD. "Skipper, new course is two seven zero, a one-hundred-ten-degree turn to port. Speed is thirteen knots."

Jerry noted *Chakra*'s new course, and he didn't like what he was seeing. "UUV operator, what's Minot see?"

"Minot's information matches ours, it's turned to two eight five and gone to maximum speed. The logic is trying to compensate for the maneuver, but *Chakra*'s faster. Range is decreasing rapidly."

## INS *Chakra*

"There you are!" the sonar operator announced triumphantly. "Submerged contact, bearing two zero five, slow left drift, down Doppler!"

"Confirm down Doppler. It's headed away from us?" Samant asked quickly.

"Yes, sir, it's trying to open the distance, but we're faster. Range is decreasing. It's headed westerly."

"Good, I'll hold this course, then. What does it look like?"

"I can't say, sir. Only a weak tone around forty hertz. Maybe an electric motor?" Lieutenant Rajat had put the senior sonar rating on the set. The captain trusted his ears.

"Nothing else?"

"It's not like any submarine I've ever heard. It's far too quiet. Forty hertz suggests a relatively high rotation rate if it's a propulsion motor, but that's all I can say. Contact is drifting slowly to the left."

"What, we're being shadowed by a blender?" An idea began to form in Samant's mind. "Right ten, steer three one zero. I don't want to get too close. Current range?"

"Just under three thousand meters."

Samant ordered, "Confirm there are no other contacts close by."

"Confirmed, Captain."

"Very well. Go active with the port flank array. One pulse."

## USS *North Dakota*

"Skipper, *Chakra*'s gone active! She's pinging Minot! Skat-3 sonar!" The UUV operator's report mixed surprise with dismay.

"At that range, he'll see the vehicle," Covey remarked.

"Just keep us in trail. I'll worry about the UUV," Jerry ordered. "UUV operator, send Minot shallow, periscope depth." The only chance of the vehicle breaking contact was to mix in with the surface return. If the Indian's sonar beam had to point up, it would reflect off the surface, just like a radar beam from above the water. Hopefully, Minot could imitate a wave top.

"*Chakra* is turning again, this time to port." As the sonar operator reported the sub's movements, Covey turned *North Dakota* accordingly. At this point, they were expecting radical maneuvers.

"She's headed straight toward Minot," sonar reported.

"Active signal from a Mouse Squeak sonar. She's turned on her mine-hunting sonar!" the UUV operator warned.

"Minot is well and truly busted," Jerry concluded. *Chakra,* and most subs, including *North Dakota,* had a sonar fitted in their sail specifically designed to look for submerged mines in the submarine's path. Operating at high frequency, it was worthless for area search, but it would provide high-resolution bearing and range information about nearby objects, exactly like Minot.

## INS *Chakra*

The MG-519 display showed a very small object 2,450 meters directly in front of them. It was about the size of a torpedo, but it was moving far too slowly.

"It's a damn UUV!" Captain Samant shouted, banging his fist on the console. "That's what's been spoiling our attacks! It's not Chinese, or Vietnamese, for that matter. And Japan and South Korea are our allies. They have no reason to shadow us with this thing."

"We won't be able to hit it with a torpedo," Lieutenant Commander Jain complained. "The torpedo seeker will reject anything that small as a decoy."

"Then we'll ram it, Number One," Samant said grimly. He was smiling, but Jain thought his expression was a little disturbing.

"Sir, may I respectfully remind you that the bow sonar dome is only fiberglass. We don't know what this thing is made of."

"Helm, left fifteen, steer two nine seven, make your depth five zero meters, increase speed to fifteen knots." Samant turned to face his executive officer. "I understand the risk, Number One, but I intend to strike it with the upper part of our bow or the sail. It's my decision."

"The contact is drawing left, new course two five zero, still at ten knots. That may be its maximum speed."

Samant smiled wickedly. "Number One, read off the contact's bearing every fifteen seconds. Helm, match the bearing."

The MG-519 operator reported, "Range is decreasing rapidly!"

Jain picked up the microphone for the ship's announcing circuit, and looked to Samant, who nodded. He warned, "All hands brace for impact!"

## USS *North Dakota*

"OOD, keep us behind him. Use whatever speed you need." Jerry couldn't worry about Minot right now. *Chakra*'s radical maneuvers made it hard to stay behind the Indian sub. With the other boat increasing speed like that, Jerry could risk going faster himself, as long as he could keep astern.

"She's pointed squarely at Minot," the sonar operator announced. "Intercept course."

"UUV operator, wait until the last minute and zig Minot to port."

"Understood, skipper. Zig to port. UUV is still rising."

Contact depth was hard to read with passive sonar, especially for a contact maneuvering like the Indian sub. With Minot rising, the question was, how well could the Indian skipper match the UUV's depth? The only thing in their favor was that submariners were not taught ramming tactics.

"Zig to port sent," the UUV operator reported hopefully.

The sonar rating called out, "Contacts have merged." And Jerry found himself holding his breath.

## INS *Chakra*

They braced for almost a full minute, long after the calculated time of impact. To the first officer, Captain Samant looked even angrier than he had yesterday when he'd lost the Chinese submarine.

Samant ordered, "Make a wide turn to starboard. Leave the MG-519 sonar on, and transmit on all three active arrays, maximum power. I expect it to maneuver, but it can't get far with a maximum speed of ten knots. We're going to get a longer run at it and build up enough speed so it can't dodge out of our way."

They waited as *Chakra* swung around the compass. At speed, nuclear submarines are agile—true sea creatures. They'd be pointed back at the vehicle in less than a minute.

"Sir, new active sonar contact, range ten kilometers, bearing one one five."

"What? That can't be the UUV." Samant's puzzled expression became one of alarm.

"It's a weak return, sir, but it's got to be much larger than the UUV if we can see it. Course is to the north, below us. It's maneuvering."

"Track him, but keep watching for the UUV. If he hasn't shot at us by now, he's not a threat. I think I know who that is."

The mine-hunting sonar operator reported, "I have the UUV. Range is two kilometers. It's much shallower, and above us, near the surface."

Samant smiled. "He's trying to hide it, but we'll get there first. Helm, increase speed to twenty knots and match the contact's bearing and depth."

"Match the contact's bearing and depth, Helm, aye."

"Captain, rising at that angle, whether we hit the UUV or not, we'll broach."

"Sod that!" Samant answered. "I want to smash that thing while its master watches."

## South China Sea

Xing Bao knew there was a war going on. The television said so, but the empty ocean told him that as well. His fishing junk normally worked well south of the shipping lanes, but there were always merchant ships on the horizon, or sometimes passing by. Occasionally they'd get too close, and he'd have to quickly pull in his nets.

But for the past few days, aside from other fishermen, there'd been nothing but the flat horizon. And since everyone had their own spots, he'd worked his junk alone since just after dawn.

Luckily, warships didn't care about fishermen. And with the war scares, prices had been—

"Captain, off the port quarter!" The lookout's call became a scream of fear, and by the time Xing had put down his tools and turned aft, everyone topside was shouting, although the words made no sense.

Three hundred meters away, maybe less, maybe more, a patch of the sea was boiling, white with froth. As Xing and his crew watched, a round black shape roared out of the water and grew quickly until he could see the entire bow of what had to be a submarine. Other parts of it appeared, the conning tower on top, and a fin aft. Almost a quarter, perhaps a third of its length was out of the water.

It was immense, many times the length of his own boat, and he had one of the larger junks in the harbor. Behind him, he could hear his crew shouting, "I see it! What's it doing?"

The vessel stopped rising, and the bow began to fall, landing heavily. Tons of water, enough to swamp the harbor, much less his boat, splashed out from the bow, and as quickly as it had appeared, the submarine was gone. The waves reached them, and he clutched a railing for support as the deck suddenly bucked wildly under him.

The patch of water remained disturbed, like a ship's wake, for several minutes, until the waves finally erased the last traces.

All thought of work was gone from his mind as he tried to grasp what he had just seen. The vessel had been painted black overall, with no way to tell who it belonged to.

Xing had been raised on the sea, and he accepted its wonders as a part of normal life. But now his mind whirled as he tried to imagine some colossal struggle, taking place in the depths right below him.

### USS *North Dakota*

"Minot is not responding," the UUV operator announced. He sounded like a heart surgeon searching for a nonexistent pulse.

"Understood," Covey answered. He looked at his skipper, still seated calmly in the chair.

"Open the range, OOD, before he stabilizes his depth and starts looking for us. It's time to report in."

### 7 September 2016
### 1000 Local Time
### Okutama, Nishitama District
### Tokyo, Japan

There was a car waiting at the Okutama station, the driver holding a sign saying HIRANO. Komamura was not the only passenger. A Korean in civilian clothes named Choi Jang-Kang was already in the car. One of the staff for the Korean delegation, he recognized Komamura immediately, and asked respectful questions about his book as they drove away from the train station. The professor pushed himself to answer intelligently, but his fatigue made speaking an effort.

The car quickly left the small town behind and began climbing through the thickly forested foothills.

Although technically part of Tokyo, Okutama was in the Nishitama District, the westernmost district in Tokyo. It had taken the professor forty-five minutes by train to reach Okutama station, the end of the Ome line.

The mountainous terrain was sparsely settled, and the area was laced with deep valleys and sharp peaks. The slopes were completely covered by trees, now brilliant with their fall colors.

The road took them north and west of town, first simply climbing, then switching back and forth through dense woods several times before coming to a pair of soldiers manning a barrier. After the driver and passengers had produced identification, they were allowed to pass. One final switchback took them to a timber-covered carport and a set of worn stone steps.

Their driver led the way up. "Please excuse the climb, but right now it is the only way to reach the estate. I understand a sloped path will be added in a few weeks."

"This was a private estate?" Komamura asked, steeling himself for the ascent.

"Yes, *sensei*. The alliance purchased it because of its privacy and because it is relatively close to Tokyo. It is also within the footprint of Tokyo's ballistic missile defenses."

"But away from any population centers," the Korean added.

"That, too," acknowledged the guide. "Security here is very strict. Please refrain from making any cell phone calls or using the Internet until you have been briefed by Captain Madarame. That's scheduled right after the meeting."

The house was hidden by the hill until they were almost on top of it. The stairs took a hard turn to the left, leading around a sharp corner in the hillside, almost a wall of rock, before becoming a more or less level path.

Komamura, grateful to be at the end of his quest, looked up to see a large tile-roofed structure, in the Edo style, built into the hillside. Oversized eaves sheltered a wooden walkway that surrounded the structure and blended with the path. The wooden frame of the building, although well maintained, had weathered so that it appeared to be part of the forest. Many of the house's outer walls had been folded back to take advantage of the warm weather.

Admiral Kubo, in uniform, and Hisagi Shuhei were both waiting on the veranda, along with several other members of the working group. Everyone bowed a welcome, and came forward to greet Komamura. After he'd said hello to Kubo and others he knew, a small, thin, dark-skinned man in uniform came forward. It took the professor a moment to recognize him, but then he greeted the newcomer warmly. "Captain Giring! You must have left for Japan immediately after my visit. I hope this means that Indonesia has made a decision."

Giring nodded, smiling. "You were most persuasive, Doctor. I am the naval representative to the working group. Our civilian representative will be Minister Ganesha. He arrives tomorrow."

Komamura smiled broadly. "You have made part of my report obsolete," he said happily.

Kubo took his arm. "I'm sure you are very tired, but if you can last a short time longer, we would welcome your presence. Events are carrying us forward rapidly."

The professor was exhausted, having visited three countries in a day and a half. It was possible that parts of him resided in different time zones. All he wanted was a quiet cup of sake and a long soak, but his obligations came first.

They walked into the central hall. Dark polished wooden floors contrasted with the brightly painted wall screens. They mirrored the fall scenes outside, making the room feel spacious, almost open.

Each delegation sat at a low table, with support staff behind them, and Komamura saw a table with the Indonesian flag and Captain Giring already seated. Another held the two representatives from the Republic of the Philippines, who had joined immediately after the Littoral Alliance had declared its existence.

*More ships to add to the new crest,* thought Komamura. He wondered what colors they would use.

The working group had a rotating chair. This time Minister Nehru, from the Indian delegation, ran the meeting. Gray-haired and just a little overweight, he wasted no time on formality. "Welcome back, Professor. We've received your reports during your travels. Do you wish to add anything?"

The professor stood and bowed. "I was going to say that my proposals were warmly received and that I was optimistic about all three countries joining our alliance." He turned to Giring. "I am very pleased to be proven at least partially correct so quickly, and I am also pleased that I can thank Captain Giring personally for his hospitality during my visit."

He sat down as the other members applauded, and Nehru announced,

"We must decide on priorities for those submarines capable of firing land-attack cruise missiles . . ."

Suddenly very tired, Komamura poured himself a cup of tea from a pot by his elbow. He wanted to be pleased with the results of his trip. Indonesia had immediately joined, and he believed the other two nations, Malaysia and Singapore, would also. But that meant their armed forces would join the fight, and the war would grow. There were rumors that Pakistan's military was assisting the Chinese, and Iran and North Korea were noisily promising their assistance. The economic costs . . .

"Professor?" Minister Nehru's question startled him from a half-doze. "I'm sorry, sir. I know it isn't within your expertise, but what do you think? Given the increasing lack of tanker targets, should submarines capable of firing land-attack missiles start attacking naval bases, or continue to use torpedoes against warships and what merchants they can find?"

"Neither," Komamura answered quickly. "Please excuse me, but sinking warships will not hurt the Chinese economy. And the loss of merchant ships carrying random cargoes will have only a superficial effect. China has already suffered deep wounds in her energy sector—specifically oil. I respectfully suggest that we remain focused on that goal.

"If there are few productive merchant targets at sea, cruise missiles should destroy oil facilities within their range, especially oil refineries. The distillation units would be particularly vulnerable to precision munitions. We must continue to hunt down tankers, even if they are empty, and sink them, even in harbor. We should also consider attacking China's deep-ocean oil-drilling rigs. Naval experts can provide guidance on the best method of attack.

"Although we are united, we still cannot beat China's military. She could lose her entire navy and just build another one." Bowing toward the Vietnamese table, Komamura said, "Your brave ships stopped the southern prong of the Chinese offensive, but only after the Chinese seized Spratly Island, and at the sacrifice of four vessels. We cannot afford many such victories."

Like the others, the South Korean naval representative, Admiral Park Uchin, nodded agreement, but countered, "There are some military targets that would benefit our campaign, Professor: Command and control centers, patrol aircraft bases for example. Taking the long view, these attacks would help reduce our own losses, and thus we would have more boats available for the campaign."

Komamura replied, "You have seen part of the way toward the goal, but are still intent on striking your opponent's sword and shield. Better to strike at the man holding them. Weaken him quickly, and his blows will cease." Komamura paused and took in all the delegates. "Time is against us, and our task is difficult. We have made the largest country on earth our enemy, and we must bring him down quickly."

Admiral Park nodded. "Thank you, Professor. Your logic is indisputable."

Nehru asked, "When will you be able to give us an updated estimate of the Chinese economic situation?"

Jetlagged as he was, the discussion had revived the professor. "I can tell you right now. I've kept in touch with my staff during the trip." Komamura stood, as much to clear his head as to be better seen. "Our campaign is having effects. I expect to see rationing soon, the increased use of alternative fuel sources, and efforts to find new sources of oil from other countries. We know they have tried to buy more oil from Russia, so far unsuccessfully."

"How will we know when they are near the breaking point?" Minister Hisagi asked.

"When their attempts to compensate for shortages are no longer effective," Komamura responded quickly. It was the schoolbook answer, and he owed them a better explanation. "They won't know themselves, until their increasingly desperate measures to make up for energy shortages cease to be effective. Spot shortages in food and energy will become widespread, leading to a rise in black market activity, civil unrest, and internal struggles for scarce resources.

"Internal security considerations will become an important factor in their decisions. The leadership will be under great stress, which will make their domestic political situation unstable and unpredictable. Their ability to reach consensus decisions, including a decision to cease hostilities, will be impaired. This will be the time of greatest danger."

Komamura tried to hide his discomfort as he described the effects. He knew exactly what awaited the Chinese people if the Littoral Alliance was successful. It was hard to see hunger and hardship as a worthy goal. But there was more. This was what had kept him from sleeping on the plane. He hated himself, but he had to tell them.

"The Chinese government's greatest nonmilitary energy priority in the short term will be the harvest, which has already begun in some places. Fuel stocks dedicated to that goal should have the highest targeting priority. Also, attacks by 'other means' should be concentrated here as well." They all knew he meant spies, and sabotage.

"And how much longer?" Minister Nyguen's tone was firm. The professor could tell he expected an answer. "We are bearing the brunt of the Chinese anger."

Minister Hisagi countered, "We have all been attacked, and suffered damage."

"Not by ballistic missiles or airstrikes! We also have armored formations massing across our border. We just want to know—must we plan again for an extended war?"

"China will probably reach a crisis point in about a month, but not less than three weeks," Komamura replied carefully. That was his staff's best estimate, and he agreed with their numbers. "That is an economist's answer. I have told my staff to brief your intelligence people on what you call 'indicators.' They will know what to watch for. I encourage this working group to develop plans and policy to take advantage of the situation, whenever it appears. Other alliances have missed fleeting opportunities to seize victory."

Nehru asked, "Are you still opposed to the United States joining our side in this struggle? Some here have proposed offering inducements to the Americans to join us, or at least stop interfering in our operations. Perhaps economic incentives could be found."

Komamura fought the urge to answer immediately, and paused, as if considering the idea, but then responded, "We cannot replace the economic pull of China. There is also the widespread destruction that would come with open war, and the issue of nuclear weapons. These days, my nightmares are uranium-fueled.

"If more nations join the alliance," he said, bowing slightly toward the Indonesian and Filipino tables, "our political strength will become a useful tool. China is seen as the aggressor now, and has few friends.

"Our task is to not only stop Chinese expansion in the South China Sea, but convince them that the cost of any future adventures will be more than they are willing to pay. They attacked because they thought we were weak and divided, but we have shown unexpected strength. That surprised and shocked the Chinese leaders, and we must continue to do so. Only such a shock will compel them to face the true situation, and make them cease their aggression."

Komamura sat down, a little heavily, and first one delegate, then all of them, applauded. Surprised, embarrassed, he shook his head and motioned for them to stop. Nehru, smiling, led the applause for a few more moments, then as the minister spoke, it stopped immediately.

"Your leadership inspires us all, Professor. In keeping with your doctrine, can you provide our staff with a list of targets, based on your economic expertise?"

Komamura nodded tiredly. "Of course. And I will also include facilities that could help the Chinese compensate for their lack of oil." Even as he said it, he hated what he was doing. But it was necessary.

7 September 2016
1600 Local Time
Luzon, Republic of the Philippines

The reporter was young, in her mid-twenties, and her wide-eyed excitement carried over into her report. She stood in front of a wide concrete tarmac, with the whine of jet engines a constant background to her narration.

"Today, Clark Air Base saw an amazing scene as U.S. fighters were joined by Japanese aircraft in reinforcing the Philippines' air defenses.

"Following President Myles's condemnation of the seizure of Spratly Island by the Chinese, the U.S. has promised to deploy air, ground, and naval units to the area to 'guarantee the territorial integrity of its longtime ally and to deter further Chinese aggression.'" As she spoke, images flashed by of F-22 Raptors lined up at the air base, then supplies being unloaded at a port, and finally a U.S. aircraft carrier, in formation with other warships.

"As U.S. forces began arriving, and without any prior coordination, Japanese F-15Js entered Philippine airspace. According to a Philippine government spokesman, the Japanese reinforcements include not only a squadron of fighters, but patrol aircraft, surface-to-air missiles, engineers, and JDS *Kirishima*, an advanced Aegis destroyer with ballistic missile defense capabilities." An image of the slab-sided warship cutting through the water at high speed appeared.

"In a related development, the U.S. secretary of state, Andrew Lloyd, gave a speech yesterday at Wesleyan University articulating the American position on the conflict. While he encouraged both sides to 'find a path to peaceful resolution' of the conflict, the speech also carried a blunt warning to China."

A clip of Lloyd at a podium showed him speaking forcefully. "U.S. forces are deploying to guarantee the security of our longtime allies. There should be no misunderstanding about the dire consequences to China of further aggression."

The reporter continued, "There has been no official communication between the Littoral Alliance and the United States, but an ad hoc conference between the on-scene commanders is taking place as I speak. These two onetime enemies, flying from a former battleground, must find a way to coexist in a volatile international situation and work toward the goal of guaranteeing Philippine security."

# 16

# DEPRESSION

7 September 2016
0500 Local Time
By Water
Halifax, Nova Scotia

---

Mac returned to his computer with a fresh steaming cup of coffee. It had been another long night, and he was still feeling a bit groggy. Looking out his office window, he could see the sun just peeking over the horizon. It was a glorious sunrise, with dazzling fiery oranges and deep reds. He frowned as the old adage "Red sky in morning, sailors take warning" popped into his mind. He'd have to check the weather forecast; it looked like a storm was brewing. But that would have to wait; there was a major blog entry he had to finish on the storm raging on the other side of the planet. Mac turned and looked again at the images on the flat-panel display. The photos of the two ships showed they'd both gone through hell.

The first photo was a crisp close-up shot of a Vietnamese Molniya-class guided missile boat, hull number HQ-380. The PTG had limped into port some four hours earlier, displaying incredible damage to the super-structure. *Hell, the entire superstructure has been practically stripped off,* Mac thought to himself, shaking his head. It was a miracle the little boat even made it back.

He shifted his gaze to the second photo. It had been taken from farther away, and while not as sharp, the ship was still easily identifiable. The Type 052C destroyer was under tow. Three huge blackened holes contrasted starkly

with the pale gray hull. Streaks of soot along the upper decks spoke of a severe fire. Mac shuddered as he imagined the men desperately fighting the raging inferno. They had little choice; there is nowhere to run on a ship at sea. He took another sip of coffee before setting the cup down, his fingers slowly returning to the keyboard.

The Great Pacific War of 2016
Posted By: Mac
Subj: New – The Battle of Spratly Island

Evidence of a pitched naval engagement off the Vietnamese-claimed Spratly Island started to surface earlier this morning. According to eyewitness accounts, the Vietnamese Navy sortied one of their Russian-built Project 11661 Gepard 3.9 frigates with four Molniya (Project 1241.1/Tarantul V) guided-missile patrol boats in an attempt to relieve the garrison that was under siege from a PLAN amphibious assault force. Battle was joined late in the afternoon on 5 September and culminated in a massive exchange of missile fire. Patrol boat HQ-380 <<see photo>> returned to the naval base at Cam Ranh Bay early in the afternoon (Hotel time) on 7 September with massive damage to the superstructure; evidence of a direct hit by an anti-ship cruise missile. Initial reporting indicates this ship is the sole surviving member of the Vietnamese squadron.

Vietnamese sources claim they sank four Chinese ships and crippled two others. While these claims have not been verified, a photo of the PLAN destroyer *Lanzhou,* DDG 170 (Luyang II class, Type 052C) <<see photo>> under tow shows extensive damage from at least three missile hits. Another report from a fisherman near the scene of the battle indicated that a Yuzhao-class LPD (Type 071) and an unidentified container ship had also been hit and were on fire.

This is, without a doubt, the largest naval battle of the missile age, with the Vietnamese squadron alone carrying 72 SS-N-25 Uran anti-ship missiles. Assuming the PLAN formation carried approximately the same number of YJ-62 and YJ-83 missiles, casualties on both sides would be significant. The losses the Vietnamese have suffered are consistent with this assumption. There are no reports of collateral damage; however, if a fishing boat were hit by any of the aforementioned missiles, it would be obliterated immediately. Only time will tell if any innocent civilian vessels fail to return to port.

Finished, he paused to read the entry one last time before posting. Suddenly, Mac felt cold. Here he was, writing a sterile, dispassionate article about the greatest sea battle since the Pacific campaign of World War II. And while it was his "job" to give as accurate a depiction as he could, he'd largely ignored the cost in human life. Undoubtedly several hundreds of sailors on both sides had perished in that incredibly short, but equally intense battle. When one added the loss of life from the two PLAN frigates and over thirty-six Chinese merchant ships that had been torpedoed, the grand total was somewhere on the order of two thousand souls. At first, the number "felt" small, then Mac remembered that the war was only in its ninth day and he hadn't included any of the casualties on land. Depressed, Mac hit the "Post" button on the screen, and then went to the kitchen to find something to fortify his coffee.

7 September 2016
1915 Local Time
Squadron Fifteen Headquarters
Guam

Captain Glenn Jacobs hurried into the conference room and sat down by Simonis; he still had five minutes to spare. The commodore said nothing; he just took another sip from his insulated travel mug. Judging by the smell, he was drinking peppermint herbal tea.

"Good evening, Commodore," greeted Jacobs.

"Is it, CSO?" Simonis grunted quietly.

"It's no worse than the others."

Simonis only snorted. He then looked around the room, taking roll of the required attendees. After the first pass, a frown appeared on his face. When he finished the second, he looked at his CSO with irritation. "Where's the OPS officer?"

"Rich stopped by the comms shack. We've received a message from *Santa Fe*. He should be here in a couple of minutes."

"About time Halsey reported in," growled Simonis. "He's been out of touch for nearly forty-eight hours. I was about to declare him missing."

"Warren's had a pretty rough time, Commodore. His boat's material condition has been a challenge for the past year. She's an old boat that needs an overhaul."

Simonis sneered. Halsey wasn't his favorite commanding officer—the man had problems keeping to the schedule and his boat always seemed to have mechanical issues at the most inconvenient time. Jacobs's defense only irritated the commodore more. "You don't hear Dobson complaining. And his boat is even older."

"That's true, sir, and while *Oklahoma City* isn't fresh out of an overhaul, she also isn't overdue for one either."

Simonis let it go. There was no point in discussing the issue further. At that moment, Walker entered the conference room, walking briskly. He made a beeline to Simonis, a single piece of paper in his right hand.

"Commodore, *Santa Fe*'s got a major problem," said Walker, handing the paper to Simonis. "The aft bearing on the port main engine is overheating again."

"I thought that deficiency had been repaired!" fumed the commodore.

"We made temporary repairs, sir, just before *Santa Fe* sortied with the rest of the squadron. Apparently it didn't hold. On top of that, Halsey is reporting the same thing the other three skippers have already noted. The Littoral Alliance boats aren't backing down anymore."

Simonis snatched the paper from Walker and read the message from *Santa Fe*. His eyes narrowed as he read Halsey's description of a near collision with a Japanese *Soryu*-class sub. *Santa Fe*'s skipper remarked that it was his opinion that the very close pass was intentional. Without speaking, Simonis handed the message to Jacobs. The CSO scanned it quickly, shaking his head as he read.

"Commodore, we've got to get our boats out of there. This spoiler tactic has run its course and is no longer effective," Jacobs said with a mixture of concern and frustration.

"No shit, Sherlock!" snapped Simonis. "That is exactly what I'm going to do, even if I have to ram the point down the CNO's throat!"

"Commodore," interrupted the IT petty officer, "Washington is up on the VTC."

"Understood," Simonis replied. "Bring us online."

"Aye, sir," answered the petty officer. "White House, Squadron Fifteen is up online, how do you receive?"

"We have you on both audio and visual. Please stand by."

Simonis watched as two small sub-displays, with the CNO's conference room in the Pentagon and COMSUBPAC at Pearl Harbor, popped up in the lower corners. It was just a minute longer before Admiral Hughes, Rear Admiral Burroughs, and Dr. Patterson were all in view. Simonis reached over and hit the mute button on his control console, activating his microphone. He saw no purpose in waiting any longer.

"Good morning Dr. Patterson, Admiral Hughes, and good afternoon to you, Admiral Burroughs."

"Good evening to you too, Commodore," Patterson replied. The two admirals also sent their greetings.

Without waiting, Simonis launched immediately into his report. "Since my last SITREP, the situation in the South and East China Seas has continued to deteriorate. Two more Chinese merchant ships have been sunk, one medium-sized tanker and one bulk carrier. This brings today's total to four ships thus far. While this represents a slight decrease in the number of sinkings from yesterday, I attribute the reduction to the continuing decline in overall shipping traffic in the affected areas.

"There is growing evidence that the Littoral Alliance has deployed more submarines into the East China Sea now that the Indian blockade has effectively closed down any approaches to the South China Sea. It is also apparent that China is deploying her own submarines, probably to interdict Japanese and South Korean shipping. My only asset in the East China Sea area has reported nearly a one hundred percent increase in submerged contacts."

"Chuck," interrupted Burroughs, "do you have any idea on what China is deploying?"

"Our best estimate, sir, is at least three Type 039 Songs, and a like number of Type 035 Mings. *Oklahoma City* held four Chinese boats at one time as they passed through his patrol area. The commanding officer indicated that a Ming appeared to be heading toward South Korea, while three Songs were heading southeast out into the Pacific."

Burroughs shook his head. "The situation is getting worse by the day. Dr. Patterson, I recommend that a warning be issued to U.S. merchant ships to avoid Japanese and South Korean ports. We don't want our ships steaming into an expanding war zone."

"Concur with the recommendation," echoed Hughes.

"All right, gentleman, I'll forward your recommendation to the president," Joanna responded.

"Thank you, ma'am," said Hughes. Burroughs nodded his approval.

"Commodore, what is the current status of the spoiler campaign?" Joanna asked, moving on.

"Frankly, Dr. Patterson, it is rapidly losing effectiveness. All four commanding officers have reported it is getting harder and harder to break up any attack by a Littoral Alliance submarine. Within the last twenty-four hours, we have only forced a couple of their boats to withdraw *without* attacking. That's about a thirty-three percent effectiveness rate. In addition, my COs have noted a significant increase in the use of active sonar by alliance boats, as well as aggressive maneuvering. As I reported in my last situation report, Commander Mitchell lost one of his long-endurance UUVs this morning when it was rammed and sunk by the Indian Akula. Now, Commander Halsey has just recently reported a very close pass, a 'near collision,' as he called it, by a Japanese *Soryu*-class submarine. In Commander Halsey's opinion, the maneuver by the Japanese boat was intentional."

Simonis paused momentarily to let his message sink in, but he wasn't finished yet. Not by a long shot.

"Ma'am, it is clear that we have exhausted the element of surprise, and that Littoral Alliance submarines have been instructed, at the very least, to ignore us. Furthermore, I view the recent aggressive maneuvering as a more explicit warning for us to get out of their way. Finally, with the increased deployment of hostile units into the South and East China Seas, the risk to our submarines continues to grow, while mission effectiveness has declined sharply. It is my professional opinion, Dr. Patterson, that we can no longer sustain the spoiler campaign, and that the probability of us losing a submarine is becoming more and more likely. I, therefore, most strongly urge the president to order the withdrawal of my squadron from the declared war zones."

There, he'd said his piece. He'd been respectful, but Simonis hoped the bluntness of his message would finally shake some sense into the senior decision-makers. Patterson nodded slightly, while Hughes and Burroughs both looked composed. This wasn't the first time they'd heard the squadron commodore's strong views on the matter.

"I appreciate your views and concerns, Captain," replied Joanna. "And to be equally frank, the recent actions taken by Littoral Alliance submarines isn't the only warning we've been given. Late last night, we received demarches from Japan, Vietnam, and India denouncing our uneven treatment of their forces involved in the conflict." There was no longer any pretense that the United States was not involved; the Asian alliance missives had demanded that they make it official, openly announcing their position.

"All three feel we were providing aid to the Chinese in their war, and they insist that if we were going to officially stay out of the fight, that we needed to declare our neutrality and withdraw our forces from the area. They would not be responsible for the consequences if we did not do so."

Simonis looked relieved. He wasn't the only one delivering unwanted news to the president. "This merely reinforces my point, Doctor. They don't want us interfering, we have little ability to influence their actions, and we are unnecessarily putting our people at greater risk. For God's sake, let's get the hell out of there!"

Patterson took a deep breath. She was in complete agreement with Simonis. The submarines of Squadron Fifteen had done everything asked of them, and more. It was time to cut their losses and get out. But on the other hand, she was also a loyal subordinate to the president, who desperately wanted to stop the fighting, somehow. She didn't like finding herself at odds with her loyalties, and the fact that Jerry was one of the people who would conceivably have to pay for the president's decision didn't help matters at all.

"I hear you, Captain Simonis," she empathized. "I will inform the president of your recommendation, and I will endorse it."


7 September 2016
2100 Local Time
MV *Tamilnadu*
Fifty Nautical Miles Southeast of the Port of Nagoya, Japan

Captain Somnath Manogar sucked nervously on his pipe; the whistling sound it made proved he was only moving air, the tobacco having been consumed hours ago. They were still in what the Japanese Maritime Self-Defense Force called the "danger zone," and over four hours from safety. The warnings issued over the last two days by the Indian government were now showing up in the Notice to Mariners. The submarine war with China was expected to expand into the Pacific Ocean; the approaches to Japan were now considered a war zone. Manogar wondered what those idiots in Mumbai were thinking. *Why would anyone want to intentionally anger the giant dragon to the east!* It made no sense to him. All he wanted to do was get his ship tied up to a safe berth, then he could think about taking a hot shower and a long nap. He'd slept little once the ship entered the danger zone, two hundred nautical miles out from Japan.

Manogar walked over to the helmsman, checking their course and speed for the tenth time in the last hour. It was totally unnecessary; the automatic pilot had them squarely on course for the port of Nagoya at twelve knots. The young mate at the helm smiled. He knew his captain was a compulsive worrier. If there were such a thing as sea monsters, Captain Manogar would fret over them. The war that he feared was far away, near China. The warnings were merely a precautionary measure the Indian government felt compelled to issue. Ever since the 2008 terror attack in south Mumbai, they'd started proclaiming warnings every time they thought something bad *might* happen. If the government felt the potential risk for severe sunburn was high enough, they'd issue a warning. *A bunch of paranoid old men,* he thought to himself.

"We're *still* steady on course three three zero, speed twelve knots, Captain," he reaffirmed sarcastically.

"I can read, Helmsman," Manogar replied tersely. Annoyed by the young man's flippant report, Manogar marched over to the bridge windows. Staring out into the dark overcast night, it wasn't even ten seconds before he felt the overwhelming urge to raise his binoculars and conduct a search. It was pure habit, one he had acquired since his time as a junior mate. He doubted he'd ever see a submarine's periscope, but a stupid fisherman cruising around the ship lanes without his running lights on was another danger that he had to keep in mind.

He'd completed a full forward scan and had turned to look at the bridge's radar repeater when suddenly the ship shook violently. Both men were knocked off their feet; the helmsman suffered a nasty gash to his head and was bleeding profusely, but he was still conscious. Manogar pulled himself up on the control console and saw the alarm panel had numerous red lights flashing. The audible alarms pierced the quiet night. Through the din, the ship's internal phone rang. The captain silenced the alarms and grabbed the phone. "Bridge."

"Captain, Engineer here, we're taking on water in holds two and three. We've also lost the main engine, not sure what the problem is."

"Engineer," Manogar spoke quickly, "we've been torpedoed. Get your men topside immediately!" He hung up before the engineer could reply.

"Jack, pass the word, prepare to abandon ship!"

The woozy helmsman responded and headed over to the shipwide PA system. Manogar reached over and grabbed the ship's radio mike and moved the frequency band selector to "16," the international distress channel.

"Mayday. Mayday. Mayday. This is Motor Vessel *Tamilnadu*. We've been hit by a torpedo, forty-eight nautical miles south-southeast of Irago Suido. Location, latitude, three three degrees, five zero minutes north. Longitude, one three seven degrees, two five minutes east. Repeat. Mayday. Mayday. Mayday. This is Motor Vessel *Tamilnadu*. We've been hit by a torpedo, forty-eight nautical miles—"

The second torpedo exploded aft, right under the ship's superstructure, abruptly cutting short Captain Manogar's distress call.


7 September 2016
1300 Local Time
White House Situation Room
Washington, D.C.

Secretary of Commerce Joyce McHenry pulled up the next chart in her brief. The diagram showed a disheartening trend.

"Trade with China has been severely reduced due to the Littoral Alliance submarine campaign. Even though the alliance was only targeting tankers initially, insurance costs have gone through the roof for any ship transiting through a war zone—and Lloyd's of London includes India in that mix. The bottom line is the number of Chinese ships entering U.S. ports is down to a quarter of the normal level, and many of the ships that get here don't want to leave. We've also seen a decrease in the number of Japanese and South Korean vessels arriving, by about one-third."

President Myles rubbed his forehead; he dreaded asking the obvious question. "Joyce, what is your best estimate on the damage to the economy?"

McHenry sighed deeply. "Mr. President, China, Japan, and South Korea are in the top ten of our global trading partners. Indian and Taiwan are in the top fifteen. *If* the merchant traffic doesn't decrease further, we're looking at an estimated loss of sixteen billion dollars in exports to the countries directly in the war zone each month. Unfortunately, Europe was still in a weakened condition and it has been bludgeoned by this crisis. Many of the European Union economies have dropped back into recession—resulting in a similar reduction in our exports. An *optimistic* figure would suggest that we are looking at a fifteen to twenty percent reduction in monthly exports."

"And the unemployment rate?" groaned Myles.

"Mr. President, we have a 'just-in-time' economy," emphasized McHenry. "It is predicated on an uninterrupted flow of goods, in and out of the country. There is little in the way of stored inventory. Since we produce only a small fraction of the consumer goods sold, particularly in the electronics, appliance, and clothing sectors, you're looking at two weeks, tops, before many stores will have little or nothing to put on the shelves. Add in the impact of a precipitous drop in exports, and significant job loss is all but inevitable. Initial estimates suggest the unemployment rate will probably exceed twelve percent. Perhaps as high as seventeen percent."

Myles winced. Many of the other cabinet members sat in shocked silence.

"And that's an optimistic assessment, correct?" asked Myles hesitantly.

McHenry looked downward, disheartened. "Yes, Mr. President, I'm afraid so," she answered.

"I see." The president paused, absorbing the dreadful news. Myles removed his glasses and rubbed his eyes, then clearing his throat said, "All right, Joyce, just skip to the bottom line."

"Yes, sir. If this war continues for another two or three weeks, the economy will very likely drop into a major recession, with unemployment rates exceeding the historical norms for the last seventy-five years. If the fighting goes on for more than a month, two months at the outside, the possibility of a depression becomes . . . unpleasantly high."

"Two months?" cried Geisler in disbelief. "How can our economy be ruined in such a short period of time?"

"As with mechanical systems, Malcolm, economic trends also experience inertia," explained McHenry. "Even if we could stop this war right now, its aftereffects would still be felt for months, perhaps years. The longer the fighting goes on, the steeper the downturn in our economy becomes, which means a deeper bottoming out further down the road—one that could take us a decade to crawl out of."

The cabinet meeting abruptly went quiet; everyone's morale was in shambles, crushed by McHenry's devastating projection. Uneasy with the depressing silence, Kirkpatrick moved on to the next topic; there was still more ground to cover.

"Mr. President," he began. "We've confirmed that the PLAN was able to secure Spratly Island, and the airfield is largely intact. China did lose a Yuzhao-class amphibious assault ship, an old Jiangwei II-class frigate, and a container ship carrying the garrison's equipment, so their hold is a bit tenuous."

Myles nodded. "Casualties?" he asked.

"High, Mr. President. The Chinese probably lost more men because of the amphibious assault ship, but the Vietnamese squadron was all but annihilated. Only a single damaged patrol boat returned to port this morning." Kirkpatrick saw the pained expression on Myles's face. "They did stop the Chinese southern thrust," added the national security advisor.

"I gathered that, Ray," exclaimed Myles testily. "But the cost in territory and blood is making it even harder for either side to see the folly of this war. Both sides are blind to the fact that there can be no winners in this conflict, only losers." Kirkpatrick's jaw tightened slightly, as he struggled for words. The president saw his advisor's reaction and realized the man was just as frustrated as he was.

Sighing deeply, Myles said, "I'm sorry, Ray. I know you're just trying to do your job."

Kirkpatrick bowed slightly, silently accepting the president's apology.

"How is our submarine spoiler campaign coming along?" inquired Myles, changing the subject.

Kirkpatrick turned to Joanna, and gestured for her to address the question.

"Not as well as we would like, Mr. President," she began. "It's getting more difficult for our subs to break up an attack."

"They're getting acclimated to our presence," Myles observed.

"Yes, Mr. President. I spoke with Captain Simonis this morning and he said their effectiveness had dropped considerably in the last couple of days. On average, they were only able to interrupt Littoral Alliance submarine attacks about one-third of the time. And there has been a noticeable increase in aggressive behavior as well."

Myles's forehead wrinkled. "Aggressive behavior? Explain, Joanna."

"Littoral Alliance submarines now typically use active sonar to track and harass our submarines while they carry out their attacks against Chinese merchant ships. Extensive use of active sonar is very atypical submariner behavior; they are making it clear that they know we are there, and they aren't being shy about it.

"Captain Simonis has also seen a disturbing new tactic involving Littoral

Alliance submarines maneuvering very close to our boats. There was a close pass this morning by a Japanese submarine with USS *Santa Fe*, a 'near collision,' as the commanding officer called it. When combined with the deliberate ramming of one of Commander Mitchell's UUVs by the Indian *Akula*, the squadron commodore believes that a new, and more dangerous phase of the spoiler campaign has begun."

"I'm probably going to regret asking this next question, but does Captain Simonis have any recommendations?"

"Yes, Mr. President. He strongly recommends getting our boats out of the war zone," Joanna replied quickly. Then, taking a deep breath, added more slowly, "And I, reluctantly, agree with him."

Myles was surprised by Patterson's admission, and it showed. "I must say, I'm a bit astonished, Joanna. I thought you were supportive of the spoiler strategy. What changed your mind?"

Joanna was torn, emotionally. She desperately wanted to be a loyal subordinate, and supportive of the president's policy. But now, she felt another equally strong force pulling at her, placing her loyalties in tension. Her bonds to the submarine community ran deep, and she had many friends who still served on the black boats. Subconsciously, she was very protective of the men and women who made up their crews, and she had difficulty putting them in harm's way, especially when the military or political gain was so meager. It didn't help that her husband and Charles Simonis, both former submarine commanding officers, had such diverse views on the matter.

Lowell Hardy, on the one hand, had counseled her to work hard to advance the president's goals even when she had nagging doubts. The officers and crews on the submarines served at the pleasure of the president; he had the moral authority to place them at risk if he felt it was necessary. Simonis, on the other hand, objected to putting his people on the line with rules of engagement so restrictive that the loss of one of his boats was a very distinct possibility. He'd salute and carry out his orders when told, but until then he'd fight like a rabid dog for his people's well-being. Patterson respected both men's views, and it didn't help that both men were right.

And then there was Jerry Mitchell. Jerry's boat was up against the best submarine in the Littoral Alliance. Normally, his advanced *Virginia*-class submarine would be the hands-down winner in any fight against an Improved *Akula*. But the spoiler campaign required Jerry to give up many of his advantages, thus significantly leveling the playing field. The thought of Jerry's boat being sunk because she blindly supported the president's strategy left her cold. And tucked away in the back of her mind was the memory of another run-in with an Akula-class submarine, one that nearly killed *Memphis* and everyone on board, including her. More than once in the past week she had awakened from a troubled sleep, sweating, after reliving that nightmare.

"Mr. President, I *begrudgingly* supported your policy because there was a legitimate political benefit to the United States, and the risk to our people was fairly low. I no longer believe that is the case. The risk has grown significantly, while the benefit has all but disappeared. And to be frank, I have a very good friend who is putting his life, and those of his crew, on the line, for what I see as little to no gain." Patterson swallowed hard after she finished her explanation.

Myles nodded soberly. "Thank you, Joanna. I appreciate your candor. But as hard as that decision was, I still think putting some brakes, however small, on this conflict is in our best interests."

"Mr. President," Alexander interrupted. "As much as I hate to argue with you, how can you say we're having a slowing effect on this war? From where I sit, it's accelerating away from us. The Philippines' decision to join the Littoral Alliance was a very rude surprise. And now there is evidence that their 'prophet,' Dr. Komamura, went to Indonesia, and possibly Malaysia, to convince them to join as well. If both countries do sign on, China will be completely surrounded along her maritime border by a hostile alliance."

Andy Lloyd picked up right after Alexander. "The demarches we received yesterday accused us of being rather one-sided in our execution, as the vast majority of the attacks we've interfered with are those by the Littoral Alliance. If we continue with the spoiler strategy, we are risking alienating countries who have been our allies for decades."

"Ones whose economies, when combined, rival China's and will probably recover faster once this is all over and done with," added McHenry.

Myles grimaced unhappily, his voice loaded with frustration. "Andy, I know you and Joyce have presented arguments that we should join this alliance and help rein in China's aggressive behavior. But do you *really* want to go to war with another nuclear power?"

Before Lloyd could respond, Kirkpatrick barged in. "I don't think that's a viable option, Mr. President, for the simple reason that I don't believe the Littoral Alliance wants us to join."

"Ray, what do you base that on?" cried Lloyd, clearly miffed.

"Andy, everything this new alliance has done is in complete conformity with Dr. Komamura's book. If he is their guiding light, their 'prophet' as Greg put it, then he will be strongly advising the alliance leadership to *not* include us. The chapter in his book that addresses relationships with the United States, 'Sailing Alone,' is a strident argument for Asian countries to distance themselves from our 'overbearing' policies. Have you had a chance to read it yet?"

Irritated and embarrassed, Lloyd replied, "No, no, not in its entirety. I've only skimmed some of it."

"I strongly recommend it to all of you," Kirkpatrick insisted firmly, as he looked around the conference room table. "This book provides considerable insight on the beliefs and goals of this new alliance. Sun Tzu put it best—know your enemy, people."

"All right, Ray, you've made your point," admonished Myles while gesturing for Lloyd to calm down. "So why don't we just cut to the chase and have you provide your recommendation. Not that you have a strong opinion on the matter."

Kirkpatrick chuckled; the president's light humor successfully dispatched the growing tension amongst his key advisors.

"My apologies, Mr. President. I didn't mean to preach. But there is one point of agreement between the People's Republic of China and the Littoral Alliance—neither side wants the United States to become involved in this conflict. Therefore, I recommend we comply with their mutual desire and withdraw our forces from the South and East China Seas. Regardless of which side ultimately prevails, it is in our best interests, *long-term* interests, to be perceived as neutral."

Myles leaned back in his chair as he considered Kirkpatrick's suggestion. The president knew that his national security advisor never took a strong position on anything without first dissecting every fact. And yet, Lloyd and McHenry also had strong arguments. The president loathed situations such as this when he had a diametrically opposed cabinet. It made the job of making a decision far more difficult, as he respected the views and opinions of each of his closest advisors. This time, Myles chose to do something he hated almost as much—he'd kick the can down the road.

"Okay, Ray, I'll make a deal with you. I'll postpone a final decision on the spoiler campaign until after Andy and I meet with the Japanese ambassador this evening. After I hear the alliance's position from the horse's mouth, then we'll sit down and hammer it out."

Kirkpatrick nodded his head, disappointed. But a delay did make some sense, particularly if the Japanese ambassador confirmed his understanding of Komamura's writings.

Lloyd was equally unhappy, but more vocal. "Mr. President, this will reinforce your opponent's view that you are a fence-sitter. You're taking a beating in the polls. The perception is that you are too weak to take a strong stand, or that you don't know what to do. The election is only two months away; this perception has to be changed, and soon."

"Andy, I'm being pilloried by both parties for not articulating a firm position—they want me to choose sides," Myles remarked. "Regardless of what I do, someone will be unhappy with it. If both my own party and the Republicans are upset with my actions, then maybe, just maybe, it's the right one. I'm going to go with my instinct on this one, Andy. We'll wait till after our meeting tonight. Then we'll know where we stand."

# 17

## EXECUTION

Chen had agreed to let General Hu present his plan, not because he intended to approve it, but because he was frankly curious. The Second Artillery Corps controlled China's nuclear ballistic missiles, but it also had an impressive arsenal of conventional weapons. They were already being used against Vietnam with some effect, but Hu wanted a much broader strike against the entire alliance, one with political, as well as military effects.

"The alliance nations have made it easy for us to avoid killing Americans," Hu argued. "They've evacuated the bases they operate jointly with the United States. The only exception is Clark Field in the Philippines, but the CJ-10 cruise missile is accurate enough to attack only areas where the Japanese units are located."

Hu brought up the last slide. It was a summary, showing arrows reaching out from China toward South Korea, Japan, and the Philippines. Only India was spared, to avoid any possible nuclear misunderstandings.

"We will strike ten targets in three countries, a mix of military and economic targets related to their own energy infrastructure. The plan uses ninety-four missiles, approximately one-fifth of our conventional long-range inventory. It does not call on our standing forces near Taiwan, and does not affect our campaign in Vietnam. With this heavy blow, we will bring the war to the citizens of the Littoral Alliance." Hu sat down with a pleased expression.

General Shi Peng did not look pleased at all. At Chen's request, he'd listened to Hu's plan, but the instant the missile commander was finished, Shi quickly spoke up. "I know you're eager to bring your forces into the struggle, General, but this 'heavy blow' is also an open challenge to the United States. We already have U.S. military units deploying to the Philippines, where before there were almost none, and they're reinforcing their troops in South Korea."

Shi turned to General Xi. "Have your intelligence people considered whether the Americans are using these deployments to mask a surprise intervention on the side of the alliance? If they decided to join—"

"They won't," Chen interrupted.

"You all read the ambassador's report," Shi argued. "I'm alarmed with the level of detail the Americans possessed."

"I'll send them my copy of the plan," Vice Chairman Zhang replied acidly. "It's old news now. We went over all this when we first received Yang's report. Even perfect knowledge of the enemy is not enough. One must have the desire to act. They don't." Others, including Chen, nodded agreement.

"But you will still not approve my plan," Hu predicted.

"No," Chen answered. "A deliberate attack like this might—no, likely would provoke the Americans into action. I understand their reluctance to fight, and I share it. A war between our countries would be a calamity, even if we won. It's bad enough we have to deal with India, but they only have a limited nuclear strike capability; they'd destroy a few of our cities while we would annihilate their entire country. A nuclear exchange with the U.S. would be profoundly different . . ." Chen shuddered.

General Su, chief of the General Staff added, "President Chen and I have had many discussions about the Americans. They will not join this war, which leaves us no excuse for not winning. We are developing plans to punish Indonesia for joining the alliance, which will also serve to deter Malaysia and Singapore from making a similar foolish decision. They are not under American protection, and indeed have no military alliances to speak of. General Xi is working with Pakistan to increase pressure on India, and do not forget that phase one of Trident is nearly complete, in spite of our setback at Spratly Island."

"All we need to do is endure for a little longer," Chen insisted.

8 September 2016
Littoral Alliance Headquarters
Okutama, Nishitama District
Tokyo, Japan

The television kept distracting him. Like so many others, he simply left it on a news channel all the time. Even with access to the intelligence resources of the alliance, he was afraid of missing something. Things were happening too quickly.

The sound was off, but a map of Russia showed army units moving toward the Chinese border, but so far all the analysts agreed it was precautionary. NATO was arguing about its role, too. The war had nothing to do with European security, but was deeply and adversely affecting Europe's economy. When did an economic threat require a military solution?

Perhaps his next book would be about the interrelated nature of the world economy. No, that was too obvious. Of course they were interrelated. It took at least two countries to engage in any sort of trade, and there were trade groups, and don't even get him started about the Common Market . . .

No, Komamura realized, it wasn't that one country's fortunes affected others', it was the speed at which the shockwaves from the Pacific War were traveling. That was what his next book had to describe: as countries developed and grew, trade and economic ties also grew more numerous and more diverse. And just as sound travels faster in a denser medium, economic shocks were felt more quickly in highly integrated economies.

The war had already provided plenty of data. World energy prices were whipsawing. China, desperate to replace her trade losses with other sources, was paying almost any price for whatever it could obtain, either domestically or from its neighbors. On the other hand, without Chinese purchases, oversupply had caused world oil prices to crash. Speculators were making billions short-selling oil futures.

It was also a bonanza for China's trade rivals. With Chinese-made exports evaporating, competitors were scrambling to ramp up production. Except that many items were built with Chinese-made components that were now unavailable.

Companies in the United States and Europe especially had been cut off from their biggest customer. Domestic consumption couldn't take up the slack, and layoffs were now endemic. Eventually, if the imbalance lasted long enough, demand from the expanding industries would absorb many of those laid off elsewhere, but in the meantime, the headlines shouted about record unemployment and shortages.

And there were problems that couldn't be solved. Chinese rare earth materials were vital to high-tech manufacturing around the world, and there simply were not that many other sources. Komamura had read about ventures springing up, exploring for new deposits or going after what had been marginal sources, but those would take months or longer to come on line. In the meantime, industries requiring those resources would be depressed, and the loss of efficiency—

A knock on the doorframe pulled him away from his calculations. Miyazaki Nodoka, one of his doctoral students, caught his attention and bowed slightly, brushing away the hair that hid her face. She was a brilliant student with a precise mind, but not a shred of fashion sense.

Miyazaki spoke Russian and Chinese, as well as Japanese. Komamura regretted his own lack of language skills, and relied on graduate students to bridge that gap for him.

"Here's what I've been able to find on Russian oil sales to China," she reported. "It's all black market, and the Russian authorities appear to be severely punishing anyone they can catch who is involved. Sales are still growing, though, because the profits are so high, especially for refined products. A lot of the cases involve tanker trucks 'getting lost' between the refinery and their destination."

She handed him the analysis. "It's not going to help the Chinese economy. It's too little, and too unstable," she added. "I believe Beijing may not even know about most of it. The local officials along the border are looking for their own sources of supply, or starting private stockpiles."

"Which implies . . ." Komamura prompted.

"Shortages. Lack of confidence in the national government," she reasoned. "Local corruption, although that's no surprise."

"And if it's affecting the border regions, what about provinces with oil refineries?" the professor asked.

"Local officials in those provinces may be diverting part of the output into private stockpiles, further reducing national supplies." She brightened. "My next research project?"

He nodded, smiling approvingly. "Look at energy distribution inefficiencies as a measure of government control. The oil fields are all clustered in the north and far northwest. I expect you'll find the worst shortages in the south. You'll need to see what the alliance intercept people have been able to pick up. Has Captain Madarame approved your security clearance yet?"

She bowed. "Yes, *sensei*, and thank you for your endorsement. I'm sure it made all the difference."

"Nonsense, you're more than trustworthy."

She bowed and left, almost at a run. There was urgency, of course, but also the excitement of a new task and his encouragement. This was what he loved, exploring the mysteries of human commerce and teaching those skills to his students.

No, he decided. Once this was over, if he lasted, he'd stick to what he loved most. No more books.


7 September 2016
2000 Local Time
Harry S. Truman Building, State Department
Washington, D.C.

President Myles was waiting with Secretary of State Lloyd, which evidently surprised the Japanese ambassador. Myles explained, "I'm sorry to have asked you here instead of the Oval Office, but a 'consultation' with the secretary of state will attract less media attention."

Ambassador Urahara's handshake was firm, but his face was a mask. He might have been reading a street sign for all the meaning in his expression. "I've come in response to your summons, Mr. President. I assume you wish to discuss some aspect of the present crisis."

Lloyd motioned them to a group of high-backed chairs. His staff had wasted almost half an hour arranging the three of them so the two Americans weren't crowding the ambassador, but didn't seem far away, or ganged up two-to-one, which is why Lloyd winced when Myles moved his chair closer to Urahara before sitting down.

Myles spoke carefully. "Mr. Ambassador, since Japan is now a declared member of the Littoral Alliance, can you carry our message back to the other alliance members as well as Japan?"

Urahara paused for a moment before responding. "I have no authority to speak for the alliance, but I can certainly share our discussions with the other members, if that is your wish. Indeed, I would not do so without your express permission."

"Unless you know of someone who can speak for the entire alliance, Mr. Ambassador, I do not believe I'll find a better messenger," Myles replied with a smile.

"I'm sure that with time, the alliance will choose an individual to fill that role. The current crisis came upon our countries too suddenly, before we had time to properly establish the machinery of the organization."

During this exchange, the ambassador's expression had not changed. "Our foreign policies, at least in the matter of our relations with China, are in complete unity."

Myles read that message clearly. Don't even try "divide and conquer." But that hadn't been his intention.

"We'd rather discuss Japan's long-standing and excellent relations with the United States," Lloyd replied. "I must reluctantly and officially inform you of our displeasure regarding Japan's participation in an armed conflict with another nation without consultation with the United States, as required by our long-standing mutual security agreement."

Urahara's reply was as carefully phrased as Lloyd's statement. "Japan understands that our actions have violated the letter of the treaty, and regrets the necessity, but circumstances compelled our decision. Consultation with America was carefully considered by Japan, and the other alliance governments, but in the interests of security, we decided that it was not possible. It was also not necessary, since at that time we did not require, or desire, U.S. assistance in this matter."

That was the opening Lloyd had been waiting for. "Yet the United States is providing valuable assistance to Japan, South Korea, and the Philippines. Our formal military treaties are shielding your countries from direct Chinese attack. At the same time, if the Chinese do attack your territory, under the terms of those treaties, we are obligated to join you in a war we did not choose, and which would have the gravest consequences for all of us."

"If the United States does not wish to become involved in this war, why are your submarines interfering with attacks by alliance vessels? Protecting the Chinese will not earn you their gratitude. Some in the alliance . . . excuse me, some in Japan believe you have chosen sides." Urahara's expression changed just a little, and Myles saw anger beneath the mask.

Myles answered, "My orders were to frustrate all attacks, whether by Chinese or alliance vessels, with the goal of reducing the loss of life on both sides, in the hope that a diplomatic solution could be found."

"As much as you wish it to be even-handed, your submarines are not powerful enough to stop Chinese air or ballistic missile attacks. They also prevent us from hurting Chinese naval surface forces and stopping their campaign of conquest. And since the alliance has the advantage at sea, your actions help the Chinese more than us. The last two tankers to reach Chinese ports did so because attacks on them were disrupted by American submarines."

Urahara paused for a moment, before stating flatly, "I have been told that at the moment, Japanese submarines are under strict orders to avoid firing at any vessels other than Chinese. Other alliance countries have given similar directions. American interference in the war also increases the risks to our submarines and their crews, and prolongs the war. That is unforgivable."

When Urahara used the word "unforgivable," Myles understood that in the Japanese language the word meant not just "offensive," but "is not permitted." In other words, the United States had crossed the line. There could be no recompense.

The ambassador continued, "In discussions with other alliance members, the Japanese Foreign Ministry has observed the very prevalent opinion that the United States is attempting to preserve the status quo, that is, a Pacific dominated by American military power. Japan recognizes that for decades, she has grown and flourished under such an arrangement. But would your country have stood against Chinese ambitions in the South China Sea?"

"Because Japan and America's other allies did not consult with us first," Myles answered sharply, "that specific question can never be answered."

"You would have pressured us to wait, to give diplomacy a chance, to confront China with what we had learned. It was too late for that. There was no time."

"So, Japan believed that the U.S. would not stand with her," Myles stated flatly.

"Risk open war with another nuclear power when your vital interests were not threatened? Over 'disputed territories'?" Urahara almost spat the words out.

"If U.S. security is so worthless, then withdraw from the treaties. Relieve us of our obligation."

"Join us," Urahara countered. "China is reeling now. The alliance is winning. If the United States openly sides with us, the political shock alone may be enough to convince the PRC to cease hostilities. Your military power, although less than in the past, would help end the war swiftly."

"I agree that China is near the edge, but that makes this the most dangerous time." Myles was harsh. "You were willing to predict America's behavior before the war started. Can you correctly guess how Chen Dao and the Politburo will act facing the abyss of defeat and economic ruin? They're losing much more than just 'face.' Besides, I don't think Dr. Komamura would approve of our involvement."

Urahara's eyes narrowed perceptively. Myles had struck a nerve. Still, the irritation passed quickly and the ambassador continued. "The Littoral Alliance wants a short war. That limits the suffering, and maximizing the violence has the best chance of delivering the sharp blow that will convince Chen and the others to abandon their expansionist plans. The United States, with its strange 'neutrality,' is prolonging the conflict and frustrating our aims. If you want to end the war quickly, help us. If not, at least stay out of our way."

Myles's voice hardened. "Mr. Ambassador, you've read the American newspapers, seen the debates in Congress. There is a growing movement in this country that wants the U.S. to simply withdraw from all mutual security treaties with Japan, South Korea, and now the Philippines—declare them null and void. That would remove the risk of a war between two superpowers, but it would also be a signal to China that it could do as it pleases. Can the Littoral Alliance really prevail against the unrestrained power of China's armed forces? The damage and loss of life in Japan alone could—"

"Now you threaten us!" Urahara almost shouted. "Japan and her allies have acted to protect ourselves against Chinese aggression, and instead of supporting us, as America so often promised, you have done everything possible to frustrate our victory."

"I'm trying to find a way to end this war on terms fair to both sides. You know we've demanded that China evacuate all the islands she's seized. She won't do that unless the alliance also agrees to a cease-fire. You've inflicted massive damage on the Chinese economy. She's seen your power. Present your demands over a conference table."

The Japanese ambassador paused for a moment, then replied carefully, "I will convey your entire message back to my country, as well as our allies." He relaxed a little, and continued, "If I may be allowed a personal observation, China abandoned the conference table when she committed to her surprise assault. I do not believe her leaders will accept another course until they have been forcefully shown that their aggression incurs a painful consequence. They must be humiliated, shocked—only then will they change their path. And she is not yet at that point."

Urahara stood and bowed deeply, then left.


7 September 2016
2345 Local Time
Georgetown, Washington, D.C.

Lowell Hardy sipped at his glass of port. It had been a long day and all he wanted to do now was decompress. Catching up on the news, he moved the cursor to his bookmarks folder and pulled down to the Bywater's Blog entry. Once the Web site opened up, he clicked on the sub-blog covering the war and started reading the newest updates. As usual, he'd completely lost track of time, as he didn't realize it was well after midnight until the lock on the front door clicked.

Stumbling through the door, Joanna stopped just long enough to dump her purse and valise on the floor and kick off her shoes. She looked exhausted. Hardy got up, walked over quickly, and gave her a big hug. She almost collapsed in his arms, but returned the embrace along with a kiss.

"Tough day at the office, dear?" joked Hardy.

"Don't even go there," Joanna whined.

"Sorry. Have you had any dinner?"

"No. Didn't have time," she replied wearily.

"Right! You come sit down while I find something edible in the fridge." Hardy escorted her over to the easy chair by the computer hutch. "I think the leftover spaghetti is still mold-free."

"I'll eat anything you put in front of me. Just as long as I don't have to make it."

Hardy laughed and made his way to the kitchen. As he started rustling about, he called back to her. "If you've got any mental energy left, you might want to look at that blog that's up on the screen."

"Do I have to?" whimpered Joanna.

"No, of course not," Hardy said as he returned with a glass of port.

"Oh, bless you, my love!" cried Joanna as she graciously accepted the drink. After a sip, she gestured toward the screen. "What's this blog about?"

"It covers the war, of course, and does a right fine job of it."

"Lowell, dear, I read enough about this damn war at work. Why would I want to look at something here at home?"

Hardy leaned over and gave her a kiss on the forehead. "Trust me, you won't get articles like this at work."

As her husband went back to the kitchen, Joanna struggled out of the easy chair and shuffled to the computer hutch. Plopping her bottom into the chair, she began reading. Almost immediately, a confused frown appeared on her face.

"Lowell, who is this Bywater guy?"

Beeping sounds came from the kitchen as Hardy started the microwave. "Say again?" he called out.

"Who is this Bywater guy?"

"Oh, yeah, I had to look that up too." Hardy chuckled. "The blog is named after Hector C. Bywater, an early twentieth-century reporter in England. Part spy, part naval correspondent, and part best-selling author, Bywater had an extensive network of contacts, worldwide, that fed him information for his articles. Apparently, he really knew his stuff, and had a knack for communicating complex naval issues to laymen and politicians alike.

"The Web administrator of the blog is a Canadian, up in Halifax, and he's just as well connected. He's done some interviews for CNN, and for a talking head, he's pretty damn good. I've been following his blog now for the last few days and he has information I don't get in my intel briefs. His last entry will be of particular interest to you, given your passions, my dear."

Intrigued, Joanna took a sip and scrolled down to the most recent article. The title grabbed her attention immediately.

The Great Pacific War of 2016
Posted By: Mac
Subj: New—The Environmental Consequences of War

Some of my readers may remember BRIT48, a frequent contributor. He has been working as third mate on a Panamanian-flagged bulk freighter, which was one of dozens of ships in the South China Sea that went to ground (pardon the pun) in the closest port they could find. His ship (name withheld) is now anchored out at Kuala Belait, Brunei. As you might know from his previous posts, Nate doesn't like staying in one place for more than a few days.

While Kuala Belait is a pretty town, after two days anchored out, and with no answers from the owners on when they would get under way again, Nate went in search of other diversions. I'll let BRIT48 tell the story from here:

Mac, I'm back at sea, although I've never had a billet like this. Three nights ago, I went with a mate to a private house in an upscale sub-urb of Kuala Belait, very hush-hush. The place looked as dark as a tomb, but my friend whispered a word into his mobile phone and the front door was opened by a sturdy-looking chap, who gave us a careful look-over before allowing us inside.

It was nothing more than a dimmed entryway, bare except for a few beat-up chairs. I noticed a TV camera in one corner of the ceiling. We each paid $20BD (Brunei dollars, about the same as your Canadian dollar, Mac) to gain entrance to the inner sanctum. With the front door firmly closed and barred, Mr. Big opened an-other door, and immediately we were awash in light, deafening rock music, tobacco smoke, and the wonderful smell of stale beer. It was amazingly un-Islamic.

Brunei being a dry country, I was suffering from terrible thirst, and did my best to make up for my enforced abstinence. My mate introduced me around, and I met a mix of longtime expatriates, with a few trusted locals, also non-Muslims.

One of the many people I met was a fellow Brit, from Ports-mouth, and we hit it off splendidly. He was looking for experienced sailors in need of work, and since I fit his rather loose requirements, he made me an offer. The pay was good, and when could I start?

Some undefined time later, in what was either the very late evening or very early morning, the two of us staggered to one of the commercial piers at the south end of the city. I'd brought my kit ashore, and I actually remembered to retrieve it from the badly overpaid taxi driver.

It wasn't a big ship, maybe forty meters, with a hull that had been painted black and white some time in the past, but not re-cently. Her stern bristled with electronics, and a van, covered with tarps, had been lashed to her deck aft. She had a high freeboard, and looked seaworthy enough. Did I forget to mention I hadn't asked what I'd be doing?

"You'll be our first mate, and our navigator, and take orders from me," my employer explained as we struggled up the brow. I won't give his real name, and I won't tell you the name of the ship, either. It wasn't the same one she'd owned before this trip, and it would change every time she came back to port.

The next morning I woke up, at sea, and found that my captain, "Adam," was a petroleum engineer from Greenpeace! The helmsman, "Karl," gave me a hard look from top to bottom as I staggered onto the bridge.

Andy was all business. "There's our GPS, and the chart table, and," tapping the chart, "our first destination." It was in open water, a few hundred miles northwest of Brunei. I saw a zigzag line leading from one point to the next, heading generally north.

"Get us there as quickly as possible," he ordered, and I nodded automatically.

"What's our speed?" I asked out loud, looking for the pitlog. Karl pointed to a panel over the bridge windows, and I spotted a digital readout: seventeen knots.

"That's best we can do," he said in accented English. Scandinavian, I guessed. "We stay at full speed all the time, unless we're surveying."

"Surveying what?" I asked.

He just smiled. "You'll see."

We were still a good hour from "Point Alpha" when the sea changed. Mac, I've been at sea long enough to see plenty of oil slicks, but this was another world. As soon as the lookouts spotted it, we slowed and approached at ten, then five knots, while "Adam" and other scientists took samples and other readings.

We entered the slick at bare steerageway, and what started out as a thin oily sheen quickly became a thick yellow-brown foam, dotted with seaweed, and the occasional fouled seabird or fish. The fumes became so thick we had to wear respirators. The layer increased in thickness quickly, rising from a few centimeters to what Adam measured as fifteen centimeters. As this point, I was worried for the engines, and said as much to Andy. He agreed, and we turned back and increased speed until we were in open water.

After that, Andy had us follow the edge of the slick while he gauged its size. On one of his stops on the bridge, he explained, "That was most likely *Tai Chuan*, thirteen thousand tons dead-weight, over eighty-five thousand barrels of crude oil. A relatively small slick." It took us half a day to circle part way around it, Mac, as well as getting thankfully upwind.

We found one more that day, and we're headed for another one as I write this, although it may be from two separate tankers.

Mac, I'm not a big fan of Greenpeace. They get in my face while I'm trying to do my job, and they have kittens every time a pipe sprouts a leak, but I don't need a diagram to recognize a catastrophe when it's in front of me.

Think of the last tanker accident near shore, and all the things that were done to contain the spill and reduce the amount of oil that reached the water. None of that's been done for any of the two dozen-odd tankers that have been sunk. Huge oil slicks are endangering some of the most fertile fishing grounds on the planet, one of the things everyone's fighting over. The oil's going to reach the shores of hundreds of islands and poison anything that lives there.

I don't know if there's anything that can be done about this, Mac, but tell everyone on your blog that a cease-fire, while a fine start, certainly won't solve all our problems.

Joanna finished reading just as Hardy brought out a tray with her food. Looking up at her husband, there were tears in her eyes. "My God, Lowell, I hadn't even stopped to think about the oil slicks! How could I have missed that?"

"Gives a whole new definition to the term collateral damage now, doesn't it?"

"We've got to do something!" she cried.

"Yes, we do. And the first step is to stop the fighting."

# 18

# EXPANSION

Milt Alvarez had to pull the president out of a meeting with his economic advisors, so everyone knew it had to be important. Myles trusted his chief of staff, who refused to explain, except to say that he had a special visitor, and Secretary Lloyd was also en route.

That was useful information. The secretary of state's presence meant foreign relations, and Myles felt a little bit of the tension leave. His private nightmare was a surprise meeting with a television reporter, armed with an exposé and a cameraman recording every moment.

Several people were waiting in his secretary's office, but Evangeline quickly shooed them off when Myles appeared with Alvarez in trail. Both were moving quickly, and just nodded in passing to Myles's faithful gatekeeper.

The Oval Office was empty, and as Alvarez closed the door behind them, he explained, "Ambassador Leong is in your private study. We brought him in through the west entrance. Only half a dozen people know he's in the building, and I've sworn them to secrecy. We had five minutes' notice of his arrival on what he described as a 'secret and vital matter.' Alison's in with him right now." Alison Gray was deputy chief of staff.

"Where's Andy?" the president asked.

"At least ten minutes away," Alvarez sighed. "He had that speech at Georgetown this morning."

"That's too long," Myles decided. "Let's not keep the ambassador waiting."

The presidential study was not small, but it was much more private than the Oval Office. It had a desk, where Myles actually did a lot of his work, and several overstuffed chairs.

Ambassador Kenneth Leong was chatting with Alison Gray as Myles opened the door. He immediately put down his teacup and stood, while Gray faded back and made a quiet exit. Myles knew she'd be right outside, in case either of her bosses needed anything.

"Mr. President." Leong bowed deeply. "Thank you for seeing me on such short notice, with so little warning, but this was necessary for security reasons."

"Mr. Ambassador, you are always welcome here." Myles didn't bother wheeling out his Mandarin skills. Leong had started the conversation in his flawless English, and they continued that way.

With Leong's mention of security, Alvarez turned to leave the two men alone, but Leong stopped him. "There is no need for Mr. Alvarez to leave, if he can keep a secret for another fifty-three minutes." The ambassador smiled, but it was strained.

Myles motioned for them to take seats, and Leong gratefully sat down again, with the president close by on his right. Alvarez stood near the door, as if to guard against eavesdroppers.

Even as they sat, Leong began what had to be a carefully rehearsed speech. "Mr. President, at 9:00 A.M. your time today, which is 9:00 P.M. in Taipei, President Lee will announce that the Republic of China is abandoning its state of neutrality and joining the Littoral Alliance."

Myles stared at the ambassador, absorbing the news for a moment, before speaking. "I can see the need for secrecy."

Nodding toward Myles, Leong explained, "We felt obligated to notify our longtime American friends, but at the same time we cannot let Beijing learn of our decision until our preparations are complete. Our armed forces have been at combat alert since the Littoral Alliance began its submarine campaign, but we have taken extra steps."

Leong's explanation had given Myles the time he needed to organize his thoughts. "Mr. Ambassador, are you sure that this course of action is fully supported by your entire government? Once you've done this, any chance of a peaceful accommodation with Mainland China will be gone forever."

"With respect, Mr. President, our 'peaceful accommodation' with the mainland has turned the Republic of China into an armed camp. And what do we have to look forward to? Hong Kong has shown us the value of Beijing's promises. No, the Littoral Alliance is winning, and the sooner it is victorious, the better. A humbled mainland will give us the freedom that they will not now."

Myles shook his head. "That may be true, but she is not defeated yet. My intelligence people have noted that the military units across the straits from your country have remained in place."

"We have been watching those same units for a long time, Mr. President. They are a hollow threat, and may be more defensive than offensive. Fully involved in one war, with her economy near breaking, she will not embark on any new adventures. I am sure the United States military will not be needed to defend our security."

"We have been guaranteeing that security for decades," Myles observed.

"But the situation is changing. The Littoral Alliance is on the path to becoming a new superpower, with its roots and interests in Asia. We belong with them. And we will remember who supported us for so long. But I agree, Mr. President. Beijing will not ignore us. While there will be inevitable damage, in the long run, we feel this is the better choice."

Leong stood suddenly. "I must excuse myself, Mr. President. I have other calls to make before nine o'clock."

As Myles stood, Leong produced a folded document and handed it to Myles. "As partial recompense for the distress our actions will regrettably cause, this is a list of Chinese agents we know of operating covertly in your borders. The information is reliable. The sources that provided it have been withdrawn. We are 'burning our bridges.'"

Myles took the document carefully, almost reluctantly. "I wish I could agree with your reasoning, Ambassador Leong." He reached out to shake the ambassador's hand, and said, "Please be assured of America's continued friendship, and our best wishes for the future of the Republic of China."

They both then bowed, and Alvarez escorted the ambassador out.

Myles sat quietly, considering the implications this move would have on an already volatile region. He didn't have long to wait before there was a quick rap on the door, and Alvarez opened it for a breathless secretary of state. "Milt said the Taiwanese ambassador was here."

Myles nodded. "They're joining the Littoral Alliance."

"Crap." Lloyd's face fell. "Think the Chinese will leave them alone?"

"Not a chance." Myles glanced at his watch. "He's given us forty-eight minutes. Let's not waste them."

8 September 2016
2200 Local Time
Littoral Alliance Headquarters
Okutama, Nishitama District
Tokyo, Japan

The Hirano estate included a garden, more correctly a forest glade, but beautifully tended. Komamura had been encouraged, no, commanded by Admiral Kubo and several others to take time there at least once a day. He was spending too much time indoors.

Now he sat on a roughly carved stone bench, sharing tea with the new Malaysian minister. Someone different seemed to show up every evening at about the same time, offering to walk with him and chat about anything other than the war or economics. Minister Azhar was a rabid soccer fan, but Komamura barely followed the sport . . .

"*Sensei*!" Komamura heard her voice before he saw her. She was still calling excitedly when she turned a corner and found them. It was Miyazaki, flushed and excited, and wearing another shapeless tracksuit. "*Sensei . . .*" She stopped to bow deeply. "Please excuse me, *sensei*, Minister. Please come to the dining room right away. It's very big news!" Barely allowing time for the sound waves to reach them, she ran off, presumably in search of other unsuspecting victims.

"We'd better go back," Azhar suggested, and the pair headed for the main house.

They could soon hear excited voices, then staff and other alliance functionaries greeted them with broad smiles, and urged them toward the dining room.

The large central room had been filled with tables. A wide-screen television at one end of the room was kept on the news, normally with the sound muted. Komamura could hear the set now, though. ". . . have taken this action in the belief that Mainland Chinese aggression can no longer . . ." They were speaking in Chinese, but he could see the text at the bottom scrolling in English, and on the right side in Japanese.

As he stood in the back, someone recognized Komamura and urged him forward. Kubo and Hisagi both spotted the commotion around him and waved. Advancing silently and half crouched, he discovered they'd saved a space for him in the center front, almost too close to the screen. At the back of the room, people continued to pour in, and he could sense an air of celebration. Had the Chinese abruptly surrendered?

Kubo saw the question in his expression and whispered, "The broadcast started exactly on the hour, 9:00 P.M. in Taipei." Kubo stopped and smiled. It was the happiest he'd ever seen the admiral. "They've joined us, *sensei*! Taiwan is joining the alliance. Our encirclement is complete!"

Hisagi leaned over from the other side. "I just heard from the communications department. Their delegation to the alliance is already en route. They'll be landing at Narita in a little over an hour!"

Ever since he'd realized that the alliance might actually come to be, Komamura had struggled with the question of Taiwan. Normally, the more members that belong to an alliance, the stronger it becomes. And Taiwan not only had a small, but capable navy, it had economic power, and was a major trading partner with both Mainland China and the West.

But Beijing still considered Taiwan a "rebellious territory," part of China. It had long been accepted that if Taipei ever formally declared independence, it would trigger a long-dreaded invasion of the island. This was worse than mere separation. Taiwan had joined in a war against her "mother country." Beijing would—must—react.

By joining, Taiwan added her military power, economic power, and political power to an already complex set of simultaneous equations. Komamura didn't think anyone truly could comprehend how all the variables would work together—he certainly did not. How would the results from those equations change?

The professor watched his colleagues. Kubo was almost euphoric. Why couldn't he share their excitement? All he could see was the danger. Suddenly weak, he sat back in his chair, forcing a smile and trying to follow the subtitles. Information. He needed to know the details.

The Taiwanese minister had finished his prepared remarks, and was answering questions, still in Chinese. The image shrank to an inset and was replaced with two Japanese analysts. Komamura listened to them repeat the obvious facts for a few moments, but then one held up a map of the western Pacific. Tracing arcs with a pen, he drew a single line from Indonesia in the south to Hokkaido in the north, all of it controlled by the Littoral Alliance.

China's access to the open sea was now completely blocked. She'd tried to seize the resources in the South China Sea, with future designs on the East China Sea. Instead, those two and the Yellow Sea were now war zones.

It was getting harder to find worthwhile targets at sea for the alliance forces to destroy. They'd already started attacking China's oil processing infrastructure on land, but while the professional military figures agreed with the revered academic publicly, he sensed it was begrudgingly.

The urge to go after military and political targets would become even stronger, now that the alliance had added another three countries to their ranks. The combined militaries of the alliance would not want to wait for the inevitable effects on the Chinese economy. They would ask for new targets, new ways to inflict pain on their enemy.

On the screen, the two journalists were interviewing another journalist about the chances of China suing for peace, now that the Littoral Alliance had grown so strong. Economically, the clock was ticking. The big unknown was the determination of the Chinese leaders. "If they do the math," the guest was saying, "they know they can't win. But the men in charge may not want to hear that. They have too much to lose."

Kubo was right. Taiwan was the final straw.

8 September 2016
2130 Local Time
August 1st Building, Ministry of National Defense Compound
Beijing, People's Republic of China

Chen almost lived in the conference room now, so he'd seen the broadcast almost from the beginning. None of the CMC members were ever far from a television, and unlike most of China, they could watch the uncensored transmissions. Chen knew this news would be blocked. China's censors did not have to wait for permission to block foreign media.

He wasn't sure how the ordinary Chinese citizen would react. The party spoke of Taiwan as a wayward child, misguided, lured astray by foreigners. Disappointed, but always hopeful that eventually she would realize how wrong she'd been and would return to the loving arms of her true mother.

It would be well not to push the "mother and child" analogy too far, Chen realized, because it was the way of the world for children to leave their parents.

The chairman of the Central Military Commission and the president of China shook off his musings, as if regaining consciousness. The others seemed as shocked as him, most sitting silently. General Wen was calling urgently to an aide. General Shi was writing furiously. As the head of the political department, he would be most affected. He looked angry.

Other members of the commission started to arrive from their offices elsewhere in the building. Not everyone was there, of course. The announcement had caught them by complete surprise, which meant uncomfortable questions for General Xi Ping, chief of intelligence. They hurried in, asking questions that brought the rest out of their stunned silence.

Vice Chairman Zhang spoke first. "Why do I feel betrayed?"

"It's because Taipei initially declared neutrality," General Su explained. "I was relieved then. It meant one less enemy, and at least one possible path out for our trade. But after that traitorous announcement, I feel it as well."

Shi had stopped writing, and his angry expression had softened. He spoke sharply. "Before the war, if Taipei had done this, we'd be ordering military action. Comrade Vice President, your anger is well founded. Taiwan saw which way the wind was blowing. Her neutrality helped us, to some small degree, withstand the alliance. That will now be turned against us as she tries to hasten our end."

Zhang asked, "How will this news affect the population? How will they react?"

Shi shrugged. "I've been a political officer for thirty-four years, and all I'll predict is that it won't be to our advantage." Shi paused for just a moment, then added, "Comrade President, members of the council, the Political Department recommends that we break all connections with the Internet immediately. As we sit here and discuss the effects of Taiwan's defection, the rest of China is doing the same thing."

Some at the table rose in protest, but Shi waved them down. "I understand the value of the Internet in commerce and government, but this stream of bad news is damaging the morale of the people."

Instinctively, Chen agreed. The Chinese-controlled media was censored, of course, and her cyber security services blocked the great majority of objectionable sites. But it was impossible to completely block word from outside her borders, not with the Internet. And worse was the citizenry using it to talk among themselves. The CMC was well aware of the role that social networking had played in the collapse of other governments.

There was plenty for them to talk about. Hunts for foreign spies, industrial sabotage, the losses at sea, and now energy shortages all powered the rumor machine. The new fuel rationing system was already corrupt, rife with hoarders and profiteers.

Protests and riots were endemic, with no relief in sight. Ethnic groups like the Uyghurs in Xinjiang province and Tibetans were restive. Dissidents throughout the country were quick to claim that the communist party's ambitions in the South China Sea had started the war. The information supporting that argument had come from outside China.

General Shi was still explaining, but Chen cut him off. "Comrades, I believe General Shi is right, and becomes more right with each passing moment. Does anyone else wish to comment?"

A few shook their heads, and others muttered their agreement with Shi.

Chen waited for a full minute, then said, "General Shi, your recommendation is accepted. Will you please give the necessary orders?" Shi nodded and left quickly, almost at a run. Chen was sure it was the right thing to do, but why did it feel like another loss? Damnit, he was still shaking off the news about Taiwan.

General Su, the chief of staff, stated flatly, "We have to change our grand strategy." When there was no immediate agreement, Su explained, "I'm a soldier. We're trained to make an estimate of the situation, evaluate possible courses of action, and then choose the best one. My estimate of our situation is that we are losing this war. The trends are all in the wrong direction. What do we do about this?"

Chen answered him. "There are only two choices. We either agree to a cease-fire, which amounts to a surrender, or escalate."

There was dead silence in the room as the others absorbed the idea. Chen reasoned, "We must evaluate both courses before we choose. Adopting either one has benefits, and costs.

"To remove the risk of anyone being accused of disloyalty or defeatism, I will discuss the benefits of a cease-fire. The damage to our economy stops. Oil begins flowing again. The losses of equipment and men cease. What are the costs, Comrades?" He gestured to the others at the table.

Zhang said, "Unbelievable loss of prestige. The world would accuse us of being a failed superpower."

"The failure of Trident," General Su added.

"But the plan has already failed," General Ye Jin countered. "We will never be able to exploit the South China Sea's resources, as we had planned."

"We could use a cease-fire to mobilize and reposition our forces, then aim for a more limited objective," General Wen suggested.

Su quickly shook his head. "It won't work, Minister. Trident depended on surprise, on getting strong forces in place before our opponents could react. I don't think anyone here truly appreciated just how vital a factor surprise was."

Zhang added, "And we didn't expect such a unified response. The sudden appearance of the Littoral Alliance has completely changed the political calculus in this region. If we had known of its existence, would we have even started the operation?"

"That is not the issue, Generals," Chen insisted. "What are the costs to China of a cease-fire?"

Zhang looked thoughtful. "I've already mentioned the loss of prestige abroad. Domestically, we face widespread unrest. Energy supplies will be tight this winter, even if we restart imports immediately. Many industries are damaged, and our export markets will be lost for years, perhaps a decade. Unemployment, especially in the cities, will rise sharply."

"The best we can all hope for, personally, is resignation," Chen observed, "followed by a retirement in disgrace. That may not be the end of it, though. The next government will be looking for ways to assuage the citizens' anger. Accusations of criminal conduct and show trials are one method of placating the masses." Chen had stated the uncomfortable truth. Nobody expected justice in China, unless it served the party's purposes.

"Our economy crumbling, our citizens angry, the world turned against us. Regardless of my own fate, this is not what I dreamt of for China." Zhang's voice was hard. "If this is the aftermath of a cease-fire, then we must keep fighting."

"But we cannot win," Su reminded him. "The South China Sea is lost to us."

"Then we change the war," Zhang explained. "Instead of three or four countries, we are fighting an expanding coalition that now encircles us. We must recognize our new situation."

Chen asked, "Then what is our goal? How do we win?"

Zhang replied, "We bring enough force to bear to make them ask for a cease-fire, on our terms. We demand free passage of the ocean straits and removal of all economic sanctions.

"They haven't faced our full power yet. We've limited ourselves because of the military ties some countries have with the United States. We know America doesn't want this war. There's pressure in the American government to renounce the treaties. Let's call the alliance's bluff."

"We change the war," Chen repeated, testing the idea in his mind. "A full range of attacks against all alliance members, short of nuclear weapons. We remove the restrictions we've placed on our submarines. Allow them to attack any alliance shipping—it won't matter that they've disabled the automatic identification system. Any ship approaching an alliance port will be attacked. And we withdraw from the territories in the South China Sea we've captured."

"That was one of the alliance's demands," Su reminded him.

"The garrisons on those islands have been under constant siege. They can only be supplied by air, which costs fuel we can't spare. They are also at considerable risk from Japanese fighters staged in the Philippines."

Su nodded his agreement. "You're right. They can be sustained only with great effort, but cannot not be expanded, or exploited for further gain. What about Vietnam?"

"I see no reason to suspend that campaign," Chen replied. "Indeed, with the cancelation of Trident, we should be able to allocate more resources to that front. And where is General Hu?"

An aide left, in search of the Second Artillery commander. Chen said, "I remember his briefing argued for missile strikes on Japan, South Korea, and the Philippines. He can now add Taiwan to the list."


8 September 2016
1310 Local Time
North American Air Defense Directorate
Peterson Air Force Base
Colorado Springs, Colorado

They'd been on high alert since word had come from Washington about Taiwan's decision. Not that they hadn't been on high alert before, with half the Pacific shooting at the other half.

"Heaven help us, they went and did it!" the controller announced, hitting the audible alarm and calling the duty officer. "Multiple launches from within China!" He didn't even try to count the dots on the screen. The computer kept track, but the number kept climbing. Finally, he reported, "I'm seeing sixty-plus launches."

The duty officer, a major, didn't wait to see where they were headed. They wouldn't know that until after boost phase ended, a couple of minutes from now.

"Make sure PACOM's seeing this," the major ordered as he picked up the red phone. "This is Major Markowitz at NORAD. I have flash traffic for the NMJIC duty officer."

8 September 2016
1315 Local Time
White House Situation Room
Washington, D.C.

Ray Kirkpatrick was keeping vigil when the word arrived. When he phoned the residence, Myles answered after one ring.

"It's happened, Mr. President. Multiple Chinese ballistic missile launches."

"Do we know where they're going?" Myles asked, sounding resigned.

"Not yet, sir. It's too early."

Myles appeared in the situation room five minutes later, dressed in maroon sweats that had UNIVERSITY OF CHICAGO printed on the shirt. The call had caught him just as he was getting ready to go to the gym.

Kirkpatrick greeted him with, "None of them are headed for U.S. territory. Targets are in Japan, Taiwan, South Korea, and the Philippines. NORAD says they're DF-21s."

The president nodded an acknowledgement as he studied the display. "That's one nightmare avoided, then. Where will they hit first?"

Kirkpatrick pointed to a window on a side display. "Taiwan. Time of flight is six minutes. They'll be hitting about now."

"Taiwan's got Patriot," Myles observed.

"Yes, Mr. President. I was reviewing their order of battle. Eight batteries on line, with PAC-2 and PAC-3 missiles. And three Sky Bow batteries."

As they spoke, the display operator zoomed the view in so that the island of Taiwan filled the screen. Nine hostile missile symbols crawled in from the west. Their apparent slow speed was deceptive. Much of their movement was in the vertical plane.

Projected targets appeared, and Kirkpatrick called them out. "Two at Tsoying Naval Base where their submarines are berthed. Three at the BMD radar on Leshan Mountain, and . . . the Mailiao oil refinery. Four missiles headed there." Surprise filled his report.

"Payback. Makes sense." Myles's tone changed to puzzlement. "What's happening? Shouldn't the defenses be engaging them?"

"Yes, sir, they're just in range." One hostile missile headed for the sub base disappeared, then another, but that was it. As the two watched, the remaining seven symbols merged with their projected targets, then disappeared.

"I don't get it." Kirkpatrick's tone mixed worry and confusion. "The display showed at least three batteries in range. Only one engaged. The sub base is untouched, but the other two targets . . ."

"Find out what happened," barked Myles. "If the Chinese have put a hex on our interceptors, we need to find out."

Kirkpatrick turned and started walking quickly toward the watch floor, when Myles's voice called him to a stop. "And Ray, get our submarines clear of the area. This war is now beyond our abilities to stop."

9 September 2016
0211 Local Time
JDS *Atago* (DDG-177)
Off the Noto Peninsula, in the Sea of Japan

Captain Okubo Atsushi checked his watch and smiled. Four and a quarter minutes to battle stations manned and ready. Of course, they had good reason for being so quick.

Okubo picked up the shipwide PA microphone. "This is the captain. Our national air defense network has detected ballistic missiles fired by China, headed for targets across Japan. They will enter our engagement range in a little over a minute. We are the first line of defense. Center your thoughts, do your jobs. Today you will all be heroes!"

"Sir, Seasnake Two is airborne." The helicopter controller's voice came over his headset.

"Tell him to watch for suspicious surface craft, as well as submarines." Okubo had been flying the rotors off his two helicopters since they'd assumed this station. He was uncomfortable with the "bathtub" he'd been assigned, a box on the map just ten miles square. Warships were designed to move. Staying in the same area while radiating his radar nonstop was an open invitation to the Chinese.

But it was necessary. The central display was zoomed well out, showing the entire Sea of Japan. Okubo could see not only his ship, but also *Myoko* to the north and *Ashigara* to the south, their missile coverage overlapping to protect all of Honshu and Shikoku, and part of Kyushu. He'd asked for, and been honored with, the center station: the hot spot, guarding Tokyo. Unfortunately, to prevent gaps in the coverage the defending ships were glued to their stations.

Lieutenant Takagi, the missile officer, reported, "Our radar has detected the missiles. We have a good track." The hostile symbols on the display shifted slightly as the secondhand data from the air defense network was replaced by information directly from the destroyer's own SPY-1D radar. *Atago* could have fired using the other sensor data, but this was better.

"Radar detects five targets. Engaging closest three." Takagi's voice was even. He had said those words hundreds of times in synthetic exercises. Okubo depended on that familiarity now.

"Use standard firing doctrine." Takagi acknowledged the order with a nod. The system would assign two missiles to each target. In full autonomous mode, the Aegis fire control system would fire automatically when the hostiles were in range.

The only limitation was that they only had three illuminators, so their first salvo would only engage three of the five possible targets. A second salvo would go after the other two, plus any stragglers from first engagement, but it would follow ten seconds later, and the hostiles would be farther downrange.

"Captain! Seasnake's radar has multiple high-speed contacts, inbound! Range forty-seven nautical miles, bearing two nine two."

Okubo looked at the display. Datalinked from the helicopter's radar, four "unknown" contacts had appeared on the screen, but he could see the symbols move across the display, much too fast for a surface vessel. The helicopter's surface-search radar beam was pointed down. Normally it wouldn't even see aircraft. These were clearly air contacts, but they must be skimming the surface.

How fast? It took the computer two beats to get enough information to calculate the speed, and numbers appeared next to the unknown contacts. Almost six hundred knots. Large, subsonic, but no radar emissions? Were they cruise missiles? But fired from what? Then they disappeared from the display. Okubo's insides turned to ice.

Normally, *Atago* could deal easily with aerial contacts like these, whatever they were, but the Aegis fire control system was in ballistic missile defense mode. It couldn't engage aerodynamic contacts at the same time as ballistic missiles, and the Chinese were taking advantage of that. And he couldn't shift from aerial targets to ballistic missiles and back quickly enough to deal with both threats. He was committed.

"Launching in thirty seconds." The missile officer's voice was steady, focused.

"Tell Falcon flight to radiate and engage," Okubo ordered quickly. The unknown contacts were very low, and still over *Atago*'s radar horizon. Falcon flight, four F-2 fighters silently loitering at high altitude, was only ten miles to the east. They were high enough to see the intruders as soon as they lit off their radars.

A siren on the weather decks sounded, loud enough to be heard even in CIC. The controller announced, "Ten seconds," and Okubo reflexively braced himself, although there was no need.

The first missile's roar was background for the air controller's report. "Falcon flight's radars are on." After a moment's pause, "They have our unknowns—classified as Flankers. Falcons are firing." All through the narrative, Okubo could hear *Atago* launching SM3 missiles, each roar following another at one-second intervals.

The four air contacts reappeared on the screen, now labeled as "hostile aircraft." They were accelerating, and climbing. "Still no radar emissions from the aircraft," the air controller reported.

The last of six SM3 missiles left *Atago*, roaring toward the incoming hostile missiles.

Okubo saw new contacts on the display at the same time the air controller made his report. "Four new, very small contacts, evaluated as missiles. Range to *Atago* twenty-five nautical miles."

Okubo immediately ordered, "Falcons, engage the new contacts." He told the CIC crew, "Stand by missile defense stations. Stand by chaff." As he gave the last order, Okubo realized he still hadn't seen any radars from the hostiles. Of course they didn't need radar to find him, not with his SPY-1 energized. And the threat must be anti-radar missiles, homing in on his radar's signal. He was right to have Falcon flight shift targets.

Anti-radar missiles wouldn't care about chaff. They simply homed in on the SPY-1's radar signal, using it like a spotlight. And he couldn't turn the radar off because his own SM3s needed it to find their targets.

Another roar echoed outside, the beginning of the second salvo, another six missiles following ten seconds behind the first.

The Chinese Flankers had turned away, diving back down to low altitude now that they'd launched their missiles. One of them suddenly disappeared, and the air controller reported, "Splash one."

Okubo felt no joy in revenge. The incoming missiles were fast; labeled now as Kh-31Ps, speed Mach 3. He knew his air cover had shot at them, but it was a four-way race now.

"Splash one, splash two!" The missile officer's near-shout was overtaken by a rattling sound. *Atago*'s Phalanx point-defense guns firing. One long burst from each, then a second burst from the forward mount.

He had to see. Okubo left CIC and ran forward, but as he stepped onto the bridge, the windows were suddenly filled by black smoke laced with orange streaks. He'd felt no shock, but now there were metallic bumps and bangs, as if someone were throwing rocks, large ones, at *Atago*'s side. The doors to the bridge wing were open, and acrid smoke made them all cough.

Holding on to the doorframe for support, he fought for air, and finally cleared his lungs. Looking up, he saw the night sky outside the bridge.

The bridge phone talker reported, "Captain, damage control says we've taken a secondary hit. Ship control is good, but the radar's been hit!"

There was nothing to do here. He was back in CIC in moments, but many of the displays were dark. The main display still showed the tactical situation, but it was all secondhand data.

"We missed the last two, sir," Takagi said, upset, almost shaking. "I'm sorry, sir. The radar went offline before the terminal seekers were in range. The secondhand data wasn't as accurate, and we only splashed one more missile. Air defense was watching, they'll engage with Patriots soon." He was breathing hard, fighting for control. "I should have—"

"Forget that. What happened to the radar?" Okubo demanded.

"We lost two radar faces to fragments. The datalink showed missiles from Falcon flight splash two of the Kh-31s, and our Phalanx systems got the other two, but one was so close we got caught in the fireball."

"Sir, those missiles were aimed at Tokyo." Takagi was staring into space. "If . . ."

"No," Okuda said sharply. "It couldn't be helped. You did well. And whatever will happen is already under way."

9 September 2016
0215 Local Time
Littoral Alliance Headquarters
Okutama, Nishitama District
Tokyo, Japan

There was no siren. They hadn't been there long enough to have a warning system installed. Instead, every cell phone, tablet, and computer suddenly beeped, buzzed, and rang while displaying the simple message: *Take cover immediately.*

Komamura's shelter was in the house, but farther back, where the structure burrowed into the hillside. It was solid rock, they said, and would withstand anything short of the unthinkable.

The shelter had been used for storage until quite recently, and even as he'd hurried in, staffers were shifting boxes and cartons to make more room for the thirty-plus people, most of them in pajamas, crowded into a space the size of a large bedroom.

In deference to his rank, or age, or both, Komamura had been ushered to a fairly comfortable spot in the far corner, farthest in and farthest from the door. Sitting on a sturdy crate, he waited with the others, his back leaning against the cool rock wall. It had already become stuffy, and he could only wait for— What? An explosion? An all-clear?

The air defense people had promised them about fifteen minutes' warning. According to his cell phone, the alert had been sent almost that long ago. It had taken them far too long . . .

There. He felt a sharp, sudden movement in the rock behind him, and for a moment he thought of earthquakes, but it lasted only a fraction of a second, and then the sound reached them all a moment later—a deep, hard, boom loud enough to prevent speech, if the surprise and fear hadn't stopped it anyway. There was no sensation of blast, but a little dust fell from the ceiling.

A few people tried to speak but were hurriedly shushed, as if to not attract attention. The all-clear signal, like the alert sent to everyone's cell phone, made most of them jump, then laugh nervously. Everyone started to file out, and some made space for Komamura to go ahead of them, but he waved them on. He was comfortable, and suddenly reluctant to leave his place.

He was the last to leave, and had planned to head straight back to bed. Instead, a commotion in the hall outside carried him forward to the front of the house. Shouts and sirens prevented him from asking any questions, and he finally worked his way into the open.

A hundred meters away, on the hillside, a missile had struck. The impact point was easy to find by all the blown-over, burning trees. There was a lot of smoke, and small fires littered the nearby blast area. Helmeted rescue workers in bright-colored vests were already working with fire hoses to stop them from spreading.

He was still working to grasp the force of the explosion. A DF-21 supposedly had about a half-ton warhead. If that had stuck the building . . .

"*Sensei!*" It was Miyazaki, running again, but tearful and breathless. There was a dark, shiny patch of blood on her blue tracksuit, and the alarm must have shown on his face, because she quickly stopped and shook her head. "No, *sensei*, I'm fine, but the admiral . . ." That was all she could say before her legs gave out.

With Komamura on one side and a staffer on the other, they lowered her to the ground. She sobbed, then pointed, back toward the explosion. "The storage shed, they were in there."

Komamura knew she meant another one of the shelters, separate from the main house, but solidly built, with rock walls and a timber roof. Admiral Kubo had been in that shelter, along with many others. Hisagi was in a third. They'd collectively decided that if the alliance headquarters were attacked, no country should have its entire delegation in the same shelter.

He noticed rescue workers now, reflective white vests marked with red crosses, running around to the far side of the estate. Some of the staff headed in that direction too, but the professor stayed put. He didn't want to see.

Breathing carefully, Miyazaki spoke softly. "It was the closest shelter to the blast. After the all-clear sounded, I ran over to see how they were, but there was no shed, just rubble with the roof collapsed on top. We tried to pull it off, and some of it came away in pieces. Then I found Admiral Kubo, or at least I could see the top half of him. The rest was buried, and he wasn't breathing, but his eyes were open . . ."

She started shivering, and the professor found himself putting an arm around her shoulders. He intended to comfort her, but he found some strength in it as well. "There were more people killed, I think, and everyone in there must have been hurt. I'm sorry I didn't stay to help. I don't know first aid and when I saw the admiral I just panicked."

"It can't be helped, child." Komamura stood, then helped her to her feet. "We must move forward. Go change your clothes, then find Minister

Hisagi for me. I'll wait here." Blinking and still sniffling, she bowed quickly and ran off. By the time she came back, he'd have thought of some other chore for her.

Keeping busy was the best tonic. He tried to do the same thing, making a list of tasks, but found himself tripping over the first item: notifying Kubo's family. His wife was dead, but he had three children. But could they even release such news? Wouldn't the Chinese brag about such a thing?

His thoughts jumbled together. The oldest was a girl. Natsuki. She lived outside Ueda. As he tried to remember the other two children's names, Kubo's face and voice filled his memory and the tears came.

9 September 2016
0130 Local Time
41st Group Army Forward Headquarters
10 km South of Pingxiang, Near the Vietnamese Border

Lieutenant General Luo Shi found his chief of staff waiting outside the communications tent. "If we have to go tonight, are we ready?"

Qu Ding almost saluted. "Yes, sir. Everything is in place."

"Good, because General Su himself just gave me the order. Get the staff together. I'll speak to them in five minutes, but get word to the first-echelon units now. The infiltrators and engineers have to step off within the hour."

The ground campaign for Vietnam was under way.

# 19

# EVACUATION

9 September 2016
0120 Local Time
USS *North Dakota*
West of Hainan Island, South China Sea

The captain was in a foul mood. Jerry paced silently around the confined control room looking first at the sonar operator's screens, then the useless fire control displays—still no trace of *Chakra*. After putting some distance between them and the Akula following Minot's sinking, *North Dakota* had lost contact, but that was expected. Some forty hours later, Jerry's sonarmen still hadn't reacquired the elusive Indian. The only clues they had of *Chakra*'s whereabouts were two sets of distant explosions leading them northward, toward the Gulf of Tonkin.

Jerry paused by the UUV control console. "Anything from Fargo?"

"Sorry, Skipper, nothing," replied the petty officer.

Sighing deeply, Jerry gave the enlisted man a solid pat on the shoulder and made his way back to the CWS—the starting point for yet another lap. Thigpen watched as his captain beat a well-trodden path in the linoleum deck, and after almost two hours, his patience was gone. Inching closer to Jerry he whispered quietly, "If you want the watch, Captain, I don't mind turning it over. I have plenty of other stuff to do."

Jerry closed his eyes and took a deep breath. Thigpen's tone and the use of the word "captain" were a clear indication of his frustration. It was Thigpen's watch as the command duty officer, Jerry's had ended at midnight, but his silent lingering was putting everyone in control on edge.

"Sorry, XO," said Jerry. "It just grates me that we can't find this guy."

"Join the crowd, sir," Thigpen responded flatly. "But with all due respect, Captain, your rambling about is driving everyone in control crazy; and you know how short a trip that is for me."

Thigpen's quip took most of the bite out of his comment, but the message was loud and clear. Jerry was distracting the watchstanders with his moping about, and as CDO, Thigpen was completely in the right to put a stop to it.

"All right, all right, XO," replied Jerry, chastened. "I'll . . . just sit over here if you don't mind." Jerry pointed to one of the empty fire control chairs.

"As long as you behave yourself," jabbed Thigpen sternly. Lymburn desperately tried to stifle a laugh, but ended up emitting a loud snort instead.

"Something wrong, Q?" Jerry asked with mock annoyance.

"No, sir. Just clearing my throat. *Ahem, Ahem,*" replied the young lieutenant, smiling.

"Hmph! Insubordinate twits," Jerry muttered.


INS *Chakra*
50 km West of Hainan Island, South China Sea

"Report, Number One," demanded Samant as he strode into central post. He'd ordered *Chakra* to action stations just before he left the torpedo room, where he had supervised the loading of the first six land-attack cruise missiles.

"Yes, Captain, all compartments report they are at action stations. All torpedo tubes are at action state, with the exception of opening the bow caps. The target's coordinates have been successfully loaded into the missile's guidance computers," Jain answered promptly.

"Did you double-check that the missiles' navigation systems are selected to use Beidou satellite guidance?"

Jain nodded vigorously. "Absolutely, sir! The Klub missiles will use the Chinese's own navigation satellites to guide them to their targets."

"Excellent," smiled Samant with satisfaction. When India first purchased the Russian Klub missile system, the deal included the 3M-14E land-attack cruise missiles. As received, the 3M-14E missiles' onboard navigation system could only use the American GPS and Russian Glonass satellite navigation systems. However, before the missiles were loaded on Indian submarines, DRDO technicians replaced the Russian receiver with a home-built unit that could use all four satellite navigation systems, including the military signal from the Chinese Beidou, or "Compass" system.

Indian cyber spies had stolen the receiving chip design from a Chinese vendor's network, and when it was exploited, discovered that the Beidou system had an accuracy degradation feature similar to the U.S. Global Positioning System's "Selective Availability." The Ministry of Defense ordered the chip to be reverse-engineered and installed in all Indian military navigation systems and applicable weapons—particularly missiles. The wisdom of this decision was justified early in the war.

Soon after the Littoral Alliance announced its existence, the CMC ordered the jamming of GPS and Glonass signals over selective areas of the Chinese mainland. The degradation to the satellite's guidance signals reduced the effectiveness of some of the alliance's early missile strikes, but once India passed on the schematics and some examples of the new receiver to her allies, Vietnamese and South Korean cruise missiles were soon fitted with the modification. The Chinese were just about to find this out.

"Helmsman, make your depth twenty meters. Prepare for a safety sweep," announced Samant. "Open bow caps on all torpedo tubes. Stand by to fire, firing sequence tubes one through six, five-second intervals."

### USS *North Dakota*

"CDO, new contact, designate Sierra-five two, bearing zero three eight," cried the sonar supervisor. "Contact is faint, just a few mechanical transients."

Thigpen turned and looked over his shoulder. "Do you have a range?"

The sonar supervisor shook his head. "No, sir. I only got a few hits on the TB-33, definitely mechanical in nature. Nothing on any of the hull arrays."

Jerry had shot out of the chair as soon as he heard the news and stood next to Thigpen. "Sounds like our boy, XO."

"It's a good bet, Skipper."

"Hell, I'd take *any* bet right now. This guy is pretty cagey. If we've picked up mechanical transients, it's only because he's about to shoot someone."

"But that's just it, Skipper," complained Thigpen. "There is nothing else out there even close to that bearing to shoot at!"

"Not even a Chinese sub?"

"No, sir, not that we can see. And we've had no problem picking up lots of transients and strong tonals from Chinese boats long before we get broadband contact."

"So, if it isn't a surface ship, or another submarine, then . . ." Jerry just stopped, letting his statement dangle. He had a coaxing expression on his face, pushing his XO to finish the thought. Thigpen caught on immediately.

"Wait a minute, are you suggesting . . ."

"That's what I'm thinking."

"Oh, shit," Thigpen uttered quietly.

"Yup, that's about right," concluded Jerry.

Lymburn looked back and forth at the two men, totally confused by their cryptic conversation. "What!?" she exclaimed. "What's the matter . . . sirs?"

Thigpen held up his left hand, signaling for her to wait. "Patience, Grasshopper," he said as he pivoted back toward the command workstation. "Pilot, right full rudder, steady on course zero five zero. All ahead standard."

As the pilot responded to the orders, Thigpen grabbed an interior communications handset and punched in the number for the engineering officer of the watch. "Maneuvering, Conn. Shift reactor coolant pumps to fast speed. Stand by for flank bell."

*North Dakota* heeled slightly as she accelerated through the turn. Swinging toward the contact, and gradually picking up speed, she began to close the distance.

Thigpen shook his head as he looked at the electronic plot on the port VLSD. He was not happy with the geometry. Glancing over to Jerry, he said, "Assuming it's our friend, and assuming he's still headed in a northerly direction, I'm biasing us to come in behind her. But I really dislike putting whatever it is in the towed arrays' forward beam. Our bearing data will suck."

"Do we have a choice?" Jerry asked stoically.

Thigpen sighed. "No, sir."

"Then we don't have a problem, XO."

"Yes, sir," he replied. Then more defiantly added, "But I still don't have to like it."

Jerry rolled his eyes; Thigpen was just being stubborn. "Very well, XO, permission granted to not like it."

"Thank you, sir," replied Thigpen, satisfied.

Lymburn, sensing a break, moved closer. "Captain, XO, I still don't understand what's going on."

"Ah, yes, sorry about that, Q," Thigpen apologized. "Here's the deal. We think Sierra-five two is the Indian Akula. If so, then the mechanical transients we've detected are likely torpedo tube preparations. As we hold no other contacts near the bearing, the Skipper is guessing that our friend out there is about to . . ."

"Launch transients!" sang out the sonar supervisor abruptly. "One weapon . . . two, solid rocket ignition. XO, Sierra-five two is launching missiles."

". . . launch missiles," said Thigpen dryly, completing his sentence. He then leaned forward, and acknowledged the report. "Very well, Sonar Supervisor. Did we get a range?"

"No, sir. Sierra-five two is still in the wide aperture arrays' baffles. Contact is drawing left, bears zero three five."

"Sonar, were you able to get a weapon count?" interrupted Jerry.

"Not a good one, Skipper. At least two missiles, probably more. The noise from the rocket motors drowned everything else out."

"Orders, Skipper?" asked Thigpen.

"He's not done yet, he's probably reloading for another salvo," Jerry opined. "Time to let him know we're here, XO. Put the spurs to her."

"Aye, aye, sir!" Thigpen responded enthusiastically. "Pilot, left standard rudder, steady course zero three five, all ahead flank. Sonar, stand by to go active on Sierra-five two."

## INS *Chakra*

"First missile salvo launch complete, Captain. Bow caps are closed on tubes one through six, and the loading of the second salvo is under way," reported Jain.

"Very good, Number One, but tell the boys in the bomb shop to be quick about it. We just broadcasted our location to the world, and I have no desire to tarry here more than is absolutely necessary," Samant demanded.

"Aye, Captain."

Samant was pleased. They'd gotten off the first six land-attack cruise missiles without a hitch, and the loading of the second salvo was well under way. In another few minutes, he'd be finished launching the last of the twelve-missile strike. Some fifteen minutes later, the oil refinery at Beihai would receive a very nasty surprise. The Chinese undoubtedly expected any

Littoral Alliance cruise missile that used GPS or Glonass to miss their target. How ironic that their own satellite navigation system would foil their plan. He reveled in the fact that this was the first strategic strike by an Indian submarine on Chinese soil; his place in the history books would now be secured. But Samant had little time to fully appreciate his achievement, as the intercom speaker suddenly blared.

"New contact, number eight seven, bearing two one eight. Contact is submerged and closing at high speed!"

*Damn the American!* cursed Samant silently. It had to be him; they would have surely heard a noisy Chinese SSN long before now. Samant's patience was exhausted, the American had become more than a mere nuisance and he intended to deal with this interloper once and for all.

"Number One, begin tracking the new contact. Stand by for rapid-fire torpedo attack, tube eight."

Jain looked incredulous, he seemed confused by the order. Samant didn't appreciate his hesitation. "You heard me, Number One. Prepare to attack contact eight seven."

"Captain," replied Jain forcefully. "With respect, sir, I must remind you that we are not authorized to fire on *any* American vessel."

Samant was irritated on the one hand by his first officer's response, but impressed on the other. Jain was proving to be a fast learner. He'd already figured out the likely identity of the new contact.

"Very well, Number One," Samant conceded with a slight smile. "Would you condone a warning shot?"

"A warning shot, sir? With a torpedo?" Jain sounded incredulous.

"Yes, Mr. Jain," answered Samant, using the first officer's name to reassert his authority. "We'll fire a single torpedo, but the seeker will be disabled and we'll offset the weapon ten degrees to starboard. That should suffice to make it impossible for the torpedo to hit the American submarine."

"It's still bending the rules a bit, sir," said Jain carefully. "But given the circumstances, I believe a review by a higher authority will find it acceptable."

"Splendid!" cried Samant. "Track contact eight seven, stand by for deliberate torpedo fire. Disable the seeker on the torpedo in tube eight."

"Torpedo seeker is disabled, Captain. And tubes one through six are loaded, rear doors are secured," reported the primary fire control operator.

"Bring tubes one through six to action state, and open the bow caps." Samant picked up the intercom microphone and selected the sonar room. "Sonar, go active on the port flank array, three pulses."

## USS North Dakota

The alarm from the WLY-1 acoustic intercept receiver beat the sonar supervisor by only a couple of seconds. "Skat-3 transmissions, three pulses, correlates with Sierra-five two, classify the contact as an Akula class SSN."

"Answer in kind, XO," Jerry commanded.

"Aye, sir. Sonar, go active on Sierra-five two, three pulses."

Three invisible, but intense sound waves shot out from *North Dakota*'s active conformal array. Upon reaching the Indian submarine, the sound waves bounced off the air-filled pressure hull. Even though the Akula was covered in anechoic coating, the sub was too close for the coating to have a significant effect. *North Dakota*'s passive conformal array got three good returns.

## INS Chakra

"Captain! Confirm American BQQ-10 sonar, bearing two one zero. Matches bearing to contact eight seven, range eight thousand seven hundred meters and closing rapidly!" The sonar officer sounded ruffled over the intercom.

"Solution status, Number One," barked Samant.

"Contact is pointed right at us. Course, zero three zero, speed, thirty-two knots. Solution is ready!"

"Set torpedo course, two two zero."

"Course set!" Jain replied.

Samant nodded. "Stand by . . . FIRE!"

Inside tube number eight, a Russian UGST torpedo was violently expelled by a sudden wave of fast-moving water. At first, it coasted downward in a shallow arc as the onboard computer started up the engine. Once up to speed, the torpedo turned hard to port and began climbing back to its ordered depth. Soon it was roaring toward the American submarine at fifty knots.

## USS North Dakota

Jerry and Thigpen looked at the command display. The active sonar had no trouble detecting the Akula. It was just a little under 9,500 yards away, moving slowly to the northwest.

"Ping him again, XO. Let's make him feel uncomfortable about staying here."

"Aye, Skipper. Sonar, go active on Sierra-five two, three more pulses," ordered Thigpen. Once again, three pulses went out, and three good returns were detected. But the Indian wasn't reacting; his course and speed were unchanged.

"Nothin', Skipper," Thigpen grunted. "He's ignoring us."

"He's a cool one, that's for sure. I think he knows he'll be able to launch his second salvo before we can get too close."

"He certainly is a cheeky fellow," remarked Thigpen.

Jerry ignored his XO's comment, choosing instead to focus his thoughts on his alternate number. The man knew how to handle his boat; of that there was no doubt. But what was he like? Where did he get his education, his training? What motivated him? All these questions, and more, swirled around in Jerry's head. And all of them were, at the moment, unanswerable.

"Skipper, you want me to hit him again?" Thigpen's question jerked Jerry from his musings. He'd have to deal with his questions later.

"Yes, XO, but this time, hammer him. Go continuous, keep pinging him," Jerry said resolutely.

"Aye, sir. Sonar, go continuous active on Sierra-five two."

Jerry's head snapped up immediately; he didn't hear the expected repeat-back of the XO's order. Looking toward the sonar station, he saw the supervisor and a senior sonarman staring intently at the same screen. Thigpen saw it too.

"Talk to me, Sonar Supervisor," the XO demanded.

"XO, there's another contact in the general direction of Sierra-five two. It's hard to make out with all the flow noise on the towed arrays, but there is definitely something out there."

"Petty Officer Andersen, do I need to start being worried?" Jerry was able to sound calm, but his heartbeat had just shot way up.

"I'm not sure, sir. It kind of looks like . . ." The sonar supervisor stopped in mid-sentence as another set of faint lines showed up on his display. After some quick manipulations of the controls, the lines were enlarged and matched against the acoustic database—a flashing red "Torpedo Warning" indicator popped on the screen. Andersen's face went white.

"Torpedo in the water! Same bearing as Sierra-five two!" he shouted.

"Captain has the conn," thundered Jerry. "Pilot, right standard rudder, steady on course . . ." He paused as he looked quickly at the geoplot on the big screen. "... one four zero, maintain flank speed. Torpedo defense, launch an ADC Mark 5 and mobile decoy, standby ATT."

*North Dakota* heeled sharply to starboard as the rudder kicked over. Even with fly-by-wire controls, the submarine rolled heavily into the turn, vibrating noticeably as she swung around. Jerry knew speed was his main advantage, and he'd intentionally used less rudder to keep his speed up. The only indication that the countermeasure and mobile decoy had been launched was the blinking of icons on the large display screen. For a few tense minutes, everyone held on in silence, with only the sonar supervisor's reports breaking the tense quiet.

Finally, he called out, "Captain, torpedo has passed CPA and is opening. *Whew!*"

A collective sigh of relief was heard throughout control.

"Sonar, did the weapon ever enable?" Jerry asked tersely.

"I don't know for sure, Skipper. I don't think it went active, but we had the ADC pretty much in our field of view during the whole turn. We could have missed it."

"Very well." Jerry was unconvinced; he knew his sonar operators were good. And it would be unlike them to miss something so loud as an active torpedo seeker even with the countermeasure in the way. Turning toward the rest of the control room watchstanders, he announced loudly, "Attention in Control. I intend to stay on this course for a little longer, then we'll slow and take a look around. I don't believe the Akula will pursue us, but we can't afford to make that assumption, so stay sharp, everyone. Carry on."

Thigpen pulled up beside Jerry. "I can't believe that son-of-a-bitch fired at us! We're lucky he misjudged the distance, the weapon probably enabled after it passed us."

Jerry laughed cynically. "He didn't misjudge anything, Bernie. He's too good to make that kind of mistake. He deliberately fired the torpedo with the seeker off. A warning shot, with a very clear message—keep off the grass."

"What do we do now, Skipper?"

"We report in, XO," stated Jerry flatly. "The rules of this weird game appear to have changed yet again, and we need to let our bosses know. You have the conn. I'll be in the radio room if you need me."

9 September 2016
0145 Local Time
Squadron Fifteen Headquarters
Guam

Simonis took a healthy slurp of coffee while he read the initial intelligence reports on the missile attacks. It didn't look good. He'd been called at his residence as soon as NORAD put out the warning. Fifteen minutes later he was in his office. His staff came in dribs and drabs a few minutes behind him. After a quick review of the situation, the CSO sent half the staff back home, but not before announcing that they were now on a port and starboard watch rotation. A sharp knock at the door pulled Simonis's attention from the reports. His operations officer was in the doorway with a carafe in his hand.

"Need a recharge, Commodore?"

"Sure, Rich, come on in."

Walker strode over and poured fresh hot coffee into Simonis's half-empty mug.

"Did you see these reports?" Simonis inquired, pointing to the intel assessments.

"Yes, sir. It would appear this war is taking a turn for the worse."

"Ha!" Simonis blurted. "Mr. Walker, you are a master of the understatement!" The commodore picked up the last report and read from its key judgments.

"At 1710 Zulu time PLA Second Artillery units executed multiple ballistic missile strikes against targets in Japan, Taiwan, South Korea, and the Philippines. While ballistic missile defenses were moderately effective, numerous missiles still reached their targets. Moderate to heavy casualties are expected."

Simonis threw the paper back down onto his desk. "That's not just a turn for the worse, Mr. Walker. It's the first step on a very slippery slope that will lead to a nuclear exchange!"

The operations officer was surprised by Simonis's fierce outburst. The attack on the Littoral Alliance nations was shocking, to be sure, but they were still limited, given China's conventional ballistic missile capability. If China really wanted to plaster the targets they were after, the strikes would have been much larger. Furthermore, the attacks were largely on legitimate alliance military and oil infrastructure facilities—missile strikes on civilian population centers were a rare occurrence. In the operations officer's mind, this attack was long overdue, a logical reaction to Littoral Alliance cruise missile attacks on Chinese oil refineries and tank farms.

Come to think of it, Walker didn't remember Simonis reacting so strongly to the initial strikes by alliance cruise missiles, and those were attacks against targets on Chinese soil. For the commodore to suddenly jump straight to the conclusion that the war would inevitably go nuclear seemed a bit of a stretch. China didn't need to go down that path, and indeed seemed to be avoiding it, as India hadn't been targeted at all.

"Sir, how can you say that?" Walker protested. "This attack was expected, or should have been, given the Littoral Alliance's strikes on Chinese oil refineries. And yet, China didn't fire a single missile at India. That tells me China is trying hard to keep this conflict conventional."

Simonis shook his head vigorously, his face grim. "Rich, you're completely missing the big picture. When the Communist Party figures out they're losing, they'll go nuclear—they will have no other choice!"

Walker was stunned by Simonis's conclusion that China was losing the war. The PRC had certainly been stung, but militarily they still had an advantage over the Littoral Alliance. However, before he could respond, the commodore's yeoman knocked on the door.

"Sorry to interrupt, Commodore, but Dr. Patterson is on the secure line."

"It's about time," Simonis mumbled as he grabbed the handset. "Dr. Patterson, good afternoon."

"Good morning, Commodore, although the 'good' part is seriously being debated here in Washington," she replied.

"I completely understand. The situation is deteriorating rapidly. However, I'm hoping you have some good news for me."

"You're correct. The president wants you to recall your submarines. They are to return to Guam as fast as the tactical situation allows. We've done what we can and it's time to evacuate the area."

Simonis's shoulders relaxed noticeably, as if a heavy weight had just been removed. "I will do so with pleasure, ma'am. The order will go out in ten minutes. Please express my gratitude to the president."

"I will when I get the chance. Good luck, Commodore."

"And to you, Dr. Patterson." As the handset hit the cradle, Simonis looked at Walker and said, "Rich, I want a flash precedence message ordering all our boats to return to base. You have seven minutes."

9 September 2016
0215 Local Time
USS *North Dakota*
West of Hainan Island, South China Sea

Jerry sat in the back of the radio room, replaying the last encounter with the Indian Akula in his mind. He ran through the scenario over and over again, trying to see where he'd made a mistake. The critical decision was to close the faint contact at high speed. On the one hand, if he hadn't charged, the Akula wouldn't have detected *North Dakota*. On the other, if he hadn't, the Indian would have fired off his second salvo and possibly cleared datum before Jerry could reacquire him. *Damned if I do, damned if I don't,* he said to himself.

"Skipper, sorry to disturb you," interrupted the information technician, "but we have flash traffic coming in."

Jerry looked at his watch with confusion; it hadn't even been four minutes since they sent in their report. "That can't be in response to our last message—way too quick of a turnaround."

"It's not, sir. This message is a recall order. I'm printing it out now."

The printer behind Jerry's head whined to life and kicked out a single sheet of paper. Grabbing it, he called out to Thigpen, "XO! Flash traffic!"

Thigpen stuck his head into radio seconds later. He too looked perplexed. "My, that was fast! Has our commodore moved a cot into the radio room?"

"No, XO. This isn't about our incident report. It's a recall order," said Jerry as he handed the message to Thigpen.

"Seriously?"

"Absolutely. Simonis refers to 'continued escalation,' no further explanation provided, as the reason for the president to order a withdrawal. We're to return to base ASAP."

The XO frowned, his voice heavy with cynicism. "It would have been *nice* to have gotten this an hour earlier!"

"Yeah, well, what's done is done, Bernie. Send the 'return home' signal to Fargo, and select a rendezvous point away from our last meeting with the Akula."

"Aye, aye, Skipper," responded Thigpen. He handed the message to Jerry and darted back to control.

With his XO's voice in the background, Jerry scribbled a response on the message printout and handed it to the IT. "Send this. Message received. Rendezvousing with UUV, will advise when we begin transit back to base."

"Aye, aye, sir," the petty officer replied.

As the young sailor typed out his captain's response, Jerry wondered what had happened to change the president's mind. Whatever it was, he knew it had to have been really bad.

9 September 2016
0345 Local Time
Squadron Fifteen Headquarters
Guam

Simonis paced tensely in the back of the Squadron Fifteen operations watch floor. There was still no reply from *Santa Fe* acknowledging the recall order. Grumbling about Halsey's ineptness, the commodore kept walking back and forth, stopping only to refill his mug. Between fatigue and overcaffein-ation, his patience was virtually nonexistent, his temper on a hair trigger.

Walker kept a watchful eye on his commodore. He knew Simonis was barely holding on, and had instructed all the watchstanders to give him a heads-up first when *Santa Fe* finally responded.

Out of the corner of his eye, Walker saw one of the duty ITs signaling him—the message was in. Shielding his right hand from view with his body, he made a typing motion. The petty officer nodded, clicked his mouse, and held up one finger; the message was coming out on printer number one. Walking slowly over to the printer bank, the operations officer pulled the message and read it quickly. His heart sank.

Simonis saw Walker's expression, and demanded loudly, "What is it, Rich?"

"*Santa Fe*'s reported in, Commodore," he answered.

"Well, it would seem that Commander Halsey likes to take his sweet time responding—"

"She's been attacked, sir," Walker added quickly.

"What?" Simonis's expression changed instantly from anger to concern.

"Yes, sir." Walker elaborated as he walked up the stairs to Simonis. "She got bounced by a Y-8 patrol aircraft, and took two depth charges close aboard. The port main engine is down, there is a bad main propulsion shaft rub, and both towed arrays are gone. Halsey also reports some personnel casualties, but nothing life-threatening."

Simonis snatched the message from Walker, but before he even began reading it, barked, "What's her position?"

"Sir, she's currently near the western edge of her patrol zone, approximately forty nautical miles due east of the northeast tip of Hainan Island," answered one of the watchstanders.

"She's deep in Indian country, Commodore," Walker observed, looking up at the large flat-panel display.

"I can see that, Rich," snapped Simonis. "What's the closest boat to her?"

"Theoretically, *Texas* is the closest. But Pascovich was the first CO to respond and he's undoubtedly gone deep by now. He won't be back up for a comms check for another ten hours."

"What about Mitchell?" asked Simonis.

"Nothing since his acknowledgement of the recall order, sir, so he's still in the process of recovering his recon UUV. Given Mitchell's rude encounter with the Indian Akula, he's probably moving cautiously," Walker answered.

"A wise course of action," said Simonis, nodding approvingly. He paused and looked first at the message, and then at the electronic plotting board. There really was no other option.

"Very well, Rich, send a flash precedence message to *North Dakota*, copy *Santa Fe*. Provide a rendezvous point and have Mitchell link up with Halsey; keep *Santa Fe*'s speed to no more than ten knots. I want *North Dakota* to escort *Santa Fe* out of the South China Sea. You have—"

"Yes, sir, I know. I have seven minutes," shouted Walker as he leapt down the stairs. "Jeff! Get me a position that both boats can reasonably make given *Santa Fe*'s mobility restrictions. Use *North Dakota*'s last position and shift it to the west by fifteen miles. Move, people. We've got a hurt boat to get home!"

9 September 2016
1430 Local Time
USS *North Dakota*
Southeast of Hainan Island, South China Sea

They'd initially detected *Santa Fe* half an hour earlier at the ungodly range of thirty-five thousand yards. Even at ten knots, the shaft rub was very noisy and Jerry wondered how the Chinese could possibly miss it. Still, he prayed that their acute deafness would continue, preferably for the next several days. Guam was a long way away.

"Skipper, new contact, designated Sierra-six three, bearing north," announced the sonar supervisor.

Jerry and Thigpen both looked over the supervisor's shoulder as he pointed to a few tenuous lines on his display. "What do you have, Chief?" Jerry asked quietly.

"Don't know, sir. The narrowband is really unstable," replied Chief Halleck. "There's no discernable bearing drift as well. It could be a distant surface contact, but that's just a SWAG."

"That bearing isn't in the direction of the normal traffic lanes, or any harbor that we know of," Thigpen remarked. "Why do I have the sneaky suspicion this isn't a coincidence?"

"Because luck hasn't exactly been running in our favor lately, XO," admitted Jerry with a hint of irritation. "Mr. Covey, begin tracking Sierra-six three."

"Aye, aye, sir."

For the next six minutes, Jerry stared intently at the port VLSD, as if pure concentration could conjure up more information. Nothing. Absolutely nothing. There was no bearing drift at all, and sonar was still only picking up a couple of unstable tonals. But as each minute passed, Jerry became more and more agitated. There was something wrong here; his intuition was ringing with alarm bells. Finally in frustration he growled, "Chief, I'm starting to get really annoyed with this situation. I think we're on an intercept course with Sierra-six three. Do you concur?"

"It's a good possibility, Skipper. I'm not seeing, or hearing, any screw noise from the contact. If we've been constantly staring at his bow the whole time, that would explain the lack of any main-propulsion-related noise."

Jerry walked over to Halleck and tapped the chief on the shoulder. He needed the man's undivided attention. "Chief, I'm going to cut across the line of sight to try and generate some bearing rate. But I think we need to come shallow as well. If I remember correctly, we had a weak layer on the last SVP, but that was taken earlier this morning. If the layer has gotten stronger, and deeper, that would explain why we aren't seeing more tonals."

"Yes, sir, it would indeed."

"Have your guys glue their noses to the stacks. I'll bring us around," Jerry said while patting the chief on the shoulder.

Turning back toward the ship control panel, Jerry called out, "Pilot, left full rudder, steady course three two zero. All ahead two-thirds, and make your depth one hundred and twenty-five feet."


Moments after *North Dakota* reached her new depth, Chief Halleck sang out, "Broadband contact, Sierra-six three. Bearing zero zero six!"

"Very well, Chief," Jerry replied with satisfaction. Then whispered, "Gotcha!"

"Tracking Sierra-six three, initial range, twenty-one thousand yards," reported Covey.

Before Jerry could acknowledge Covey's report, Halleck jumped in with unwelcome news. "Skipper, there are two contacts close together. Designate the second contact, Sierra-six four, bearing zero zero four!"

"Begin tracking Sierra-six four!" commanded Jerry. "Chief, I need a classification ASAP."

"Working it, sir."

Jerry watched the port VLSD as the fire control system's output settled down to a consistent solution. Inwardly, he groaned. Whatever they were, the two contacts were headed straight toward *Santa Fe*. When Halleck made his report, Jerry already knew what he was going to say.

"Captain, both Sierra-six three and six four have two five-bladed screws."

"Warships," Jerry concluded grimly.

"Yes, sir. One is a possible Type 052 destroyer, the other looks like a Type 053 frigate," answered the chief.

"Makes sense," Jerry remarked. "Classic high-low mix."

Thigpen also heard the report. His face showed his anxiety. "Skipper, I don't think *Santa Fe* knows those two ships are even there!"

"I suspect you're right, XO," granted Jerry. "Without a towed array, Halsey doesn't have an effective sensor. Between the strong layer and the increased noise from her shaft, *Santa Fe*'s spherical array probably hasn't detected them yet."

"Can we warn him?"

Jerry shook his head. "*Santa Fe*'s still too far away. And even if she did hear us, we'd have to transmit at such high power on the underwater comms gear that those two yahoos out there would hear it too."

"Then . . . then what can we do?" pleaded Thigpen.

Jerry turned toward Thigpen. His expression was hard and determined. "We'll do what we have to, XO. Copilot, sound general quarters!"

As the general alarm rang throughout the ship, Jerry added sternly, "If either of those ships even look cross-eyed at *Santa Fe,* I'll put a Mark 48 into them."


Control became abuzz with activity as the battle stations watchstanders filed in and took their positions. Jerry immediately began issuing orders to prepare *North Dakota* for battle. He hoped it wouldn't come to that, but he still had to be ready for the worst. Even though there was plenty of activity going on, time seemed to crawl by for Jerry, as the distance between him and the Chinese warships wound down ever so slowly. The problem was that he was at the wrong end of the triangle; the warships were closing faster on *Santa Fe* than he was on them. If he wanted to close the gap, he'd have to kick their speed up a notch or three, but that only raised more alarm bells. Thigpen was thinking along those same lines. He was worried and said as much.

"I've got a bad feeling about this, Skipper. Why haven't the Chinese warships gone active yet? Their hull arrays can't be that good in passive mode."

"They're not, XO. One of those ships has a towed array. That's how they've been able to track *Santa Fe.* I'm certain of it."

"They could have an MPA in support."

"A patrol aircraft would have attacked by now, and there's no reason to expose your ships to a possible torpedo attack if you can engage from a distance. Those ships are closing in together, positioning themselves to execute a coordinated attack. You can bet there's at least one helo in the air," summarized Jerry.

"So what's the plan, sir?" queried Thigpen.

"First off, XO, we need more information. An eye on the target," Jerry replied. Then looking over at Covey he demanded, "What's our status, Weps?"

"Sir, torpedo tubes one and two are ready in all respects with the exception of opening the outer doors. A Sea Tern UAV has been loaded into the number one signal ejector and is ready for launch."

"Very well, Mr. Covey," acknowledged Jerry. Moving back to the center of the control room, he cleared his throat and spoke loudly. "Attention in control. My intention is to launch a Sea Tern UAV to get a better view of the tactical picture. We need to watch this situation carefully. We don't want to cause an incident, but if any of the Chinese units fire on *Santa Fe,* we will engage immediately with Mark 48 ADCAP torpedoes. Stay sharp; this ride may get a bit bumpy. Carry on.

"Pilot, all stop. Make your depth sixty-five feet."

"All stop, make my depth sixty-five feet, Pilot, aye. Skipper, Maneuvering answers all stop."

"Very well, Pilot." Jerry watched as the speed started to drop. *North Dakota* had to slow down considerably before he dared to raise a photonics mast. Even at ten knots, the maximum safe speed for the mast, it would leave a huge wake—easily visible to an airborne helicopter.

To save time, Jerry used the residual speed to plane his boat up to periscope depth. It was only a few minutes until the pilot reported, "Captain, on ordered depth. Speed is six knots."

"Very well, Pilot. Ahead one-third, make turns for five knots." While the pilot repeated the order, Jerry faced Covey. "Weps, launch the Sea Tern. Then take the UAV station. XO, you can double up as weapons officer."

"Aye, Captain," answered both men simultaneously.

As soon as Covey hit the launch button, a slug of water forced the canister with the UAV out of the signal ejector. Floating to the surface, the canister's end cap blew off as soon as the pressure sensor detected it was clear of the water. Milliseconds later, the micro-UAV was propelled out of the canister by a small charge. Once airborne, it climbed to five hundred feet and turned toward the Chinese warships. Based on the Switchblade micro-UAV, the Sea Tern was just over a foot long, with a small battery-powered motor that could get the tiny vehicle up to a maximum speed of seventy-five knots. But its best endurance was at half that speed. With its minuscule size and slow speed, the Sea Tern looked like a seabird to a modern radar. Thus, any reflected energy would be filtered out by the radar's signal processor, essentially rendering the vehicle invisible while in plain sight. It wasn't long before its electro-optical and infrared sensor data was relayed to *North Dakota*'s exposed mast.

"Skipper, the Sea Tern has acquired the Chinese ships," Covey announced. "Sending the output to the starboard VLSD."

Jerry and Thigpen looked at the large screen and saw the two warships in a line of bearing formation with the destroyer in the lead.

"Good call, Chief," Jerry complimented his sonar supervisor. "We've got one Type 052B Luyang I destroyer and one Type 053H3 Jiangwei II frigate."

Thigpen leaned forward, then pointed toward the screen. "Skipper, look at the Luyang on the IR display. See that black line streaming from her stern? You were right, she's got a towed array!"

"Then she is our primary target. If we have to shoot," Jerry replied calmly.

"Conn, ESM Bay," squawked the intercom speaker. "I hold two surface-search radars from the warships, low signal strength, but no airborne radars."

Jerry turned to Thigpen, perplexed. "They don't have a helo up? That doesn't make any sense."

"Maybe they've got a mechanical glitch. The Chinese have been flying them pretty hard lately," Thigpen suggested.

"Going after a potentially hostile submarine with just two surface ships and no helicopters? That's not too bright. There has to be another explanation," argued Jerry.

No sooner had Jerry said this, than Chief Halleck shouted, "Lamb Tail transmissions, bearing zero three seven, same bearing as *Santa Fe!*"

"I'm on it," cried Covey as he instructed the UAV to turn toward that bearing. It didn't take long before the large screen showed a Ka-28 Helix helicopter down low, hovering over the water, a dark line dropping from its fuselage.

"It's dipping," said Thigpen.

"And it's got *Santa Fe,*" Jerry added. Suddenly, a small object dropped from the helo's underside.

"What was that!?" barked Jerry. "Chief, what do you hear?"

"Nothing, sir. It just hit the water and sank . . ." Halleck stopped in mid-sentence, his face turning white. "Torpedo in the water! It's pinging, but no propulsion noises!"

"Damn it!" groaned Jerry angrily. "It dropped an APR-2E rocket torpedo! Snapshot! Sierra-six three, tube one!"

The fire control technician at the weapon's console began rapidly punching buttons. "Outer door on tube one open!" he cried. The sailor watched, his hands shaking, as the remaining indicators turned green. "Stand by . . . Shoot!"

Jerry felt the subtle vibrations from the ejection pump winding up; the torpedo was on its way. He'd just launched a weapon in anger.

"Normal launch, wire is good," reported the petty officer.

Jerry could see the position of the torpedo on the port VLSD, sprinting off at high speed toward its target. "Very well," he said.

"Captain, *Santa Fe* has deployed countermeasures. She's turning," reported Halleck.

"What about the APR-2, Chief?" asked Jerry anxiously.

"Still searching . . . No, wait, rocket motor ignition! It's homing!"

Helpless, a mere spectator, Jerry issued a silent prayer while he waited with the rest of the people in control for the seemingly inevitable outcome.

"It missed!" shrieked Halleck. "The APR-2 missed her!"

"Praise be!" whispered Thigpen. But his relief was short-lived as Lymburn pointed to her display. He looked and immediately understood. Dejected, he said, "Skipper, *Santa Fe* has turned *toward* the Chinese warships!"

Jerry closed his eyes and rubbed his forehead, Halsey had turned the wrong way. Jerry's mind raced for anything that he could do to help the stricken U.S. boat. Looking up at the port VLSD, he saw his Mark 48 was six thousand five hundred yards away from its target; one thousand five hundred yards from the enable point when the seeker would activate. "XO, command enable own-ship's unit."

"Command enable, aye," answered Thigpen. Followed shortly by, "Sir, weapon has enabled."

Glancing over at Thigpen, Jerry nodded wearily. "Maybe I can scare them off," he said quietly.

"Skipper!" yelped Covey. "Both ships have launched torpedoes!"

Jerry's head snapped up toward the starboard display. He could see the remaining wisps of smoke drifting aft from the Chinese ships.

"Concur!" Halleck blurted out. "Torpedoes in the water! Bearing zero one five! Two Yu-7 torpedoes—damn! They do sound like Mark 46s!"

There was nothing left to do but watch, and wait. Like watching a fight in slow motion, Jerry stared at the screen as the three torpedoes crept toward their respective targets. His Mark 48 would reach the Luyang I destroyer first, but that would be of little help to Halsey and the crew of *Santa Fe*.

"Detect. Detect. Detect. Homing! Own ship's unit has acquired the target," shouted the fire control technician. "Target bears zero one six, range three thousand five hundred yards."

Jerry acknowledged the report; his eyes remained fixated on the large display screen on his left.

"*Santa Fe* is deploying more countermeasures, Skipper," reported Halleck. "Now she's launched ATTs. Yu-7s have enabled, they're searching."

As the Mark 48's icon merged with the one representing the Luyang I, Jerry turned toward the starboard VLSD. Suddenly a large white disk jumped up beneath the destroyer, as the explosive shock wave reflected off the sea surface. Two grayish pulses soon followed, the second one ripping its way through the destroyer's hull and climbing high into the sky. Mortally wounded, the ship wallowed as her forward motion came to an abrupt stop. The Jiangwei II frigate peeled off hard to port, accelerating. Jerry could only imagine the fear they were feeling after seeing their larger brother blown in two. No one in control cheered.

Halleck didn't bother reporting on the demise of Sierra-six three; his mind was on *Santa Fe*. His tense shoulders leapt forward quickly, his eyes and ears straining to pull information from the acoustic sensors. "Skipper! One of the ATTs hit!" he shouted excitedly.

"Yesss!" hissed Thigpen. An anti-torpedo torpedo had just taken out one of the Yu-7s. Just one more weapon to evade, but it was not meant to be.

Halleck's face suddenly scrunched up, contorted with grief. His report was superfluous. "Loud explosion bearing zero three one. I . . . I hear breaking-up noises. Loss of propulsion plant tonals . . ."

Jerry reached over and gently squeezed the sonar supervisor's shoulder. "Enough, Chief," he added quietly. A depressing silence descended on the control room. Many of the men had tears welling, two of the young women were openly weeping. Thigpen fought to retain control. "What about the frigate?" the XO asked, his voice shaky.

Jerry shook his head. "Let it go. Sinking it won't bring Halsey and his crew back. Set course for Guam."

# 20
## INDECISION

"The second wave of missiles did the real damage." The air force colonel was running through the slides a little too quickly. It was hard to see details in the photos, but the colonel's point was still well made. "With the alliance nations still putting out fires from the first ballistic missile strike early this morning local time, China followed up with a second salvo around noon that concentrated entirely on economic and political targets. And they used twice as many missiles," the briefer explained.

The colonel pressed his controller, and a map of Tokyo replaced ground-level photos of what had been the Tokyo Stock Exchange. "Second Artillery launched seventy-two DF-21s at Japan, and as far as we can tell, every one was aimed at something in Tokyo. They used supporting air- and submarine-launched cruise missile attacks again, designed to disrupt the Japanese air defenses, but with less success. The Japanese were ready for them this time."

The colonel's dress blues had the customary "fruit salad" on the left, showing long and distinguished service. The name tag on the right side of his uniform blouse read CHAMBERS. He was not wearing pilot's wings, however. Instead, on the left, under the rows of decorations, was a stylized silver rocket, surrounded by a wreath, with a star on top. The Master Missile Operations badge was awarded to officers with at least nine years' experience in operational ballistic missile units. This was a new kind of war, with different skills required.

"Because their missiles were concentrated in one small sector, the Chinese were able to overwhelm the batteries defending Tokyo. The Japanese had another missile ship damaged by the supporting attacks, but altogether the defenders destroyed fourteen incoming hostiles. That left sixty missiles with six-hundred-kilogram warheads hitting the city, and the Chinese chose places where it was impossible to *not* hit something."

He pointed to a cluster of yellow dots. "For example, of the nine missiles aimed at the Tokyo Stock Exchange, four fell on the exchange proper, effectively leveling the building. One landed a little to the southwest, flattening a securities company, two to the north shattered an elevated expressway that is a major traffic artery, and one outlier to the west collapsed a high-rise apartment building. Casualties from this one cluster of hits alone are going to be in the high hundreds, at least.

"In addition to the stock exchange, the Chinese targeted the Tokyo Shinkansen train station, the busiest in Japan, the National Diet Building with five warheads, the business district in Marunouchi, and the Tokyo Bay Aqualine. It's a bridge-tunnel across Tokyo Bay, and although they didn't get a direct hit, the warheads acted like depth charges and collapsed the underwater tunnel.

"It was the same story in other countries. According to our best accounting, Seoul was hit with thirty-two missiles, Taipei with forty-seven, Manila with thirty-three. A total of at least twenty-two Chinese IRBMs were shot down by national air defenses and the U.S. units at Clark Field.

"Aside from the Chinese ballistic missile strikes, the three ocean basins—the South China Sea, East China Sea, and Yellow Sea—are all battlefields. Strike aircraft and submarines hit anything flying the other side's flags. The Chinese are even strafing alliance-flagged fishing craft. But they're keeping most of their fighters close to home to block alliance air and cruise missile raids.

"The Chinese ground offensive in Vietnam is all about speed. They're taking heavy casualties, but they're making decent progress, better than they did in 1979. They've committed six group armies to the initial assault wave, that's approximately equivalent to sixteen divisions. There are another three group armies marshaling in the rear area, and we've seen indications several more are getting ready to transfer to the Guangzhou military region. The Vietnamese are putting up a good fight, but they were pounded by Chinese air attacks for several days before the invasion began. The terrain is probably Vietnam's best defense. It is very unfriendly to heavy mechanized units.

"And of course, the cyber attacks and the sabotage continue."

Colonel Chambers's last slide showed the seal of the CJCS with the word QUESTIONS.

"Are any of the alliance nations retaliating?" President Myles asked.

"South Korea, Vietnam, and India have land-attack cruise missiles, but they haven't targeted Chinese cities, either before or after these attacks. They've been aimed at China's oil infrastructure: refineries, storage areas, even a company involved in experimental oil extraction techniques. The entire alliance remains focused on the Chinese oil supply."

Senator Frank Weitz asked, "Colonel, you didn't say how many civilian casualties you think the alliance countries suffered."

Chambers sighed. "It would be an estimate, Senator, and probably a poor one. It's only been three hours since the second wave landed. We don't even have firm casualty figures for the first set of attacks. The missiles hit on a workday morning. The commercial and business establishments were fully occupied. The roads and trains were full, although it wasn't rush hour. Certainly thousands of souls have been killed in each city, with several times that wounded. We haven't seen anything like this since the mass bombing raids of World War Two."

Malcolm Geisler, the secretary of defense, asked, "Why did the Chinese change their tactics between the two raids?"

"As I mentioned earlier, it enabled them to swamp the defenses in one narrow sector. I believe it was also a correction of their targeting philosophy. The Chinese don't have an infinite number of missiles, and in the first wave, some shots simply missed their targets and were effectively wasted.

"A DF-21C has a fifty percent chance of striking within a hundred and thirty feet of its target. For example, the Chinese fired four missiles at the Leshan Mountain ABM radar in Taiwan. One hit and damaged some of the outbuildings, but the other three were clean misses. Military targets are small, and often designed to resist damage. Civilian targets are not." Chambers sounded grim.

"How many missiles do the Chinese have?" Weitz asked.

"They could do this two or three more times, tops. This probably represented a maximum effort, based on our estimates of the number of launchers they have."

Congresswoman Karen Sanchez asked, "Those three group armies you mentioned. Why are they being held back?"

"Most likely as tactical reserves," replied the colonel, "in case the Chinese need to shore up one of their main attacks, but they can also be used as garrison forces and blocking troops. This allows the main effort to just keep on going without having to worry about their rear."

Weitz asked, "What about the media in the alliance countries? How are they reacting? The Littoral Alliance declared itself on the fifth and four days later the Chinese are pummeling the alliance capitals."

"That's not really my specialty, sir, but what I've seen is what you'd expect—anger and horror."

Gregory Alexander, the director of national intelligence, added, "Seoul has been prepared for an attack since the end of the Korean War. This is just coming from a different direction. Japan, with seventy-plus years of pacifism, is having a tougher time of it. There's always been a strong anti-nationalist sentiment in Japan, a reaction to the militarism of World War Two. Now that's building, with a sort of 'see what you've gotten us into!' theme. Manila's in between. And with the Internet, it's all happening at light speed."

Chambers nodded. "Absolutely. We got some of our best information about the damage caused from personal photos posted online."

Myles seemed concerned at that news. "Greg, do you think the Chinese are taking advantage of that?"

"Absolutely," the DNI replied. "Fast feedback from the first strike undoubtedly affected their targeting decisions. And it's possible that the Chinese are also salting the forums and chat boards with provocative posts."

"Strategic trolling," Myles remarked. "And damage assessment provided by the target. It's a real advantage for China. They can see exactly what effect their attacks are having, physically and psychologically."

"In World War Two, the governments kept detailed information about bombing attacks out of the media," Alexander replied. "All they'd print was, 'Portsmouth was bombed with some damage last night.' Can any democracy do that today?"

Nobody had an answer for that.

"And these attacks are expected to continue?" Geisler asked.

"There's no reason for them not to," Chambers answered firmly. "It takes several hours to check out a launcher and load another missile, and each brigade can only reload so many launchers at the same time. We could see another salvo in five to eight hours."

Sanchez raised her hand. "One last question, Colonel, or maybe Mr. Alexander. How close are the Chinese to breaking? Will we be able to tell? What will we be able to do if that happens?" Chambers raised his hands and stepped back, shaking his head.

Myles nodded to Alexander. "Tell them what you told me, Greg."

"Ma'am, that's three excellent questions, not one. Large-scale civil disorders or significant electrical blackouts would be the easiest to spot, but other signs could be sudden changes in the leadership, even problems in their banking system. It's a systemic failure, so it's like what doctors see when someone's dying and their organs begin shutting down.

"That's in addition to what we can find out about their oil and other energy supplies. As to what we'd do, we're not waiting for the event. That's what we are talking about here."

"And how long can they last?" she pressed.

"I'd hoped you wouldn't notice me not answering your first question." Alexander paused, contemplating how to deal with the representative's question. "The problem is that we are not looking at a military defeat. Both sides could keep smacking at each other for months. China has the advantage in manpower and materiel, but they aren't fighting the war they planned for. That was focused largely on deterring us from becoming involved in an invasion of Taiwan. Now, they are facing a multi-front conflict against a unified opponent who is single-mindedly focused on crippling them economically. So, the real question is, 'How long can China go before her economy has rolled too far downhill to prevent it from becoming an avalanche?'"

Sanchez motioned that she was following his line of thought, but her arced eyebrow showed she was still waiting for an answer.

Alexander sighed. "All right. If nothing changes, maybe three weeks. Not less than two weeks, probably not more than five. A change in alliance strategy, or, heaven forbid, some sort of random event like a natural disaster . . ." He shrugged.

Myles nodded to his fidgeting chief of staff. "That's all, Milt," and then, "Thank you, Colonel." As the JCS briefer left, the others, silent during the brief, stirred. Myles explained, "Lady and gentlemen, you now know as much as I do. Frankly, I'm amazed at the reaction here in the U.S. It's as if we're the ones being bombed."

Senator Weitz, the democratic majority leader with four terms in the Senate, waited half a moment, then said, "I believe it's the overt and destructive nature of this latest development. Japan, Korea, and the Philippines have all been our friends and allies for what? Seventy years. A naval war, especially with submarines, is out of the public's sight. The sea claims the wreckage. As the good colonel pointed out, there are photos and videos all over the Internet, not to mention firsthand accounts. We can see and share our friends' pain firsthand."

"And it's the last straw," Sanchez added. She was the House majority leader, with only two terms in office, but impressive political skills. "As Senator Weitz has pointed out, the Chinese are now intentionally killing noncombatant citizens of allied nations, hurting our friends. There is a large Asian population in my district, and in many American cities. The U.S. has military, economic, political, and blood ties with the countries being attacked."

"What about the ethnic Chinese?" Myles asked. "There are a lot of them in California and the U.S. in general."

"A valid point, Mr. President. But China is not a democracy. Ethnic Chinese in the U.S. either have American attitudes, being raised here, or chose to emigrate because they rejected the communist regime. And all the citizens in my district now see that communist dictatorship directly attacking democratic countries with bloody results. My staff has received thousands of e-mails and messages since the first attacks yesterday, demanding that the United States of America act."

Milt Alvarez asked, "What about the rest of the Congress?"

Representative Sanchez shrugged. "This war has developed and changed so rapidly that it's hard to form a consensus and put any decision into action. I know of at least seven bills being circulated demanding everything from trade embargoes to your impeachment."

"The voters may take care of that last item shortly," Myles remarked.

Weitz added, "It's been the same in the Senate. My sense was that party support for your policies was strong until the Littoral Alliance declared itself. Since then, the Democrats are fractured, either urging some level of support or formal neutrality—renouncing our Pacific alliances as invalid, overtaken by events. They're worried about the precipitous drop in trade, too. Unemployment in my district is too high as it is, and the common belief is that it's about to fall off a cliff. I can't predict how frightened people will vote.

"If you were to ask for hard numbers, Mr. President, I would say that it's fifty percent or more in favor of some level of support for the Littoral Alliance, thirty percent for cutting all ties, twenty percent are just plain confused, but one hundred percent are worried." The senator shrugged. "Of course, that was before this latest round of attacks on the alliance capitals. The wanton destruction and loss of life may drive more people into the 'support the alliance' camp."

"The Republicans are divided as well, along similar lines," Sanchez remarked.

"And your personal recommendations?" Myles asked.

Weitz replied, "Frankly, I'm in the 'do something' camp. Internationally, as a global power with interests in the region, we have to take some sort of constructive action or the world will think we can't, or worse, don't care. Domestically," he paused, but then reluctantly admitted, "you're being perceived as indecisive, and that's having an economic as well as a political cost. Wall Street's in free fall, but they can recover if you show them where you're headed, and why."

Sanchez nodded emphatically. "There are good reasons for any course you take. The party will follow your lead—well, most of them will," she corrected, smiling. "After all, we're Democrats."

Myles sighed. "I wish I had better options. Military action brings us into direct conflict with a nuclear superpower. The first time Chinese forces kill Americans, or vice versa, this war takes a dangerous turn."

As he spoke, the senator seemed to make a decision. "Mr. President, I'm counting votes in my head, and if you want to take us in on the side of the Littoral Alliance, I can almost guarantee a Senate resolution supporting your actions. It will silence the fire-eaters on both sides of the aisle, and it's the kind of big decision presidents make. The average man on the street doesn't like dictatorships, and there are some particularly nasty aspects of the Chinese version. You know we can beat them." He straightened in his chair. "That's my official recommendation."

Karen Sanchez looked thoughtful. "The problem is, we could really do without the expense of another war—human and economic. We could spin a decision to nullify the treaties into a 'take care of the home folks' message. We can work with that. More than one president's been elected by promising mothers that their sons wouldn't be sent to die in some foreign land."

"And how many kept their promise?" Myles asked. "This war will be over by the election, but the shockwaves will be with us for a very long time afterward." He stood, and the rest stood with him.

"I apologize for the late hour, but things are moving very fast. I'm grateful for your insights and support," Myles said, shaking their hands. "I need you to ask your colleagues for a little more patience. There's a lot going on under the surface. If I'd picked the obvious answer three days ago, I would have been wrong. And remind your fellows there is a price we pay with any choice."


Andy Lloyd waited until they'd left and Myles was sitting down again. As the president poured another cup of tea, the secretary of state said flatly, "I think we should join the alliance."

"Then you've changed your mind," Myles observed. His tone wasn't critical, but it invited an explanation.

"I keep thinking of what the Japanese ambassador said about short, violent wars being better than long ones. The Chinese are losing; their economy is tilting over the edge. If we throw our weight in, the Chinese will lose all the more quickly, or perhaps, even sue for peace. That's a good thing. And the Littoral Alliance has grown very powerful. I'd rather have them remember us as an ally than a judgmental bystander."

"As we work with them to crush our second biggest trading partner," Myles replied, smiling. "If we're lucky, losing fifteen percent of our export market will only put us in a recession."

"That's going to happen anyway, if and when the alliance wins."

"The Chinese losing is what scares me, Andy. But do we want to add the cost of another war to that?"

Ray Kirkpatrick, who'd organized the briefing, and suggested inviting the congressional leaders, said, "I'm going to have to officially disagree, Mr. Secretary. The Littoral Alliance is winning at sea, but their entire war is premised on the belief that the Chinese government, at some point, will cut their losses and agree to terms.

"We don't know how far the Chinese leadership is willing to fall. Admitting defeat has personal consequences for the guys in charge. They're not monsters, but they may be willing to let things go to hell if it keeps them in power. And here's what I'm scared of: Do the Chinese want a postwar world where their country's a wreck and the alliance is strong? If the Chinese think they're going to go down, they'd almost certainly want to pull the Littoral Alliance countries down with them. I think we should keep clear."

"Thank you, gentlemen. I appreciate your opinions, as always. You both have good arguments to support your views. My problem is that I have to reconcile the wildly diverse recommendations and make a decision," Myles admitted wearily.

After a short pause, the president turned to his two most trusted advisors and said, "The only choice that's entirely bad is doing nothing. Ray, I'm sure the joint chiefs have been updating the contingency plans for China. Tell them to get ready."

Kirkpatrick didn't look happy, but he nodded.

National Security Adviser's Office
West Wing, the White House
Washington, D.C.

Patterson was waiting in the outer office when Kirkpatrick returned from the briefing. He nodded and wordlessly waved her in behind him.

After entering and closing the door, she found a chair. Kirkpatrick wearily dropped into his seat and she asked, "So no decision, then?"

"No." Kirkpatrick shook his head reflexively. "On one level, I can't blame him. Neither choice is what he wants, which is a cease-fire. We tell him he can either join the fight or sit back and watch until it's all over.

"He's scared, Joanna. Did you know the president has asked Greg Alexander for intel projections of a nuclear attack by China on the alliance? First, what a 'demonstration' might look like, and second, for a full-blown nuclear strike." He nodded at Patterson's horrified expression. "Thinking the unthinkable."

"I've been away from the grid for an hour and," Kirkpatrick checked his watch, "seventeen minutes. What's new?"

"New casualty figures, higher of course. Someone posted a video from the traffic cameras inside the Tokyo Aqualine tunnel as it flooded."

Kirkpatrick held up a hand as if warding her off. "That's okay, I've got a thing about tunnels. What about governmental reaction?"

"Nearly identical statements asking their citizens to bear up under the attacks. 'The alliance is strong, the Chinese are on the ropes,' and so on. They promise new attacks that will bring the war to a swift and successful end."

Kirkpatrick shook his head in disbelief. "They should have been in with us at the briefing. Greg Alexander gives the Chinese at least three weeks, possibly five, maybe more."

Patterson read from one of the documents in her lap. "'The end of our struggle is at hand. These attacks against our cities are China's last gasp before they either see reason or collapse, exhausted and broken.' This was released less than an hour ago in all the alliance capitals. Same wording."

"China is nowhere near that far gone. It's a bad sign if the alliance is lying to its own people."

"Unless they think it's true," she countered.

"If they think China's close to the edge, then this Komamura's dropped a decimal point. Our briefer said the Chinese are preparing to move more group armies to the Vietnam border. That'll take a lot of time, that's a lot of people and gear to pack up, ship, and unpack. That takes scarce fuel and shows long-term planning."

Patterson agreed. "They're still committed to the fight. Can we pass that report on to the alliance somehow?"

Kirkpatrick took off his glasses, and rubbed his face with both hands. "Dunno. Cooperation's been way down since the alliance declared itself. We're still collaborating on the missile-warning stuff, but neither side is sharing any operational-level data, or even information on our own side's movements. They might just take it and sit on it."

Patterson brightened. "What if we released it publicly?"

"Another press release from the U.S. government? Would anyone even notice?"

"What if it wasn't from the government," she asked, "but a respected source?"

"Walter Cronkite died in 2009."

"Ray, I'm serious. I know someone who can get our information out to a wide audience on the Internet. He's respected and from what I can tell, knows what he's doing. And he gets stuff from all over the world. Our information could just be folded in with the rest."

He nodded, smiling. "I like it. The Internet. Citizens in the Littoral Alliance find out they're in for a long haul, not a quick victory. Maybe they'll push their governments for a cease-fire. Americans find out China's not a pushover, and the president gets a little breathing room. Maybe it even gets into China somehow and the man on the street finds out what's going on."

Kirkpatrick nodded and called his assistant. "Denise, I need ten minutes with the president ASAP. Yes, before he goes to bed. Tell them it's about improving our options. I'll stand by."

He hung up the phone and pulled out a notepad. "All right, tell me about this respected Internet source."

"Well, he's Canadian . . ."

9 September 2016
0800 Local Time
Ground Floor
West Wing, the White House
Washington, D.C.

Joanna hadn't come home last night, and Hardy worried, as was a husband's prerogative. It wasn't about her fidelity so much as her health.

His cell phone rang exactly three minutes after the clock alarm, and he was relieved to hear her voice. "Lowell, it's been a long night. Can I see you for breakfast, say at eight? In the West Wing."

"Of course. I'll be there earlier, if I can arrange it," he answered. She sounded tired, which made sense if she'd been up all night. He felt guilty, then silly. It didn't do her any good for him to lose sleep.

A taxi from Georgetown got him to the White House by seven forty, and he was waiting in the ground floor lobby when Joanna found him. Her good morning hug was especially welcome, but she did look tired.

When he looked up, her boss, Ray Kirkpatrick, was standing nearby. Suddenly flustered, Hardy said, "I understand. Go help your boss, we'll have breakfast another time."

"No, Lowell, Dr. Kirkpatrick and I both need to talk to you."

Now he was curious, as well as hungry.

There were several small dining rooms on the ground floor, along with offices for people supporting the situation room. The three ate alone at a table big enough for six, one of two in the room. She'd ordered for him, and thus Hardy had his familiar cereal, toast, and juice. She liked fruit and a muffin. The familiar meal made Kirkpatrick almost a guest, but the national security adviser tore into bagels and lox while Patterson explained.

"Lowell, would you be willing to pass some information from us to a CNN reporter? It's the one you told me about."

"Laird? The one who made so much noise with Bywater's Blog?" Even as he spoke, confirming the reporter's identity, alarm bells sounded in his mind, enough to form chords.

"What kind of information?" he asked carefully.

"Information about the war, security-related information," she answered guilelessly. "Freshly declassified. *Very* fresh."

Hardy's expression must have given him away, because Kirkpatrick explained, "This has the president's permission and full support. In fact, he's enthusiastic. Everything we give you will have been personally reviewed, maybe even chosen by him."

One of the bells shut off. Leaking classified information was endemic in Washington, but it was also illegal as hell. If, for whatever reason, you were identified and prosecuted, there was nowhere to hide. But the president could declassify whatever he wanted to. Kennedy had used his authority to declassify photos of missiles in Cuba. If Kirkpatrick—no, if Joanna said this had Myles's imprimatur, then it was all right.

"We want to get some background material onto the Internet and into the news. Too many people think the war's going to end in a week, or that the Chinese are just going to say 'uncle.' We'd like you to contact Ms. Laird and offer her 'background' information. She will know what to do from there."

There was no question of him saying no. Not to Myles, and especially not to Joanna. But he felt uncertain. "I'm a little new at this," Hardy explained. He asked Kirkpatrick, "Can you recommend a good parking garage?"

After Kirkpatrick stopped laughing, he said, "Deep Throat didn't have e-mail. We'll give you a cell phone with an unregistered number. Use it only to speak with Laird, of course. You can also use a special e-mail address. If anyone else tries to trace it back, it will go to a different IP address each time."

Joanna added, "While we want to make sure that your role can't be traced, it will be obvious to Laird that this information is being deliberately leaked. Once she sees its value, she won't be able to resist using it."

She slid a small box over to him. "Cell phone and charger. A flash drive is in there as well. Her contact information is already loaded into the phone, and the drive has the first file, along with a fact sheet on Laird." Joanna smiled. "She sounds nice."

Kirkpatrick said, "I'm going to insult your intelligence, Senator, only because you said you're new at this, and I think you're too much of a straight shooter. You speak only to Laird directly. No staff, no messages, and definitely no voice mails. She has to know it's you, of course, but no explanations about how you came by the data, or why you're offering it to her. She will press you, hard, but you will have to be reluctantly unhelpful. Your identity as a senator is her guarantee that the information is worth looking at. If she shares your identity as a source with anyone, it's instantly over. She should know the rules. If she breaks them, throw the phone away and tell us."

The national security advisor added, "We need you to move on, this, too. The sooner this is on the street, the better."

9 September 2016
0845 Local Time
CNN New York Bureau
Time Warner Center, New York

It was a Washington, D.C. area code, but Chris Laird didn't recognize the caller. She was already behind schedule. A piece on an industrial accident in Malaysia that might actually be Chinese sabotage was supposed to be ready for the 9:00 A.M. feed, but part of being a journalist was never ignoring a lead, or a call. And how did they get her personal cell number?

"This is Chris Laird," she said carefully.

"Ms. Laird, this is Senator Lowell Hardy. I'm about to send you a file that you may find very useful."

And that was why she always answered the phone.

# 21

# PARTICIPATION

9 September 2016
0915 Local Time
By Water
Halifax, Nova Scotia

The phone rang, and the only reason he answered was because it was Christine.

"Mac, I'm sending you a file I've received about the Battle at Spratly Island. I'd like you to look at it and tell me if the information is worthwhile."

"What kind of information is it?" he asked. Christine had proven to be a sharp reporter and a fast learner. If she thought it was worth looking at, he'd take the time.

"Detailed. You'll probably understand it better than me. I'm sending it now. You'll have it in a few moments."

"Fine," Mac replied. "Who's it from?"

"I can't tell you, and for the moment, don't send the file to anyone else."

Now he was curious. "Seriously? I can't use it on my blog?"

"Look at it first, then please, call me back."

After promising to call, Mac hung up and checked his e-mail inbox. He found the file, downloaded and opened it.

His first impression was of a patchwork of blocks of text, then names and terms started to pop out at him. "DRAGON EYE" and "PLANK SHAVE" were NATO code names for Chinese- and Russian-built radars.

One missile was described as the "CSS-N-8 SACCADE." That was the NATO designation for the Chinese YJ-83, and was linked to a "seeker activation" time. In fact, he realized most of the document was a timeline listing when different radars had been detected and then when the signal was lost, correlating the radar types with different ships, like "LANZHOU" and "YULIN." The only time he'd ever seen names in all caps like that was in U.S. Department of Defense handouts . . .

9 September 2016
0920 Local Time
CNN New York Bureau
Time Warner Center, New York

Chris Laird snagged the phone on the first ring. "That was four and a half minutes," she observed, smiling.

"Where did you get this?" Mac demanded.

"Mac, I said, I can't tell you."

"This looks official."

"Exactly how official?" she asked.

Mac sighed. "I'm not a military expert, but I know that the U.S. has planes that can eavesdrop on foreign radar and radio signals. This file is an electronic record of the battle, and looks like exactly the type of things those aircraft would do. It lists Chinese and Vietnamese ships that took part in the battle by name, even the weapons they fired at each other. I'm not sure that the two combatants have such a complete picture."

"And it matches what you've received from other sources?"

"It's more like, 'Does my other data match this?' and the answer is yes."

She relaxed a little. For whatever reason, Hardy was giving her good stuff—maybe very good. "Okay, then. Mac, let's go ahead and work on a joint piece, something you can post on your blog and I can use as well." She checked her watch. "We can aim for the noon feed."

"I need to talk to your source."

"Absolutely not!" she said. "They made it very clear that they'd speak only to me."

"Christine, this smells like halibut a few days after the refrigeration fails. Why are they giving us this information?"

"The source hinted there might be more stuff after this."

"More?" Mac's voice was rising, and Christine could hear him pause and take a breath. "All right. Think it through. This type of information is normally highly classified. Someone with access to classified data is giving it to you. Wouldn't you like to know why?"

"I remember some Chinese proverb about gift horses. We are at no risk. We do not have clearances, so we're under no obligation to keep it secret," retorted Christine.

"That's the reporter in you," Mac replied. "And I feel the same way. But I don't want my blog turned into some sort of tool for someone with an ax to grind. I've heard too many horror stories. Let me speak to him or her and clear up a few questions. Otherwise, you can do what you want, but I will not partake of the mysterious fruit."

"All right," Laird conceded reluctantly. "I'll have to call them, and then they'll call you. Stay close to your phone."

9 September 2016
0930 Local Time
By Water
Nova Scotia, Halifax

The caller ID read as UNAVAILABLE, but Mac grabbed the phone. This wasn't a telemarketer. "This is McMurtrie."

"Mr. McMurtrie, I understand you're reviewing the information I sent to Ms. Laird." The voice was male, strong, and the speaker was probably not a young man. Mac couldn't tell anything more than that. It wasn't being electronically altered, as far as he could tell, but anything was possible.

"It's very impressive, and I should thank you for your generosity. But I'm concerned about your motives."

"I don't suppose you'd be satisfied with my desire to support your blog? I am a fan, by the way. You've done a lot of good work."

"Thank you," Mac replied automatically, "but this information comes from within the U.S. government, and was or is classified."

"Was," the voice replied. "I'm not breaking any laws, and neither are you by publishing it."

"That's a relief. I don't want to appear as a witness at your trial, whoever you are, thank you very much. I'll take you at your word that's it's an 'authorized,' if unconventional, release of sensitive information. Will you also guarantee that this is not fabricated or altered?" pushed Mac.

"This and anything else I send you will be factual to the best of my ability."

"Anything else? There's more?" Mac tried to suppress his excitement and failed completely.

"Yes, there is. For example, your theory about the loss of *Vinaship Sea* is correct. She was sunk by two Yu-6 torpedoes fired by a Chinese Shang-class SSN. That's the NATO designation. The Chinese call it the Type 093 class."

*Migod!* Mac felt amazement mixed with satisfaction. *And he reads my blog.*

The voice continued, "This touches on my purpose, and I'll share some of that with you. There's a lot of misinformation about the war out there. Most is noise, but some is harmful; for example, the staying power of the Chinese. People with bad information make bad decisions. A poorly informed public might demand that their politicians do the wrong thing."

"How does information on the Battle of Spratly Island correct that?"

"It doesn't, but it shows you and Ms. Laird that I can provide something of worth, and when you post it, enhances your blog's reputation as a valuable source of information. First we will get their attention, then tell them what they need to know."

"I'm not a U.S. citizen, but I'm no enemy of America, either. Do you promise that this information is not meant to harm U.S. interests?"

"For what it's worth, I can promise, absolutely, that the information I give you is meant to advance U.S. interests. In this case, that includes ending the 'Great Pacific War,' as you call it, as quickly as possible. I'm sure Hector would be honored." Mac smiled at the reference to his personal hero.

"I'll even answer questions, within reasonable limits."

Mac felt a small thrill, remembering what he'd already been given. But he couldn't pass up the opportunity. He mentally ran down the popular topics on the blog forums. "A lot of people are asking about *Liaoning*, the Chinese carrier. She hasn't left harbor since an engineering casualty on August eleventh. Can you tell me her current status?"

"That's a very good question, Mac. I'll see what I can do. It's been a pleasure, but I don't expect I'll speak to you again, at least not for the foreseeable future. You can pass any future questions through Ms. Laird. I enjoy reading your blog. Keep up the good work."

Whoever it was broke the connection before Mac could thank him or say good-bye.


**9 September 2016**
**1200 Eastern Daylight Time**
**CNN Headline News**

"This is CNN breaking news. In a massive series of predawn airstrikes, Indian air force planes attacked Pakistani air bases, ports, and army installations. At the same time, reports from crossings in the northern and southern border areas with India have described sharp fights between Pakistani border police and Indian regular army units. It's clear the Indian Army is crossing the border in strength, but the Indian government has only released this short statement."

The anchor was replaced by the recorded image of an Indian Air Force major, reading a prepared statement. "The Indian armed forces have begun a series of defensive operations designed to protect Indian territory from further outrages like the Pakistani-sponsored assault on our navy base at Visakhapatnam. Our intelligence has information that even more vicious raids are being planned, so we have taken this action to protect our homeland."

A map of southwest Asia appeared, and the anchor explained, "India has declared the entire coast of Pakistan to be a war zone, and that ships of any country in those waters risk being sunk without warning. An official Notice to Mariners was filed by India a little over two hours ago saying that the ports of Karachi and Gwadar are mined. A similar Notice to Airmen covers commercial flights to Islamabad, Lahore, and Karachi, stating an aircraft using the fields may be shot down."

The anchor's image returned. "The only response from the Pakistani government has been to condemn the Indian attack and promise to repel 'every invader from our holy ground by all necessary means.'"

"In another breaking development, CNN journalist Christine Laird has provided a new, more complete description of the Battle of Spratly Island." An image appeared, of the now-famous photograph of a shattered Vietnamese missile boat. It had become one of the defining images of the war.

"This battle, waged four days ago between the Vietnamese and Chinese navies, is credited with stopping the Chinese advance in the South China

Sea, although at high cost. According to the narrative, which is posted on the now-famous Great Pacific War of 2016 Web site, on Bywater's Blog, the Chinese amphibious assault ship *Jinggang Shan*, a civilian container ship loaded with supplies, and the escorting frigate *Xiangfan* were all sunk by Vietnamese cruise missiles. Another warship, the guided missile destroyer *Lanzhou*, was crippled by a newly-revealed antagonist, which fired a different type of anti-ship missile, the 'Yakhont,' while the Vietnamese ships fired the 'Uran' missile. Both types are manufactured in Russia, but the Vietnamese ships are only fitted with Uran.

"The depth of the analysis on Bywater's Blog, a privately operated Web site, has added to the reputation of its administrator, Hector McMurtrie, a naval expert and author. Sales of his most recent book, *Steam Propulsion Plants of the Cunard Line Ships*, have soared in the past week.

"Chinese and Vietnamese officials refused to comment on the accuracy of the information, although the Vietnamese naval spokesman did admit that he was aware of the report, since he read the blog every day."

9 September 2016
1300 Local Time
White House Situation Room
Washington, D.C.

The ambassador's expression was all they needed to see. They'd set up the VTC less than half an hour ago, based on the earliest time the U.S. ambassador to Pakistan could reach a secure terminal. She was hurried, almost breathless. She didn't bother trying to look pleasant. "I just came from a meeting with the foreign minister. It's chaos over there. This has caught them completely by surprise."

"Us as well, unfortunately," Kirkpatrick remarked.

"You'll have to take that up with my counterpart in Mumbai," Ambassador Wright snapped. "The only reason the minister would see me at all was that we already had something set up for today. We had about fifteen minutes. He shared some information, I offered moral support, and got out.

"According to the minister, there have been attacks all along the border with India, most probably diversions. They know a large column of vehicles has crossed in the north, opposite Lahore, and is driving west. They've also had reports of crossings in the south, but it's so sparsely settled that they're sending reconnaissance units to find out what's going on."

"What about their nuclear forces?" Patterson asked. She sounded worried, and the ambassador acknowledged her concern.

"I asked, as politely as possible, 'If they were comfortable with the security of their nuclear forces.' The minister said they'd been on heightened alert since India's affiliation with the Littoral Alliance was revealed, and have been dispersed to safe locations."

Wright added, "The minister made a point of telling me that no nuclear-weapons-related sites have been struck so far. Air bases, vehicle parks, road junctions in the north and south have all been hit hard. Based on what he was the most angry about, their air force has especially suffered. Our attaché in Karachi also reported a frigate in the harbor was sunk at the pier by precision-guided bombs."

"But no nuke missile sites," Kirkpatrick observed. "They don't want to give the Pakistanis a reason to launch."

"How about invading their country? Doesn't that count as a sufficient reason?" Patterson countered.

Wright, listening to the conversation, shook her head sharply. "No, Doctor, the Pakistanis won't launch unless the situation is dire. They can hurt India, of course, but India can destroy Pakistan as a modern nation. They only have three cities with populations over a million, with most of the educated population and almost all the commercial, scientific, and military infrastructure. For Islamabad, it's virtually a doomsday option. Frankly, they depended more on Chinese support to deter a conventional invasion."

"And the Chinese have their own problems right now," Kirkpatrick completed. "What's your assessment of the military situation?"

"If you mean what my attachés think, they unanimously agree that the Pakistani armed forces have been completely surprised and are reacting poorly. My attachés were just as surprised. Everyone assumed India was involved with the war in the South China Sea, and most of the Pakistani intelligence assets have been tied up with supporting the Chinese."

"Including the terror attacks."

"Entirely true, sir. Excuse me, but I have things I must attend to," Wright said, a little impatiently. "Do you or the president have any special instructions?"

"None beyond safeguarding U.S. citizens and keeping us informed."

"With the ports and airfields at risk, the land routes to Afghanistan are the safest option left. We're getting our people moved here and to Quetta, and then across the border to Kabul and Kandahar. All the civilian flights that usually land in Pakistan are using those airports as well."

"Good luck, Madam Ambassador. We'll talk again at . . ." Kirkpatrick glanced at the clock. "0500, your time."

"We'll be here," she responded, trying to sound positive.

10 September 2016
2200 Local Time
Littoral Alliance Headquarters
Okutama, Nishitama District
Tokyo, Japan

Miyazaki found him sitting in one corner of his office on a cushion. "*Sensei,* Admiral Orihara is here. He has arrived."

Komamura started, as if waking from sleep, and looked at the clock. "Oh no! It's ten o'clock already?"

"Yes, sir. Minister Hisagi was there to greet him, and will bring him here after the admiral has greeted the other members of the working group." She sounded a little impatient.

"I will have to apologize to the admiral. I have been disrespectful. I should have been there, too."

"You were missed, *sensei,* but I told them you were very fatigued."

He smiled, and bowed slightly toward her. "Nodoka-*chan,* you are a great help to me. And may I compliment you on your appearance?" She blushed, but his remark was accurate. She'd replaced her customary tracksuit with a skirt and blouse more appropriate to the occasion.

A knock at the door made them both turn to see Minister Hisagi with an unfamiliar officer in his dress blue uniform. Steadied slightly by Miyazaki, Komamura quickly rose.

Hisagi said, "Dr. Komamura, may I present Vice Admiral Orihara Izaya, Japan's new military representative to the Littoral Alliance working group."

The professor thought he was much younger than Kubo, maybe in his late forties, and taller, although that wasn't a challenge, but he still wasn't as tall as Komamura. His hair had hardly any gray . . .

Komamura realized he'd been silent too long, and bowed. "It is a pleasure to meet you. I am in your hands."

Orihara returned Komamura's greeting, bowing deeply. "It is an honor to meet you, *sensei*. I look forward to working hard together." As he straightened, the admiral noticed the small shrine in the corner of his office, near where Komamura had been sitting.

A small table against the wall held a portrait of Admiral Kubo Noriaki bordered in black. It was flanked by incense holders, and different items had been placed in front of the photo: a bottle of Kirin lager beer, a set of the admiral's shoulder boards, a referee's fan from a sumo game, several white chrysanthemums, and a dagger, to keep away impure spirits.

A pair of small sake bottles sat on a tray next to the cushion. "I was having a drink with Admiral Kubo," Komamura explained.

"My deepest condolences on the loss of your good friend," said Orihara. "It is regrettable that his death must be kept from the public, at least for a time."

Komamura nodded, grimly. "His family understands the need for security. Their sacrifice will be honored as well when he is finally given a proper funeral."

Miyazaki had picked up the tray and turned for the door when the professor said, "Wait, please. Gentlemen, will you have a drink with the admiral and me?"

Hisagi and Orihara each took a small cup from the tray and Miyazaki filled all three cups, then added a few drops to a cup in front of Kubo's photo.

"He died in battle, you know, as surely as if he'd been on a ship," Hisagi remarked. "That's what they're saying at the ministry."

Orihara quoted, "'Duty is heavier than a mountain, death is lighter than a feather.' He can rest now."

They drank, and Miyazaki collected their cups. Komamura set his down a little unsteadily, and Hisagi and Orihara nodded to each other. After arranging to meet at breakfast tomorrow morning, and Miyazaki promising to make sure the professor got to bed, the two quickly left.

They walked in silence for some time, until they were finally in Orihara's newly assigned quarters, and Hisagi had closed the door. The admiral said, "I had no idea he was this bad. I'd heard stories, but this . . ." His sentence trailed off into silence as he sat. "I feel as if we've lost our compass."

Hisagi replied, "Admiral Kubo's death would be difficult to bear under normal circumstances, but the civilian casualties from the strikes yesterday were another heavy blow. He believes that since his book inspired the alliance, he must take responsibility for them, and therefore the war. He is also uncomfortable with taking an active part in the strike planning. *Sensei* told me himself that every time he recommends targets, he feels like a mass murderer."

"I was in Tokyo yesterday morning when the missiles landed," Orihara told him. "None landed close to the ministry, but their impact was still cataclysmic. The trains and roads are all paralyzed. Only the emergency services are able to move at all. I had to use a SDF helicopter to get here."

"And we sit here and wait, helplessly, for the next salvo," Hisagi mused. "They've been ready for over a day, there's nothing we can do but wait."

Orihara nodded his solemn agreement. "The missile defense forces did their best, but we have all learned an important lesson, both about China's power and our own vulnerability. After I was given my new assignment here, I met with the heads of the other services, and then the minister of defense and the prime minister. They told me that Japan is taking new steps to protect us from Chinese ballistic missiles."

Hisagi sighed. "Then I hope they do it quickly. I can't decide what would be worse, another strike on Tokyo or a different city."

"It really doesn't matter," concluded Orihara. "We lose people regardless of the city. An interim measure has been deployed, an electronic countermeasure system, but all that will do is provide some protection to key military and civilian installations. It does nothing for the general population.

"The ministry's estimate is that the Chinese will wait until things start moving again in Tokyo, and then hit it again. The refugee problem is unbelievable. Anyone who can leave the city is fleeing to more rural areas." The admiral paused for a moment, then continued, "It can't be helped. Heaven decides our fates. Let us work hard together on problems closer to us."

"The professor," Hisagi replied. "Yes. He is grieving, as I am, but it has been less than two days since Admiral Kubo was killed. I believe that with time, Komamura's spirit will return."

"Do we have the time for that?" Orihara asked. "This war changes day by day."

"But his strategy has never wavered. That is one of his lessons. We must avoid distractions and focus our attacks on China's greatest vulnerability. He's trained his assistants well. Certainly we can follow *sensei*'s guidance for a short time without his direct supervision."

Suddenly the new air raid siren began to wail, and both men's cell phones buzzed—another missile attack was incoming. Orihara shook his head, a rueful grin on his face. "So much for the ministry's estimates! Come, let's get to the shelters."

11 September 2016
1200 Eastern Daylight Time
CNN Headline News

"NATO ministers met again today to consider possible reactions to the worsening economic situation caused by the Pacific and now Indian-Pakistani wars. Although both conflicts are well outside the NATO charter's area of responsibility, the economies of all NATO countries are being battered by wildly fluctuating energy prices, and shortages of all kinds, especially finished goods that are largely only available from Asia. With ever-increasing shipping losses, and the blockade of the Pacific sea lanes, global trade has all but ground to a halt. Although initially content with the role of 'concerned observer,' demands from European citizens, as well as business leaders, have grown to near-deafening proportions. NATO may be compelled to act. They're just not quite sure how.

"The normally busy shipping lanes, stretching from the Cape of Good Hope east all the way past Japan, are now a war zone. While some merchant ships continue to sail east of Good Hope, they do so at great risk, and without insurance.

"The British Royal Navy and French Navy have started to move warships from the piracy patrols in Africa, and from their home bases, to the Cape of Good Hope. They plan to begin convoying nonbelligerent merchant ships safely through the war zone, but questions have been raised about what ships will be allowed to sail in the convoys. Also, what if Chinese or Littoral Alliance submarines attack the merchants being escorted? Will the warships escorting the ships be allowed to sink them?

"China has also announced that it will begin convoying ships bound for Chinese ports, but has not released any details, or whether they will be coordinating with the NATO effort.

"NATO has ruled nothing out, although direct intervention in either conflict seems unlikely. In addition to possible further sanctions against China, seen as the aggressor in that war, and against India, NATO could authorize emergency transfers of arms to the Littoral Alliance countries, except India, and Pakistan, and sharing intelligence with the Littoral Alliance and Pakistan to assist in their defense.

"Newton Thursbury, the U.S. Representative to NATO, has lobbied aggressively that any measures should be defensive only, and designed to encourage the combatants in both wars to seek an immediate cease-fire. The U.S. representative spoke strongly. 'A war between five countries in the South China Sea was bad enough. We now have ten countries involved in two separate wars. The last thing we need is to add NATO to the mix.'"

"In a follow-up to this morning's report, new photographs from last night's massive ballistic missile attack on Littoral Alliance capitals have been posted on the Internet. These photographs, many of which are extremely graphic, reveal a disturbing change in Chinese targeting strategy. Instead of striking military, political, or economic targets, the missiles largely hit the residential sections of Tokyo, Taipei, Seoul, and Hanoi. Initial casualty estimates are in the thousands, but an accurate count is proving to be difficult as a number of residential areas and schools were hit in this latest attack. Due to the high number of casualties from previous missile barrages, and damage to some of the hospitals, medical facilities in those cities have been filled to capacity, forcing the use of public buildings as emergency medical wards.

"Civil authorities have brought in rescue dogs to aid in finding survivors, but the destruction is so great that heavy equipment cannot get close to the disaster scene, forcing rescuers to dig through the wreckage with hand tools.

"A Littoral Alliance foreign affairs spokesman issued a statement saying, 'This latest attack shows just how desperate China has become. They are unable to counter our combined militaries, so they resort to terror attacks against our citizens. Their defeat is near, we will continue to press on!'"

12 September 2016
0800 Local Time
Littoral Alliance Headquarters
Okutama, Nishitama District
Tokyo, Japan

With eight nations making up the Littoral Alliance, the sixteen representatives to the working group, with the necessary translators, took up a fair amount of room. Admiral Orihara could not use the commons area for his briefing, given the level of security, but luckily the Hirano estate's dojo made an excellent venue. The weapons racks, although empty, still gave the place a martial atmosphere, a perfect setting.

The representatives of each country sat in pairs at western-style desks, complete with national flags. The only jarring feature was the sight of dozens of cable runs taped to the floor carrying power and secure data to each delegation. This information was most definitely not going on a Wi-Fi network.

"Gentlemen and ladies, thank you for your time this morning. This is my first official duty as Japan's military representative to the working group." He bowed slightly. "Please take good care of me."

The first slide said simply "Project Ryusei," and below in English, "Project Meteor." He quickly brought up a second slide, a map of China with symbols marking oil installations.

"We've been striking oil refineries along the coast with submarine-launched cruise missies, as well as unconventional sabotage and cyber attacks. The refineries at Juijang, Ningbo, Zibo, Beihai, and Panjin have all been reduced to below twenty percent output, effectively crippling them, but this takes time and great effort. There are also many refineries that are simply outside our reach.

"The South Korean land-attack cruise missile, the Hyunmoo 3, can only fly fifteen hundred kilometers after being launched from a submarine. While this sounds like a great distance, it is not compared to the vast expanse of China." He pressed a control and an irregular red line appeared on the map, a little less than one-third of the way across China from its eastern coast. "Of greater concern is the land-attack Klub missile, employed by the Vietnamese and Indian navies, which has a far more limited range of three hundred kilometers. This severely restricts our ability to strike critical targets in the South China Sea area. All of the refineries that have been hit lie within this area," Orihara pointed out.

He called up a picture of the South Korean missile, along with its specifications. "The Hyunmoo 3 has a five-hundred-kilogram warhead, which is enough to destroy most individual targets, but many oil refineries cover one or two square kilometers, with hundreds of components."

An after-strike photo appeared of the Huabei Petrochemical Company petroleum refinery in northern China. "This is a major refinery, with an output of a hundred thousand barrels per day. It was struck by nine missiles fired by the submarine ROKS *Ra Kyungji*. Aiming for vital components like distillation towers and piping manifolds, the installation's output was reduced by twenty-seven percent, and repairs are estimated to take several months.

"But the Korean Hyunmoo-3 and the Russian Klub, like most cruise missiles, are subsonic, and although both have very small radar signatures, they can be detected if the searching radar is close enough. The Chinese air defenses discovered the Huabei raid, which took just under twenty minutes to fly from the launch point to the target, and destroyed three of the missiles, or one-quarter of the twelve missiles launched. This is essentially the submarine's entire load, the maximum number of missiles most subs can carry while still leaving an adequate torpedo loadout for self-defense.

"Another issue is the time it takes a submarine to load weapons in port, sail to the launch area while evading enemy defenses, and return to port after launch. While it is engaged in this type of mission, it's not doing what it does best: sinking other ships and subs."

Orihara turned and bowed slightly toward the South Korean delegation. "While the strike went well, and did great damage, we need to reach targets farther inland, with greater striking power, and less chance of interception."

His next slide drew a surprised murmur from the delegates. It was a photo of a rocket, an orbital launch vehicle, with labeled arrows pointing to different components. The arrow pointing to the nose read "warhead."

"This is a Japanese H II-series launch vehicle. It was first used in 2002, and has proven to be a dependable heavy-lift platform. Even the basic version can lift four metric tons to a high orbit."

He changed the slide to show a cutaway diagram of the nose section. "The Self-Defense Agency, working with the Japanese Space Exploration Agency, has developed a simple modification that allows the vehicle to act as a ballistic missile, able to reach any location in China. Since it doesn't have to reach orbit, it can carry a payload of six metric tons of explosive. Instead of a single unitary warhead, it will carry sixty one-hundred-kilogram charges, which will spread out over an area hundreds of meters across. Each charge includes an incendiary component as well as a high-explosive blast and fragmentation warhead."

As he'd been describing first the vehicle and then the payload, Orihara had heard soft voices, then discussion, and finally the Filipino military delegate spoke. "How can you even consider this when your constitution explicitly forbids offensive weapons?" Other delegates were nodding as well, with expressions ranging from curiosity to concern.

Orihara looked to Minister Hisagi, who stood. The minister explained, "The self-defense clauses of the constitution were intended to prevent Japan initiating a war of aggression. They do not have any provision for what Japan should do if it is involved in a war of self-defense, or an alliance like this one. 'Invincibility lies in the defense, the possibility of victory in attack.'"

Everyone understood the quote from Sun Tzu, some nodding their agreement. Hisagi pressed his point. "Only offensive weapons like this," he said, pointing to the screen, "can carry our fight to the Chinese where they have been safe before."

He paused, taking the time to look at each delegation. "The Japanese Diet has met in secret session, and is prepared to amend our constitution to allow the construction and use of offensive weapons." This created a stir, and Hisagi quickly continued, "But we acknowledge and respect the security concerns of our allies and neighbors. The Diet has also agreed that any offensive weapons developed by Japan will be placed under the joint control of the Littoral Alliance, and will be used only against targets approved by the alliance."

Orihara was watching the group, and could see their expressions change from concern to relief. Confusion was replaced by approval. Almost all the delegates looked convinced, including the Filipino general who'd raised the question. Targeting was already jointly controlled by the alliance. This would simply be another weapon in their arsenal, and a powerful one.

Hisagi sat, and Orihara continued his brief. "Work on Ryusei began soon after the Chinese missile attacks on our capitals. We have reached the point where we are confident the weapon can be successfully developed, and are therefore asking for the working group's permission to complete the work. We expect to have three missiles ready for launch in several days."

He brought up the map of the Chinese oil refineries again, but now an arc appeared, reaching from the Japanese launch facility at Tanegashima deep into the Chinese interior. "We are recommending that the first target be the Yumen Refining and Petrochemical plant in western Gansu province, and that it be attacked by all three missiles. Not only is this a major refinery serving western China, but a pipeline from this refinery supplies the Lanzhou refinery to the east.

"We can launch two missiles simultaneously from the Tanegashima facility, and the third six hours later. They should reduce the facility's output to near zero, and the best part is that the Chinese are virtually powerless to stop them."

# 22

## PREEMPTION

12 September 2016
1400 Local Time
USS *North Dakota*
Apra Harbor, Guam

Standing on the flying bridge, Jerry watched in silence as his boat entered Apra Harbor. Even though he was physically present, he felt detached from what was going on around him. Part of his brain recognized and understood the conning orders that were given, the radio exchanges with the tugs, and the reports from the OOD. But the rest of him was some two thousand miles away, in the South China Sea. He spoke only when absolutely necessary, and even then it was usually just a curt, emotionless, "Very well."

Bernie Thigpen looked up from the deck and saw his captain standing ramrod straight up on the sail. Since the loss of *Santa Fe*, the skipper had become withdrawn, reclusive; he seemed to intentionally shun human interaction. He took the normal reports as required by his duties as a commanding officer, but that was all. He hadn't attended even one meal in the wardroom during the last three days. Hell, Thigpen wasn't sure he ate much at all. He knew Mitchell had hardly slept; the light in his stateroom had been on the whole time. The only thing delivered to his stateroom was one carafe of coffee after another.

The XO had tried to get his captain to talk, but he didn't have much success. On those rare occasions that Thigpen did get a response, it was always cryptic. During his last attempt, he pressed the issue: "What could you have done to change the outcome, Skipper? The situation was completely out of your control! You can't hold yourself accountable for what happened."

Jerry's reaction was completely unexpected. His face flashed with intense anger. Seething, he replied in low, guttural voice, "*Santa Fe* was my responsibility! I was ordered to get her home safely. I failed! And I left her entire crew behind."

Although shocked by the explosive, visceral response, Thigpen saw past the anger and noted the pain in Jerry's eyes. Coming to his senses, Jerry apologized to Thigpen, and thanked him for his concern. Despite the XO's best efforts, Jerry refused to talk about it again. However, while in the head one evening, Thigpen overheard his skipper talking to himself. Leaning quietly against the door, Thigpen heard, "In times of adversity, you can turn to no one else." He immediately recognized the phrase from Senator Hardy's speech at the change of command ceremony.

*North Dakota* eased slowly into the inner harbor, and as the tugs turned her about, Jerry noted two *Virginia*-class submarines tied up to the submarine tender's starboard side. Raising his binoculars, he looked at the name placards on the sails—USS *Texas* and USS *North Carolina*. Ironically, he hadn't noticed the *Burke*-class Aegis destroyer anchored in the outer harbor.

Before the brow was even in place, Jerry swung over the top of the sail, and climbed down the ladder to the deck. Thigpen was waiting for him by the brow with a locked pouch and a key. Jerry nodded as he took the key and put it in his pocket. Reaching for the pouch he said, "Do what you can to get fresh provisions, XO. Right now, I have absolutely no idea what's going to happen next, so we might as well get ready for anything."

"Aye, aye, sir," Thigpen replied. "Good luck with the commodore."

"Thanks. I'm going to need it."

Jerry saluted the ensign, and strode across the gangplank. On the pier, standing at attention, was the same petty officer that had picked Jerry up during his previous visit. The young sailor stood rock steady, patiently holding the car door open. But this time, Jerry firmly shook his head no, pointed forcefully down the street, then turned sharply and started walking. The shocked look on the petty officer's face caused Thigpen to laugh out loud. "That poor kid is going to have a heart attack," he mumbled to himself.

\* \* \*

Simonis paced back and forth in his office. The clock read 1525. *North Da-kota* had tied up over twenty minutes ago—Commander Mitchell was late. The driver the CSO had sent down to the pier called back in a panic: *North Dakota*'s skipper insisted on walking to squadron headquarters. Both Jacobs and Walker found it amusing, and understandable. Even Simonis begrudg-ingly admitted that a good leg-stretching walk after a stressful patrol was therapeutic, but he had little patience for such self-indulgences. He'd lost a boat assigned to his squadron, and he desperately wanted to know more of the details, the ones that weren't included in *North Dakota*'s initial report.

Except for the clock's ticking, and Simonis's occasional grumble, the office was quiet. The commodore was in no mood for casual conversation and Jacobs and Walker knew better than to try and start one. Fortunately, it wasn't long before the yeoman knocked at the door.

"Commodore, Commander Mitchell is here."

"Send him in," Simonis demanded.

Jerry stepped smartly into the office and proceeded directly to Simonis. Stopping just short of the commodore, he came to attention and reported. "Commanding Officer, USS *North Dakota* reporting as ordered, sir."

Simonis appeared to approve of the formal greeting. Nodding, he ex-tended his hand. "Welcome home, Captain," he said.

"Thank you, sir," Jerry replied as he grasped the commodore's hand.

"I trust you remember my chief staff officer and operations officer," said Simonis, gesturing first to Jacobs, then Walker.

"Of course." Jerry reached over and shook their hands.

Simonis then motioned toward the conference table. "Be seated, gen-tlemen."

As soon as Jerry sat down, he opened the locked pouch and pulled out an annotated chart, a bound report, and a DVD. Unfolding the chart, he positioned it so that Simonis could see it clearly.

"Before we start," interrupted Jacobs, "would you like some coffee, Captain?"

"No . . . no, thank you. I think I've had my annual allowance already," Jerry responded hesitantly.

The commodore held up the discussion briefly while he looked the chart over. After a short examination, he looked up at Jerry and said, "Walk me through the engagement, Captain."

"Yes, sir."

For the next half hour, Jerry went step by step through the encounter, beginning with the initial acquisition of *Santa Fe*. Walker grimaced when he saw the unbelievably long detection range, and Jerry commented that the excessive noise from *Santa Fe*'s main propulsion shaft not only enabled the Chinese to find her, but almost certainly degraded her spherical array. When combined with the strong layer, it was understandable how Halsey could have missed the approaching ships.

Simonis grunted, and gestured for Jerry to continue. Turning to the page in his report with a video freeze frame from the Sea Tern UAV, Jerry showed the commodore the cable for the towed array streaming from the Luyang I destroyer, and emphasized that the prosecution was done passively. Only the Ka-28 Helix went active, and then probably only to verify *Santa Fe*'s position before dropping the rocket torpedo. That statement got a noticeable reaction from the commodore, as well as Jacobs and Walker. The Chinese had not demonstrated such sophisticated tactics before; the war was forcing them to learn quickly.

Jerry then walked Simonis and his staff officers through the Chinese attacks. When he got to the point where he described Halsey's evasive maneuvers, Simonis roared indignantly, "Halsey turned the wrong way! What was he thinking!?" Walker's face turned red with anger, but he remained silent.

"I thought that at first myself," Jerry quickly interjected. "But my team found this in the post-engagement analysis. Look at the geometry, Commodore." Jerry turned to a blown-up section of the chart in his report and pointed to the Helix's position. "See here. The Helix dropped the APR-2E on *Santa Fe*'s port side. Warren did exactly what he had been trained to do. He turned away and launched countermeasures."

"The helo was herding him?" Simonis asked incredulously.

"That, or the Chinese were just plain lucky," answered Jerry. "Either way Warren reacted in accordance with doctrine, and it drove him straight into the two warships, here. Each ship launched a Yu-7, staggered so they wouldn't interfere with each other. Warren intercepted one, but missed the other. That weapon hit *Santa Fe*. I think any one of us would have been hard-pressed to successfully handle three homing weapons in such a short span of time."

Simonis slowly leaned back into his chair, suddenly quiet. Jerry's description of the event had hit his preconceived notions hard—he had much to consider. Jacobs saw his boss's reaction and knew Simonis was done, but the CSO had one question.

"Captain, the chart shows that you command-enabled your weapon, why?"

Jerry nodded. "Yes, I did. I was trying to scare the warships off. But they either didn't hear the seeker's transmissions or didn't understand what it meant." He looked down at the table briefly, then added, "I . . . I didn't know what else I could do."

At that point the discussion abruptly ended, the office becoming suddenly silent. Jerry looked at the three Squadron Fifteen officers and realized it was over. Pushing the chart, report, and DVD toward the operations officer, he said, "Commander Walker, this is for your reconstruction analysis team. The DVD contains digital copies of my ship's sensor, fire control, and event logs, the UAV download, and my report with the annotated chart. I'd appreciate it if you'd send a copy back to my parent squadron, SUBRON Three. I know Captain Corina would like to see them."

"Certainly, Captain. I'll have the files e-mailed over the secure network."

"Thank you," replied Jerry.

"Gentlemen." Simonis spoke as he rose. "If there is nothing else, I'd like to speak to Commander Mitchell alone, please."

Jacobs and Walker quickly collected their notes and the patrol report, and after shaking Jerry's hand again, headed for the door. As Walker was about to exit, Simonis called out to him, "Rich, shut the door please. Thank you." The click of the doorknob latch seemed particularly loud.

Simonis marched over to the carafe on a side table and refilled his mug. Grabbing a second cup, he poured one for Jerry. "How do you take your coffee, Captain?"

"Uh, black, sir," said Jerry, a little confused. He was sure the commodore had heard him decline earlier. "I'm not an advocate of highly adulterated coffee."

"Excellent!" responded Simonis, pleased. "Somehow I knew you weren't a mocha cappuccino latte kind of guy."

Jerry smiled slightly. "I think that's three different drinks, Commodore."

"Whatever," shrugged Simonis. "All I know is that you can't taste the coffee with so much milk, chocolate, or other crap mixed in." He placed the steaming cup in front of Jerry, raised his, and said, "Cheers."

"Thank you, sir."

"How's your crew holding up?" asked Simonis casually, taking his seat.

"Hmmm," Jerry uttered, sipping his coffee. "They seem to be doing okay. None of them were exactly thrilled watching *Santa Fe* being attacked and sunk. Some are taking it harder than others."

"And how are you taking it?"

Jerry's cup stopped just short of his mouth, and he slowly lowered it to the table. "I, uh . . . I guess I would put myself in the harder than others category."

"I suspected as much," grunted Simonis. "You implied in your initial message that perhaps you could have done more to help *Santa Fe,* and just a few moments ago you reinforced that impression. You've had three days to study the logs and the after-action report, weren't you able to find *anything*?"

Embarrassed, Jerry shook his head no.

"Really?" replied Simonis with a condescending tone. "You disappoint me, Captain. I thought you were smarter than that."

Rage suddenly filled Jerry; his stomach churned and his jaw drew up tight. Fighting to keep himself in check, he looked at Simonis with intense anger. Through clenched teeth, he was just barely able to choke out the words, "And what should I have found, Commodore?"

Simonis leaned forward, his gaze equally intense, his voice just as stern. "That you were not in control of the situation, Captain."

Stunned by Simonis's statement, Jerry found himself unable to speak. The young captain's blank expression told the commodore that his first volley had hit home. He had Mitchell's undivided attention.

Simonis quickly rose again, pacing as he spoke. "In one of my previous assignments, I was the head of tactics development at DEVRON Twelve. For two years, I reviewed every event reconstruction from boats on both coasts. By the time I left, I could dismantle an after-action report in a couple of hours, three tops. I can say with reasonable confidence that after reading your initial message and hearing your brief, there was absolutely *nothing* more you could have done to help Halsey. Furthermore, there were a number of bad decisions that you *didn't* make that potentially could have cost me two boats. And your attack on the Luyang I was well executed. All in all, Captain, I'm quite impressed with your performance."

Jerry was awestruck; his anger washed away as fast as it had formed. He heard Simonis's words, but he had trouble wrestling with their meaning. It was not what he expected.

"But, sir . . . I failed to get *Santa Fe* home. I left them all behind," Jerry croaked, his voice heavy with emotion.

Simonis stopped and looked at Jerry. "Captain, get it through your thick skull, there was nothing you could have done that would have changed the final outcome. Given the circumstances, there was no way you were going to pull that rabbit out of the hat. I know it sucks, but this was a no-win situation."

"But, sir . . ."

"But nothing!" exclaimed Simonis firmly. "I know about your ties to the SEAL community. They are damn fine warriors, and they have a right to be proud of the fact that they bring everyone home. But Jerry, we don't have that kind of luxury."

Simonis then raised his right arm and made a large sweeping motion toward the Pacific. "We lost fifty-two submarines out there during World War Two, and you can add *Scorpion* and *Thresher* to that tally. In almost every case, we lost entire crews, every single last man! And, we lost them permanently! There's a reason why we say they are on eternal patrol. In our line of work, Jerry, if a boat goes down, *everyone* on board is left behind. That's just the way it is."

Swallowing heavily, and fighting back the tears, Jerry nodded stiffly. Simonis was right, but that wasn't much comfort at the moment. A boat had been lost, colleagues, fellow submariners were dead, all because of the misfortunes of war. And then there were the Chinese sailors on the destroyer he had torpedoed; most of them probably died as well. Ironically, there were no indications the Chinese ships knew it was an American sub they were attacking. Life seemed so damned unfair at times.

As the emotional turmoil settled down, Jerry was finally able to talk. "I hear you, sir. I don't like it. But I understand, now."

"Good," replied Simonis, satisfied. "I need you firing on all cylinders. This war is getting worse by the day, and if the rumor mill is correct, we'll soon be in the thick of it. I'll need every boat to be operating at one hundred percent, and that includes their skippers."

Jerry pushed himself away from the table and stood. He needed to get back to his boat. He had to get her ready for war. Extending his hand, he responded confidently, "Understood, sir. *North Dakota* will be ready to set sail, whenever you give the order."

"Very good, Captain. That's all I can realistically expect."

"Thank you for the coffee, sir, it was really good. So was the advice," Jerry added sheepishly.

"You're welcome, Jerry. Just let my staff know what your boat needs, and I'll see to it that you get it ASAP."

A slight smile popped on Jerry's face. "If I know my XO, sir, your staff already has all the requisitions. Good afternoon, Commodore."

12 September 2016
1700 Local Time
August 1st Building, Ministry of National Defense Compound
Beijing, People's Republic of China

General Xi Ping walked wearily into the CMC conference room. It had been a long two days, and judging by the way the war was progressing, the days were likely to get even longer. He saw President Chen and General Su sitting at the conference table; each was reading one of the myriad of daily reports. Xi signaled an aide to bring him coffee, and an army major rushed a cup over to him. The general gulped the contents down quickly and returned the cup to the aide. Fortified with caffeine, Xi approached the two senior members of the Central Military Commission.

"Good afternoon, President Chen, General Su," he greeted.

Chen looked up; his serious expression immediately became one of surprise, then concern. "General! Please forgive me, but you look dreadful!"

Xi chuckled lightly. "That's because I feel dreadful, Comrade President."

"I take it you have the final analysis of the third missile attack?" Su asked impatiently. They were all fatigued, thought the chief of the General Staff. And if Xi had to work extra-long hours to support final victory, well, that was the price of his promotion.

"Yes, General Su," Xi answered testily. "And it's as we feared. The Littoral Alliance nations are jamming the Beidou navigation system signals over their territories. The accuracy of our ballistic missiles was severely degraded. We missed most of the targets of interest in the last attack."

"But how?!" Chen demanded. "General Hu assured us that the satellite navigation systems on all our missiles were highly resistant to jamming!"

"He was partially correct, sir," Xi explained. "The receivers are upward-looking and are very resistant to jammers *on the ground*. Unfortunately, the Littoral Alliance has put the jammers in high-altitude, long-endurance UAVs. The receivers on our missiles looked right at them and accepted the more powerful, flawed signals as valid. It threw the missiles far off course."

"Wonderful!" replied Su sarcastically. "So now instead of hitting important military and economic targets, our missiles are destroying hospitals, schools, and civilian residences—with photographs posted instantly on the Internet for the whole world to see!" Su's face became crimson with anger. "Do you have any idea as to the magnitude of the propaganda bonanza we've handed the Littoral Alliance!?"

Xi became equally angry and stood his ground. "I believe, General, I explicitly briefed this commission that we would have two or three attacks before the Littoral Alliance would probably deploy countermeasures. General Hu disagreed, and you, sir, accepted his argument!"

"Generals!" shouted Chen Dao. "Fighting amongst ourselves will not help us win this war!"

Vice Chairmen Tian and Li, and General Shi, heard the president's raised voice and immediately came over to the conference table. Su was silent, but obviously fuming. President Chen looked at Xi. "Do you have any recommendations on how to counter the jamming?"

"I have some ideas, but I need to discuss them with General Wang," Xi responded. "Until then, I would recommend delaying any further large-scale ballistic missile attacks. Our inventory is now limited and we must husband our remaining resources."

"I agree with General Xi," said Tian. "We may have to look at using more missiles to support our attacks on Vietnamese defensive positions. We lost fourteen aircraft this morning during the saturation attack on their line at Cao-bang. Our bombers delivered their ordnance and were suddenly pounced on by low-flying fighters. We were ultimately successful in smashing through the Vietnamese defenses, but the losses in the air and on the ground were higher than we expected. We'll have to reinforce both the air regiments and group armies with our reserves."

Chen was perplexed. "How did the Vietnamese muster the necessary forces to oppose the strike? I thought we had command of the air over the front?"

"It would appear that a squadron or two of Indian Flankers have deployed to Vietnam, Comrade President," a chagrined Li volunteered. "General Xi's people suggested this was a possibility. But I discounted it as a foolish notion given India's massive assault on Pakistan." Li faced Xi and bowed. "Please accept my apology, Ping."

Xi silently bowed in return.

"President Chen," interrupted General Shi, the head of the political department, "while I agree we need to exercise caution in conducting future missile strikes, we can't afford to lose the momentum we've achieved. Militarily speaking, the situation has turned to our advantage. We've plunged nearly fifty kilometers into Vietnam across the entire border in only three days. We've largely gained air and surface dominance in the seas around China, and Admiral Wei reports that he has confirmed the sinking of three enemy submarines. And, of course, we've inflicted considerable damage to our enemy through ballistic missile strikes. However, as positive as these indicators are, our position is far more tenuous from an economic and political perspective.

"According to General Ye in the logistics department, we've lost approximately fifteen percent of our tanker fleet, and about twenty percent of our refining capacity. We've sustained less damage to our storage and production facilities, but it is still noteworthy. And, of course, we have been completely cut off from any external sources of petroleum. Even if the war were to end right now, the long-term damage to our economy will be considerable, but ultimately recoverable.

"Current estimates point to a five-to-ten-year period required to regain our pre-war gross domestic product. However, the longer this war continues, the more damage our economy will suffer and the longer that recovery period becomes. Some of the analyses suggest there is a tipping point where economic collapse becomes likely, and that we are closer to that point than we think.

"Politically, we have a growing internal security issue looming before us. The people are getting more and more restive. The short-term economic downturn is causing significant anxiety, the fuel rationing policy is highly unpopular, and they are absolutely incensed about the complete cutoff of access to the Internet and social networking sites. If we do not successfully conclude this war soon, we may have an internal crisis on our hands as severe as the external one."

Chen nodded his understanding. "Thank you, General Shi, your wisdom is greatly appreciated." Turning toward the other members of the CMC, Chen continued, "We must regain the initiative in the aerospace dimension. We've started to turn the tide on the seas, and we've made great progress on land, but it is our air and missile strikes that will ultimately give us victory. General Xi, please work with General Wang's staff to implement your ideas. As for the rest of you, any suggestions that you can come up with will be considered. The sooner we can resume effective missile attacks, the better."

"Yes, Comrade President, I will attend to it immediately," Xi replied. Then he hesitantly added, "But . . . there is another issue that I wish to bring to your attention."

Chen was momentarily confused, then quickly realized that the conversation had wandered far afield shortly after the intelligence chief's initial report. "I'm sorry, General, we became so fixated on the missile problem that I didn't realize you had additional business. Please go on."

Xi shuffled a little, uncomfortable with the topic he needed to raise. "Comrade President, I have an intelligence officer who is particularly gifted. He is socially inept, rude, and lives like a hermit in the basement of our building. In fact, his only redeeming quality is that he thinks darkly, and does it extremely well."

The president and the other members of the CMC looked at Xi with a mixture of impatience and curiosity. Only Su seemed mildly amused. "I don't know if I would call the ability to think evil thoughts a redeeming quality, Ping," he said, smiling broadly.

"Normally, General Su, I would completely agree with you. But this intelligence officer is the one who wrote the assessments on the jamming of the Beidou system and the Indian Flanker deployment."

The smile abruptly disappeared from the general's face; the other members were suddenly keen to hear more. "Please continue," ordered Chen.

"In the folder I just gave you, sir, there is a synopsis of Major Geng's latest work. In this paper he presents a frightening argument as to why Japan will develop nuclear weapons, and will do so soon."

The members of the CMC all looked at Xi with surprise and shock. It was several moments before some even tried to speak; Xi politely cut them off. "Please, listen to me first, then we can debate the merits of Geng's work.

"First of all, their constitution does *not* forbid Japan from possessing nuclear weapons. Yes, it has been their national policy since the mid-1950s to forbid their development, but that is only a piece of paper. Yes, their national psyche is still scarred and that has had a significant influence on their past decision to not pursue them, or even allow them to be transported through Japanese territory. But that memory has dimmed. It's been over seventy years since the Hiroshima and Nagasaki bombings. Most important, however, is that these two factors are predicated on the belief that Japan does not need to produce nuclear weapons because they are under the American nuclear shield. Geng argues that may no longer be the case.

"The Japanese, indeed the entire Littoral Alliance, has snubbed the American president's attempts to broker a cease-fire. They have boldly told the Americans they are no longer needed to ensure Japan's security, and yet they made the hypocritical assumption that they would still be covered by America's nuclear deterrent. Our recent ballistic missile attacks have shaken this belief badly. The fact that we have not launched any ballistic missiles at India, a nuclear power, reinforces their perception of vulnerability.

"Furthermore, Japan possesses the technological base and knowledge to develop a nuclear weapon. A number of their civilian reactors use mixed oxide, or MOX fuels, which use a mixture of plutonium and uranium. What most people do not realize is that while the plutonium only makes up about five to seven percent of the reactor fuel by weight, it is of weapons-grade quality—at least ninety percent pure plutonium-239.

"As of last year, Japan has increased its production capacity of MOX fuels to one hundred and forty metric tons a year. Simple math suggests that Japan has access to tons of weapons-grade material. Depending on the sophistication of the bomb design, only a few tens of kilograms are needed to produce a fission weapon. Japanese engineers also have access to weapon design expertise through India, should they run into problems.

"Comrades, Major Geng has argued that there is now a strong political motivation to develop nuclear weapons in Japan. When coupled with their technological capabilities, and the close alliance with India, this becomes a substantial new strategic threat to the People's Republic of China."

An awestruck silence greeted Xi's finale. The senior members of the Communist Party looked back and forth at each other. Some had the look of disbelief, others shock, a few, outright fear. It was General Su who finally broke the silence. "Is there any evidence the Japanese are pursuing this path?"

Xi took a deep breath and answered, "No, General. But I must caveat that by saying we really haven't looked all that hard. Our collection assets have been heavily tasked to support the war effort."

"Then, General Xi, this becomes your number-one priority," announced Chen sternly. "We must know if Japan has an active nuclear weapons program, and we need to know soon."

12 September 2016
2045 Local Time
USS *North Dakota*
Apra Harbor, Guam

---

"My God, Bernie! What the hell are you doing! We have to be there in fifteen minutes!" shouted Jerry; there was a distinct note of panic in his voice.

"I had to shower, Skipper! I was filthy!" cried Thigpen from his stateroom. A towel came flying out and landed on the floor of the head the two men shared. Sounds of drawers being opened and slammed shut echoed from the XO's quarters. "Now where did I put my cover?"

Jerry collapsed into his desk chair and cradled his head in his hands. "Simonis will just shoot me!" he moaned. Looking up at the clock on the bulkhead, he saw the seconds relentlessly ticking by. The thought of being late sent a chill down Jerry's spine.

"You know, XO, it is not considered career-enhancing to show up fashionably late for a video teleconference WITH THE PRESIDENT OF THE UNITED STATES!" he bellowed.

"Keep your shirt on, Skipper. I'm almost ready," Thigpen squealed as he walked into his captain's stateroom.

Jerry took one look at Thigpen and emitted a guttural cry of frustration. "Gak! XO!!"

"What!?" yelled Thigpen, completely confused.

"Your shirt!"

"Huh?" Thigpen looked down and saw that he had buttoned his shirt incorrectly. "Oh shit!"

While Thigpen wrestled with his buttons, Jerry shoveled him out into the passageway, and drove him toward the control room. The two made a comical entry with Thigpen still trying to button his shirt and Jerry mimicking a tug pushing him toward the ladder well. As they passed through control, the occupants watched with amusement as the two senior officers acted more like a comedy team than the boat's command element. As Jerry propelled Thigpen through the door, he called to the ship's engineer. "Mr. Sobecki, the ship is yours until we get back. I'll expect it to be here."

"Aye, aye, Skipper. Have a good time," shouted Sobecki as he desperately tried to keep a straight face. The control room watchstanders all attempted to stifle their laughter; Lymburn failed and uttered a loud snort. From the behind the door, the XO's faint voice wafted through. "I heard that, Q!"

Everyone in control lost it.


They barely made it in time. With only a minute to spare, Jerry and his XO hustled into the Squadron Fifteen conference room. Simonis's stern glare sent a clear message: *I am not amused!* Jerry shrugged an apology as he shuffled by the commodore.

The two quickly took their seats and looked up at the large display screen. Jerry noted that the connection with the White House Situation Room had been established, and the display showed a number of people milling about and talking. In the background, Jerry saw Joanna Patterson and her boss, Dr. Kirkpatrick. Jerry remembered fondly his meeting with the national security advisor soon after the Iranian incident.

Suddenly, a harried-looking man appeared in the camera's field of view. He strode quickly up to the mike and announced, "Squadron Fifteen, this is the White House, stand by for the President of the United States."

"Attention on deck!" commanded Simonis. Everyone in the conference room jumped to their feet and stood rigidly at attention.

Within seconds, President Myles appeared on the screen, followed by Vice President Randall, and the secretaries of state and defense. Myles took his seat with Randall to his right and Kirkpatrick to his left. Pulling the microphone closer, the president addressed the Guam-based squadron. "Good evening, Commodore. Thank you for getting everyone together on such short notice. As you can imagine, we're in full-fledged crisis mode here. Meetings like this tend to occur at the last minute. Please, be seated."

"It was no inconvenience at all, Mr. President," Simonis replied as he sat down. "We are honored to have you with us tonight."

Myles slowly shook his head. Jerry thought the man looked exhausted. "No, Commodore. It is I who am honored. Your squadron has shouldered the load of this crisis, and I am very grateful for your exquisite service. You took on a very difficult and unusual assignment to buy me time; time to learn why the war started, who the belligerents were, and to attempt a diplomatic resolution of the conflict. My orders tied your hands behind your back, and yet your squadron executed their mission brilliantly and gave me the time I asked for. It is unfortunate that I wasn't as successful in negotiating a cease-fire."

Jerry saw the bitter disappointment on the president's face. *He's holding himself solely responsible,* thought Jerry to himself. The president's admission was a harsh judgment on himself, perhaps too harsh. In diplomacy, it takes two to tango, and it's really tough if one of the partners doesn't even want to dance.

"That is why I wanted to have this VTC, Commodore," continued Myles. "To personally thank you and your crews for all your hard work and sacrifice, and to express my sincerest regrets and condolences on the loss of USS *Santa Fe* and her crew. I know your command is grieving. I only wish there was something I could do to ease the pain."

The president paused for a moment, totally silent. Jerry couldn't tell if he was trying to compose himself or praying. Either would be acceptable given the circumstances.

"Commander Mitchell," called Myles.

"Yes, Mr. President." Jerry stood as he replied.

For the first time that evening, Myles had a smile on his face. "You continue to amaze me with your resourcefulness and dedication, Captain. I've been briefed on your engagement with the Chinese destroyer, and both Captain Simonis and the CNO strongly endorse your actions. You followed, to the letter, the restrictive rules of engagement I placed upon you, and I commend you on your sound decision-making skills. I only regret having placed you in a position where you had to make such a decision. Taking lives is never easy to do."

"Thank you for your kind sentiments, sir," responded Jerry. In the background he could see Joanna wiping her eyes.

President Myles then acknowledged Dobson, Pascovich, and Simonis for their diligence and skills in successfully executing the spoiler campaign. Once again the president noted that the combined efforts of the squadron exceeded all expectations. Finally, he concluded his remarks with a short awards presentation. "Captain Simonis, moments ago I authorized the awarding of the presidential unit citation to Squadron Fifteen and the four participating submarine crews. Individual personal awards will be forthcoming. It is the least I can do to acknowledge your efforts on behalf of the United States of America."

"Thank you, Mr. President, for your kind words. They are greatly appreciated," accepted Simonis.

"Now, Commodore, before we end the VTC, do you have any questions for me?"

"Just one, Mr. President. There is a lot of scuttlebutt, rumors, which suggests that we will soon be at war with China. Are we truly that close?" asked Simonis with deep concern.

Myles sighed. "I'm afraid, Commodore, that we are on the brink of war. There are already rumors on the Internet concerning the loss of *Santa Fe*. References to the sinking of USS *Maine* and Pearl Harbor are coming up frequently in the media, with much the same result. I daresay that with the formal acknowledgement of a Chinese attack on one of our submarines, there will be significant congressional and public pressure for the United States to become an active participant on the side of the Littoral Alliance. I will keep *Santa Fe*'s loss secret for as long as I can, but the release of basic information in the near term is unavoidable."

"It seems incredible!" remarked Simonis. "Do Congress and the public comprehend the risks of going to war with another nuclear superpower?"

"Some do. But most assume we'll be able to 'control' the escalation, that China won't risk national destruction. I find this assumption to be preposterous. Too much blood has been spilled; neither side has any inclination of backing down. Thus, escalation is all but inevitable. And yes, I firmly believe nuclear weapons will ultimately be used."

Simonis looked shaken. "Surely this has been brought up in negotiations?"

Myles nodded. "Lord knows we've been beating that drum, Commodore. I've struggled hard to retain our neutrality, so we could serve as an uninvolved mediator. We've been soundly rebuffed by both sides—no one wants to listen."

The president paused and took a deep breath. "I've studied Asian cultures for most of my life, Commodore, and the only way to get them to listen at this stage is to deal them a serious emotional shock. The last time we did this, in 1945, we had to use nuclear weapons to get our point across. That's not an option today."

When Jerry heard the president's last statement, an off-the-wall idea popped into his head. Briefly considering it further, it seemed crazy. But it wasn't any crazier than going to war with China. He knew he'd catch hell for this, but it sure beat the alternative.

"Mr. President, if I may," Jerry interrupted.

Simonis whipped his head about in Jerry's direction, shocked by his intrusion.

"Yes, of course, Captain," Myles said.

"Mr. President, I've listened carefully to your explanation of the situation, and the significant limitations you're facing in dealing with this conflict, so I have to ask this question." Jerry swallowed hard, preparing himself. "Why don't you use nuclear weapons to end this war?"

Both rooms erupted in chaos. Jerry saw the president's stunned expression. Joanna's jaw dropped in amazement at what she heard. A number of people were shouting. Simonis thundered, "That's enough, Mitchell!"

"Quiet, please!" shouted President Myles. The roar slowly died down as the president also motioned for silence. "All right, Captain, please explain yourself."

"Certainly, Mr. President, but you have to admit that my mere mentioning of the idea was a bit of a shock."

Myles chuckled. "It most certainly . . . was." The president's tone and expression told Jerry he had his foot in the door.

"Mr. President, you've stated your conviction that this war will inevitably result in a nuclear exchange. If that is indeed the consensus of you and your advisors, then the preemptive use of nuclear weapons, as a demonstration, becomes a viable option. You've struggled to maintain the neutrality of the United States, consistently and openly pushing for a cease-fire and a negotiated settlement; neither of the warring parties are particularly happy with you or your policies right now. This means you are in the ideal position to actually employ nuclear weapons in a demonstrative fashion, and get away with it."

As Jerry spoke, he saw Kirkpatrick lean forward, intrigued by what he was hearing, his right hand stroking his chin. Tilting toward the president, the NSA whispered something. Myles's head snapped around. There was a hushed exchange, and Jerry noticed Kirkpatrick's head nodding ever so slightly.

Myles turned back toward the mike. "What are you suggesting, Captain?"

"That you authorize the detonation of a number of nuclear weapons in the deep-water areas adjacent to the South and East China Seas. It will have to be more than two. You need to be more shocking than the last time, but your experts will have to determine the exact number. The weapons should be detonated simultaneously along the war zone. No one will miss this. The blast energy from the detonations will be conducted acoustically and seismically; they will literally be shots heard all around the world. If we explode them deep enough, there will be little venting of radiation into the atmosphere.

"Once you have the warring parties' undivided attention, you give a speech that graphically articulates where this conflict is going, and the devastating consequences that will inevitably follow. You know better than I, sir, but I would think this would be *highly* shocking to the Japanese and Chinese at the very least. The beauty of it all is that if we do this properly, there is little risk of anyone getting hurt from the demonstration, and a reasonable chance that you'll be able to stop the fighting."

Jerry ended his proposal and sat down. Thigpen, just as stunned as everyone else, leaned over and whispered, "Skipper! Are you nucking futs!?!"

"Shh," said Jerry.

After an awkward period of total silence, Myles spoke. "Commander Mitchell, I've already mentioned your resourcefulness, but this idea of yours is, well, a bit outlandish. However, my national security advisor is more than a little intrigued by your proposal and believes it has merit. Therefore, we'll take it up for further discussion over here. If we have any questions, we know how to get ahold of you."

Jerry nodded. "I'll be here, Mr. President."

"One last thing. That took a lot of courage, Captain. And I appreciate your candor and concern for our great nation. I won't forget it. Good evening, everyone."

Without a word, everyone in the conference room came to attention as the president departed. And before the connection was terminated, Jerry saw Kirkpatrick smile and give him a thumbs-up.

As the assembled officers filed out of the conference room, no one even came near Jerry Mitchell.

# 23

# DESPERATION

12 September 2016
1000 Local Time
White House Situation Room
Washington, D.C.

"Mr. President, you cannot possibly be considering such a reckless and ir-responsible proposal!" blurted Andy Lloyd.

"And yet, you support our direct involvement in the war against China," Kirkpatrick shot back. "The result is the same, Mr. Secretary. Only the timing differs."

"Nonsense, Ray! Escalation control may not be an exact science, but we have decades of experience in keeping the lid on the nuclear genie."

"Try 'black art,' sir, a purely academic exercise. We have no practical experience of escalation control under the conditions of open conflict with another superpower—none whatsoever!"

"Gentlemen, *please*," Myles exclaimed loudly. His raised voice commanded everyone's attention, and the shouting ceased. "Thank you. Now, let us turn to the issue at hand. First, Andy, yes, I am considering it. Why? Because Commander Mitchell's proposal is the only other option I've been given other than going to war with China or sitting back and doing nothing. Neither will end the fighting quickly, which is my ultimate goal."

Lloyd and Kirkpatrick both slowly sat back down; chastised like young schoolboys caught fighting on the playground. Myles looked over at Patterson and waved for her to take a seat at the table. "Dr. Patterson, please join us. You're the expert on environmental and nuclear issues, I'll need to hear your views on this option as well."

Joanna grabbed a chair next to her boss. She was still reeling from the VTC. Jerry's proposal was shocking, to say the least, but that the president was seriously considering it compounded her amazement. Participating in an honest-to-God discussion on actually using nuclear weapons was surreal.

"All right, Andy, you lead off," said Myles as he pointed to the secretary of state.

"Mr. President, nuclear weapons are the option of last resort, not the first. A demonstration right off the bat can be too easily misinterpreted, potentially leading to a hasty and poorly thought-out decision by an adversary to retaliate." Lloyd paused, looking down at the table before finishing his argument. "And on the domestic front, Mr. President, a decision to employ nuclear weapons would be political suicide. Even *if* Mitchell is correct and the fighting does stop, the damage to your campaign would be irreparable."

"So, let me see if I understand you," summarized Myles. "We can't use nuclear weapons immediately because they are nuclear weapons. We have to fail conventionally first before we can even begin to think the unthinkable. Correct?"

Lloyd initially opened his mouth to speak, but stopped. He wasn't happy with the president's summary, and his face showed it.

"Ray, your opinion?" asked Myles, turning away from his close friend.

"I grant the secretary of state's argument that a demonstration can be misinterpreted. However, his unspoken assumption is that the demonstration is *detected* before the weapons are detonated. If we can deliver the nuclear warheads with absolute covertness, then the first indication China or the Littoral Alliance will have is when their seismographs start twitching like crazy. At that point, there is nothing to misinterpret. They'll know the weapons were exploded far from their borders, in the deep sea, but what will grab them by the throat is that we detonated a number of nuclear devices.

"Commander Mitchell's idea is audacious, brilliant, and will be completely unexpected by the warring parties. The shock value will almost certainly be immense. You will have the world's undivided attention, Mr. President. You can make your pitch with the assurance that you will be heard," concluded Kirkpatrick.

"Thank you, Ray," Myles replied. "General Dewhurst?"

The chairman of the Joint Chiefs of Staff was calm, but he took a noticeable deep breath before answering. "Mr. President, I am uncomfortable with providing any specific guidance. Quite frankly, this is not something I've been trained for or previously considered. However, my *personal* opinion is that Commander Mitchell's proposal is very bold and will indeed shock the hell out of people. Just look at the effect it's had on us. But, Mr. President, you will be letting the nuclear genie out of the bottle. My concern is that the cork may not go back in."

"Kind of like a champagne bottle, eh, General?" questioned Myles with a slight grin.

Dewhurst chuckled. "A good analogy, Mr. President."

Facing the secretary of defense, Myles repeated his question. "Malcolm, what are your thoughts?"

"I'm with the chairman on this, Mr. President."

Myles became silent. Joanna could see the strain on his face, the magnitude of the decision weighing heavily upon him. After what seemed an eternity, he looked at Patterson and asked, "Joanna, Commander Mitchell said the radiation release would be minimal if we did this properly. Is he correct?"

'There is a precedent for this concept, Mr. President. Unfortunately, it's a single data point," Patterson began. "Back in 1955, we detonated a thirty-kiloton fission device at a depth of two thousand feet. The gas bubble did vent into the atmosphere and the surface water initially showed significant contamination levels, but as the water dispersed, the radiation decreased rapidly. Radiation exposure by the personnel in the test area was minimal.

"If you pursue this option, we'd use a lower-yield fusion weapon, say ten or twenty kilotons, which generates less fallout. If we can get the warheads deeper, that would also help," Patterson remarked.

Joanna paused briefly as she considered her next statement; it would likely have a major impact on the president. "In my professional opinion, Mr. President, the ecological damage from the detonation of a handful of these warheads would be far less than the spilled contents of a single supertanker."

Myles nodded slowly. Leaning back into his chair, he looked around the room, his advisors watching him with great expectation. He announced his decision. "I will authorize the use of nuclear weapons for demonstration purposes. We will execute the good commander's plan. Ray, I'll need the details on this operation ASAP! No, sooner."

"Yes, sir, Mr. President!" Kirkpatrick exclaimed. "I'll have DARPA, DTRA, and ONR work on the size, number, and placement of the warheads."

"Very good, Ray. But your point about absolute covertness is well taken. How do we deliver these weapons?"

"B-2 bombers will have no problems getting to the drop locations without being detected, Mr. President," volunteered Dewhurst. "We can have them in the air within a couple of hours."

Kirkpatrick shook his head. "I'm sorry, my dear Chairman, but stealth bombers aren't viable in this case. We'd need to use multiple bombers, possibly four or five, perhaps more, to deliver the warheads over such a large area. Our bomber bases are being watched, both China and the Littoral Alliance have eyes on the ground. As soon as the bombers take off, they'll be reported. We know this has happened in the past.

"Furthermore, I don't believe there is an air-delivered weapon that will meet the specific requirements." The national security advisor turned toward Patterson.

"Dr. Kirkpatrick is correct, Mr. President. The best airborne weapon we have is a B61 Mod 11 strategic nuclear bomb. But even with its special delayed fuze feature, that allows only about one hundred feet of penetration in soil, maybe a little more in water. We need over ten times more depth capability."

"I see," replied Myles. "So what other options do we have?"

"Mitchell knew," stated Kirkpatrick forcefully. "Submarines, Mr. President. The only platform that can give us the necessary stealth and deploy a weapon that can get deep enough is a submarine. He didn't say anything because he knew we'd come to this conclusion. He's already volunteered for the mission."

The president looked at Patterson. She silently nodded her agreement. Myles chuckled briefly. "Why am I not surprised? Very well, then, the attack submarines at Guam will carry out the mission. I hate to ask them to do more, but somehow I don't think they'll mind. Let's get this moving, people!"

As the president's advisors started collecting their notes, Myles called out to them. "One last thing. Andy is also correct that this decision is political suicide. Since the decision is mine to make, the consequences of that decision are also mine. Therefore, I request that you do not discuss with anyone what you've shared with me this morning. I consider the guidance you've collectively provided me to be for nonattribution. God willing, in a few days we'll have more mundane things to talk about. Now, let's hop to it!"

13 September 2016
0730 Local Time
Littoral Alliance Headquarters
Okutama, Nishitama District
Tokyo, Japan

Komamura woke with a blinding light in his eyes. He tried to close them tightly, but that wasn't enough, and he reflexively threw an arm up to shield his face. The sudden movement triggered an explosion in his head, pain so intense he thought he'd been struck. He tried to scream, but all that came out was a weak "aaaahh."

The spike of pain subsided to a deep throb, and he opened his eyes carefully. Even with his arm protectively shading his face, the light seemed unnaturally bright, and he rolled over, away from its source, and discovered he was in his quarters, in bed, with no memory of how he'd gotten there. Low-slanted morning sunlight streamed through the window.

Like any academic, Komamura cared more about where he worked than where he slept, so his bedroom was small, like a monk's cell or a dormitory room for a college student. There was a single western-style bed with a nightstand, a standing closet and dresser, and a small desk and chair. Miyazaki Nodoka sat slumped forward at the desk, her head pillowed on her arms, snoring softly.

"Miyazaki-san?" He'd meant to call her name, but it came out more as a croak and he realized his throat was dry, almost painful. He coughed, and that set off his headache again.

His graduate student and assistant stirred at the sound, then sat up, shaking her head to clear it. She looked over to Komamura, and managed to smile while also looking deeply concerned. "*Sensei,* you're awake!" She quickly knelt next to the bed. He started to speak, but couldn't get his throat working, and she picked up a glass with a straw, holding it so he could drink.

The water helped, and she put one arm behind his back to bring him to a sitting position. He said gratefully, "Thank you, child. You're always supporting me."

To his surprise, her face fell and she backed away from the bed, still on her knees. Weeping, she fell forward, knees, elbows, hands, and forehead all touching the floor. "No, *sensei.* I did not. Please forgive me." She held her pose, like a supplicant, crying and shaking with what? Shame?

"Stop this. Raise your face. What has happened?" He had to ask again before she finally lifted up her head. "It was my idea," she confessed. "I'm so sorry."

"What did you do?" he asked, confused and curious.

"*Sensei*, it wasn't good for your health. I couldn't stand seeing you like that, but you had lost your best friend, and we could all understand, but I was worried, and I spoke to the doctor here and he agreed. It turned out Minister Hisagi had even consulted the prime minister. They were considering a psychologist, but I said it was because you'd been working so hard . . ."

"Please, Nodoka-chan, what are you talking about?"

Her expression started to dissolve again, but she pulled herself together. "Your drinking. After two days and two nights, I couldn't bear it anymore. The doctor gave me something and I added it to your drink, to make you sleep. You passed out right away, and we all brought you to your room so you could rest."

Still on her knees with her head down, she backed up several feet, then rose to take something from the desk. Back on her knees, head down, she held out a folded paper in both hands. "Please, *sensei*, accept this." He looked more closely at it. It was neatly labeled *Resignation*.

"No," he said, shaking his head and immediately regretting the gesture. Then, as his brain began fitting the facts together, he asked, "How long have I been asleep?"

Still on her knees with her head bowed, she glanced up at the clock. "About twenty-nine hours. Doctor Ono has visited you several times, and gave you vitamin and fluid injections so you wouldn't get dehydrated."

"How long have I been asleep?" he repeated, anxiety rising. "Over a day?" He looked at the clock. It was morning, on the 13th!? Panic rising, he sat up quickly, and again regretted the sudden movement.

Miyazaki saw his pained expression, rose, and retrieved a bottle from the desk. She shook out a pair of pills. "For your headache," she explained, and helped him swallow them with water. After she put the glass down, she was still holding the resignation, and turned to offer it to him again. Her expression was a model of unhappiness.

Still striving for coherent thought, he said quickly, "Put that away," but when her expression became even more miserable, Komamura stopped himself and said more gently, "Your resignation is not accepted. I cannot forgive you, because you have done nothing wrong."

There was a knock on the door, and it opened a little. He heard another of his graduate students, Saotome, ask softly, "Miyazaki-san, do you think . . ." As he cautiously peeked around the edge of the door, he saw the professor and said brightly, "You're up!" and closed the door.

"Minister Hisagi and the admiral wanted to be notified the moment you woke," she explained.

"Then I'd better get dressed," he said, rising unsteadily to his feet. "Child, I have been a fool and a poor teacher. I must ask your forgiveness. I have been most troublesome. Thank you for taking such good care of me."

"We were happy to do it," she replied. Miyazaki was smiling, but still a little teary. "I'll get you some breakfast."

It took Komamura some time to dress and make himself presentable, although it felt like he was hurrying. Hisagi and Admiral Orihara were already waiting in the garden, standing next to a small table, when the professor arrived. When they saw each other, he stopped for a moment, gathering himself, then slowly approached the pair.

Bowing deeply, he said, "I have neglected my duties and caused great difficulty at a critical time. My behavior was inexcusable." His head still throbbed, but he continued to hold his bow until he'd finished his speech.

He straightened slowly, one hand on the table for support, as Hisagi replied. "Your actions are understandable and forgivable. You grieved for a friend, and nobody would ever criticize that. We accept your apology, and look forward to you resuming your duties."

There were three chairs, and Komamura gratefully sat down as the others did. Miyazaki appeared with a tray, and while the professor carefully ate, the others had tea and brought him up to date.

After breakfast, feeling humbled but also ready to work, he returned to his office. Komamura's desk had been neatened to an almost frightening degree. Several piles of documents containing ongoing projects were missing, and he could only hope that one of his assistants had taken them, or some of the alliance's deepest secrets were in danger.

Most of his assistants shared a single large workroom, but Miyazaki had been given a small office of her own. The door was open and she was hard at work, and he stood silently for a moment watching her, proud as any parent. She'd run things while he'd wallowed in grief and drink.

He knocked on the doorframe. "I came by to see if you could use any help." He smiled, and the expression felt a little unfamiliar.

She almost bolted from her chair. "*Sensei,* please come in, sit down."

With very little urging, he sat. "Hisagi and Orihara have briefed me on the situation, and your actions while I was—" He corrected himself. "—over the past few days. You've done well. We are all in your debt. Please, tell me what I have missed."

Miyazaki nodded. "We're continuing to supply target recommendations, of course. Several Malaysian and Singaporean submarines have passed to alliance control. There have been almost no merchant ship sinkings. There's almost no one left at sea. I've got Akashi reviewing data on the accuracy of SINOPEC production reports. He's detected some inconsistencies."

"Good," Komamura said approvingly.

"I had to take Kasugi off of damage analysis," she reported, then suddenly stopped herself and nodded toward the door. The professor reached over and closed it.

"I've assigned him to the Ryusei project," she continued, "along with a new Indian officer that the admiral's brought in. I'm assuming Minister Hisagi and Admiral Orihara told you . . ."

"Yes," Komamura replied. "Ballistic missiles. Surprising, but logical. But why Kasugi?"

"We needed his mathematical skills. We've never had to analyze groups of targets like this."

"May I see the requirements?" he asked.

She handed him a hard copy that described the weapon's accuracy, penetration against different types of armor, blast radius. He saw a second column. "What's this second set of figures?"

"An improved version. They say it will have an increased radius of effect, and use a different type of explosive."

"I should say so," he remarked. "It's more than four times as large, and with greater destruction within the radius." Even as he said it, a chill ran up his spine. Was he really awake? But if they wanted to hurt China and end the war, it couldn't be helped.

"Calculating the measure of effectiveness when groups of targets are involved has been difficult," she explained. "Kasugi's made good progress."

"I think you chose well. I'll take over the oil infrastructure analysis now, since I won't have my time taken up with supervisory duties."

She looked confused. "I don't understand."

"Hisagi and Orihara both suggested that you should be the new head of the economic intelligence section. They asked me to concentrate exclusively on the Chinese economic situation. I told them I approved completely. The working group will ratify it shortly."

"I'm honored by your confidence, *sensei*. I will do my best."

Back at his desk, Komamura plopped several fat folders down, returning each one to its accustomed place. His head was clear, but he could feel his body still waking up, his energy slowly returning. He looked over at the shrine to Admiral Kubo in the corner. His first impulse was to remove it, to remove temptation and banish the sadness, but then he decided he could leave it. He'd said good-bye. It was time to move forward.

He reached for the folder with the Chinese economic data, but still hadn't put away the hard copy with the ballistic missile targeting requirements. Both Hisagi and Orihara had made it clear that this was a "sensitive" program, meaning that knowledge of its existence should be limited, even within the alliance leadership. It was, literally, a "secret weapon."

Ballistic missiles were offensive weapons, forbidden by Japan's postwar constitution, but he'd argued in his book that at some point, Japan would face a circumstance that required their use, and now they found themselves in exactly that situation. Still, for it to come about so quickly, and as a consequence of his writings, was unnerving—a self-fulfilling prophecy?

He reviewed the information again. It was a powerful weapon. Even a handful would do tremendous damage, especially after the new warhead became available in a month's time. Where before they needed dozens of cruise missiles, or three of the early Ryusei missiles to destroy an area target, the improved version could flatten a refinery with one hit, and destroy a fair amount of the surrounding landscape.

How could they do it? In his new work with the alliance, he'd become familiar with different types of weapons and their general capabilities. He understood how the Ryusei's warhead worked, with many small charges, even as he shuddered at the damage it would inflict. But the details of the new warhead were not included, which was reasonable. It was still being developed, after all, but it was hard to imagine how anything short of . . .

*   *   *

Admiral Orihara had taken over Kubo's old office, of course, although it held two desks now, for the admiral and his aide. The Hirano estate had never been intended to serve as the headquarters for a multinational military alliance.

Komamura stood silently at the open door for a moment. Orihara had been an aviator, and the model of *Tachikaze,* Kubo's first ship, was gone. One wall was covered with photos of different Japanese aircraft. A photo of Kubo, bordered in black, had been added as well.

His aide, a lieutenant, noticed Komamura first, and stood, almost coming to attention. "Yes, Doctor?"

Struggling with several emotions, the professor did not respond right away. Reading Komamura's troubled expression, Orihara glanced toward his aide. The lieutenant said, "I'll bring tea," but Komamura shook his head, still silent. At a nod from the admiral, the aide grabbed a sheaf of papers and quickly left.

"Please, come in," Orihara urged. Once inside, Komamura closed the door carefully and sat down, feeling the admiral's eyes on him. He felt painfully aware of what Orihara's impression of him must be—at best, a melancholy drunk. But that could not be helped. He would not hold back.

Komamura leaned forward and laid the hard copy he'd gotten from Miyazaki in front of Orihara. "By my estimates, the improved warhead for the Ryusei has a yield of about fifteen kilotons. It's a plutonium implosion design, correct?"

He was watching for Orihara's reaction, and the admiral seemed genuinely surprised by the question. "I don't know what you're talking about. The improved warhead—"

"Cannot achieve the described level of destruction using any known conventional explosive," Komamura interrupted. Now that he'd said it out loud, he felt unexpected anger, and fought to control it. "Damage over such a large area can only be achieved by a nuclear weapon."

Orihara did not answer immediately, but instead picked up the phone and punched a number. After a short pause, he said, "Please ask Minister Hisagi to come to my office immediately."

As he hung up, Komamura asked, "How did you get permission from the Diet? I was surprised that they approved the ballistic missile, even with a conventional warhead, but this? Wait. Do they even know?"

"The prime minister, the defense minister, and the head of the Japanese Atomic Energy Agency know," the admiral answered. "As you can imagine, security is extremely tight."

"Is 'extremely tight' good enough?" Komamura asked, his voice rising. He paused for a moment, then spoke more softly. "If China learns of a nuclear weapons program in Japan, it almost guarantees instant devastation."

There was a knock on the door, and Orihara answered, "Come in." Hisagi stepped inside quickly, closing the door again.

The admiral announced, "Dr. Komamura has deduced the nature of the Ryusei's 'improved' warhead."

Hisagi's face registered surprise, then it went blank for a moment before he carefully responded. "That is unfortunate, Doctor. You were not supposed to be briefed into the project."

"I'm not surprised. You certainly knew what my reaction would be. I'm repelled by the very idea." Looking at the two, he asked harshly, "Are either of you truly Japanese?"

Both reacted to the insult as if they'd been slapped. The use of nuclear weapons in World War II had scarred Japan's national psyche. You didn't have to have family near Hiroshima or Nagasaki, or have met someone suffering from radiation-induced illness. It was enough to have been born and raised in Japan.

Orihara answered carefully, "Your opinion is respected, Doctor, even now, but this was a matter of national and alliance policy. You were never part of the decision process."

Suddenly he felt helpless. He'd caught Orihara's slight—"even now"—and the admiral had referred to him as an academic, instead of the "*sensei*" everyone else used. His message was clear. *I don't care who you are.*

"I cannot imagine a Japan that possesses nuclear weapons. What about the other alliance members? Do they know?"

Hisagi answered, "They all know. Like the ballistic missiles, the weapons will be jointly owned, and based in all of the alliance countries."

"Why not just procure some Indian ballistic missiles, then?"

"India has reservations and refused. The other nations agreed that it would be better if we developed our own nuclear technology. These will be alliance weapons, not just Japanese. We've had the technical capability; we've just chosen not to develop them.

"It will proceed very quickly. The MOX fuel used in our nuclear reactors is seven percent weapons-grade plutonium. We already have several labs at work chemically separating the element, and we only need a few kilograms for a small implosion warhead. The Indians have agreed to provide assistance, as well."

Komamura remembered the officer working with Kasugi. "And you're already picking out targets. It's unbelievable."

"We have no intention of using them," Hisagi protested, "but think, *sensei*. Not a single ballistic missile has fallen on Indian soil. The reason is obvious, as is the solution. Deterrence works, and these will be our shield against future attacks."

"Unless the Chinese decide that seven more nations with nuclear weapons is too many," Komamura argued. "We are frighteningly vulnerable now, with a secret worse than the existence of the alliance initially was. Remember our fears then of being discovered? If China learns of the program, she'll immediately strike every location she can think of that might be involved in their development."

Komamura's own words frightened him. "And how will the alliance make them public?" he continued. "A secret deterrent is useless. How many weapons do we need to have a credible deterrent against an established nuclear superpower?"

He paused, then shook his head. "No, China will never let us get that far. Even if they don't discover the program before it becomes operational, the moment the alliance announces it has nuclear weapons, the Chinese will have to strike!"

Hisagi and Orihara both looked grim. The minister replied respectfully, but firmly. "Your arguments, and more, were debated at length, and the decision was made by our national leaders, as is their duty.

"This is at least in part because of your work, *sensei*. As long as we were willing to let America guarantee our security, Japan could limit her armed forces. If we are to stand by ourselves now, as part of a military alliance, then we should build whatever we need for a proper defense."

"Please, let me speak to the prime minister," Komamura pleaded.

"What will you do, question his heritage as well?" Orihara responded harshly. "Put your skills to work and show us a way to break the Chinese economy. If we can do that quickly enough, then all of this is moot. One more opinion will not change anything. Events have moved forward. There is no looking back."

13 September 2016
1300 Local Time
By Water
Halifax, Nova Scotia

He titled the piece "Shattered Trident." Christine's source, whom he'd dubbed "Deep Voice," didn't send something every day, but everything he sent was a blockbuster. The latest one had arrived less than three hours ago, and Christine was waiting for him to proof and polish the piece before giving it to her.

There. He always forced himself to read completely through each posting one final time before sending it. With the last few corrections made, he hit the "Send" link and checked his watch.

She'd use the text he wrote almost verbatim, now that she'd given him a few journalism tutorials, but she'd still have to assemble the "visuals." That probably meant the 4:00 P.M. feed. He wouldn't post the article until then. Their arrangement was simple. CNN was the source, so CNN got the scoop.

All the news channels, and probably many of the intelligence services, now watched his blog closely. He wasn't the only source of information about the war, but he had broken enough stories now so that he was a known authority—an authority with excellent sources.

This article would only reinforce his blog's status. Laird's source had given them The Plan: a complete copy of the Chinese operations order for something called "Trident." While the military details were fascinating, the underlying purpose and goal were frightening. It was bad enough that China had intended to seize most of the disputed territory in the South China Sea by force, but beyond that, those in the East China Sea, and then the Yellow Sea. China's leaders had big ambitions.

What if the plan had succeeded? He tried to imagine the entire western Pacific under Communist Chinese hegemony. This posting would change the world's attitude about China. It could have as much effect on China's fortunes as a traditional bombing campaign.

He'd better proofread it again.

As Mac read, he imagined what the Chinese spokesman would say. It was certain that they'd be barraged with questions, just as the Littoral Alliance spokesman had been besieged after his last major release. A detailed analysis of China's oil infrastructure and its impact on the economy had spiked Littoral Alliance claims of imminent victory, changing the public debate almost overnight. He imagined that was Deep Voice's real goal, although Mac couldn't see that the pronouncements by the two warring factions had improved. Each side just used what it wanted and ignored any inconvenient facts.

13 September 2016
1430 Local Time
Pearl Harbor-Hickam Joint Base
Hawaii

Commander Garcia, the sub base XO, met Patterson's plane at Hickam with a private car. During the five-minute ride to the sub base, he briefed her on the security. "With the war, we were already at a very high level. The special weapons requirements are on top of that, of course, but they're not attracting the kind of attention they would normally."

Even as he described them, the car stopped at the gate to the part of Pearl Harbor that housed the sub base. A marine sentry examined all their identification thoroughly while a dog handler walked around the car. They even checked the trunk and searched her overnight bag.

The techs had decided to do the work at the base's torpedo shop. While moving twelve nuclear warheads from inactive storage was not a simple process, moving twelve Mark 48 torpedoes was even harder, and there simply wasn't room at the special weapons shop for twelve torpedoes, each nearly twenty feet long and weighing almost two tons.

There was more security at the torpedo shop itself, the building literally surrounded with marines, weapons at the ready. And was that a machine-gun position?

More salutes, and more identity checks at the door, but at least she'd left her overnight bag in the car. Inside, she was greeted by Captain Marino, the sub base commander, and Colonel Thomas, head of the technical team. "My people will supervise loading the torpedoes onto each sub, and the arming."

"Did you have any problems with the authorization process?" she asked. She'd been briefed about the strict rules controlling what the United States called "special weapons." There was the two-man rule, requiring that all work on a nuclear device, however trivial, be done by two people, and thoroughly documented, of course. Each weapon also had to be under positive control at all times. This meant that until it was to be launched at a target, a weapon was guarded at all times and could not be armed, which required authorization from the president.

Thomas explained, "President Myles has signed an executive order declaring that this use of nuclear weapons is not an attack on any country, but a 'controlled detonation for peaceful purposes.' The SECDEF has also verified the order. Each weapon will be prepped just before it's put in the tube, in the presence of the sub's captain, weapons officer, you, and myself."

That was why she was there. She was the president's personal representative. She carried the Permissive Action Link, or PAL security codes, for the nuclear warheads. This was definitely not the way things were done normally. But the submarines' fire control system lacked the ability to insert the PAL code while at sea, so the codes would have to be manually entered just as the torpedo was loaded into the tube. Without a proper PAL code, a warhead could not be armed. It would be by her action that eight nuclear weapons would be detonated in the South and East China Seas. It didn't seem quite real.

"Once we verify that the weapon is properly prepared, it goes in the tube and we padlock the tube door. The only way it leaves the tube is either by being fired, or offloaded when the sub returns to base. The captain and weapons officer of each sub will have access to the keys, in case of emergencies."

"But the subs only have four torpedo tubes," Patterson protested. "You'll be tying up two of them until they get back to port. Can't they wait to load them until they're in position to fire?"

"Not and maintain positive control, ma'am. Too many people have access to the torpedo room. And we'll be using three tubes, actually," Thomas clarified. He ignored her alarmed expression.

"Each sub will have a third weapon as a spare, in case there's a problem with either of the first two. So, yes, until they fire, they will only have one tube available for self-defense. But once they do shoot, they can unlock the tube doors and use them normally."

She didn't know whether to be relieved or more concerned. Of course, the four boats would not be looking for a fight when they sailed, but poor *Santa Fe* demonstrated that plans didn't always work out.

They walked down the length of the shop, escorted by Warrant Four Harris, the officer in charge of the facility. The interior was crowded with not only navy torpedomen, but the nuclear weapons specialists of Thomas's team.

Complex mechanisms filled every corner of the shop. The sounds of different tools combined to form a constant background to their conversation.

Harris explained that the warhead sections from the torpedoes were easily removed and replaced with an exercise module. It was a straightforward process, and was covered by established maintenance procedures. "We normally separate the sections as part of a torpedo's overhaul."

"They fit?" Patterson asked. It was obvious they did, but she was curious.

Harris nodded. "Easily. We're using W-80 warheads from Air Force B61 tactical nukes. The device is smaller in diameter and shorter, so volume isn't an issue. It's also not that far off weight-wise. The real challenge was securely mounting the warhead inside and then figuring out how to ballast the weapon so the torpedo's center of gravity didn't shift. That would have thrown the guidance completely off."

They reached the far end of the shop, where the torpedoes already converted were being cased for shipment. Thomas said, "We'll start loading the weapons onto the trucks shortly. There's a C-17 prepped and waiting to take the weapons, you, my team, and our security detachment to Guam. If you'd like to rest, Warrant Officer Harris's office—"

"That's fine," Patterson answered. "I'd like to stay here, if that's all right. I'll keep out of the way." Maybe if she watched for a while, it would begin to sink in. She'd been going through the motions, doing what needed to be done, but the enormity of it all was overwhelming. She couldn't decide if she was in shock or had just become numb.

She'd spent part of the flight out to Hawaii trying to determine more accurately how bad the environmental damage was going to be. Terms like "best case" and "conservative estimate" didn't really seem appropriate. In the end, she could only draw broad limits around an unhappy answer, but the damage from the nuclear explosions was still going to be considerably less than what had already been inflicted by the sinking of nearly three dozen tankers. And then there was the political "fallout" that was likely to be just as devastating. But the war had already killed tens of thousands, and threatened to slip over the edge into a nuclear nightmare.

Any choice had costs. She could accept paying this price if it could stop a war.

# 24

## PREPARATION

14 September 2016
0830 Local Time
Littoral Alliance Headquarters
Okutama, Nishitama District
Tokyo, Japan

Minister Hisagi and Admiral Orihara filed out of the Hirano estate's dojo along with the rest of the alliance's formal working group members. It had been a short meeting. There was little to discuss militarily. Attacks against Chinese merchant ships had fallen to almost zero, and those attacks that took place were very close to the Chinese coast, where defenses were more robust. The South Korean representative reported that they had lost one of their Type 214 submarines near Qingdao in the Yellow Sea.

Submarine attacks against Chinese deep-ocean semi-submersible oil rigs were also disappointing. Only one oil rig had been sunk, requiring four torpedoes before it finally capsized. Another two were seriously damaged. Although they were assessed as repairable, they had temporarily stopped pumping oil. Unfortunately, the PLAN responded quickly to this new avenue of attack and began forward-deploying ASW helicopters to the oil rigs. Freed from their responsibility of patrolling the shipping lanes, Chinese maritime patrol aircraft now concentrated their ASW searches near the drill sites, further complicating the approach for alliance submarines.

There had been no cruise missile strikes in the last two days, while the attacking ships and submarines returned to base to rearm. Orihara again emphasized that Project Ryusei would help to alleviate the gaps between cruise missile strikes. Of greater concern were the reports from South Korea and Vietnam that they were running low on land-attack cruise missiles. The Korean representative said the production of the Hyunmoo 3 missiles had been stepped up, but it would be at least two weeks before the alliance would see an appreciable increase in their inventory. India promised to see what they could do to resupply Vietnam with 3M-14E Klub land-attack missiles. Unfortunately, a significant number of India's stock had been expended in the opening attacks against the Pakistanis.

There was good news from the Vietnam front. Thanks to India's transfer of two Su-30MKI Flanker squadrons, the Chinese Air Force had suffered considerable losses to their frontline air regiments. When combined with classic Vietnamese SAM traps, Chinese ground-support air strikes had been reduced by nearly half. Deprived of adequate air support, the Chinese Army's advance had slowed significantly.

The working group took the "good news/bad news" update brief with guarded optimism, but the topic of discussion had nothing to do with the execution of the war. No, it dealt with the growing civil unrest in several Littoral Alliance nations. Tokyo, Seoul, Taipei, and Hanoi had all had large civilian demonstrations demanding an end to hostilities. Much of the anger behind the protests was directly tied to the Chinese ballistic missile attacks on the capital cities, but a number of Internet blogs and social networking sites were throwing gasoline on the fire. One Japanese Web site had leaked the existence of the Beidou jamming system, and claimed the military was using the civilian population as a shield. Hisagi was incensed.

"The individual responsible should be tried for treason," he hissed.

Orihara laughed cynically. "The leak was undoubtedly a Chinese information operation targeted against the people of our nations' capitals. They either discovered or deduced the countermeasure we put in place, and are now trying to shift the blame on to us for the civilian deaths."

"The Internet is proving to be a curse," Hisagi grumbled.

"Indeed, and some Web sites are far more damaging than others. Take that Bywater site, for example."

"You mean the one run by the Canadian?"

"Yes! He is particularly well informed. He must have spies all over the world!" Orihara vented. "His recent analysis on the mining of *Liaoning* was disturbingly accurate. It was as if he was reading our own after-action reports."

Hisagi stopped dead in his tracks and grabbed the admiral by the arm; there was great concern on the foreign minister's face. "Are you suggesting someone in the alliance is feeding him information?"

Orihara sighed. "I don't know, Shuhei-san. It's a possibility, but this McMurtrie fellow is, by all accounts, a very bright man. His rendition of the Battle of Spratly Island was even more detailed than the Vietnamese Navy's official report. Regardless, his blog has a huge following within the alliance and throughout the world. And now that he's working for CNN, his postings carry even greater weight, and they are not necessarily in our best interest."

Both men suddenly went silent as they saw Komamura walking down the hall toward his office. His head was down, his posture slumped, and his feet moved in uneven small steps. Hisagi shook his head in disappointment and pity. "He's been drinking again."

"I'm afraid so," Orihara replied sternly. "He's been very depressed since his discovery of the improved warhead. That knowledge is weighing heavily on him."

"It's the memory of his mother," Hisagi volunteered. "She died from cancer caused by radiation from the Nagasaki bombing. Her death was slow and painful. Her death haunts him."

Orihara looked again at the retreating figure. His face now showed understanding and compassion instead of disdain. "I did not know this. It explains much," he said.

The admiral turned back to Hisagi. Orihara stood almost at attention and swallowed hard. "Forgive me, Minister, for what I'm about to say, but I must. I believe Professor Komamura is becoming a significant security risk. His questionable mental and emotional stability is becoming a threat to the very alliance his genius has inspired."

Hisagi's expression suddenly became pained, and he turned away from the admiral. Orihara expected the minister to lash out in anger, but instead he slowly looked back; there was a sad look on his face. Nodding, he said, "As much as I hate to agree with you, Admiral, I find your concerns to be valid. We cannot remove him, though. The other alliance members would never tolerate that. But we can watch him closely. For his own good, as well as that of the alliance."

14 September 2016
0800 Local Time
August 1st Building, Ministry of National Defense Compound
Beijing, People's Republic of China

General Su pointed to the map of northern Vietnam with his laser pointer. "As of early this morning, PLA units now control all five northeastern provinces and most of Lai Chau, an adjacent northwestern province. Our rate of advance has slowed, due to the arrival of Vietnamese reinforcements and reduced air support." Su made sure he had eye contact with General Wang, head of the PLAAF, when he finished the sentence.

"Our casualties are running higher than expected, but not excessively so," Su continued. "The 13th, 41st, and 47th Group Armies have suffered the most and have been reinforced by the 20th and 31st Group Armies. This leaves only the 54th Group Army as an operational reserve; however, three reinforcement group armies have finished embarking their trains and are en route to the Guangzhou Military Region. That concludes my summary. Are there any questions?"

"General Su," opened the minister of defense, "in committing two of the reserve group armies to the northeast so soon, I'm concerned that we are leaving the northwest flank open to counterattack. How long before the reinforcements arrive and are combat ready?"

Su nodded and illuminated that area on the map. "General Wen, once the reinforcements arrive, I plan to shift the 54th Group Army to the west to shore up that front. This should be accomplished in approximately one week. Fortunately, the hideous terrain affects Vietnamese tanks as much as it does ours. Moving mechanized units just takes more time. While there is some risk with this deployment, I believe it is acceptable."

Ye Jin, the head of the logistics department, was next. "General, with the reinforcements, we will have committed two-thirds of our frontline army units to the assault on Vietnam. Shouldn't we consider mobilizing some units of the ready reserve?"

Su frowned. Mobilizing reserves was a political hot button. Militarily it was the right answer, but some members of the CMC argued that it would have a negative effect on an already unhappy people. *To hell with their concerns,* Su thought. He was a soldier and he would give a soldier's answer. "You are correct, General Ye. We'll need more troops as garrison forces for the provinces we've occupied. I don't have an accurate number for you right now, at least several divisions, but the sooner we start, the better."

If Zhang or Shi were unhappy with Su's response, they didn't show it. Chen had been ambivalent on the issue, his views shifting back and forth depending on who had talked to him last. However, it was the president who responded. "Very well, General Su. This commission will consider your recommendation. Please provide us with the force requirements and mobilization timetable and we'll discuss it later."

"Yes, Comrade President. You'll have the figures by this afternoon," replied Su. The president's answer wasn't what he wanted to hear, but at least the topic was now formally on the commission's docket for discussion.

Chen rose and cleared his throat, commanding the commission's attention. "Fellow members, I appreciate the effort and forethought you put into your progress reports. But while they are encouraging, I'm beginning to sense stagnation in our war effort.

"We've finally contained the submarine threat in our waters, and Admiral Wei has said that the first convoys will be ready to set sail in a few days. However, the performance of our own submarine campaign is less than impressive. I understand there are many reasons for this, but comrades, we have to find a way to do better.

"And I'm not just singling out our navy. The picture in the air and on the ground shows progress, but the rate of improvement is slow. Let me be blunt. Our military position in this war has improved, but it's not improving fast enough."

Chen walked over to the theater map on the large-screen display and pointed to three formations in the middle of the Philippine Sea. "The Americans now have three carrier strike groups within a day's travel of the South and East China Seas. All four of their SSGNs have deployed, and the two in the U.S. Pacific Fleet are likely within striking distance as I speak. Their submarine forces in the Pacific have also been sortied—there are currently four attack submarines at Guam. Three of them are of the new *Virginia* type. The United States has amassed a huge armada on our very doorstep, and should they become directly involved, we will be hard-pressed to stop them."

Alarmed, General Xiao interrupted, "But Comrade President, surely our anti-ship ballistic missiles will keep them at bay?"

"We are still in the process of developing the entire system," cautioned

Hu. "The missile flies, and flies well, but there are problems involved with targeting the weapons that we are still working on. In addition, we've redeployed many of the launchers to augment the attacks on Japan, South Korea, and Vietnam. We might be able to handle one carrier, but not three."

"It's their submarines that will break us," interjected Wei firmly. "They can wreak far more havoc than the Littoral Alliance could ever conceive of doing. The two SSGNs alone can carry more land-attack missiles than have been fired on us thus far. If the United States joins the Littoral Alliance, and follows their strategy, the vast majority of our oil infrastructure is within range of their Tomahawks."

"This is an unnecessary academic discussion," objected Wang, obviously frustrated. "Ambassador Yang's reports clearly show the United States is heavily divided. Many of its people and political leaders are strongly advocating neutrality, particularly after the Littoral Alliance rebuffed their president. And history shows that when America is divided, it usually doesn't act."

"You're correct in saying America is divided, General Wang," observed Shi Peng, the chief of the political department. "But the ambassador also notes the division is almost a fifty/fifty split between neutrality and joining the alliance. In short, President Myles will anger half of his population regardless of what he does. This makes him potentially very dangerous, much more so than the statistics would suggest. And may I remind you that we haven't accepted his proposals either."

Vice President Zhang Fei looked depressed. "If the Americans are considering joining the alliance, perhaps a limited nuclear demonstration, say on a Japanese target, would give them something to consider."

Both Chen and Su strongly disagreed. "Absolutely not!" cried Su. "My apologies, Comrade Vice President, but if the United States is sitting on the fence, then such a move would only push them over onto the alliance side."

"I agree with General Su," stated Chen strongly. "Such a move would almost certainly work against us."

"Then what can we do?" asked Zhang.

"We must push harder, move faster," declared Chen. "Commanders, we currently have the advantage, and we need to exploit it to the fullest extent possible. I expect you to be bold, even daring. We must take more risks if we are to conclude this conflict in our favor. If this war descends into a long-term struggle, then even if we win, we lose."

14 September 2016
1030 Local Time
Squadron Fifteen Headquarters
Guam

The summons to the squadron headquarters arrived mid-morning. Frankly, Jerry was very surprised that the call hadn't come earlier—it had been over thirty-six hours since the VTC on Monday night. He suspected Simonis was still deeply troubled by his recommendation to the president to use nuclear weapons as a war-ending strategy. The commodore had been in a state of total disbelief when the VTC ended, and left without saying a single word. Everyone stood in amazement as he just walked out of the conference room. No ranting, no orders, nothing.

Jerry again skipped the car ride and walked to the squadron headquarters building. It was a pleasant morning and the stroll helped to clear his head. He fully expected a major blowout with Simonis, and he needed to be thinking clearly. After signing in at the quarterdeck, he collected his visitor's badge and passed through the turnstiles, taking the left-hand passageway toward the squadron admin spaces. As he passed by one of the offices, a voice called out to him, "Commander Mitchell!"

Jerry turned to see someone poking his head out of an open door. It was Commander Walker, Simonis's operations officer. "Do you have a minute, Captain?" he asked.

Glancing at his watch, Jerry saw he still had five minutes before his meeting with Simonis. "Yeah, sure. What can I do for you?"

Walker motioned for Jerry to come into his office, then closed the door behind him. He looked a little agitated. "The order to implement your nuke demo suggestion came in earlier this morning. We've been tasked to carry it out, and the commodore is *not* a happy camper. He's been bubbling like a stopped-up volcano all morning. Your meeting won't be very pleasant, I'm afraid."

Jerry nodded. "I figured we'd get the job. I was pretty sure the air force didn't have a weapon that could get as deep as we need to go."

"Well, I wouldn't admit that if I were you. It'll only make him madder."

"I'll keep it in mind, although I don't think it will matter one iota what I say. He's not very open to people who disagree with him."

Walker smiled wearily. "You got that right."

"Thanks for the heads-up, though. I'll try not to antagonize him any more than I already have." Jerry turned to leave, but Walker spoke up again.

"Ah, Captain . . . I also wanted to thank you for sticking up for Warren Halsey the other day."

Jerry pivoted to face Walker again. Confused, he said, "I wasn't aware that Halsey needed defending. I only presented what I believed had happened."

"Warren was a close friend," Walker explained slowly. "He wasn't the best submarine skipper, but he was a competent one. Unfortunately, that's not good enough for our commodore. It didn't help that *Santa Fe* was not in the best of shape. Warren and Captain Simonis had a pretty tumultuous relationship; the commodore can be brutally harsh at times. I just wanted to let you know that I appreciated someone, other than myself and the CSO, speaking up for Warren, that's all."

"You're welcome," Jerry replied. "And I'm sorry that you lost a friend. It's never easy, is it?"

"No, it's not," responded Walker quietly. Jerry could see there was still pain in his eyes. Clearing his throat, he added, "If there is anything I can do for you, just let me know. I like to pay my debts."

Initially, Jerry was going to tell Walker that wasn't necessary. But before he could say anything, a nagging question resurfaced in his mind. "Now that you mention it, there is something I'd appreciate you looking into."

"Name it!" Walker said eagerly.

"Can your intel shop get me any information on the current CO of the Indian Akula, INS *Chakra*? The guy is a certified pain in the ass, and we're likely to run into him again. I'd like to know who I'm dealing with."

"I'll get the request into the system immediately and ask for an expedited response."

Jerry thanked Walker and shook his hand. Jerry then marched quickly to the commodore's reception area. The first-class yeoman in the outer office saw him approaching and immediately rose. "Good morning, Captain. I'll let the commodore know you're here."

Jerry smiled and nodded. His eyes wandered around the outer office as he waited for the yeoman to return. He didn't have to wait long.

"Sir, the commodore will see you now."

Thanking the yeoman, Jerry walked smartly into Simonis's office and snapped to attention. "Commanding Officer, USS *North Dakota*, reporting as ordered, sir."

Simonis was over by his side table, refilling his coffee mug. Without even looking in Jerry's direction he ordered, "Please close the door, Captain. Then take a seat."

Jerry carefully shut the door and strode quickly to the conference table. He pulled out a chair and sat down. Simonis walked slowly by his desk, and picked up a folder. He threw it onto the table and sat down. Jerry noticed the commodore hadn't bothered to offer him any coffee this time, a bad omen.

"Congratulations, Captain, your harebrained scheme has been approved by the president," Simonis began sarcastically. "And it gets even better. My squadron has been ordered to carry out this fool's errand. Your ditsy buddy, Dr. Patterson, is leaving Hawaii within the hour with twelve modified Mark 48 torpedoes. She'll arrive around 1930. Shortly thereafter we'll begin loading three nuclear-armed torpedoes on each submarine. *North Dakota* will be the first to depart at 1200 tomorrow."

Jerry was angered by Simonis's disrespectful tone when he spoke of Joanna, but Jerry kept his response short and professional. "Understood, Commodore, we'll be standing by to receive the weapons by 1915. Is there anything else?"

"Anything else? I would think starting a nuclear war is quite enough, don't you, Captain?"

"I don't believe this demonstration will trigger a nuclear exchange, Commodore," Jerry answered tersely. "And apparently neither does the president."

"Well, I'm sure that will be of great comfort to the survivors after a city or two is vaporized," sniped Simonis.

Jerry had had enough. "Permission to speak frankly, sir."

"By all means, Captain."

"If you disagree so strongly with this course of action, why don't you ask to be relieved?"

"Because it wouldn't do any good. They'd just bring in someone who'd follow the orders of an asinine academic who's trying to get reelected!" Simonis replied angrily.

"So, you'll just sit here and badmouth the president, the deputy national security advisor, or anyone else who happens to disagree with you. Contempt of an official is a UCMJ violation, Commodore, Article 88 if I remember correctly," Jerry shot back.

Simonis became enraged. Jumping to his feet, he howled, "HOW DARE YOU LECTURE—"

"YES, COMMODORE! I DO DARE," shouted Jerry just as loudly. "Your behavior is unprofessional and a disgrace! *IF* you are so convinced these orders are a disaster in the making, then show some courage and ask to be relieved! Otherwise, stop this passive-aggressive bullshit and do your job!"

Simonis sat back down, stunned; he was unaccustomed to subordinates fighting back. His jaw was tight, his fists balled, he was visibly shaking. "And what makes you so damn sure this will work? How do you know you're right!?" he growled through clenched teeth.

"How do I know it will work, Commodore?" replied Jerry with a lower, less adversarial tone. "Honestly, I don't know. But in looking at the president's likely options, it seems to be the path with the least risk."

"Least risk!?" Simonis wailed. "You obviously don't see the big picture, Captain. The least risk is for us to remain neutral. Stay out of the fight completely!"

"Is that really true, Commodore?" pushed Jerry. "Let's analyze that hypothesis. Staying neutral all but ensures the fighting goes on for a whole lot longer. Eventually, China will likely win, but their economy will be down the toilet. This will cause a global economic meltdown as bad, or conceivably even worse, than the Great Depression of the 1930s, that will drag us down as well. Just look at the economic impact the war has already had on the U.S. and Europe. A collapse is unavoidable; our economies are too interconnected. Every newspaper article and official government report I've read all say the same thing—unprecedented unemployment, soaring poverty, and the government safety net can't possibly catch them all.

"Politically, the U.S. will be viewed as untrustworthy. At the very least we'll be pushed out of the Pacific Rim, because we refused to honor our treaty commitments. I know that doesn't make a whole lot of sense, but the blame game isn't exactly logical. We'll be blamed for their loss, even though the Littoral Alliance rejected the president's repeated attempts at mediation. This will also raise doubts with other countries as to whether we'll honor our security agreements with them. Coupled with our own economic problems, U.S. influence will be severely compromised.

"And I haven't even begun to address the humanitarian disaster this war will cause if it continues. Every continent will be affected, some far worse than others. Definitely China and the Littoral Alliance will suffer more civilian casualties, but the impact on developing nations following the economic collapse will be catastrophic.

"No, sir. The *bigger* picture painted by staying neutral is dismal, even if we ignore the significant loss of life, worldwide, this war will cause. The U.S. will emerge from it fiscally broke, politically feeble, a superpower in military terms only. Which is why the president has already chosen not to adopt that strategy, you know this better than I. PACOM has already started implementing major parts of OPLAN 5077. Come tomorrow, one way or another, my boat leaves for war.

"So, either we shock the crap out of both the Chinese and the alliance, get them to see the oncoming train wreck, or we start shooting Chinese targets. And once we push their back up against the wall, the Chinese will feel compelled to resort to a nuclear demonstration to stave off defeat. That's when a city or two will be vaporized. They may not be ours, but that distinction won't matter a whole hell of a lot. After that, things will go downhill really fast."

"I don't buy the use of nuclear weapons, period, Mitchell," said Simonis, still strained. "It is too easy to misinterpret the message we're trying to send."

"I'm not saying there isn't any risk, Commodore," argued Jerry. "All I'm saying is that the risk of a preemptive demonstration out in the middle of the ocean is *lower* than escalation to the point where nuclear weapons are used against an actual target.

"Think about it. There really is very little to misinterpret. The first warning the Littoral Alliance and China will have is when the warheads detonate. They'll know they went off, and they'll know they went off far from their homelands. That's why our squadron got tasked with this mission; we've got the stealth and the weapons to pull it off. This has to be a bolt out of the frickin' blue, no warning, just a lot of big bangs that will shock the living daylights outta them, hopefully enough to bring everyone to their senses."

Simonis didn't respond immediately. He just sat there, his mind working its way through Jerry's explanation. On the plus side, the crimson hue had drained from the commodore's face and his hands were no longer clenched tight. After nearly a minute of silence, Simonis took a deep breath; he seemed calmer, but his voice was still tense as he spoke. "Thank you for your explanation, Captain. I'm still not completely convinced this is the right thing to do, but I now see there is some logic behind it. I must admit that I'm greatly concerned about the possibility of a Chinese retaliation. This island makes for a splendid demonstration target."

Jerry smiled weakly. "The thought had occurred to me as well, sir. I just didn't think it would be very constructive for me to bring it up."

"You're correct, it wouldn't," replied Simonis sternly. "I have a lot of

people and their families here, Captain, and I'm responsible for their welfare. It's difficult for me to watch this situation as it deteriorates, and know
that I have absolutely no control over what's going on. It's not a pleasant
feeling being helpless."

"I completely understand, sir. I believe that was the point you had to
ram down my throat earlier." Jerry grinned as he spoke. To his relief, Simonis broke out laughing.

"I guess I'd make a rather poor psychiatrist. Beating one's patients
about the head and shoulders is usually frowned upon."

"Well, I can certainly vouch for the effectiveness of the treatment,"
Jerry said with a wink. "But your bedside manner could use some work."

Simonis smiled as he nodded. "Got it. I'll make sure it's on my next
counseling form."

Rising, the commodore extended his hand to Jerry, who grasped it firmly.
"I expect you and your crew to carry out your assignment flawlessly, Captain," remarked Simonis firmly.

"Understood, sir. I'll try not to disappoint you."

"I know you won't, Captain."


14 September 2016
1930 Local Time
Andersen Air Force Base
Guam

Simonis watched as the C-17 Globemaster III transport aircraft pulled up
to the hangar. The immediate location was swarming with air force security
personnel. The roads to the submarine piers had been closed to civilian traffic, and marines lined the entire route. Security was so tight, one would
have thought the president of the United States was coming for a visit.

As the aircraft's turbine engines wound down, the cargo ramp began
lowering; more security personnel jumped out of the back of the aircraft and
quickly set up a perimeter. Marine guards ran forward with the trucks as they
moved into position to receive the "special torpedoes." Soon Simonis saw
the forward crew door open. The access ladder extended out and reached for
the tarmac. Once the ladder was down, Dr. Patterson emerged from the air-
plane along with a small entourage. Simonis walked briskly up to meet her.

"Welcome back to Guam, Dr. Patterson."

"Thank you, Captain," she replied. Joanna then pointed to the two officers accompanying her. "Captain Simonis, this is Colonel Thomas and Chief Warrant Officer Four Harris, they're in charge of preparing and supervising the loading of the weapons. Gentlemen, Captain Simonis is the commodore of Submarine Squadron Fifteen."

After a brief exchange of greetings, both Thomas and Harris excused themselves and marched over to the cargo ramp to supervise the unloading. Patterson, her two guards, and Simonis headed toward a row of parked cars.

"The entire route from here to the submarines has been cordoned off, and there are Marines stationed in armed HUMVEEs every half mile. The air force security forces squadron has set up patrols all around the base perimeter. To quote the base commander, 'a seagull would need a pass to get in here,'" Simonis reported.

"Excellent, Captain. Did the governor give you any grief?"

Simonis chuckled. "There was some friction at first. He wasn't happy with us shutting down several of the main streets for a couple of hours, but the call from the secretary of state solved that problem."

"Good! The sooner we get these weapons on the boats, the happier I'll be," Patterson exclaimed.

For the rest of the brief walk to the cars, Simonis and Patterson were silent. But as Simonis opened one of the car's rear doors for Joanna he finally said, "Dr. Patterson, I must admit I'm not a particular fan of Mitchell's proposal. It would make my job a lot easier if I knew this plan had been thoroughly discussed with the president before he made his decision."

Joanna initially looked puzzled, then a grin slowly lit on her face. "Ohh, yes, Captain, there was a long, and at times very heated discussion. The president basically convened an impromptu meeting of the NSC right after the VTC and he heard everyone's views. I can assure you the topic was discussed in detail, and his decision was not made lightly."

"I see," said Simonis, somewhat satisfied. "If you're allowed to say, I'd like to know what some of the objections were."

"I'm sorry, Captain, but I'm not at liberty to go into details of the discussion with the president," replied Joanna. She saw the disappointment on his face, but she was also sympathetic to the issue he was wrestling with. Joanna took a deep breath and spoke softly. "What I can tell you is that there were two strongly held opinions. But by the end of the meeting, only one member objected to implementing Jerry's idea. The rest, including myself, felt it was the best option available to us."

Simonis nodded his understanding. "Sounds very much like the same conversation I had with Commander Mitchell this morning. He doesn't back down much, does he?"

Joanna laughed, clearly amused. "No, Commodore, Jerry has a stubborn streak in him. He's also not the greatest at being tactful, a trait I fear he learned from my husband."

"Your husband?" asked Simonis, confused. "I'm afraid I don't understand."

"You know my husband was Jerry's first CO, on USS *Memphis,* don't you?" she asked tentatively.

"Yes, I'm aware of Mitchell's record," Simonis responded, still uncertain as to what she meant.

Patterson nodded and continued with her explanation. "Lowell ran a *very* tight ship, and even he admits he could be a difficult man to work for. He and Jerry went at it, hammer and tongs, on more than one occasion. Both men can be stubborn as mules, God knows. But Jerry was able to hold his own, largely by being brutally honest and straightforward, and Lowell begrudgingly respected him for it. They are now very close friends. No, sir, if Jerry Mitchell has a strongly held position on a topic, he won't back down, regardless of the personal cost. Which is why the president finds him so refreshing."

Joanna slowly scooted into the backseat, and after she'd been flanked on either side by her marine escort, Simonis closed the door and walked quickly to the passenger side. As the convoy left Andersen Air Force Base, Simonis was mentally chewing on the new information Patterson had provided. There was more to Jerry Mitchell than he'd originally thought, much more. And if the vast majority of the president's advisers felt Mitchell's idea was their best option, after fighting about it amongst themselves, then perhaps it really was the right thing to do.

14 September 2016
2230 Local Time
Squadron Fifteen Headquarters
Guam

"Attention on deck!" shouted Captain Jacobs. The assembled group quickly came to attention as Simonis and Patterson walked into the conference room.

"As you were," Simonis boomed. The commodore marched straight up to the podium; he wasted no time in getting the predeployment briefing started.

"My apologies for the late hour of this briefing, but it was unavoidable. As you know, Dr. Patterson has been jumping from boat to boat getting the special weapons prepared and loaded into the torpedo tubes. As her presence was absolutely necessary, we had to wait until she had finished inserting all the PAL codes and had witnessed all the torpedoes being locked in their tubes before we could drag her away for some dinner. I may be able to flog you guys like rented mules, but I have to be a little more lenient with senior administration officials."

The audience's laugh was genuine, and Joanna just shrugged her shoulders. Simonis then punched a few buttons and brought up the first briefing slide on the large-screen display. In big, bold letters, the slide was titled OPERATION MINERVA. A low murmur grew from the crowd, along with some snickering.

"All right, pay attention. 'Operation Minerva' is the code name for the deployment of eight modified Mark 48 torpedoes with nuclear warheads in the deep-ocean areas adjacent to the South and East China Seas. And I don't want to hear any guff about the name. I don't write this crap, so we'll just have to suffer together. Some faceless bureaucrat named the operation after the Roman goddess of useful knowledge and wisdom—which would be apropos given the goal of this mission. Now, moving on . . ."

Jerry was following along with the copy of Simonis's presentation in his briefing binder, but as he turned to the page, he found a single sheet of paper sitting on top of the second slide. It was a hard copy of an e-mail from ONI concerning the commanding officer of INS *Chakra*. Jerry eagerly began reading its contents. Simonis's voice faded into the background.

Samant, Girish, CAPT, Indian Navy
- Graduated from Indian Naval Academy in 1995
- Extensive junior officer tours on Project 877E KILO-class submarines, as weapons officer and navigator
- Member of Indian Navy Klub missile acceptance team
- First Officer INS *Sindhuvir*, S 58
- Graduated from Kings College, Department of War Studies, United Kingdom in 2010
- Commanding Officer, INS *Sindhukirti*, S 61

- Completed Royal Navy Submarine Command Course "Perisher" in 2014
- First Indian submariner to complete the course
- Promoted to Captain in 2015
- Assigned as INS *Chakra* Commanding Officer in June 2015
- Strengths: Brilliant tactician, competitive, rated highly by "Perisher" instructor
- Weaknesses: Short-tempered, slightly egotistical

Jerry's eyebrows rose when he read the line about completing the Perisher course. When he got to the part where it said the Indian was highly rated, he whistled softly and whispered, "Whoa!"

Thigpen heard his skipper and looked over with curiosity. Jerry gave him a stern look and waved a finger at him, signaling that he should be paying attention to the commodore. One of them had to, but at the moment Jerry was busy getting to know Mr. Samant.

After finishing the e-mail, Jerry immediately ran through the three encounters he'd had with the Indian captain. Everything in the ONI e-mail matched his impressions. Samant was as good as Jerry suspected. No, scratch that. If a Royal Navy Perisher Teacher thought he was good, then the Indian was *damn* good! It suddenly became obvious that Jerry had seriously underestimated the man during the last two meetings. *Which is why I lost*, he thought to himself.

The rest of the briefing was basically a blur for Jerry. His mind was elsewhere, in the middle of the South China Sea, and focused on a very capable adversary. Strangely, Jerry felt encouraged by the e-mail. He now had something to work with, a man's identity, an idea of his capabilities. Information Jerry could use to begin planning for their next encounter. And he was absolutely convinced there would be another.

Suddenly, Jerry was jerked back to the predeployment briefing by Simonis's loud voice. He was a little shocked to find out he'd missed all of Joanna's presentation. Chagrined, he looked over at Thigpen's steno pad and saw his XO had taken copious notes.

"L-hour is tomorrow at 1200 local time," Simonis announced. "Commander Mitchell, *North Dakota* sorties first. You've got the farthest to go and you'll have to fly at flank speed for a good portion of your transit."

Jerry nodded as he acknowledged the order. "Understood, Commodore."

"Commander Nevens, *North Carolina* will leave four hours later. Followed by *Texas* and *Oklahoma City*. In seventy-two hours you have to be in the launch boxes articulated by Dr. Patterson. H-hour is 1200 local time on 18 September. At precisely that time, each submarine will fire two nuclear-armed torpedoes on the assigned courses and at medium speed. You'll then promptly put your ass to the blast, come shallow, and run like hell. Clear?"

"Yes, sir!" answered the four commanding officers.

"Very well," replied Simonis. "Now I suggest you finish up any preparations you may have left before you deploy tomorrow. I've augmented the duty staff and they'll assist you with whatever you need. Just call and get things moving, we'll follow up with the paperwork later. Any questions?"

There were none.

"All right, I'll see you all tomorrow morning at *Santa Fe*'s memorial service. Afterwards, we'll honor our shipmates by ending this war. Dismissed!"

14 September 2016
1800 Local Time
By Water
Halifax, Nova Scotia

The Great Pacific War of 2016
Posted By: Mac
Subj: New—Book Review: *Navies for Asia* by Dr. Sajin Komamura
One of the most vexing issues about the current conflict in the seas surrounding China is how did it start? At the time, it seemed to spring forth out of nowhere. And while we know a little more now about the opening moves—Operation Trident, the mining of *Liaoning*, the sinking of *Vinaship Sea*—there is still a gap in our understanding of the intent, the motivation behind the war. Well, I'm ashamed to admit that the impetus behind the formation of the Littoral Alliance, as well as its covert submarine war, was right under my nose, available months before the first shots were fired.

A careful examination of the official statements and military strategy of the Littoral Alliance will show they are in perfect harmony with a recent book written by Dr. Sajin Komamura, an economics and history professor at the University of Tokyo. Dr. Komamura's book, *Navies for Asia,* is a masterpiece of argumentation as to why the nations surrounding the Chinese littorals need to band together, in a formal alliance, to resist the aggressive tendencies of the People's Republic of China. Furthermore, Dr. Komamura strongly believes this alliance must be free from the restrictions affiliated with existing security agreements with the United States, whose national interests are not necessarily in concert with Asian countries'.

Dr. Komamura's formal argument is quite powerful and explains fully how the Littoral Alliance came into being. And yet for all its brilliance, there are two fatal flaws that seemed to have gone totally undetected by senior civilian and military officials of the nations within the Littoral Alliance. The first flaw is an assumption made by Dr. Komamura, and to his credit it is an explicit one, that a military conflict with China is inevitable. This is a powerful, and insidious assumption, as it predisposes the alliance away from investigating the potential uses of their collective diplomatic and economic power. Indeed, while Dr. Komamura extols many of the "virtues of the NATO alliance" in Europe, he misses several key political and diplomatic aspects of that alliance that effectively helped deter a war with the Soviet Union.

The second flaw deals with the total exclusion of the United States from their alliance. I'm Canadian, and there are times when my neighbor to the south aggravates me with their policies. However, in the grand scheme of things, belonging to a formal alliance that includes the U.S. has largely been for the good. The sheer military power of the U.S., both conventional and nuclear, was critical to NATO's deterrence credibility. Yes, there have been periods of tension in the past between other members of the NATO alliance and the United States, but tension forces us to think hard about an issue. It's a natural brake that helps prevent rash decisions, even if it makes the decision-making a messy and frustrating process. At the end of the day, deterrence is served.

By adopting Dr. Komamura's writings so completely—indeed his book is often referred to as the Littoral Alliance's "bible"—the alliance policy-makers have severely restricted their options to purely military ones. Is the book *Navies for Asia* a self-fulfilling prophecy? Perhaps. Did it have to be this way? Regrettably, it did not.

# 25

# END GAME

They'd held the memorial service for *Santa Fe* early in the morning, just before the squadron sailed. Who could say when the four boats would all be in port at the same time again? And everyone needed to begin healing. As important as their mission was, it would keep for a few hours.

There were far too many people for the base chapel. The submarine crews, minus their duty sections, from *North Dakota*, *Texas*, *North Carolina*, and *Oklahoma City*, and the families from *Texas*, *Oklahoma City*, and of course *Santa Fe* attended. Adding in the Squadron Fifteen staff, it came to over fifteen hundred people. *North Dakota* and *North Carolina* were home-ported out of Pearl Harbor, so their families were not present, and Jerry missed having Emily beside him.

So they'd taken over a nearby parking lot, setting up chairs, awnings, a podium, flags, and sound system. Volunteers from the Squadron Fifteen boats had made short work of the preparations, so that by the time the last torpedo had been locked in its tube, everything was ready for the service. The mess crews on the four submarines worked all night to prepare the refreshments. They wanted to do this right.

It was going to be a warm day. It got into the eighties in Guam, even in

September, so it was a short service, but that was fine. The crews had places to be.

The navy hadn't lost a ship for a long time, but they hadn't forgotten how a memorial service should be done. Honoring a fallen shipmate, admittedly an entire crew in this case, was a tradition the navy clung to fiercely. The base chaplain had begun the service, followed by readings from each of the Squadron Fifteen skippers. Captain Simonis gave a short speech about service and sacrifice, and that the greatest sacrifice was made by the ones left behind—the families.

Joanna Patterson, at the direction of the president, read a short message praising *Santa Fe* and its crew, who had accepted the risks inherent in their work, and, in faithfully carrying out their duties, "had upheld the finest traditions of the U.S. Navy." She'd held it together while reading the president's message, but the deputy national security advisor wept silently through the rest of the service.

The base band played the navy hymn, and then serenaded the attendees as they enjoyed the refreshments. Jerry had sought out Joanna, who gave him a quick hug, wished him luck, and told him to be careful. Simonis found him as he was talking with Patterson. Upon seeing the commodore waiting, she quickly excused herself. Joanna knew the two had business to discuss. Simonis approached Jerry and offered his hand.

"Good luck, Jerry. I'm sorry about sending you back to the same patrol zone, but *North Dakota* has the best chance against that Akula. I'm assuming Samant's still annoyed, so it makes the most sense to send someone with experience up against him."

"Oh, he's still pissed, Commodore. That's a safe bet. I'll do my best to stay out of his way."

"Just do what's needed and come home. I don't want to lose another one of my boats."

Less than an hour after he returned to *North Dakota*, they were under way. Half an hour later they were submerged, with a flank bell on, speeding for the South China Sea.


Jerry had begun running drills as soon as they were clear of the harbor. The memorial service had left his crew thoughtful, and he needed their heads fully in the game. Feeling sorry for *Santa Fe*, or worse, sorry for themselves, was a good way to get dead. Better they were sweating the next drill, or mad at him for working their tails off.

He ran snapshot torpedo exercises that morphed into damage control drills. He inserted *Chakra*'s recorded acoustic signature into the sonar's computer, exercising his team until even his most junior sonarman knew exactly which tonals would show up first.

He also had the torpedomen run rapid reloading drills. With only one tube available, if he had to shoot, he wanted to make sure it wasn't the only chance he'd get.

In spite of the long distance, *North Dakota* was still close to its assigned station two hours ahead of time. They'd decided to wait inside a box five miles square, centered on their designated launch position. That meant they were never more than half an hour from the launch position at ten knots.

In the infantry, a unit would simply dig in for protection and concealment, but all the crew of *North Dakota* could do was stay quiet, mill about smartly, and wait.

Thigpen and his fire control team had plotted every bit of information on *Chakra*'s patrol patterns, but there was no observable pattern, and besides, their launch position was dictated by geography and hydroacoustics. For this torpedo shot, tactics had to take a backseat.

He'd run the boat at Condition II, port and starboard watches, since leaving Apra Harbor. An hour before launch time, Jerry ordered general quarters. At thirty minutes before H-hour, he went to periscope depth for a final look around. After three slow sweeps with a photonics mast, Jerry was satisfied there wasn't a soul near him. They headed back down to launch depth.

18 September 2016
1140 Local Time
INS *Chakra*
South China Sea

"New contact, number seven three, bearing zero four nine. Hull-popping noises, contact is likely submerged," blared the intercom speaker.

Samant quickly grabbed the mike. "Sonar, is the contact the American submarine?"

"Captain, contact is very weak. We can't tell what it is yet."

Samant threw the mike onto the desk and bolted to the sonar room. Opening the door, he thrust his body between the two operators. "Show me what you have."

Lieutenant Rajat pointed to the slight trace on the waterfall display. The tonal was weak, unstable. The lieutenant was right, it was too hard to tell whether the new contact was a submarine or a ship, but the hull-popping noises meant a submarine was changing depth. And if it was a submarine, it was probably an American. All of the Chinese boats he'd detected thus far had been much farther to the north. Until proven otherwise, he had to assume it was an American attack submarine.

Jain's voice came from behind him. "What is it, Captain?"

"We don't know for sure, Number One, but I think our nemesis is back," answered Samant.

"What!? We haven't seen hide nor hair of him in over a week! Why would he be back now?" Jain asked, surprised.

"I have no idea, Number One, but please be so kind as to bring the boat to action stations."

## USS North Dakota

"Captain, new sonar contact, designated Sierra-one three. The contact is in the forward end fire beam of the TB-33, bearing is two two zero, but it's really sketchy, sir," reported Chief Halleck.

Jerry chuckled cynically and rolled his eyes. "Figures."

"Do you think it's your buddy Samant?" questioned Thigpen.

"Who else? You couldn't get any more inconvenient if you tried. It looks like Murphy is working overtime!" Jerry grumbled. "Attention in Control, I'm about to come left to get Sierra-one three out of the forward end fire beams of our towed arrays. Things could get ugly quick, so keep alert. Carry on.

"Pilot, left fifteen degrees rudder. Steady on course east," ordered Jerry.

"Left fifteen degrees rudder, steady course zero nine zero, Pilot aye."

## INS *Chakra*

"Captain, contact seven three is classified as an American SSN. Contact is altering course, turning away from us," Lieutenant Rajat reported over the speaker.

"I knew it!" Captain Samant's exclamation made Jain and several others in the central post jump. "I had a feeling he'd be skulking around here somewhere, he knew we'd have to head south eventually to find more targets! Has he detected us yet?"

"At this range and in these water conditions, it's likely, sir. He's moving away from us at low speed," said Jain.

"Of course he is," Samant remarked acidly. "He'll try to stay at the edge of his sonar's detection range, following us, and then, when we find a potential target, he'll do his best to interfere. I wouldn't put it past him to put a radio antenna up and warn a ship we were attacking!"

Jain, his first officer, suggested, "Sir, if he's moving east, let's just move westward and break contact."

"Absolutely not!" Samant shot back. "He'll use his acoustic advantage to trail us, and we won't be able to tell whether he's there or not until it's too late. I don't want to play underwater tag with this man for the rest of the war. Let's scrape him off our shoe so we can get back to business. I'll make him regret his career choice," Samant promised grimly.

"Helm, left twenty five, steer zero four five, increase speed to twenty-five knots. Sonar, go active and track the American."

## USS *North Dakota*

"Confirm target zig by Sierra-one three. He's changing course and increasing speed, Skipper. WLY-1 has Skat-3 active transmissions."

"Then there's no point in going east now," Jerry remarked. "Pilot, hard left rudder, steady course north. All ahead two-thirds, make turns for ten knots. I want a little more energy if I have to maneuver suddenly." Even as he said it, he realized that even after all this time, he still thought in aviator terms.

"Sonar, go active as well, and track *Chakra*. I want the best information we can get on his position and speed."

Jerry marveled at the situation. Submarines rarely used active sonar, because it revealed their position. But in this situation, stealth was the last thing on either captain's mind.

He could see *Chakra*'s position on the VLSD. A projected course line ran from her toward and past *North Dakota*. Jerry's turn to the north had shifted the line behind him; his intention was to open the range between the two subs. Now, as they watched, *Chakra*'s course line swung to the left again and steadied in front of the American boat's bow.

The computer's estimate of the closest point of approach was no more than a hundred yards, the approximate length of either sub. "I don't like the look of that," Thigpen remarked.

"At least it's not an intercept course," Jerry answered.

A few moments later, sonar confirmed the Indian sub's course change. *Going active was the right move*, Jerry thought. *Passive tracking takes too long for this business.*

"Pilot, make turns for fifteen knots." Jerry could see Thigpen's worried reaction to the speed change, but the XO remained silent, and Jerry took that as a compliment.

*North Dakota*'s speed built up quickly, but *Chakra*'s projected vector continued to stay just ahead of *North Dakota*. *That's his active sonar tracking*, Jerry thought. *He can see small changes in my course and speed as well. Good.* It also showed Samant didn't want to ram them, just make a dangerously close pass.

"Two minutes to CPA," Thigpen reported. "We're still well within our box."

"Then we're done maneuvering for now. No surprises until after they are clear. Attention in Control, stand by for rapid maneuvers by both boats."

## INS *Chakra*

As he closed, the American's sonar pulses became noticeably louder. It was an unusual sound, but Samant welcomed the noise. He felt he could almost gauge the boat's distance and direction through the hull.

"Closest point of approach in thirty seconds," Jain reported. His first officer was tense, but all business.

The active sonar gave them an unrealistically clear picture of the American sub's position, course, and speed. In Perisher, he'd had to keep this all in his head based on periscope observations, but then again, this was going to be harder than lining up for a simple torpedo shot against a frigate.

Jain's voice was steady. "Loss of active signal! We're in his baffles! Ten seconds, Captain. Five seconds. At CPA . . . *now!*"

Rajat reported, "Captain, the U.S. boat is slowing and turning to the right. He's changing depth, going deeper."

*He's trying to open the distance between us as we pass,* Samant thought. *I don't care. I've got the speed I need to compensate.* The correction came to him instantly.

Samant ordered, "Left thirty, steer zero zero five, make your depth one three zero meters."

"We'll pass two hundred meters astern, and we should be slightly higher than him in depth, perhaps twenty meters," said Jain, looking at the fire control console.

"Perfect." Samant smiled.


## USS *North Dakota*

"He's turning to the left again, Skipper, blade rate's unchanged." The chief paused for a moment, then added, "Sir, he may have changed depth."

"Continue the descent," Jerry ordered. There was little else he could do. If Samant had immediately turned back toward him, then they were dangerously close. No zigging or zagging.

Jerry flashed back to Captain Rudel's maneuvering duel with *Severodvinsk*. He'd been just the navigator then, as he watched *Seawolf*'s captain skillfully maneuver his boat during the Russian sub's insanely close passes. Rudel had done his best to stay out of the Russians' way, and yet they still collided.

"He's going co-depth, sir, matching our change . . ."

Before the chief sonarman could finish his report, a slight jolt ran through *North Dakota*, and half the sonar displays went dark. Alarms rang and Jerry felt a surge of fear. "All stations, report!"

There was no flooding, no apparent effect on their propulsion, but the TB-33 thin-line towed array was gone, snapped off cleanly.

"He's on our port side now sir, bearing two nine zero. Speed is slowing to ten knots. His active sonar is off now."

"Maintain active sonar contact," Jerry ordered. "I don't trust that SOB. Bernie, best course to launch point?"

"Two one zero, Skipper. At ten knots we're there in four minutes, with four minutes to spare. *Chakra* is still heading away from us, steady on course zero zero five at ten knots."

"Understood, XO. Pilot, right fifteen degrees rudder, steady course two one zero."

"Right fifteen degrees rudder, steady course two one zero, Pilot, aye."

"Skipper, what if he's still nearby when we have to shoot?" Thigpen asked.

"I can't see him interfering with the actual launch, and being nearby is a good thing . . . for him," Jerry answered. "That means he'll be clear of the blasts."

"Good point," the XO observed. "But why was he messing with us to begin with? We weren't interfering with one of his attacks."

"It's preemptive, and smart. He's told us to get lost, and took away our primary search sensor. He can break contact and we won't be able to find him as easily. Our TB-34 towed array was short enough to be clear of him, but it isn't as good as his array. We're even now."

"Yeah," grinned the XO. "For another eight minutes, anyway. Luckily, we don't need our thin-line array to shoot our two little friends." Thigpen paused, then suddenly realized that he'd have to document the lost towed array. "Wait a minute! That bastard! Now I've got to do the paperwork for Minot *and* the TB-33! Are you sure we can't shoot him, sir?"

## INS *Chakra*

"All stations report no damage, Captain," Jain announced.

*Perfect.* He'd crippled the American's sonar capability, and incidentally cost the U.S. Navy a million dollars or so. Samant had held his breath when they'd rammed the towed array. It was the exact opposite of what submarine captains were trained to do.

Running into another sub's towed array was something one usually avoided at all costs. There'd been a very real risk of fouling *Chakra*'s screw with the array's cable. That would have been embarrassing at the very least, and potentially deadly if they'd been forced to surface and request a tow back to a friendly port. But he'd bet and he'd won. *Take that,* he thought happily.

"What's he doing now?" Samant demanded.

Lieutenant Rajat reported, "He's come right, steadied on two one zero at ten knots, Captain."

"Still at ten knots?"

"Yes, sir," Jain confirmed. "He's not leaving."

Samant's face slowly turned red. He looked ready to explode. "Can't this fellow take a hint? He is not welcome here! We must convey that message to him in the strongest possible terms. Set up another UGST torpedo shot. Bring tube one to action state. Disable the seeker, five degree offset. He won't dare ignore this!"

"It worked before," Jain added hopefully.


## USS *North Dakota*

"Launch transients! Torpedo in the water!" shouted Halleck. "UGST torpedo bears three five zero. Weapon has not yet enabled."

"Pilot, hard left rudder, steady course south! All ahead flank! Torpedo defense, launch an ADC Mark 5 and mobile decoy, stand by anti-torpedo defense system!"

The deck tilted under his feet as *North Dakota* turned sharply to port.

"Sonar, what's the weapon doing?"

"Slight right drift, but the bearing rate isn't changing as we change course."

"So he's steering the weapon, following our movements," concluded Jerry.

"Yes, sir."

"Just like before. XO, course back to the launch point?"

"We're good, Skipper. On this course we'll pass within five hundred yards of the launch point in two minutes. With five minutes to spare!"

"It was four minutes before!" Jerry protested.

Thigpen shrugged. "Sorry, sir. That last burst of speed caused us to close the distance a lot faster than anticipated."

"Skipper, the torpedo is on our starboard quarter, and it's going to pass astern," reported a relieved Halleck.

Jerry relaxed a little. "Very well, Chief, reestablish active contact on Sierra-one three. Pilot, all ahead two-thirds."

## INS *Chakra*

"Sir, the American is slowing again." Jain paused, studying the displays, but then reported, "He's ignoring the weapon, Captain. His course and speed are not consistent with evading our torpedo."

Samant stiffened, as if fighting to control his anger. "Damn him! He can't ignore me! Fire control operator, put the weapon on an intercept course and command activate the seeker."

"What?" Jain's question startled everyone, including Jain himself, but he persisted. "Sir, we can't sink him. Our orders—"

"Are very clear," Samant interrupted, completing the first officer's sentence. "I understand that! It's my decision, on my authority, Number One." Samant turned back to the fire control operator. "Do it!"

## USS *North Dakota*

"Weapon has changed course! Weapon has enabled!" yelped Halleck. The WLY-1 acoustic intercept receiver began beeping loudly as well.

The chief's report sent lightning through Jerry. "Launch ADC Mark 5 and ATTs! Pilot, left full rudder, steady on course one three zero, all ahead flank. Snapshot, tube one, Sierra-one three. Minimal enable run!"

Thigpen watched as Covey's team quickly flooded the torpedo tube and opened the outer door. Seconds later the Mark 48 ADCAP torpedo was ejected into the ocean and accelerating in *Chakra*'s direction.

"Normal launch, wire is good. Firing range is fifty-five hundred yards, run time is two minutes thirty seconds."

A deep rumble came through the hull. "One of the ATTs hit, sir. Incoming weapon destroyed."

Jerry exhaled. He realized he'd been holding his breath.

## INS *Chakra*

"Captain, the American has counterfired! A single torpedo, and it's already active. Bearing one seven zero. Our own torpedo has been destroyed," reported Jain with excitement.

Samant reacted instinctively. "All ahead flank, steer two seven zero, launch decoys." He added to Jain, "That's it. Once we get clear of this weapon, I'll give him a spread that will leave him in pieces."

## USS North Dakota

Jerry looked at the port VLSD. The tangled mess of submarine and torpedo tracks made it hard to figure out which way to go. Looking over at his XO, he saw Thigpen pulling his hair out trying to keep track of a very contorted and confusing situation.

"Which way do I need to go, XO?"

"Ah, um, recommend course three zero zero at fifteen knots. That should get us pretty close, I think. Time to launch, three minutes with no margin."

"Close is good enough, Bernie. These *are* nuclear weapons we're launching. Pilot, left fifteen degrees rudder, steady course three zero zero. All ahead two-thirds."

As they watched *North Dakota*'s turn on the tactical display, Thigpen asked, "Skipper, do you think that was a deliberate setup? You know, fool us into believing it was like last time, then enable the torpedo at the last minute?"

"I don't know and I don't care," Jerry replied angrily. Then, after a moment, he added, "I doubt it, but we don't have time for this."

"He's still evading our weapon, sir. We can command-shutdown the unit."

"We've still got the wire?" Jerry asked skeptically.

"Surprisingly, yes. Even after all that pirouetting."

Jerry shook his head. "No. Just cut the wire. I won't give him another chance to shoot at us. If it hits him, so be it." Jerry paused to consider the issue. "An Akula getting hit by a Mark 48 ADCAP torpedo. The Russians build them tough. It might not sink right away. They may have time to get to the escape chamber. If they're lucky."

"Real lucky. One minute to launch, Captain, five hundred yards from launch point," Thigpen reported.

"Pilot, right full rudder, steady course north. Make turns for ten knots."

As the pilot echoed his command and *North Dakota* swung onto firing course, Jerry ordered, "Make tubes three and four ready in all respects. Confirm selection."

"Tubes three and four selected." Thigpen stood behind the torpedo console operator, watching. He nodded to Jerry.

"Captain, tubes three and four are ready in all respects, outer doors are open," said Covey. "Torpedo course is set, medium speed selected, maximum depth selected, seeker set to acoustics off."

The torpedo's course, speed, and depth had been predetermined by the engineers back in Washington, and all Covey's people had to do was make sure the fire control system had the same values. One torpedo would head due east, the other due west, to the maximum length of their run. There was only one thing left to do.

"Firing point procedures, tubes three and four," announced Jerry.

"Weapon ready," replied Covey.

"Ship ready," reported Rothwell, the ship's navigator.

Jerry looked around control; this was it, "Stand by . . . SHOOT!"

"Tubes three and four normal launch, weapons running hot, straight, and normal."

"It's out of our hands now, XO. Pilot, hard right rudder steer course one eight zero, all ahead flank, make your depth one hundred feet. Sonar, cease active transmissions."

"What about the Akula, sir?" Thigpen asked. "We could warn him."

"Not a chance. He's at flank speed. He'd never hear us."

## INS *Chakra*

They were still alive after three minutes, and Samant slowed *Chakra* a little so their sonar would function. As they fell below twenty knots, he could hear the relief in Lieutenant Rajat's voice. "It's confirmed. The American weapon is going after one of the decoys, bearing zero two five. It's in a constant reattack pattern. We are outside its acquisition cone."

But then his alarm returned. "Torpedoes in the water! I have two more torpedoes!!"

Fighting panic, Samant demanded, "Where are they? What are their bearings?" Which way should they dodge? Was there time to react, or were they about to die?

Rajat's tone suddenly changed from fear to confusion. "Captain, one torpedo bears two four five, drawing right, the other bears one two zero, drawing left."

"What?" Samant was totally confused.

"I have down Doppler from both American torpedoes. They are headed away from us in opposite directions. Speed is also considerably slower than the first weapon."

"And where is the American submarine?" Samant asked.

"It's headed due south at high speed. He's also changing depth, coming shallow."

The Indian captain almost shook his head to clear it. "Jain, he's fired two torpedoes, evidently not aimed at us, to opposite ends of the compass, and is now heading away from us at high speed. Does that make any sense to you?"

Lieutenant Rajat's voice came over the speaker again. "The American's speed has stabilized at thirty-two knots."

"And on top of everything else, he's going so fast his own sonar is useless." Samant was working the problem, but it just didn't fit together.

"Don't forget the depth change, sir. I don't understand it, and I don't like it."

"Neither do I. Helm, new course one eight zero, flank speed," Samant snapped. "Make your depth forty meters."

He turned to Jain. "I don't know what he's doing, but if he thinks this is a good idea, so do I."

They watched *Chakra's* speed build quickly. "We're going to be leaving a wake on the surface, Captain."

Samant nodded. "Understood, but if he's not concerned, then neither am I. He launches two torpedoes, then runs away from them at maximum speed . . ." Samant's expression changed from confusion to shock, with Jain's face mirroring his half a second later. "Sound collision! All hands brace for shock!"


At forty knots, it took the U.S. torpedoes nearly half an hour to reach the end of their eighteen-nautical-mile range. The weapons were set to run deep, so deep that the explosive pulse would just barely break the surface. This not only minimized the potential damage to any surface ships, but made sure that the majority of the warhead's energy was transferred to the water and the ocean floor—in other words, a massive sound wave.

*North Dakota* was eighteen miles away from the two detonations. *Chakra*, a few miles in trail, was sixteen miles away. The ten-kiloton underwater burst was only lethal out to a few thousand yards, but would have damaged either boat if they'd been within four or five nautical miles.

While they were waiting, braced, Samant and Jain took the time to review other possible scenarios, and came up with none. Working it through, they knew the time the American had launched his weapons, and the range and speed of the U.S. Mark 48 torpedo. They could calculate the time of detonation, assuming a maximum run. Jain even added in a time/distance calculation for the speed of sound in water. They could relax for a short while. Sort of.

The only thing they could not estimate was the size of the warhead. At this distance, they should be clear, probably, unless the torpedo was fitted with a really large nuclear device. How big was it? These were the Americans, after all.

Twenty-seven minutes after the U.S. torpedoes were fired, Samant ordered again, "All hands, brace." He waited, watching the seconds pass, and prayed that if he was right, all of his assumptions were right.

After a minute and fifteen seconds, Jain called on the sub's announcing system, "Stand by for shock wave, any second now."

Samant could feel his hands sweating, slick on the metal surface. He was thinking about wiping them off, one at a time, of course, when the deck suddenly rose and fell, as if they'd ridden over a speed bump too quickly.

Lieutenant Rajat started to speak, but a second jolt, as hard as the first, rattled them again, but then it was past, and that was it.

As they all began to breathe again, Rajat began his report. "Captain, the sonar's flooded with noise. All frequencies are being drowned out. It's completely blind."

"Go to active mode. See if you can find the American sub."

Rajat pressed a switch and watched the screens. "It's no good, sir. The echoes from the active pulses are drowned out as well. Our sonar is completely useless."


18 September 2016
2405 Eastern Daylight Time
CNN Headline News
Washington, D.C.

"Ladies and gentlemen, the President of the United States."

Myles walked to the podium slowly, deliberately. It was done, and nothing could change that. He'd rolled the dice. It only remained to tell the world, and see if it was enough.

His staff had put out the word that he would make a major announcement about the Pacific War, and every news feed that mattered was listening. The fact that the news conference was set for just after midnight only fueled the wild speculation.

Some partisans predicted he would finally throw in with the alliance, which showed he was opportunistic. Others opined he would finally declare neutrality, which would prove how weak America was.

Myles began his speech by glancing at his watch.

"Exactly six minutes ago, on my orders, eight ten-kiloton nuclear devices were detonated in the depths of the South and East China Seas."

The gasps and uproar in the press corps went on for almost ten minutes. Myles made no attempt to stop it. He simply waited silently for the commotion to die down, and when they were quiet again, he continued.

"These devices were placed by four U.S. Navy submarines, deployed to carefully plotted positions in the South China Sea and East China Sea, where they each fired two specially modified torpedoes, each fitted with a nuclear warhead.

"The torpedoes were not aimed at anything or anybody, and were detonated at a depth that minimized the blast and radioactive contamination from reaching the surface. They presented no danger to nearby ships, and based on reports from U.S. aircraft monitoring the operation, did not cause any injuries or damage."

Myles was watching the audience as he read from the teleprompter. They were completely silent, almost transfixed. They were full of questions, he knew, but also curious as hell. Why, then?

"One effect of these weapons, which we did our best to maximize, was something called 'blue-out.' The shock waves from these eight blasts will reverberate through the entire South and East China Sea basins for days, completely blinding all sonars. Submarines cannot find their prey or detect another ship, save by short-ranged periscope or radar. Surface ships cannot hunt for submarines, and cannot know if they are about to be attacked, unless they spot said periscope. Aircraft cannot hunt for subs except by radar, visual search, or magnetic anomaly detectors, which are very short-ranged and unreliable.

"Since this war began, the United States has done its utmost to convince the warring parties to quickly end the conflict, before the violence escalates to a level no rational human wishes to see.

"In spite of our best efforts, both sides have repeatedly refused to consider any negotiations to end their dispute, or even declare what their definition of victory was. Today, the United States has imposed at least a partial cease-fire at sea. The Littoral Alliance's most powerful weapons, its submarines, are virtually impotent. But as impotent as they are, the Chinese Navy cannot ignore, or even detect, a submarine, if it happens to be nearby."

Myles paused for a moment, and looked at the line of television cameras at the back of the room. His image was being seen around the world.

"To the leaders of the Pacific nations engaged in this war, if our use of nuclear weapons, even in this nonlethal way, has shocked you, then pause in your struggle and consider the horror that lies inevitably in front of us. The death tolls in Seoul, Tokyo, and other cities thus far will be trivial compared to the holocaust after a nuclear weapon strikes them.

"The environmental damage caused by our eight detonations is not as great as the harm already caused by one wrecked supertanker. The South China Sea, the major prize in this struggle, is losing its luster daily as war's ruin fills it with poison.

"We have not done this from some altruistic desire for peace. This is naked, if enlightened, self-interest. A Chinese economy in ruins is a global catastrophe that could drag the rest of the world down with it. A nuclear exchange would be far worse. The world is too small now for wars such as this, and only a fool would think that the belligerents would be the only ones to suffer."

18 September 2016
1330 Local Time
Littoral Alliance Headquarters
Okutama, Nishitama District
Tokyo, Japan

The delegates had all gathered to hear the American president's speech. As soon as he mentioned "nuclear devices," the room had erupted in chaos, with shouts and exclamations in half a dozen languages. Aides ran out to confirm Myles's announcement with their respective governments. Some delegates without translators asked others to confirm what seemed unbelievable. Surely their English skills weren't that bad.

By the time the aides had begun to straggle back in, Myles had finished his speech and the delegates were listening to a replay, some making notes, others just holding their heads in their hands. Not a word was spoken until Myles's speech ended again.

Lieutenant Commander Xang was the aide to Admiral Han, the Taiwanese military representative, and the most senior aide. He stood in front of the admiral, quickly bowed, and reported, "Both of our submarines currently on patrol report their sonars are completely blind. The time coincides with the Americans' announcement. On his authority, Commander Submarines has ordered both subs back to port, and forbidden any other sailings until better sonar conditions develop."

The other aides all followed in order, and their messages were similar. Ships and subs at sea were all heading for the nearest friendly port at their best speed. Some had asked the working group for their concurrence. Numbly, and by a simple show of hands, the offensive campaign at sea was unanimously "suspended, until acoustic conditions improve." Myles was right. In one stroke, they had been hobbled.

The military confirmations were hardly needed. Within minutes of Myles's broadcast, scientific stations, civilian observers, even weather satellites had posted information about the detonations on the Internet. Wild speculation about the physical effects would reverberate long after the acoustic pulse had faded.

Minister Jan Ignacio, the Filipino civilian representative, chaired the working group this week, and called them to order.

"Mister Chairman, I have a motion," cried a Taiwanese representative.

"Mister Chairman, I demand an immediate release condemning the American action," urged the representative from Singapore.

"Mister Chairman . . ."

By the time Ignacio sorted out the immediate and most emotional demands from the delegates, the anti-American release was tabled, as was a motion for an immediate cease-fire. Trying to buy time, Ignacio asked Lieutenant Commander Xang to brief them on the blue-out phenomenon. Was Myles correct? Would this last for days?

Xang deferred to a different officer, with a degree in acoustics. He expanded on the president's description. High-frequency sonars, used by torpedoes and mine-hunters, would return first, maybe in twelve hours or so, but the low-frequency bands, used for long-range search by subs and surface ships alike, were blocked for at least two days. The only thing to do was head for port and hope for the best.

The Korean minister was incensed. "The Americans have taken away our best weapon. Our aircraft can't match the Chinese Air Force's numbers, and we can only hope for a handful of ballistic missiles."

"That's why we should offer terms for a cease-fire," the Taiwanese delegate insisted. "If we continue to use cruise missiles . . ." He didn't complete his sentence, but saw several heads nodding agreement.

"We must continue," the Indian delegate argued. "We've already inflicted terrible damage on the Chinese economy. They are already deep into their strategic reserves. If we keep them on a war footing, and at the same time continue choking off their imports, they'll be faced with complete collapse soon. Then we won't have to offer terms. We can dictate them."

Minister Hisagi disagreed. "We should think carefully before we back the Chinese leadership into a corner. Desperate men use different rules. Also, Dr. Komamura has always insisted that the Chinese themselves may not know where the edge is. By then, it might be too late."

"Then perhaps the professor can give us an update. We'd all welcome his counsel."

But Komamura's chair was empty. Hisagi sent his aide to find the doctor and ask him to rejoin the meeting. But in the end, Hisagi and Orihara were the ones who went to the doctor.


They'd found him on the floor of his small quarters, Miyazaki collapsed on top of him, sobbing. They tried to help her up, but she clung to Komamura, crying, "It's too late. It doesn't matter. He's gone. He's gone."

Dr. Ono had arrived by this point, and his simple check and solemn nod confirmed their worst fears. As Ono stepped back from the body, the news passed from person to person, and a silence spread out from his room and through the halls.

Captain Madarame, in charge of security, hustled the onlookers away. Even Hisagi and Orihara had to stand outside. After asking Miyazaki a few questions, he stepped out into the hall and spoke to the two representatives.

He showed them a vial of prescription medicine. DO NOT TAKE WITH ALCOHOL was printed in red along the top of the label. The vial was empty. "There was an empty flask of sake next to him as well. Dr. Ono says that even a third of the vial would have been fatal, and there must have been at least that much in there." Madarame sighed. "It was quick. He didn't even have time to lie down on the bed."

Attendants appeared with a litter, and another confrontation with Miyazaki began. Her coworkers on Komamura's staff, fellow graduate students, interceded and gently separated her from the professor, promising that she could see him to the ambulance. They escorted her out, promising she would not be left alone.

"You should see this," Madarame said, ushering the two representatives into his room and pointing to the screen of his personal laptop computer. "He left a message. Don't touch anything. This is a crime scene until the examiner declares it a suicide."

Careful to stay back, Hisagi and Orihara bent over, squinting to read the display at that distance. After several moments, Hisagi asked, "May I print this page? It's very important."

Madarame reluctantly nodded. "Let me record which keys you press."

Word of the note spread ahead of them, so that by the time they arrived back in the meeting room, it was full, with staff crowding the sides and back until it was impossible to move. Miyazaki, red-faced after her sad good-bye, had been given a chair near the front.

Hisagi didn't bother with explanations. "This is what he wrote."

My good friends and dear colleagues, I can no longer bear the sadness and shame of this war. Even if my economic theories are correct, I was wrong to think that they must inevitably lead to conflict. We were too quick to take the path of violence, and I must take responsibility for my poor judgment. With my death, I ask that the delegates of Littoral Alliance pursue peace with the same energy that they applied to war.

Half an hour later, the Littoral Alliance declared a unilateral cease-fire, beginning at 1200 GMT, and offered to send representatives to a neutral country of China's choice to begin peace negotiations.

18 September 2016
1400 Local Time
August 1st Building, Ministry of National Defense Compound
Beijing, People's Republic of China

President Chen Dao read the communiqué from the secretary general of the United Nations. Would the Chinese accept the cease-fire? Bangkok, Thailand, and Wellington, New Zealand, had both offered to host the peace negotiations. Were either of these acceptable, or did the Chinese have a different location in mind?

Every member of the CMC had his own copy, not that it took that long to read. None of them spoke. A tomb would be noisier.

"They've put us in a very small box, Comrades. If we refuse such an offer, the world will impose more sanctions. If we continue to fight, we will quickly exhaust our store of conventional missiles, and eventually our oil reserves."

"The 'blue-out' will only last a few days," General Shi of the political department argued. "We can use the time to rest and reposition our naval forces."

"I wouldn't put it past the Americans to do the same thing again. It would be hard to stop them," Chen observed. "Or worse, should we refuse, they can join the Littoral Alliance without reservation and the rest of the world will cheer them on."

"What about the campaign in Vietnam?" General Su argued. As chief of the General Staff, he'd personally supervised the offensive. While the PLA had gained some ground, it had not yet seized the capital, Hanoi, or any of the Vietnamese oil fields to the south.

"Are you seeking victory, General, or redemption?" Chen asked. Su scowled, but didn't take the bait. "We are all at the end of our political careers, Comrades. We will be blamed for the war's start and its outcome, even those of us who did our jobs well," he said, nodding to some of those at the table.

"Then with so little to lose, let's continue the struggle," Su insisted.

Zhang Fei, vice president and secretariat of the Chinese Communist Party, answered him. "China still has much to lose, and each day we continue fighting lengthens our recovery time by months or years. We squander our wealth to no end." His voice was hard, but sad, not angry.

Chen nodded in agreement as Zhang spoke, and added in almost the same tone, "Trident has failed and our economy is in tatters. We are beaten."

19 September 2016
1200 Local Time
By Water
Halifax, Nova Scotia

---

The Great Pacific War of 2016
Posted By: Mac

SAM784 has sent pictures of the first UN inspectors to arrive at Jinhae, South Korea. This batch is a mixture of Swedish, Polish, and Spanish naval officers, who were given a grand welcome and taken straight to the piers. Jinhae is a major base for the ROK Navy, and under the terms of the armistice, the navies of the Littoral Alliance and the PLAN are to stay in port until the final peace accord is signed. I've posted photos of their welcome, and their initial visit to the base. Photos aboard the ships were strictly prohibited, of course.

The inspectors will ensure that all ships remain at the pier, with only light-caliber gun ammunition loaded. Similar inspectors will monitor the air forces of the different countries. According to SAM784, the inspectors all seemed quite keen on being in South Korea, as well as crawling about foreign warships.

We're still looking for someone who can tell us about the inspectors sent to the Chinese naval bases. Photos, personal accounts, whatever you've got. Bywater's Blog only works because of your contributions.

I've also posted photos of the reconnaissance aircraft that the U.S. government has deployed to Misawa, Japan, Clark Field in the Philippines, and Osan in South Korea. These planes are the American contribution to the newly formed UN commission that's going to tackle the environmental damage from the over two dozen tankers (click here for a list) that were sunk during the war. It's expected they'll also report on any warship or submarine movements they spot. It's probably no mistake that the U.S. Navy has donated a P-8 anti-submarine patrol squadron for the effort.

# EPILOGUE

It was hard to choose—Smithwick's or Killian's Red. Somehow, being indecisive felt good, almost a guilty pleasure.

"I like the Killian's," Joanna suggested.

"But that's made by Coors now," Hardy protested. "Smithwick's is actually brewed in Ireland."

Suddenly he knew what to do. "I'll try Siné Irish Red," Jerry announced.

"You don't want to try the others?" Hardy asked.

"I don't like having to choose between the executive and the legislative branches," Jerry explained, smiling.

Joanna had suggested Siné restaurant, "Since I missed out last time," she complained.

"That was not my fault!" Hardy insisted. "The first thing you learn in spy school is never bring a date."

Jerry smiled, both on the outside and the inside. They were all in a good, no, a great mood, following the awards ceremony at the White House. Unlike after the Iran mission, this had been a public ceremony, with a second Navy Cross for Jerry, the Distinguished Service Medal for Captain Simonis, and a Presidential Unit Citation for Submarine Squadron Fifteen and the five boats that had served in it. Rebecca Halsey had come out from Guam, with Simonis as her escort, to receive *Santa Fe*'s award.

Afterward, they'd all mixed with the president and other bigwigs at the reception, but then Jerry, Emily, and the Hardys had headed for Siné to celebrate quietly and decompress.

"I heard that the president wants to appoint you special ambassador to the Littoral Alliance," Jerry remarked. As he spoke, Patterson frowned and Hardy looked uncomfortable.

"That's what Senator Weitz said," Jerry insisted. "He was complaining about special elections and how they'll have problems finding someone for your district."

The senator's expression changed from discomfort to near-misery. "I turned him down."

"You did what!?" Jerry didn't know what surprised him more: Hardy rejecting the plum assignment, or Hardy saying no to the president.

"It would have meant either living apart for at least a year," Hardy explained, "or Joanna giving up her job and becoming 'Mrs. Ambassador.' I couldn't do that. And Ray Kirkpatrick said that he's stepping down after President Myles is reelected. There's an obvious replacement, and I don't want to deny her that opportunity."

"Not 'if he's reelected'?" Jerry asked.

Hardy shook his head. "He stopped a war, and kept the U.S. economy from going completely down the toilet. While we lost some people, and the economy took a hit as well, it could have been much, much worse. And he showed some real intestinal fortitude ordering the use of nuclear weapons; he's been getting a lot of good press for being so innovative and decisive. Sometimes the election's about war and peace, sometimes it's the economy. This time it was both."

Joanna gave her husband a gentle poke. "He didn't even ask me. He just said no—to the president. I don't even know if I'd want Ray's job. I lost enough sleep as his deputy. There's still the new Indo-Pakistani war, China's economy is a mess, as is much of the world. The U.S economy is in pretty good shape by comparison. And weapons sales are up." She sighed. "I would be gainfully employed."

"That Littoral Alliance post would be no picnic, either," Hardy countered. "The alliance will probably continue, but their guiding light is gone. Komamura's suicide note said he was 'taking responsibility' for his poor judgment. That's a big deal in Japanese tradition. By killing himself, he explicitly admitted that his actions were dishonorable, and by implication so too were the alliance's. It's really taken the wind out of their sails.

"Besides, with so many of the alliance governments in political hot water, goodness knows what shape it will take. Democracies don't like leaders that wage secret wars. Certainly Japan and Korea will have new governments by the end of the year. India's already changed, and as for Taiwan, the alliance is their only hope. If mainland China wasn't so weak . . ." Hardy shrugged.

"And that's why you should have taken the posting," Patterson insisted. "They need someone who understands the situation. Then maybe I could get on that new UN commission that's been formed to clean up the South and East China Seas. There is so much oil and wreckage! With the reparations that Japan, Korea, and the other alliance countries have to pay, we could really accomplish something. Of course, the UN is involved, so . . ."

"And how much would I get to see you then?" Hardy demanded. "I'm good with staying in Washington, as long as we can be together . . . *occasionally*." He gave her shoulder a squeeze.

Patterson patted his hand affectionately, then turned back to Jerry. "And before you know it, Jerry, a year and a half will have raced by. And Emily and I can go house-hunting. Wouldn't that be grand?"

"I don't know, Joanna," said Emily, smiling. "Oahu is really very nice. I could get used to staying out there permanently. And my job in the Ocean and Resources Engineering Department at the University of Hawaii has a lot of neat perks."

"Nonsense! You've been in academia too long. Time to get back into the real world of practice. I know several UUV project managers that would give their eyeteeth to have you on their staff."

"It's tempting," Emily said whimsically. Then more excitedly, "What locations do you have in mind for this house-hunting soirée?"

Jerry watched as the two women started making detailed plans, without so much as asking him where he'd like to go for his next duty station. He was about to inject himself into the conversation when Hardy leaned over, patted his shoulder, and said, "First, Grasshopper, you must give up the illusion of control."

"I heard that, Lowell!" sniped Joanna, as she reached over and lightly backhanded the senator.

"Well, I really don't want another tour at the Pentagon," Jerry said flatly. "I'd rather have a root canal. At least for that they give you Novocain."

"Hey! The current naval aide to the president rotates about the same time as you leave *North Dakota*. You'd be a shoo-in for that job, Jerry!" squealed Joanna.

"I don't know. I'm not well suited for the world of politics. I've been told I'm a little too blunt."

"It's just another set of skills, Jerry," Hardy said encouragingly. "All growth comes through pain. Besides, with two Navy Crosses, you're a lock for squadron commander. You know that," Hardy predicted. "And doomed for flag rank after that. But you'll have to pay your dues first."

Finally, it was time for Jerry and Emily to head to the airport, which was only a ten-minute ride away. They had a cab waiting outside the restaurant, and they exchanged handshakes and hugs with Hardy and Patterson, who wished them a safe trip back to Hawaii. "I'll be counting the days, Emily."

Jerry handed Hardy a letter. It was addressed to the Indian Naval Attaché. "Sir, would you mind putting this in the mail for me?"

"Sure, no problem. What's this about, if you don't mind my asking?" Hardy was dying of curiosity.

"It's a personal letter from me to the commanding officer of INS *Chakra*, CO to CO. I wrote that I'm willing to call it a draw if he is."

Hardy burst out laughing and slapped Jerry on the shoulder. "Nicely done, Captain! Nicely done! I'll drop it in the blue box on our way home. Joanna and I have to pack, we'll be flying out ourselves tomorrow," he added. "We're going to Nova Scotia."

"Not for the weather, I hope," Jerry remarked, surprised.

"We're going to visit a good friend in Halifax," Hardy said, smiling. "Joanna and I want to say hi and thank him for his help during the crisis."

A little confused, Jerry asked, "What kind of help?"

"Ever read Bywater's Blog?" Hardy asked. "It's very informative. Check it out."

# GLOSSARY

**ABM:** Anti-ballistic missile

**ACINT:** Acoustic Intelligence

**ADC:** Acoustic device countermeasure

**Aegis:** A U.S. Navy integrated air-defense system built around the SPY-1 radar fitted on *Ticonderoga*-class cruisers and *Burke*-class destroyers. Built by the USA, the Aegis system has now been fitted to ships of the Japanese and Spanish navies.

**AOR:** Area of responsibility

**AIS:** Automatic Identification System

**ASAP:** As soon as possible

**ASDS:** Advanced SEAL Delivery System

**ASEAN:** Association of Southeast Asian Nations

**ASW:** Anti-submarine warfare

**ATT:** Anti-torpedo torpedo. Small defensive torpedoes designed to home in on another torpedo and destroy it.

**APR-2E:** Russian-built rocket-propelled anti-submarine torpedo

**BMD:** Ballistic Missile Defense

**B61:** U.S. Air Force tactical nuclear bomb

**CCP:** Chinese Communist Party

**CDO:** Command duty officer

**CIA:** Central Intelligence Agency

**CIC:** Combat Information Center

**CJ-10:** Chinese long-range land attack cruise missile

**CJCS:** Chairman of the Joint Chiefs of Staff

**Class:** Ships built to the same design are said to be in the same "class," usually named after the first unit of the class to be built (e.g., USS *Arleigh Burke*), or after a design number (e.g., Type 052, Project 956).

**CMC:** Central Military Commission

**CNN:** Cable News Network

**CNO:** Chief of Naval Operations

**CO:** Commanding officer

**COB:** Chief of the boat

**COMINT:** Communications Intelligence

**Commo:** U.S. Navy slang for communications officer

**COMSUBPAC:** Commander, Submarine Force, U.S. Pacific Fleet

**CPA:** Closest point of approach

**CSO:** Chief staff officer

**CT:** Cryptologic Technician

**Corvette:** A warship smaller than a frigate with its weapons and sensors chosen to support a single mission, usually anti-submarine or anti-surface warfare

**DARPA:** Defense Advanced Research Projects Agency

**DCI:** Director of Central Intelligence. The head of the Central Intelligence Agency.

**Destroyer:** A general-purpose warship designed to screen larger, more vulnerable warships from attack. Destroyers that carry long-range anti-aircraft missiles, capable of protecting a group of ships, are called "guided-missile destroyers."

**DEVRON:** Development Squadron

**DF-21:** Dong-Feng (East Wind) 21, a Chinese medium-range ballistic missile.

**DDG:** Guided missile destroyer

**DEFCON:** Defense Condition

**DNI:** Director of National Intelligence. Head of the U.S. intelligence community.

**DoD:** Department of Defense

**DRDO:** Defense Research and Development Organisation

**DTRA:** Defense Threat Reduction Agency

**DWT:** Deadweight tonnage

**EEZ:** Economic exclusion zone

**ELINT:** Electronics Intelligence

**Eng:** U.S. Navy slang for engineer

**EP-3:** A variant of the U.S. Navy P-3 Orion maritime patrol aircraft fitted to do electronic intelligence reconnaissance

**EPRIB:** Emergency Position Indicating Radio Beacon

**ESM:** Electronic support measures. Electronic receivers that can detect radar transmissions, providing their direction and type.

**F-2:** A Japanese-designed and -built single-seat, single-engine fighter, looking like a slightly enlarged F-16. It first entered service in 2000.

**Frigate:** An escort vessel, smaller than a destroyer, with a more limited weapons and sensor suite. It is usually optimized for only one or two missions, e.g., anti-submarine or anti-surface warfare.

**GEnie:** General Electric Network for Information Exchange. An online service that ran from 1985 through 1999.

**GPS:** Global positioning system

**Goat Locker:** U.S. Navy slang for the living areas of a ship reserved exclusively for chief petty officers. Also used to refer to a ship's chief petty officers as a collective group.

**GRT:** Gross registered tons

**Helo:** U.S. Navy slang for helicopter

**HUMINT:** Human Intelligence

**HUMVEE:** Slang for the High Mobility Multipurpose Wheeled Vehicle (HMMWV), a four-wheel drive military automobile

**IRBM:** Intermediate Range Ballistic Missile

**IRGC:** Islamic Revolutionary Guards Corps, aka Pasdaran

**ISR:** Intelligence, Surveillance, and Reconnaissance

**IT:** Information technician

**JASDF:** Japanese Air Self-Defense Force. The name of the Japanese Air Force.

**JCS:** Joint Chiefs of Staff

**Japanese honorifics:** In the Japanese language, a suffix is almost always attached to a person's name, usually indicating their status relative to the speaker. The most common is -*san*, e.g., Komamura-*san*, roughly equivalent to "Mr." or "Ms." in English. This is even used between married couples. If the speaker then learned that Komamura-*san* was a college professor, he could then address him as "Komamura-*sensei*" which is the title for a teacher or expert. Similar titles exist for shopkeepers, doctors, etc. Use of the suffix with a person's given name or nickname, e.g., Sajin-*sensei*, denotes more familiarity. The -*chan* suffix is a term of endearment, often used for women younger than the speaker (typically used by a parent or older relative), especially for children. It can be used with either the family or given name.

**JMSDF:** Japanese Maritime Self-Defense Force. The name of the Japanese Navy.

**Kh-31P:** Supersonic, radar-homing missile launched by aircraft. Originally built by Russia, China now produces them as the YJ-91.

**LPD:** Landing platform dock. A type of amphibious assault ship.

**LPO:** Leading petty officer

**Mark 48 ADCAP:** U.S. heavyweight, multipurpose torpedo with advanced capability. Launched by submarines.

**MCIA:** Marine Corps Intelligence Activity

**MDM-6:** Russian multiple influence (pressure, acoustic, and magnetic) bottom mine

**MG-24:** Russian submarine-deployed acoustic countermeasure

**MG-84:** Russian submarine-launched mobile decoy

**MG-519:** Russian mine-hunting sonar on many of their submarines, also known by the NATO nickname "Mouse Squeak"

**MOX:** Mixed oxide. A nuclear reactor fuel that uses both enriched uranium and weapons-grade plutonium.

**MPA:** Maritime patrol aircraft

**NAE:** Naval acoustic electromechanical. An older type of torpedo decoy that generates noise mechanically.

**NATO:** North Atlantic Treaty Organization

**NMJIC:** National Military Joint Intelligence Center

**NORAD:** North American Aerospace Defense Command

**NSC:** National Security Council

**OOD:** Officer of the deck

**OPREP-3:** U.S. Navy message format used to inform a senior authority of an incident that is of national-level interest.

**ONI:** Office of Naval Intelligence

**ONR:** Office of Naval Research

**OPLAN:** Operations plan

**OPS:** Operations officer

**PAC-2/PAC-3:** Versions of the U.S. Patriot surface-to-air missile. While the PAC-2 has some ballistic missile defense capabilities, the PAC-3 was specifically designed for this role.

**PACOM:** Pacific Command

**PACFLT:** Pacific Fleet

**PAL:** Permissive Action Link

**PCO:** Prospective commanding officer

**PLA:** People's Liberation Army. This can refer to all the Chinese armed forces, or just the ground force component of the armed forces.

**PLAAF:** People's Liberation Army Air Force. The air component of the Chinese armed forces.

**PLAN:** People's Liberation Army Navy. The naval component of the Chinese armed forces.

**PRC:** People's Republic of China

**RPM:** Rotations per minute

**ROE:** Rules of engagement

**ROK:** Republic of Korea. South Korea's official name.

**SATCOM:** Satellite communications

**SINOPEC:** China Petrochemical Corporation

**SITREP:** Situation report

**SEAL:** Sea, Air, Land. U.S. Navy Special Forces

**Second Artillery Corps:** A separate service within the People's Liberation Army responsible for the ballistic missile forces, both nuclear and conventional

**SECDEF:** Secretary of defense

**SECSTATE:** Secretary of state

**Sierra:** A U.S. Navy designation indicating that a contact was detected and is being tracked by a sonar system

**SIGINT:** Signals Intelligence

**Skat-3:** Main sonar suite on Akula classes of SSNs. Also known by the NATO nickname "Shark Gill."

**SM-3:** Standard missile 3, part of the U.S. Navy ballistic missile defense system.

**SPY-1:** This radar is used with the Aegis air-defense system. It uses four non-rotating "phased array" radar antennas, one on each side of the ship's superstructure.

**SSGN:** U.S. Navy type designation for cruise missile carrying submarine with nuclear propulsion

**SSN:** U.S. Navy type designation for an attack submarine with nuclear propulsion.

**SUBRON:** Submarine squadron

**SVP:** Sound velocity profile. A graph showing the speed of sound in water as a function of depth. A sharp change indicates the presence of a thermocline.

**SWAG:** Scientific Wild Ass Guess

**TB-33:** A fully digital, fiberoptic long towed array.

**TB-34:** A fully digital, fiberoptic short towed array.

**Thermocline:** Also called a "layer," it is a sharp change in water temperature that will reflect sound at certain angles

**TSA:** Transportation Security Administration

**UGST:** Universal deep-homing torpedo. A Russian heavyweight, multipurpose torpedo launched from submarines.

**UN:** United Nations

**UAV:** Unmanned air vehicle

**UCMJ:** Uniform Code of Military Justice

**UUV:** Unmanned underwater vehicle

**VLCC:** Very large crude carrier. A subset of supertankers.

**VLSD:** Vertical large screen display

**VTC:** Video teleconference

**WLY-1:** U.S. submarine acoustic intercept receiver. It detects and analyzes active sonar emissions.

**XO:** Executive officer, second in command of a warship

**Y-8:** Chinese maritime patrol aircraft

**Yu-6:** Chinese heavyweight, multipurpose torpedo. Launched by submarines, it is a copy of the U.S. Mark 48.

**Yu-7:** Chinese lightweight, anti-submarine torpedo. Launched from aircraft and surface ships, it is a copy of the U.S. Mark 46 torpedo.

**YJ-83:** Ying Ji (Eagle Strike) 83, a Chinese anti-ship cruise missile

**1MC:** General announcing circuit, shipwide public address system

**3M-14E:** A subsonic, land-attack cruise missile offered by Russia as part of the Klub system for export ships and submarines